SUPERSHELL STORM

by

GILLIAN ANDREWS

The Future Starts Today

ISBN: 978-84-09-43662-0

DEPÓSITO LEGAL: DL PM 00657-2022

COPYRIGHT AUTOR Y EDITOR @ GILLIAN ANDREWS 2022

PRIMERA IMPRESION 2022

1.0

PART ONE

Chapter 1

Seyal felt proud to be standing at the captain's side. Proud to be part of *Nivala's* crew. Proud to be at the ceremony. She, a lowly Avarak female, was now regarded highly enough to attend this major tribute. It was hard to take in. She breathed in the fresh mountain air and closed her eyes for just a second. The sense of belonging and of being appreciated was very precious to her.

She looked around the flat platform high up in the *Siinala* monument, on the planet of Enifa. They were surrounded by Enif who had come to honour the artistic legacy of two late members of their crew. It was an emotive moment.

On the other side of the captain stood Zenzara, the Tyzaran girl who, despite being able to talk to interstellar beings, still considered herself to be his bodyguard. Zenzie was young; she found it difficult to stand still for more than two seconds together. She was fidgeting.

The captain treated her to one of his famous sideways looks.

She looked back up at him, crest lifting in a slightly confrontational manner. "What?"

He rolled his eyes. "Can't you stand still?" he whispered.

The girl's feet froze and she went slightly red. "Sorry."

They jumped as the attendant Enif all displayed their vestigial wings at the same time and batted the air so fast that a strange sound of fluttering seemed to fill the area. Zenzie peered around, looking more interested. "What's up?"

A large Enif was stalking slowly along the length of the platform. As it passed, every other Enif folded its wings back together with a sharp click and dipped onto both knees before straightening up to stand rigidly still.

Some of the youngest Enif beside her were vibrating with excitement. "The *Aliifat!*" one of them said through its translator. "The *Aliifat* has come to the ceremony!"

Seyal stared. That was unexpected. The *Aliifat* is the elected leader of Enifa. It takes decisions on behalf of all the population. It is the supreme ruler of the whole species.

"What do we do?" she whispered urgently to the Captain.

"Do something similar to that dip and incline your head as it passes."

She did as suggested and the rest of *Nivala's* crew hastily followed suit. Zenzie, as Chyzar, probably outranked even the *Aliifat* but she did the same as the rest. The captain did too, though he appeared somewhat uncomfortable.

Seyal herself was used to being self-effacing. Her humble obeisance made her virtually disappear into the background. It was one of the most important characteristics of the Avarak female. To survive on Rhyveka, females needed to be unremarkable. She had perfected the ability to fade into her background long ago and, so far, it had stood her in good stead.

Unfortunately, her recent attempts to free Avarak females from utter subservience had not gone unnoticed by the ruling male Avarak Council. Its members naturally abhorred what they considered to be revolutionary propaganda. They had become increasingly fixated on finding her and dragging her back to Rhyveka. She had been branded a traitor.

Having always previously avoided confrontation, it was curious that fate should have put her at the forefront of such turmoil, she thought.

The *Aliifat* reached the very edge of the platform, which overhung the valley far below, and stopped. It turned and inclined its own head in answer to the recognition. The four *Belofiin* she had thought would conduct the service stepped smartly up towards it in a line, forming an organic bridge between their leader and the rest of those attending the ceremony.

Enif do not have voices. They communicate through tactile exchange. This means that they speak by creating complex patterns of vibrations, which can be interpreted through cordotonal organs situated beneath their skin. They have to be touching to use this form of communication, so it is highly personal.

The *Aliifat* began to communicate with the nearest *Belofiin*. The *Belofiin* transmitted the same message onto its neighbour, and so on. There was a long pattering sound as the message was passed along almost instantaneously to the rest of the attendees, then the *Aliifat* activated the touch communicator strapped onto its forearm. This would translate its thoughts into Universal. The crew from *Nivala* breathed a collective sigh of relief. This was the only way they were going to be able to follow any of the details of the ceremony.

"We are gathered here today in recognition of the works of Dishaan. Ten of their works which have been studied by our experts have been deemed worthy of the golden standard."

How that would have made Eshaan shine! It had been devastated when the Vaers had appropriated its life's work. It had only had a short time to create new paintings, but in Seyal's opinion they were real masterpieces. Not that she was an expert, but they certainly took *her* breath away. To have one painting given golden status was the goal of all Enif. To have ten would catapult them immediately into planetary fame. She was delighted. Her friends deserved it. She just wished that they were still there with the rest of the crew to enjoy their success.

But then, there were a lot of things she would have liked to change. Her eyes slid sideways to her captain. From Mallivan's face, he was thinking the exact same thing.

The Enif are a highly intelligent race. They always live in pairs of two, known as *faliif*. One of the *faliif* is artistic and spends its life creating; the other is usually more mechanically minded and works on the functional side of Enif society. When they die they undergo something called enlightenment, during which they are said to merge into one soul. They die together and their names are forever linked from that moment on. So Eshaan and Didjal were now Dishaan and would be forever remembered as one entity.

Yet they would never be that to their friends from *Nivala*. Seyal could see them as they lay dying, Eshaan held tenderly by Didjal's thin arms. She missed them as friends. She thought she probably always would.

She missed Sammy desperately too, although she hadn't known him like the captain had. He had been like a brother to Ryler Mallivan for so long that she knew that it was actually painful for the captain to be waking up in a universe without him. Worse, Mallivan felt responsible for his death. The captain still hadn't forgiven himself and she wasn't sure if he ever could.

She saw him swallow, in an attempt to force back the sense of loss and guilt that had overwhelmed him.

A small hand touched his sleeve. He looked down.

Zenzie was smiling up at him. Her face was sad, too. She knew what he was feeling and wanted to help him.

Seyal wished that somebody could. But he was captain of *Nivala*. Captains give orders. And sometimes people die. It had happened to her own husband not long before. Despite her ambivalence toward Avarak males, she felt a lump in her throat. Solutor had tried to treat her fairly. He had even accepted her natural voice, which most male Avaraks found grating. And he had allowed her to have a job. He had been a progressive.

She lowered her head. She had recently come to realize just how hard it could be to live with the consequences of your actions. One of the female Avaraks who had joined her small revolution had disappeared. It seemed more than likely that the woman's husband had decided to dispose of her because of her convictions. The guilt Seyal felt was heavy and inescapable.

Zenzie was pinching the fleshy part of Mallivan's arm. He had missed some of the speech. The *Aliifat* had been announcing the assignation of *Siinala* vault numbers for all ten works. Those who had known Didjal and Eshaan were vibrating with pride. All the works were to be kept together and the vault numbers indicated a very high ranking in the mountain. For Enif, the higher the vaults, the more masterful the paintings. It was a posthumous tribute that any Enif would have laid down its life for.

Mallivan blew out air. He just wanted his two Enif crewmen back. And that wasn't going to happen.

The *Aliifat* turned to them. "Furthermore, the painting that is currently adorning the mess hall of the spaceship *Nivala* is hereby granted to that ship for the period of one hundred and fifty years under a free license. After that it will be available to all Enif in the remaining slot left for that purpose in the Dishaan vault here on *Siinala* Mountain."

Everyone was looking at the captain. He inclined his body from the waist and dipped his head. This was also considered a great honor. Licenses were usually made for between seventy and a hundred years and cost a lot of money. To allow them to keep the mural for a hundred and fifty years with no payment was significant. Of course, it would eventually revert back to the Enif. One of their number would present on board *Nivala* many years from now to destroy the existing work with great reverence. A new original, executed from the data pattern that would have been deposited in the vault, would then be authorized.

Eshaan had told her once that the *really* erudite Enif never even went to see a work of art. They studied the data patterns themselves — the terabits of information that described each movement the original artist had made. Each stroke, each detail of pressure and angle would be there, hidden within the bits and the bytes. They could envisage the full work of art just through the strings of information and considered this way of appreciation the truly pure form. It was hard for Seyal to accept that ability; she needed to look at the painting itself. In that respect Avaraks were like humans, whether Spacelanders or Flatlanders.

As Mallivan straightened up again, they realized that the ceremony was now over. The captain's sister and her new Tyzaran husband moved closer to the captain to see what his orders were. The *Aliifat* was proceeding back along the platform. Mallivan half raised his arm as if he were still in school and needed to ask a question, but it ignored their presence completely. Speaking in Universal was apparently as much of an acknowledgement as they were going to get.

The captain signaled to the rest of the crew and they fell in behind the mass of moving bodies that were now pushing towards the exit and the lifts. Both Enif *faliif* who had been escorting them used all four of their arms to help clear a path to the celebrity lift. It was the only one that did not have a crowd of ordinary Enif around it.

Seyal felt embarrassed to be offered such privilege, but it was certainly true that none of those present would willingly share a lift with so many foreigners. Although the Enif now ventured out into space, those who did not were unused to the different species. She knew that the Enif acute sense of smell would mean that her crew's hopefully small body odors would be almost overwhelming to the locals in an enclosed space. Indeed, they shuffled more than willingly to one side, and the loud thrumming which followed their path as the small group walked through them probably reflected their hosts' relief at not having to come any closer.

They were soon back on board *Nivala*. Zenzie walked straight up to Mel and gave her a hug.

Mel pushed the slim body away after clutching it to her for a long moment. "Get away with you!"

She wasn't fooling anybody. Even after six months, it was clear to all of them how heartbroken she was. She had been picking at her food, had lost several kilos and there were permanent huge dark circles under her eyes.

The captain walked to a console. "Anything to report?"

There was a defeated look hovering around Mel's eyes. She couldn't have slept very well. "Nothing, Rye."

The ship was on a skeleton crew because there had been multiple changes inside the Interstellar Enforcement Agency in the last couple of months. Neema and Anzany had been given a ship of their own. *Hypatia* was about half the size of *Nivala* and had been charged with patrolling the border between the Bifold and Local Shells to make sure there was no repetition of the hostilities between the Avaraks and the Human Flatlanders or Terrans. Danaa was also getting her own ship, this time from the Nepheals. She would take command shortly and would be using it mainly to dissuade the Nova Vaers from crossing the Pallas Ring and entering the Atlas Shell. As the ship was still under construction, she was currently on leave of absence on Nephealis, her home planet. *Nivala's* crew had recently received a large pallet of phyonwe fruit from her for Scout, who had become overexcited and had to be sedated for a short time.

All this explained why Mel had been alone except for Segaton, Seyal's son. Mallivan had hesitated to leave the whole ship in her hands while she was still so distracted. Even though the ship was securely docked, Seyal wasn't sure her friend was in a fit condition to notice anything much at all. Now they were back, the captain checked the consoles. He noticed a warning light over the aft starboard supply hatch. "What's this?"

Mel peered over at the console. "Oh. That. Yes, it seems to be on the blink."

Mallivan bit back the comment he had been about to make, but he was clearly unhappy. Seyal wasn't sure that she agreed. Mel's place was on the bridge. She had been left with an extremely rambunctious adolescent Avarak; she could hardly be expected to take herself all the way to the supply hatch, leaving Segaton alone near the controls. That certainly would have been a recipe for disaster.

Even Seyal herself had to acknowledge that. Segaton these days was deep into the Avarak equivalent of teenage rebellion. Seyal wouldn't have given him free range with a firelighter, let alone a starship, and *she* was his mother. Mallivan was being unreasonable. Still, she felt a prickling of unease. The captain would need to check that light out.

His expression had softened. "Get some rest, Mel. You look like you could do with a few hours of sleep."

She nodded, but Seyal knew that she would struggle with that. The Avarak female's heart melted a little in sympathy with what Mel was going through. She moved closer and touched her friend lightly on the shoulder.

Mel accepted the gesture for a few seconds. Then she pulled back, as she had with Zenzie. She was determined to remain as independent as she could.

"Thank you, Seyal."

The rest of those present watched helplessly as she left the bridge. There was no more any of them could do to help her, much though it pained them to realize their limitations. And it *was* slowly getting better; each week put Sammy's death further behind them.

The captain turned to Izan Denaraz, his sister's husband, who was staring at him with some humor. He knew Mallivan was going to have to investigate that faulty warning light, too.

"I'll come with you," Denaraz told his brother-in-law.

Mallivan nodded. They made their way off the bridge and along the passageway to the lifts and down to the middle deck. The supply hatch in question was on the off-side from the docking ring, which made it an unlikely candidate for forced entry. It was open to space. However, everything should be checked, and anomalies like this simply didn't happen on new Tyzaran spaceships. At least, everybody hoped they didn't.

When they reached the hatch everything seemed to be in

order. It was tightly fastened and completely secure. Izan raised one eyebrow at the captain. "Could this be another of Segaton's experiments?" He gave a sideways moue of apology to Seyal.

The young Avarak had recently overtaken his mother in height at the same time as he had achieved honors in disruptiveness. For the captain, he had become another problem that was going to need to be dealt with. Seyal already knew how forceful an adult male Avarak could be; the captain was learning by trial and error. And the errors were costly. Mallivan wasn't particularly enamored of the process. It had been an unpleasant surprise to find out just how fast Avarak children matured. One year for them was like five years for a human.

The captain shook his head. "Something tripped it from the outside, and Segaton was on the bridge at the time. He is now in his cabin. I checked already. I guess it could be a simple malfunction."

Izan nodded. "Do you want to do a sweep of the ship? Just to be on the safe side?"

Mallivan nodded. "Of course, but we should be quick. We need to get underway." He looked even more depressed. The captain was definitely not looking forward to their destination.

Izan's lips twitched. "You don't believe your mother will accept me as her new son-in-law?"

Mallivan looked as though he thought she would probably throw a fit. "Sure she will."

Izan tilted his head to one side. "Should I wear body armor when I meet her?"

"Of course not!" The captain hesitated and then gave a resigned sigh. "I rather think I am the one who will be needing it most. I am pretty sure my dear parent will never forgive me for losing *Faraday*. *And* I officiated at your wedding."

Denaraz grinned. "If you had a crest it would be vertical now.

You are terrified of your mother."

Mallivan glared. "I most certainly am not."

"Your body language tells me something else."

"Yeah, well let's see how *you* feel after you've met her."

Izan spread his hands wide. "What possible reason could she have to dislike me?"

He knew perfectly well. Mallivan's sister had been educated to be the next Mallivan prime. She was to have become the CEO of the family when her mother stepped down. Sibby's recent marriage to an alien meant that it was unlikely she would ever accept that burden. Her mother was going to go spare.

That was probably the reason the captain had been avoiding any contact before reaching the family shipstation, *Bellaris*. It was not a meeting he seemed to be looking forward to particularly.

But they were in the vicinity and Sibby had to return to the family shipstation at some moment. She was responsible for all their children's education. And she had already been away for nearly a year. There were things that needed to be put in place.

It was not going to be easy for any of the Mallivan family to adapt to Sibby's marriage to a Tyzaran, but it was something that had to happen. She was quite determined to travel on *Nivala* with her new husband, and she had confessed to Seyal that she would only stay on *Bellaris* long enough to get the logistics sorted out and make sure that the children wouldn't suffer too much from any changes that had to be made.

Half an hour had passed when Denaraz, who had been searching the empty cabins while Seyal checked the galley and mess hall, gave a victorious shout. He emerged, dragging a skinny Enif behind him. The Enif's carapace was scratching the metal deck with a high pitched *eeeek-eeek-eeek* with every step so that it sounded as if the Tyzaran was pulling a squeaky wagon along an iron track.

They all stared as Denaraz came to a halt near the captain and dropped his charge. It crumpled in a heap of angular limbs and stayed where it was.

Seyal made a small compassionate sound, but Mallivan froze her out of taking action with one look. She shrank and gave a squeak of apology.

"Do you often stowaway on spaceships?" The captain enquired in what he may have felt was a mild voice.

The being in front of Seyal cringed and covered its head. Perhaps it could tell that the captain was slightly irritated.

"It was the only way to get away from Enifa," it whispered, hardly able to put enough pressure on the touch pad for the software to interpret its meaning.

"And why did you need to get away?" Mallivan was guessing this was some sort of criminal.

It slumped even further towards the floor. There was a long pause. They all stared at it.

Eventually it came to a decision. Its head lifted and it met the captain's eyes. "I lost my *faliif*." It looked down. "Without it I can never reach enlightenment."

Mallivan frowned, missing something. He turned to Seyal, who had become the go-to crew member for research and information. "I know Enif come in pairs, sure, but is it really that much of a big deal if they don't?"

Seyal stepped closer to the intruder. "Did your *faliif* die without you?"

The Enif's carapace darkened. "Halaashi disappeared when it was three and I was four. We were in separate ships – they were doing an experiment about *faliif* separation and we had been chosen as test subjects – when his ship was attacked by Vaers. My ship tried … but we couldn't reach them in time." There was a thrumming sound of despair. "Most of the crew died trying to save their ship, but Halaashi had disappeared by the time we got there. And nobody has been able to find out anything about it since. Even though it may have died without enlightenment, I must always try to find it. Until I know it is no longer alive, that must be my only purpose." The Enif's translator trailed off in a feedback loop of agony. They all cringed.

"I am very sorry for your loss," Seyal told it. "What happened to you then?"

"I was not allowed to terminate myself. If Halaashi is declared dead I will be allowed to, when I am older. As it is … I may not. Yet."

Seyal nodded. She turned to Mallivan. "Captain, I have read a little about the pairing process on Enifa. May I tell you what I know?"

"Please."

"All Enif infants are assessed when they are two years old. They are tested thoroughly to see if the chemical processes necessary for color are present. This separates out the fifty percent who will have the physical ability to paint. The others will only ever be able to extrude black, which is considered to be so unpleasing aesthetically that black and white art is banned.

"Those Enif without color-producing ability are told they are to become technicians of one of the sciences. They are then paired with an artist by the time they are three. Pairing is also done by computer and is based on emotional and chemical markers. In this way compatibility is assured.

"From that moment on they live with their *faliif* and receive all their education in the same facility, although they specialize more and more either in art or the sciences as they progress, so they will study different subjects within that facility.

"They are required to attend schools far away from their parent Enif, in order to promote the *faliif* bond and avoid any chance contact with the progenitors. They are schooled until they take a posting together wherever the technical *faliif* is sent. The technician is paid for his work, which enables the artist to be free to create.

"I read that only a tiny percentage of Enif are unpaired in adulthood, since equal numbers of children are generated: one to each living Enif. The Enif population has been static for many centuries. The genes are mixed carefully to avoid interbreeding but they are not genetically altered. Enif do not approve of such alteration. However, there are occasional deaths before puberty and there have been other cases of *faliif* being unable to reach their partner in time to aid them in the death process. If enlightenment never takes place for one, both *faliif* are condemned to be alone in death. It is considered the worst thing possible for an Enif to suffer such a fate.

"The survivor of such a catastrophe is socially isolated, since it is not possible to have more than one *faliif* in their lives. If they are artists, the state will give them a pittance to enable them to survive, but very few find themselves ever able to create again. Most commit suicide in the first few years.

"If they are technicians they are expected to work alongside normal Enif and equally few can cope with the pain that even the thought of this causes. Most will put an end to their existence almost immediately. Naturally they are never put forward for jobs off-planet since they are also considered to be incomplete entities."

Seyal fell silent. Her eyes were fixed on the sorry figure in front of her and they were full of pity. She herself had been rejected by her own race, so it was natural that she would identify with the struggle this Enif must have undergone.

"What is your name?" asked the captain.

"Thagaarus, Captain. But please, you can call me Gus."

"How old are you?"

"I am twenty-one."

Mallivan raised an eyebrow at Seyal.

She understood what he was asking. "Enif are considered to be adults when they reach twenty-five. Enif schooling lasts twenty-three years."

Gus pulled itself to its feet. It was much thinner than either Eshaan or Didjal had been, and they could see that it was much younger. Its features were shinier and darker, its limbs more skeletal. It looked as if it hadn't eaten much in the sixteen or so years since its *faliif* had disappeared. "Please don't send me back, Captain. I would never be able to get away again. I will never find my *faliif* if I stay on Enifa. I have been waiting over *six* years for a suitable ship to dock."

"But you are not considered an adult."

"Exactly. If you send me back I will be enclosed in isolation. If that happens, I shall put an end to myself next year. After twenty years, missing Enif are presumed dead. It would not be questioned."

It was a factual statement, and the captain could see that Gus believed it to be a true one. He blew out air. "Why me?"

It didn't understand. "Captain?"

"Are you at least trained to do something useful?"

Mallivan knew by Seyal's expression that he had said something cruel. But how could he take on a loose Enif? What would the authorities on Enifa have to say about that? He felt anger at this stowaway for putting him in a difficult position.

"I really don't see …"

A shape barreled past him and knocked the flimsy Enif on its back, where it lay kicking its arms and legs in the air helplessly.

Mallivan lunged at the shape, finally managing to grab Scout by his collar and pull him unceremoniously off the intruder. "Scout! Stop it!"

Scout's bristles were standing vertically out from his skin. The captain examined the newcomer again, trying to see why his Geiga had fixated on it so much. Eventually he saw that the Enif's fourth arm was pointing at the ceiling and contained a small object which it was attempting to protect. It was this object that Scout seemed to be trying to get at.

"What the fitz is that …?"

"It is my pet sunflyer. Please do not let that … that … animal … reach it!"

The captain pulled Scout back and handed him over to Seyal, who began to scold the Geiga quietly. "I have never seen one before. What are they?"

"Sunflyers are insects. They are trainable, and occasionally used as pets on Enifa. Because they convert stellar power to electrical energy, they can fly even in a vacuum. Some have even been trained to carry a tiny camera. *Faliif* never have pets … they have each other … but I was allowed to pick a pet for myself several years ago. I chose this one. He is a male. You can tell because of his size; the females are much smaller. His name is 'Tsuf'. He is named after the Enif equivalent of a toothpick." He gave what the captain had come to recognize from his people as a smile. "Though, of course, we don't have teeth."

"But Geigas are not carnivorous. I am surprised Scout attacked it … him."

"They make a small buzzing sound that is outside the range of our hearing. It probably irritates your Geiga."

"What do they eat?"

"Mites. They are most useful on board a ship. They keep it clear of ship arthropods."

Seyal glared now, taking this as an insult to their cleanliness on board. "There *are* no ship mites on *Nivala!* It will starve!"

The Enif stowaway shrugged. "Not with so many skin-based organics on the ship. They like dead skin cells too."

There was a collective ripple of distaste. Seyal resolved to wash herself better in the future. She certainly didn't want to find this … this stick insect with its head buried anywhere in *her* skin. And she definitely – *definitely* – didn't want to know why it was called 'Toothpick'.

The Enif sensed that the captain was already considering keeping both of them. "I am an expert in hydraulics and propulsion thrusters," it said quickly. "But I made sure to study hull conformation, too. Apart from that, I have spent all my free time in the last sixteen years learning everything I can about astrometrics."

Mallivan was aware of several sets of eyes boring into the back of his neck. Certainly, somebody with that skill set would be useful on *Nivala*.

"My problem is your government," he said finally. "I cannot take you on as a crew member unless they agree."

The young Enif brightened. "I have thought of that. I would never be put forward by my government, but if you request me specifically for a job opening you might have, they would not be able to refuse. My government has a policy with alien ships that their preferences be followed, wherever possible."

"Very well, I will ask. Now, get that sunflyer out of my sight and keep it away from the Geiga!"

A flare of sheer happiness ran through the thin body in front of them. Its carapace shone. "Thank you, Captain! You will not regret it!"

"Huh. Make sure I don't!" Then the captain remembered something. "And I want a detailed report on how you managed to get on board."

"Certainly, Captain. We don't want just *anybody* creeping in on us unannounced!"

Mallivan opened his mouth and then closed it again.

Denaraz was laughing so much he had to hold on to a bulkhead.

Chapter 2

Ryler Mallivan, battle-hardened as he was, felt a certain trepidation as they walked into the cargo hold of his family's shipstation. His mother still hadn't forgiven him for losing the family spaceship, *Faraday*, to pirates. In fact, Mel thought she saw him gulp as he approached the imposing woman.

"Prime," he said, acknowledging her status as head of their family. "I hope you are well?"

"Who is that?" Her tone was acerbic. She showed little interest in Ryler himself. Her chin was pointing to Denaraz, who had walked out of the shuttle holding Sibby's hand.

Mallivan swallowed again. For some reason his throat had gone very dry. "That is Sibby's new husband."

There were several moments of silence. He actually felt grateful for them.

Then she hissed. "Sssoooo." She examined Izan from crest to toe, apparently not liking what she saw. "The next Mallivan prime has seen fit to take a *Tyzaran* as a husband."

Sibby stepped forwards. "Hello, Mother ... Prime."

"I won't have ... him ... on my ship."

Sibby gave a slow smile and for the first time Mallivan saw a slight resemblance to her mother. It shocked him to see his normally placid sister with just that expression. Her whole face had sort of frozen over. "You won't have to. Denaraz is not staying. And neither am I." She threaded her arm through his in a proprietorial sort of way. Izan himself resembled a rabbit caught in headlights.

Mallivan's mother swayed slightly, as if she had received a blow. "I see. Then you will never be Prime."

"No. I won't."

"In that case, you should leave immediately."

That shook Sibby. Mallivan knew she had been planning to stay for a few weeks, just to be sure that the children had somebody amenable to be around, to teach them. "I ... I ..."

"... This has always been Sibby's home," Mallivan said in a flat tone. "She will need to put arrangements in place."

Izan's crest was vertical. So was Zenzara's.

His mother didn't need a crest. Her anger was coming off her in waves and was perfectly clear to everybody present. Her lip twitched. "Why should I ever let her back on board?"

He shook his head. "How many daughters have you got?" he demanded. "Can you really afford to cut all ties to one of them?"

"This is all your fault. I should have known you would bring utter ruin on this family!" Her eyes attempted to fry her son. He felt as if he had been caught in a microwave.

Zenzie stepped forward, offended on his behalf, but he put a hand on her shoulder. "Leave it." He smiled slightly down at her. "I knew this would happen. And, in a way, it *is* all my fault. I *did* introduce them."

She dipped her eyes almost unnoticeably.

Mallivan dropped his hand. "Get the children," he told Sibby.

Both his sister and his mother swiveled to stare at him.

"—I am not leaving them here. My mother can do as she likes with *Bellaris*. It belongs to the Mallivan family. But my children and your children will be brought up elsewhere."

His mother's face was a study. It displayed shock, fury and then displeasure in an outpouring of emotion that was almost a physical wall. She gave a gasp of disbelief. "You can't do that!"

"Enough, Mother. Neither of us has to stay here. Neither of us has any obligation to leave our children with you. I shall take them to the Agazeds. They will learn a lot and probably be much happier."

He was aware of Mel's gaze on him. The Agazeds were Sammy's family. Their shipstation had been the captain's second home when he was growing up. It had been much more friendly than his own ship. He was positive that he could come to an arrangement with the Agazed prime. Although Mallivan blamed himself for Sammy's death, he knew he would be welcomed on Sammy's family shipstation. They were proud of everything Sammy had done, of the brave person he had become.

The captain's eyes were feeling unaccountably moist. Sibby was crying openly, but she nodded her understanding.

The Mallivan prime stiffened. For a moment he thought his mother was going to take her words back, that she would soften and offer to let Sibby find somebody to take care of the children. But then her eyes flashed, and he realized that she wouldn't, couldn't lose face.

"Take them," she said sharply. "I would never expect any of them to amount to much in any case. Not if they take after you two."

He smiled. "Very well, Prime. This will only take a moment." He walked over to the shipstation comlink. "This is Ryler Mallivan Bell. All my children and all Sibeal Mallivan Bell's children are to report immediately with all their belongings to the cargo hold. We are leaving *Bellaris* for good. Anything left behind will not be retrieved. Thank you."

He left his finger near the button. "You have lost your next Prime," he told his mother, "and the one after that."

Her gaze was corrosive. "I expect that is what you wanted all along." Her chin hardened. "Don't you worry, there are plenty more Mallivans in the world. Did you think you were the only ones?"

Since all Spacelanders are required by law to engender six children, she knew he didn't.

She turned on her heel. "You have one hour to clear this shipstation. I will be removing all of you and your progeny from the *Bellaris* manifest. Neither you nor they will belong to the Mallivan family after today."

"Fine."

It wasn't, of course. Sibby was being held tightly in Denaraz's arms, having sunk almost to her knees.

Ryler Mallivan watched his past stalk away and then looked around at the others. "That went well," he said brightly.

He wasn't fooling anybody. "Rye, are you all right?" asked Mel. They were all staring anxiously at him.

He was just worried about his sister. "I'm sorry, Sibby. Should I have left the kids here?"

She shook her head, though she couldn't speak through her tears.

No, he couldn't have left them here. He had spent little time with his progeny but he wasn't about to leave them at the mercy of a woman he knew to be eminently capable of revenge. They would lose a family, but he rather thought they would win in the end.

Zenzie slipped back to *Nivala*, to make sure it was ready for the children. The others all stood in that cavernous cargo bay, waiting. Nobody spoke. Sibby managed to calm herself and came over to give her brother's arm a supportive squeeze. That was when he started to breathe again.

Some forty minutes later the children began to arrive. Ryler's three, who were a couple of months older than Sibby's, led the way. There hadn't been time to pack, so they had resorted to chucking everything they could find into a storage skip and each was trundling one in front of him or her. The wheeled skips were as big as the children, who could hardly see over them. There was a higgledy-piggledy mess of clothes and screens stuffed into each container.

The first stopped and inclined his head. "Father, is this true? Are we to abandon *Bellaris*? For good?" His tone was much happier than Mallivan had expected.

"Hello, Giedi. Yes. I am sorry to say it is. I am going to ask the Agazeds if they can take you all on."

"Permanently?"

He nodded and there was a cheer from all the kids. Sibby exchanged a glance with her brother. Perhaps what had happened was serendipitous. He had not thought the children to be unhappy here, but their relief was palpable. He remembered his own youth as being fraught with his mother's rules and regulations but he had been able to find happiness by ignoring the greater part of them. Perhaps his mother had become far more inflexible with her grandchildren than she had been with her children. He should have checked up on them more often.

There was no way that the skips and the children would fit into a shuttle, so he contacted Seyal and asked her to bring *Nivala* directly alongside *Bellaris* station. The Avarak woman brought the bigger ship in very competently. She had blossomed on *Nivala*, he thought. He was delighted that she had become such a highly valued member of their crew.

By the time they edged away from *Bellaris*, they were well over the hour that they had been given. The captain didn't think that even his mother would actually open fire on her direct descendents. All the same, he asked Denaraz to go down to the weapons bridge on *Nivala*, just in case. That made the Tyzaran arch one eyebrow. He hadn't exactly come here planning to open fire on his new mother-in-law. Mallivan offered him a shrug. Plans change.

Fortunately, they undocked without any further incidents.

As they set a course for Agazed territory, Mallivan turned to look back on the family shipstation for the very last time. He felt sad.

Because, in the end, his mother was right. He *had* dynamited all of the carefully laid plans that were in place, leaving her without a successor and without a future generation. She would be forced into using the progeny of one of his uncles or aunts for the next Mallivan Prime. And that would be very hard on her.

He sighed. What had happened on *Commorancy* three years ago had changed all of their lives. The future had derailed. Yet, he couldn't help thinking that, on the whole, it was no bad thing. He suspected that they had all become entrenched in a way of life that was stagnating. That, as he was staring at a diminishing *Bellaris*, he was looking at Spacelander history.

*

When they reached the Agazed family shipstation, *Shapley*, Sammy's mother enfolded Mel in a deep hug. Yet she couldn't have known about Mel's relationship with Sammy. Perhaps she intuited it. The two women embraced for a long time.

Finally, the Agazed Prime turned to Mallivan. "Hello, Ryler."

He kissed her on both cheeks. "Prime Ohnahara." She preferred the more informal Ohnah, but this was a formal greeting. He didn't feel he was justified to use the short form. Not yet. Maybe not until they had talked about Sammy. Maybe not even then.

She looked around at all of them. Something clicked inside that sharp mind of hers. "I see you have brought your children for a stay with us. How wonderful! Our Agazed brood will be delighted to have somebody new to play with!"

Sibby grinned. "Ohnah, I would like you to meet my new husband, Izan Denaraz."

Sammy's mother turned sharply towards her and her eyebrow peaked. "Really? Congratulations. Both of you." She stretched out and pumped Izan's hand. "You are Tyzaran. How fascinating. I shall look forward to hearing all about your travels. Now, come in, come in, all of you. I expect you are exhausted."

The difference between Ohnahara and Mallivan's mother was so striking that they must have all stared at her, because she put a hand up to her face, as if to check it was still there. "What? Did I forget to brush my hair? Have I got something between my teeth?"

They hastened to reassure Prime Ohnahara and trailed after her into the conference room on the *Shapley* shipstation. She bustled around them, fussing and twittering until they had all been served something hot to drink and something sweet to eat.

Then she sat down herself, turned to Mallivan and raised one eyebrow. "Am I to educate more children, Ryler?"

"Will you?"

She inclined her elegant neck. "Of course. The diversity can only benefit our own brood. Sammy's children are very sad at the moment. Having six other pupils in their classes and in their games can only help them to get over his loss."

Tears welled up in Mel's eyes and trailed down her face. She made no noise, though. Ohnah reached across the table and patted her hand. "I know, dear, I know."

Mallivan closed his eyes. Although she was a generous person, he was still waiting for her to place the blame firmly where it belonged. On *his* shoulders.

Of course, she did no such thing. She smiled at him in a serene way. "And don't you beat yourself up about his death, Ryler. It wasn't your fault. He died saving the galaxy. He would have been very happy to have given his life for that. I knew my son very well, you see. He certainly wouldn't have been blaming you for something I am quite sure he volunteered for."

She saw from their surprised looks that her hypothesis was true, and pushed back a little more against her chair. "Well then. I hope you will come to *Shapley* whenever your schedule allows you to. You will all be very welcome here."

Ryler felt a coldness he hadn't known was there evaporate from between his shoulder blades. Sammy's mother was so warm in contrast to the Mallivan Prime that he was tempted hug her. This would be a great place for their children to grow up in. They might have lost their hereditary places in the Mallivan family, but he determined there and then that none of them should miss out by his decision to remove them from *Bellaris*. He would just have to work that much harder to make sure that each of them found their own place in the Major Shells.

His sister was smiling softly to Izan. It seemed that she felt the same way.

"Now," said Sammy's mother, "I want to hear all about everything." She grinned at the children before going on. "—And, since you will now be living on-station, I would like to invite you all to participate in the first Samuel Agazed space race, open to anybody over eight and under sixteen, to be held shortly."

There was a collective gasp from all the kids present. They were all within that age group.

Ohnah beamed. "There will be a very, very special prize for this first edition." She gave a suitable pause, just long enough for the children to exchange glances with each other. "The winner will be awarded Sammy's personal runabout. He spent all of his leaves on *Shapley* tinkering with it so it should be a worthwhile thing to win."

Mallivan's lot were hopping from one foot to the other in excitement. They could hardly contain themselves. So were Sibby's children – her oldest, Alisevola, was very handy at the controls of a spaceship. Alise's eyes were shining at the prospect of a good race.

"You stand no chance, Tadpole," she told her brother, Orin, who was three weeks younger than her. "I will wipe the decks with you."

Orin bristled up and glowered at her. "You just think you are the best! But I am intuitive. Uncle Gunnar told me I was!"

"That won't help you to win," she gave a supercilious smile.

He went bright red. "Oh really? Then perhaps you'd like to bet your universal translator on it?"

Mallivan moved between them hastily. "Now now. Nobody is betting anything on the race. If you want to take part you will each do your best and stop taunting the others." He met their eyes sternly. Orin looked down straight away, though Alisevola met his gaze for a few seconds before she directed her eyes to the floor too. Hmm. Sibby was going to have some trouble with that one before very long.

His own son was standing with his hands clenched at his sides.

"The ship will be mine," he said firmly. "Mine."

Alisevola turned on him in a flash. "I'm a better pilot than you are, Giedi. Prime said so!"

Mallivan's other two weren't convinced by Giedi's confidence, either.

"Ha!" snapped Tally.

"You wish," said Peetion. As the smallest of her brothers, he was generally known as Peetie.

"Well *you* won't win, Talitha," Giedi informed his sister in a superior tone. "A sick whale could pilot better than you!"

There was a brief skirmish. It ended up with Ryler having to separate the three, Peetie having felt that what little muscle he had was also necessary to help subdue Giedi. Mallivan shook his head at them. They had been growing up wild. He just hoped that Ohnah would be able to drill some manners into the lot of them.

Sibby's offspring weren't much better. Her youngest, Leo, had stomped deliberately on his sister's foot and was now howling because she had retaliated by jabbing her elbow in his side.

Sibby looked at Mallivan and rolled her eyes. Maybe he should have thought this through better.

Ohnah picked up on that thought. "Don't worry. They will do just fine here. I am glad to have them." Her sharp eyes travelled over all the children. "We will do it in skimmers. I will rent an extra batch of them so you can practice. There will be plenty of time for *all* of you to get better before the actual race is run. I think any one of you could win."

There was a general mumble of excitement. Skimmers are the smallest and safest type of spaceworthy craft that you can get. They are routinely used to teach children the basics of pilotage. All shipstations had one or two for their children to use. Normally spacestation children over eight are quite proficient. The captain realized that Ohnah knew just how to motivate children.

From the grin on his sister's face, she was thinking exactly the same thing. They both relaxed. This was going to be a good place for the kids to grow up.

That put him in mind of another thing. "What about Sammy's three? Won't they feel the race should only be for them? It was their father's runabout, after all."

Ohnah shook her head. "I believe in free competition," she said. "I already told them that we would be throwing the race open to neighbors. Yours will just be nearer neighbors than they expected."

"We will want to pay their bills and upkeep of course."

"Of course. We can work that out. Don't worry about it. They will be great company for our lot and I love youthful energy. It keeps me young."

If her looks were anything to go by, that was quite true. She was radiant. Even with her face falling, as it was at that moment. She had just realized the implications of their move. "So you have renounced the Mallivan Primeship, Sibby? Is that irrevocable?"

Sibby nodded. "Izan and I are going to stay with Mall, on *Nivala*. My husband's future is with the Chyzar, and mine is with him." She gave Denaraz a sideways grin.

Ohnah nodded slowly. "I see. That must have been a very great shock for your mother."

"It was. We have been struck off the manifest, and so have our children."

"So they will never succeed to the Mallivan Primeship either?"

This only applied to Alisevola and Talitha, who were the two in line for the questionably prestigious job.

Alise stopped grappling with her brothers long enough to tell them in no uncertain terms that she had no intention of *ever* becoming Mallivan prime. Tally nodded her agreement. "Who wants to spend their whole lives stuck on some grubby shipstation?" Then she lifted her hand to her mouth, realizing that she must have offended our hostess. "I mean ..." she trailed off and looked to her father for rescue. Mallivan rolled his eyes.

Denaraz stepped forwards smartly. "I feel as though I know you already. It is such a pleasure to meet you, Prime Ohnahara," he said, inclining his head over her hands in a stately fashion.

Ohnah, who had been staring at Tally with a rueful expression turned back, allowing him to distract her. "Golly, you are tall, aren't you?"

Izan looked pleased. "Thank you."

"Well, come on! Come through all of you. We'll get the young ones settled in and give you some sort of lunch before Ryler here gets bored." Mallivan started to speak, but she held up one hand. "Yes, Ryler, I know. You never could stay still in one place for more than two minutes. I can see that hasn't changed."

He must have blushed, because Zenzie, who had just arrived, giggled. This brought her to Ohnah's attention. "And you must be the new Chyzar. Our shipstation is honored to host you."

Zenzara dipped her body slightly. "Thank you, Prime Ohnahara. It is a privilege to be here."

Mallivan stared. Zenzie wasn't usually so polite. Ohnah must have made a *very* good impression on her.

By this time Seyal had managed to get everything into standby mode on *Nivala*. She joined them with Segaton. Segaton was leading Scout, who was tugging at his lead, nose twitching in huge excitement. He was giving out little grunts of eagerness and his small tail was churning around and around.

Ohnah's children, who had arrived a few moments earlier, gave a collective "Oooh!" They had never met a real Geiga before. Soon Scout was besieged by children wanting to pet him. He gave

Mallivan a long look, as if to complain of such treatment, and then submitted to their ministering. Segaton was absorbed into a mass of children, all chattering about the forthcoming race and the Geiga.

Their new Enif, Gus, was next out. Its tiny sunflyer could just be made out hovering over its head.

Ohnah's eyes went upwards and widened. Her head turned slightly to one side as she contemplated Gus's pet. "A sunflyer?" she asked the young Enif. "From Sagrest?"

Gus managed to look gratified. "You have heard of them?"

"Indeed I have," Ohnah was circling underneath the small insect, examining it in detail, "but I have never actually seen one before. You are very lucky to own one."

"My circumstances are ... exceptional."

The Agazed prime picked up on that straight away. She regarded the thin Enif thoughtfully. "You have no *faliif?*" she hazarded.

Gus thrummed to show his pleasure at her understanding. "You know something about our culture?"

"Just a little. That is why you were allowed a pet?"

"It is."

"Because you were too young to self-terminate." She nodded to herself. "Will you, when you are of age?"

"I do not believe so. I have lived nearly all my life alone. Now that I am a crew member of *Nivala*, I am hoping to find some challenges outside my star system."

Her mouth quivered. "I am sure Ryler can help you with that."

Mallivan frowned. "Hey!" That didn't seem fair.

But they ignored him. All of his crew were giggling and jostling to get to the table first. Scout won, easily.

Chapter 3

Captain Mallivan decided to stay on board *Shapley* with the children for some days, and it wasn't long before he got the first sign of what might be the fate of his first-born son.

Giedi had always been a bit of a handful, even for his mother's stern way of parenting. The young boy got himself locked inside an escape pod when he was only three, and was within an ace of being shot out into space with little air and no food. When he was six, he stole a shuttle and tried to thread the needle around their shipstation, *Bellaris*. That episode resulted in a broken arm for him and six thousand credits of damage to the shipstation. When he was nine, he decided that he would be able to survive in outer space for an hour or two with only an IEVA suit. Luckily his sister spotted him floating alongside the *Bellaris* and tattled to her grandmother. He was hauled in pretty peremptorily, which turned out to be a lucky thing, because he already had space burns on his ears. Ever since he had suffered from a lack of feeling to both ears.

So Mallivan expected fireworks when Giedi was around. He just never expected them to come from Zenzie.

The first inkling he got was when Denaraz thrust one of his bony elbows into Mallivan's ribs. The captain jumped and turned to remonstrate with the Tyzaran, only to find him nodding his head towards a strange scene to his right.

The captain's son was standing, eyes wide, staring at Zenzie. His face was flushed and he seemed unable to move. Mallivan realized that it must be the first time that they had really looked at each other. Zenzie had been keeping Segaton occupied during the trip.

Zenzara, for her part, was stock still. Her crest was vertical, her skin had taken on a purple tinge, and her eyes were shining. She looked as though she were about to cry.

Mallivan's stomach churned. It felt as though he had swallowed a spanner.

"Giedi," he said severely, "come here please."

Giedi never even heard what he had said. Neither did Zenzie.

The captain gave a sigh. "So much for the free pass until she was twenty-five," he grumbled.

Izan started to laugh. "At least your son isn't likely to stray far away from your side. The Savior Protocol will tie him to you just as much as she is." Then he smiled at them indulgently. "You can't separate soul-mixed people — not for long, anyway. *Zeuma* meant for them to be together."

"They are too young!" Mallivan was horrified. "She promised she wouldn't date for years and years!"

Denaraz gave a shrug. "And they won't. But the bond will develop and grow with them. What is simple friendship now will become romantic when they grow up. In any case, they are fated to be together."

Mallivan sighed again. "You have no idea just how much trouble Giedi can get himself into." He was offended by Izan's broad grin. "Really! I mean it!"

"I am sure you do. But I do know what soul-mixing looks like, and that is it."

"Yes, I remember. I was there when you first saw my sister, you know. But at such a young age?"

Izan spread his hands. "I'm afraid so."

He was right. Clearly, Giedi was as struck dumb as she was. Ryler could tell that some day, in what he hoped was the far future, Zenzie would become his daughter-in-law.

The scene was finally broken by Alisevola. She pointed at Giedi's face and burst into giggles. "You look like a stuck pig!" she squealed. "Do you need to go to the bathroom?" She then collapsed in a heap of amusement.

Both Giedi and Zenzie turned to her with identical expressions of utter disdain.

Alise found that even funnier and called in the rest of the Mallivan brood to share in her fun. Zenzie got a peculiarly protective look on her face and her chin came up. Mallivan could have told Alise that she should step back, but she was so taken up with laughing at Giedi she missed the crucial signs.

There was a sharp growl from a young Tyzaran throat, a quick unwinding of a thoria from a young Tyzaran neck, and then Alise found her knees trapped in a winding of leather. She had not been expecting that, so her eyes opened wide for a few seconds before the thoria brought her down heavily on the decking.

There was a brief moment of calm, before utter pandemonium broke out. Giedi leapt to Zenzara's side, Orin and Leo to Alise's. The combatants glared at each other before throwing themselves into what promised to be the worst fight the captain had ever seen between the children.

Denaraz lost his own smile. It was one thing to enjoy a joke at Zenzara's expense, quite another to see her in any sort of danger. He threw himself into the fray, intent on extricating the Chyzar.

Unfortunately, the Chyzar was enjoying herself and did not take kindly to the interference. She leapt onto his back and began to pummel his skull.

He ducked down, taken by surprise at her ferocity.

"Stop in-ter-fer-ing," she gasped. "I can take care of myself."

Giedi, who had misinterpreted the actions of Denaraz, planted a right hook on the Tyzaran's face.

Mallivan couldn't help grinning, but waded in to control his son. The boy had clearly gone too far, although Izan appeared to be more irritated than hurt. He had taken hold of Giedi's neck and was holding him off rather gingerly. Giedi was swinging at him. Zenzie was shouting him on.

"ENOUGH!" bellowed the captain, managing to pull both Giedi and Zenzara off Denaraz. "You will *both* apologize to the Spokesdesignate."

There was a long silence.

"Now!"

Zenzie gave a huff. "Sorry. Though you shouldn't—"

"—Thank you, Zenzara. Giedi?"

His son glowered at both the captain and Denaraz. "If you think—"

"I do." The captain waited patiently, holding both their feet off the ground.

"Oh, all right. Sorry."

Mallivan couldn't help thinking that the delivery was poor, but knew that he wasn't going to get anything better at that moment.

He let them both go. Their feet hit the deck with a clatter and they both turned hotly to him again.

"I just—"

"How could you—"

He held up one hand. "Stop, both of you. Your beef is with Alisevola, not with the Spokesdesignate, who was only doing his duty. And all Alisevola did wrong was laugh at you."

Alise scrambled up from the floor, "Well, of course I did. They looked silly, standing there staring at each—"

"Yes. Thank you, Alisevola. When we need your opinion we will ask for it."

She shrugged and gave a sniff. Then she and the rest of the Mallivan children abandoned Giedi and Zenzie to their fate. Mallivan realized that his kids believed in saving themselves first. That would have to be corrected, he decided.

The two culprits had returned to staring into each other's eyes.

The captain blew out air. "You are too young for all this."

Four indignant eyes met his.

"What would you know about it?"

"You don't understand!"

He turned away. He had never felt so old before.

The day didn't improve much, either. Mallivan made his way to the captain's cabin on *Nivala* to rest for a few hours. His name was not on the duty roster so he decided to catch up on some much-needed sleep. He woke up to the worst thing he could possibly imagine. Well, perhaps not the worst thing that could possibly have happened, but one of them. Seyal had knocked on the door to update him on Enifa's reluctant permission for Gus to become a member of the crew. Mallivan called for her to come in and sat up in his bunk, slipping a robe over his shoulders.

As he lifted his right arm to thread it into the robe, his eye caught a small movement against his flesh. The sunflyer was sitting on his arm, head down, casually grazing on his dead skin cells.

He gave a scream which sounded horribly like a young girl's, and leapt out of bed.

The insect was projected upwards, hit the wall, fluttered for a few moments, righted itself and then settled hovering above his head, looking at the captain rather indignantly, Mallivan thought. He gave a sigh and muttered to himself. It was not the best way to be woken up.

Seyal looked scared for a few moments, until she detected the reason for his panic. When she did, she began to chuckle.

A few moments passed and then Zenzie came storming into his cabin, not bothering to knock, of course.

"Are you all right? What's happened?" Her nivala was out and she looked fierce enough to take down a whole division of Vaers. Mallivan went slightly red. "The sunflyer," he muttered.

She stared at him in disbelief. "You gave that *almighty* screech because the sunflyer was in your cabin?"

He felt honor-bound to defend himself. "It was eating me!" he said, in an aggrieved voice. "What was I supposed to do?"

She put her nivala away and joined Seyal's laughter. "Some warrior you are!" She clutched theatrically at her concave stomach.

He felt this was getting out of control. "It wasn't you it was snacking on!"

Zenzie was still giggling. "I expect you taste better than the rest of us, Mallivan Bell" she said between sniggers.

"What can I say?" he replied with dignity, "I guess I am just irresistible."

She gave a disgusted snort and walked out of the cabin. She didn't take the sunflyer with her. Mallivan and the insect were left eyeballing each other rather crossly. It certainly seemed just as taken aback as he was.

"What?" he demanded. "You shouldn't nibble on people when they are asleep!"

It seemed to give a cheep of disagreement. He realized he was trying to have a conversation with an inch-long insect and raised his eyes heavenwards. "Whatever!"

For some reason, his cabin was no longer attractive. He ushered a still-amused Seyal out, dressed quickly and made his way to the bridge, leaving his door open.

Noting Seyal's raised eyebrows, he felt obliged to answer the unasked question. "No, I don't know what happened to the sunflyer. Yes, I did leave the door to my cabin open. I was hoping it would find its way out and go graze on some other unsuspecting soft-shell animal. Our latest Chyzar, for example." He strode away, attempting at least a little dignity.

On the bridge, his sister and her new husband were cooing at each other at the pilot's station. He glared at them.

"Got out of the wrong side of the bed, Mall?" His sister wrinkled her nose at him.

He told them about the sunflyer. They seemed to find it amusing, too. He shook his head in despair. Well, they would learn. He looked forward to the day they found the thing munching along *their* eyelids. Then the boot would be firmly on the other foot.

Because Ohnah had declared a holiday from all school tasks to celebrate *Nivala* coming to her family shipstation, there was a festive atmosphere on *Shapley*. The children were getting in everyone's way. Even *Nivala's* bridge formed part of their playground. Sibby met his gaze and gave a shrug. They needed to suggest some sort of outing, or things were going to get really out of hand.

He was right to be worried. It only took Giedi three days to wreak havoc, and this time he took Zenzie along with him.

Chapter 4

Izan was on watch when it happened. There was a distinctly unusual tone of worry in his normally placid voice. "Mallivan to bridge."

Ryler accelerated. He knew his brother-in-law well enough to realize that he should have been there ten seconds ago.

He was right. When he arrived at the command station, Denaraz was glaring at the main screen. He pointed to a moving speck on that screen. "Your son ...," he began.

The captain groaned. "What has he done now?"

"... Only decided to take Sammy's runabout for a test drive," snapped Izan.

"That sounds just like him." Mallivan's own voice was mild. He had, frankly, been expecting worse.

"He dragged Zenzara along for the ride."

Ahh. That was different. Ryler was surprised that Zenzie would have agreed to leave him on his own for that long. She normally clung, limpet-like, by his side. The Tyzaran Savior Protocol saw to that. They had slowly come to an agreement that she would give him more space, but that had not included traveling on different ships. Not to date, at any rate.

Izan's expression was grim. "Not only that, but Prime Ohnahara assures me that there is a fault in the combustion system and the ship is not currently spaceworthy."

Ohnah at that moment hurried in. "We have to get them back!" She looked at the screen and gasped as she saw their vector. "The engines could easily overload at that speed!"

"Have we a comlink?"

Denaraz shook his head. "Giedi turned off all communication channels when he left the shipstation," he said. Then he huffed. Mallivan got the distinct impression he himself was in some way being blamed for the current situation. He scowled back.

"I will take a shuttle after them," he said, "and stop them, even if I have to detonate a missile or two in front of their noses."

Ohnah looked relieved. "Thank you Ryler. I would appreciate that. I feel a little responsible, I must say."

"No! Why would you be to blame?"

She sighed. "I decided on that stupid race. That must have got Giedi thinking about the runabout. I should have told them that it was currently undergoing a repair schedule."

"You probably assumed that my children would be as well-behaved as your own are. No shame on you for that. Giedi's rebellious nature may be due to my mother's treatment of all the kids. And that is down to me. *I* left them on the family shipstation, after all."

She gave a harried nod. "Perhaps. But apportioning blame is not going to help the situation now. We need to stop that runabout and get them to turn the engine off. It could detonate at any moment."

"Where are they heading?"

Izan consulted the console in front of him. "Looks as if they are planning to follow the proposed race course. I guess Giedi is trying to steal a march on his siblings and cousins. He will be aiming to see where he can shave off a couple of seconds."

The captain sighed. "He has always has been too impatient for his own good. Send us the course, Ohnah, please. Coming?" He looked at Denaraz.

"Of course. The Chyzar's safety is my responsibility."

"You can't watch her every second of every day."

"I should. It's my job, after all." His crest which had been vertical to mirror the danger Zenzara was in, drooped slightly at the edges.

Ryler felt sorry for him. "Not your fault, Izan. How could you have known she would actually leave me behind? It is the first time she has voluntarily risked separation. Even I would have bet money on her staying on board the shipstation or *Nivala*."

"Yes. I failed to take into account the soul-mixing."

The two men had been hurrying down to the shuttle bay as they spoke. Now they swung themselves aboard the larger of their two shuttles – the one which was first in line on the FLOW stack. That stands for Fly-Loading-One-Way, and is the system used on most Tyzaran ships for cargo and shuttle bays. It is basically the simplest possible system, whereby shuttles dock from the stern and take off from the bows of the ship. It means that vessels become stacked in a certain order for takeoff. That can be altered, but it takes time and planning, because a circular revolving platform has to be engaged. In this instance, it wasn't even an option. They simply took the first vessel on the stack. Within three minutes they were out of *Nivala* and racing away from *Shapley* station.

"Come *in* Giedi," Mallivan was already transmitting, angrily. "That runabout has a faulty engine. Switch off and power down immediately. Immediately, please. You and Zenzie are in danger. I repeat: Switch off your engines."

There was no answer. He gave the instrument panel a thump. "Come ON, Giedi! Stop playing about. You know better than this."

"He should. Chy Zenzara certainly does." Denaraz's face was long. "However, becoming what we call multi-layered rather takes away the normal inhibiting impulses. They are in the process of being imprinted by the soul of the other person as well as their own," he informed the captain kindly.

"Great! So they could do anything?"

He nodded. "Their minds are not working in any sort of logical way right now."

The captain pressed his lips together. "I am not sure Giedi's ever has."

"Chy Zenzara could have had any mate she wanted."

"Hey! There is nothing wrong with my son!"

Izan treated him to a look. "He just stole a runabout," he pointed out in a pained tone.

Ryler took a deep breath. "That may be true." He tried to keep his voice restrained. "However, Zenzie clearly egged him on. I suspect she was merely showing off."

"Chy Zenzara has been in real battle. I hardly think she would need to show off to a friend."

Even as Denaraz thought about that, his shoulders lifted and fell and he grinned. They both knew that it might be exactly what Zenzie would do. She hated inactivity of any kind.

They gave a deep breath in tandem. Mallivan savagely pushed the comlink again. "Come in, Giedi. This is urgent. That engine is unstable. I repeat, engine unstable. Please abort flight and power down."

Only static silence greeted him. He wondered why, if they had progressed so much, nobody had succeeded in eliminating static from comlinks. He glared at the offending console.

There was nothing more they could do. Their shuttle was faster than the runabout, and they were bound to catch up with it sooner or later, but they might not be in time. His heart was thudding like an unsecured piece of fuselage. He felt completely impotent. It was a feeling he hated.

"There they are!" Denaraz had been scanning the space in front of their shuttle. "Twenty klicks ahead of us, on a heading around that small moon."

"Got them!" Mallivan fixed a new intercept course and then bent over the shuttle's small weapons array. It was fitted with three rail guns and two lasers. He prepped all of those. He needed to make Giedi stop. Unfortunately, since the boy seemed to have inherited his Mallivan's own stubborn character, the captain was reasonably sure he would need to make his case in the strongest possible terms.

As the shuttle Giedi and Zenzara were in finally became visible, he bracketed it with a pair of lasers and then followed up with three high velocity projectiles which detonated immediately in front of them.

"That should make them sit up and take notice!"

Denaraz's crest was almost vertical. "I thought that last one was going to hit them," he said in a strangled voice.

"Nonsense! I was just getting their attention!" Actually, Giedi had been stupid enough to accelerate instead of stopping, which had put the last projectile so close that they may have lost some paintwork. Mallivan swallowed. He had no crest, but he had to admit that the hairs on his arms stood on end.

The close shave had, however, had the desired effect. There was a satisfying crackle on the comlink.

"What the krikk are you doing?" Zenzie sounded beyond angry. "You nearly blew us out of space!"

"That engine is faulty! Stop and power down immediately!"

The silence that followed seemed to last forever, but it could only have been a couple of seconds. Then, to his immense relief, the runabout came to a complete halt in space and the orange exhaust of the engine vanished.

They navigated quickly alongside and Izan deployed the shuttle's flexible docking tube. As he walked through the airlock at the other end of the tube, an irate Zenzara stomped across the runabout towards them. Her crest was all the way up, as were her eyebrows. "You almost killed us!"

Mallivan gave her what he hoped was an imperious stare. "Actually, you almost killed yourselves, by stealing ... yes, stealing, Giedi ... that runabout."

Zenzie gasped. "After everything we have been through together recently, you accuse us of stealing a ship!" Her crest and the whole of her face paled. She was shaking.

His son bristled. "Prime Ohnahara wouldn't have minded. We were only trying out the course, seeing what the race will be like. The skimmers haven't arrived yet, so we decided to take this ship." He shot his father a what-would-you-have-us-do look. "She should have *told* us that the runabout was under repair. It isn't our fault if she didn't!"

Mallivan's voice blazed with sarcasm. "Possibly she didn't envisage the runabout being stolen?" In his defense, he was still boiling over with worry and felt like throttling the pair of them.

Izan must have picked up on that thought, for he put an arm out in front of the captain, as if to hold him back. "You are in the wrong,

Chy Zenzara," he said firmly. "You should apologize."

"Apologize? I shall not!" Her head went up, displaying her pointy little chin. "We had every right to test drive the runabout!"

"Really? Without asking permission?"

She looked away. "It was implicit."

"It was, was it? So when did Prime Ohnahara implicitly offer Sammy's runabout to the contestants?" She opened her mouth, clearly prepared to argue the point, but Ryler stopped her by holding up one hand.

"No, let me tell you, because I was actually there too, right? Never. Never! She didn't. You are completely in the wrong and you need to apologize to her. She was extremely worried."

That made him realize that she still would be. He sent a quick communication to the shipstation to reassure them all.

A somewhat subdued Giedi touched Zenzara on the shoulder. "Were we really in danger?" he asked, his face pale. "Did I nearly kill the Chyzar?"

"You came awfully close, yes."

He clutched at the nearest bulkhead and sank into a chair bolted in front of it. "I am sorry, Zenzie. It was all my fault."

This didn't appease the Tyzaran girl in the slightest. "Ugh," she snapped, "you're all just the same!" Then she clumped off the bridge, through the docking tube and into the shuttle, leaving them to stare at each other in confusion.

"What just happened?" asked Giedi. "Did I say the wrong thing?"

Denaraz and Ryler just rolled their eyes. He would get used to it. He was only a boy, really. He had no idea how complex relationships could be.

Giedi examined their expressions and then let out a huff of frustration. "I just wanted some fun," he whined. "I didn't want to cause any trouble."

It was Mallivan's turn to sigh. "You never do, Giedi. Never mind. Come on, we will tow the runabout back to *Shapley.*"

Seyal was staring at her son with reproach. "The race is only for those over eight," she said slowly. "*Of course* you won't be able to take part. You are three."

Her son was not impressed. "Three for an Avarak is like thirteen for a Human," he grated.

He was not wrong. Avaraks matured far more quickly than the humanoids. They were considered full adults at four. Three was when the Avarak teen years started in earnest.

"That may be so, Segaton, but rules are rules, and I didn't make them. In any case, what would you do with a runabout? You will be too big to fit inside it by next year. You almost are now. Why do you care who wins?"

"I could beat them all." The tone was low and angry.

Seyal sighed. "Not in a skimmer, you couldn't. You couldn't even squeeze through the door of one of those. You are being silly."

"Silly?" His eyes were tinged red with anger. Seyal took an involuntary step back – it was the first time that her son had scared her.

His lip curled. "What would any of you or your *weak* friends know about anything?"

She self-effaced automatically at the ferocity of his tone. "I ... I ... what do you mean?"

"It is *your* fault that I am not growing up with other Avaraks. You have isolated me all my life from my heritage! This is *all* your fault!"

She cringed against the passageway. "Segaton! How can you say that? The people of this ship have always been here for you. Why, they have looked after you since you were a tiny baby. You are being thoughtless!"

The eyes got, if anything, even redder. "They are not *my* people. Can't you understand anything? Why should I have to stay on this ship full of aliens? *You* might be an alien-loving traitor, but *I* am not!"

Seyal sucked in her breath. It felt as though the air was made up of small poisonous darts. "How can you say I am a traitor?"

"You have been stirring up rebellion amongst the female Avaraks. You have been clamoring for equality, for changes to our society. Or is that somebody's else's mother? No. No, of course it isn't. It had to be *mine!*" He glared at her bitterly before turning away.

Seyal knew that she was breathing too hard and too fast. She would start to feel faint if she kept up like this. But she couldn't stop. It seemed as though her entire world had crashed around her frail shoulders. This was her *son*. She lived for him. She cared for him more than anything else in her world. And yet he was turning into an entitled, arrogant Avarak male – the thing that she abhorred more than anything else in the world.

As though somebody had suddenly pushed a button and un-muted her, she found that she could speak. "How can you say that? I am only fighting for what is right! Do you know how many women die without a voice, without hope, without anything?"

He muttered something that made her blood run cold. "What did you say?" she demanded, her thin body trembling all over.

He hesitated and then lifted his chin and took a large step so that his face was thrust almost into hers. Her heart gave a small flutter of panic. "I said," he growled, his face ugly with rage, "Who cares?"

Seyal gasped again and slid away from him along the bulkhead.

She scurried away as fast as she could, her heart struggling to pump enough blood for the escape. Some things could never be unsaid. Never taken back.

Something very precious had broken inside her heart. Nothing would ever be quite the same again. *She* would never quite be the same.

She sped blindly along the passageway. She needed to leave her son behind. She was not aware of where she was heading to, where she was going.

She turned the corner sightlessly and careened into a soft body. There was an ooof of expelled air and an apologetic laugh. Seyal found her escape route blocked. She began to shake.

"Seyal? What is wrong? What's the matter?" Sibby's concerned voice came through her haze of pain. Seyal closed her own eyes, trying to cover up both the dampness in them and the pain they held.

A warm pair of arms reached around her. "Come with me. It's all right. Come on."

Seyal gave a little sob of recognition, but she couldn't manage anything more. It didn't matter. Sibby was already seating her gently in one of the big chairs in the mess hall.

"Wait here. I will bring you some Landau coffee with plenty of sugar. You look like you have had a shock. Just sit. Nothing is going to happen to you now. I will look after you."

Seyal was grateful for the warmth and for the gentle understanding in the other woman's tone. She knew she was still in shock. At the same time, she was wondering why she had never foreseen this happening. She, of all people, knew just how the male Avarak genes worked. Why had it never occurred to her that her own son would eventually portray those genes? She felt humiliatingly stupid. And she felt guilty. After all, the accusations her son had laid against her were true. She *had* been agitating to stop cruelty to female Avaraks on Rhyveka.

She eventually managed to convey some of what had happened to Sibby. The Spacelander listened attentively, then nodded. Her mouth curved in recognition of the little ironies of life. "I suppose we should have tried to include him," she said quietly. "In the race, I mean. Did you have any idea of how he felt?"

Seyal shook her head. "He grew up so fa...a...st," she hiccupped.

"For sure." Sibby smiled. "He was just a baby only a few months ago. I had no idea that Avaraks matured so quickly."

Seyal sniffed. "All of the larger species mature more quickly. Avaraks, Nepheals and Vaers are adults by three or four years old. We go through an accelerated stage of what you would call teenager. It lasts about seven months to a year. Segaton is just at the beginning of that now."

Sibby pursed her lips. "Hmm. It is difficult. Segaton can't take part in the race because of his size. But he was actually right to protest about being excluded. Maybe Ohnahara can think of something."

"No! I don't want to bother her. It is ridiculous for him to be angry about this race. The prize is a runabout that is much too small for him! He's already too big for the skimmers. In any case, he has almost no experience as a pilot. Please don't say anything to Prime Ohnahara."

"Well, if you are sure ...?"

"I am."

"This other thing ... your agitation against female oppression on Rhyveka ... are you going to stop it?"

There was a long ... long pause as Seyal considered. Finally she dropped her shoulders in resignation. "No. It has already gone too far. It is something I have to do. I would never forgive myself if I stopped now. There has been no lasting change yet, but every day more female Avaraks are supporting the cause. If we keep on we may even find a way to stop some of the worst abuses."

"Your son should be proud of you. I am." Sibby gave Seyal a little hug around the woman's bony shoulders.

Seyal gave a sad smile. "I don't know where he has got this sense of privilege from. He didn't have it before."

Sibby shrugged. "He grew up. Who knows? One day he will be able to see just how much you have done for the Avarak people."

Seyal looked decidedly unconvinced. "Maybe."

"Anyway, have some of this coffee. And here are some Tessara cakes. These are my very favorite things to eat. You will feel better after some of these."

Seyal reached across and squeezed Sibby's hand. "I already feel better. Thank you, Sibby."

"You are more than welcome. Now, let's stop all this wailing. Have a bite of cake. You have done a great job with Segaton and he will come to realize that."

"Do you think so?"

"I am sure!"

If she could have seen into the future Sibby might have been more circumspect.

Chapter 5

Some two days went by with only very mild disorderly conduct from the more juvenile segments on board the shipstation. Giedi appeared to be sorry for his appropriation of the runabout, and had conspicuously been trying to atone for his sins.

This was not the case with Zenzara, however. She clearly believed that she had done nothing wrong. She refused to talk to any of the adults except Mel and Seyal. Mallivan found it very amusing. She hated that, becoming even more angry with him. In fact her treatment of him showed clearly that she thought herself the victim of major injustice. So it was not surprising that, when she needed help, she didn't turn to him.

It had been several years since the captain had thoughtlessly saved her life and acquired a permanent shadow in the process. He loved her like a daughter, but it was sometimes a little claustrophobic to have her trail him everywhere. Even if, as Chyzar, she was the most important Tyzaran alive at that moment. Unfortunately she was convinced that she was his guardian angel and had sworn to protect his life with hers. He should have stopped it long ago, but then she became the Chyzar and everything got a lot more complicated. The Tyzaran Supreme Council wanted to shut her up in a super-secure facility and study her, which they would be able to do if she were to be released from her obligations under the Savior protocol. Mallivan had discovered that he couldn't do that to her. The horror on her young face at such a possibility was enough to convince him never to recuse or reject her, and had kept them both bound in their strange pact ever since.

He had never imagined that he would be sharing his life with a ten-year-old alien, but here they were. At least Tyzaran girls didn't normally enter puberty until their mid twenties, so he had hoped for a few more years before he had to put up with accompanying her on her own dates. Now, with this soul-mixing thing, who knew? He blew out air again.

"Cheer up, Mallivan. It may never happen."

He swung around. His brother-in-law, Izan, was standing behind him, a faint smile on his Tyzaran face.

"That's just the problem," Ryler told him. The tone must have been a little aggrieved, because Denaraz gave a bigger grin.

"Zenzara still giving you the cold shoulder?"

"She seems to think she is in the right!"

"Yes. That is because she is the age she is."

"She should know better!"

The Tyzaran raised one of his prominent eyebrows.

Mallivan deflated. "I suppose you are right. She is still a baby. It just surprises me when she reverts to a child, that's all."

"We have got used to looking at her as Chyzar and as a fighter. She is very good at both. But she needs to be a child sometimes. Don't worry about it. All completely normal." He gave Ryler a slap on the back. "Just be thankful she agreed not to sleep in the same room as you last year. You won that battle."

"She snores! I wasn't getting a wink of sleep. And she tosses and turns and mutters to herself all night."

Denaraz nodded. "We all do. Tyzarans don't sleep like humans. We are more like your dogs or cats: our limbs tremble and run when we dream. And since when we run we take a breath with each step then it makes us snort and gasp. It isn't exactly snoring, but I do it too. Your sister has taken to wearing earplugs." Now he was the one looking chagrined.

Mallivan shrugged. "The joys of married life."

"You should try it. I know that Spacelanders rarely marry these days but I can highly recommend it."

He was aghast. "No, thank you very much. Spacelanders stopped marriage contracts over a hundred years ago, and a very good thing too in my opinion."

Izan tipped his head on one side. "You never know."

"I do know. And even if I did want to marry, I am sure I could never find somebody willing to put up with Zenzie all the time. Let's face it; she *is* a bit of an obstacle."

"She's the Chyzar." It was a rebuke. Izan was from Tyzar, after all. For his race, Zenzara was almost a goddess.

"I know. Nobody is going to forget that, unfortunately. Except when she does something absolutely stupid."

Denaraz looked at the captain in a strange way, but eventually nodded. "Fate has deflected your own life from the path it would have taken."

"You can say that again."

"It has def—"

"—Yes, Izan, thanks. I was being sarcastic,"

The Tyzaran's crest twitched. "Oh. Sarcasm. Sorry."

Ryler put an arm around his neck and squeezed. "Come on, then, brother-in-law, let's get to the gym and beat each other up with those sticks of yours."

Denaraz was far stronger than the captain; he would not be in any danger. Unfortunately he knew it. His eyebrows almost reached the ceiling and his voice was pained. "Batons, if you don't mind, Rye."

"Yeah, yeah. Whatever. You always beat me, in any case."

They both grinned and then pretended to punch at each other as they made their way to the gym.

Ohnah came in while most of the crew were finishing their lunch. "Is it all right to accept that traffic now, Ryler?" She winked in Mallivan's direction. "I only ask because the second transport is carrying brand new skimmers for the kids."

Both Giedi and Zenzara leapt to their feet. "For us? Really?"

Ohnah inclined her head. "I even booked one for Chy Zenzara. They all have the same engine, but are different colors, ranging from pink to mustard."

Giedi flushed bright red. "I am *not* having a pink one," he said, his expression disdainful. "Come on Zenz, let's get there first. We can choose the best colors. If we leave it to the others, we will only get the dregs!"

With Zenzara miraculously recovered from her sullenness, they raced out of the bridge on *Nivala* and down into the docking ring of the *Shapley* Shipstation. Ohnah grinned cheerfully at the captain. "That should keep them busy for a while."

"No kidding. I doubt we'll see them again before the race."

"That's what I was hoping to talk to you about. I have more or less decided to have it while you and your sister are still on-station. It will make it more memorable for your children, I think."

"That's stellar, Ohnah, but we will have to leave soon. The Macers are getting reports of some unusual activity around Vaer Nova and want us to investigate. I promised them that we would be there within two weeks."

"Hmm. Two weeks. You will need three days in transit. How about we schedule the race for ten days from now? You can see who wins and then go back to patrolling the Major Shells. That should give the kids long enough to practice, but not long enough to get bored with the whole concept. It could work well."

It could. Mallivan was a little leery of leaving the Vaer problem too long, but couldn't help but agree with her about it being valuable to spend a little more time with the children on *Shapley* before leaving them to manage in a new environment on their own.

"Gus?"

The Enif stepped quietly forwards. "Captain?"

"Will we still be able to meet that deadline for Vaer Nova?"

"Yes Captain. The engines are primed and ready. Your sister and Ty Denaraz have been overhauling them with me. We are confident that they will respond well."

A small fluttering of wings nearby made the captain duck. "Keep that sunflyer away from my face, will you?"

"Of course. I am sorry."

The Enif stepped smartly towards him and trapped the sunflyer gently between its two hands. "Come with me, Tsuf. I have food waiting for you in my cabin."

Judging by the irate buzzing coming from his fingers, Toothpick was not convinced. He complained noisily as the Enif escorted him off the bridge. Mallivan turned back to the others, just in time to see Denaraz miming something munching on his eyebrows. The rolling eyes accompanying the gesture showed exactly what he thought of the captain's aversion to the sunflyer.

Ryler glared.

Izan smoothed his face and met the look stolidly. "Yes, Captain?"

He sighed. "Nothing. I think I'll go supervise those skimmers. I don't want a juvenile war to break out."

Denaraz maintained an inscrutable face. "Certainly, Captain."

Mallivan shot his brother-in-law a menacing look as he went out, but it had remarkably little effect.

The captain was watching a swarm of skimmers chase each other up and over and around Shapley shipstation. The sight of so many children in charge of spacecraft, even basic ones like this, was making his blood run cold.

"Don't worry, Ryler." Prime Ohnahara had stepped up to the rexelene viewscreen on her giant ship to join him. "We are tracking them, and I made sure that all the skimmers have override functions incorporated."

That *did* allow him to breathe more easily. Giedi was pretty expert, and he could see that Alise was holding her own, but Peetie's ship was juddering and yawing from side to side. It was not good for Mallivan's heart. He was finding that being with their children accelerated aging. His. "That is quite a relief. How many ships are there out there? It looks like a hundred."

She laughed. "You and your sister's children; that is six. Chy Zenzara, seven. My three, ten. Plus six from *Penrose* station and three from *Hawking* make sixteen. Then I have station personnel accompanying them in a further five skimmers, so there are actually twenty-one ships out there."

"I am amazed none of them has crashed into each other yet."

She gazed fondly out of the screen at the ships that flashed past. "My youngest grandson, Toryn, nearly rammed Chy Zenzara. Luckily the failsafes functioned as they should and disaster was averted. Anti-collision software took over seamlessly to avoid a crash. Toryn never even noticed. Of course, he is still one of the youngest. They all have ACS activated at the highest level. Those who can pilot well, such as your first son, are allowed to deactivate it."

Ryler nodded. "But the override switch is still implementable?"

"Of course. I take the responsibility for the wellbeing of your children extremely seriously. Accidents can happen, of course, but I always put into place as many safeguards as I can."

"Thank you Prime Ohnahara."

A wary expression crossed her face. "You are very formal, Captain Mallivan. Is there something you need to tell me?"

He looked at the decking. "We haven't spoken about Sammy yet. I thought you would want to know ..."

"... How he died? Yes, I suppose you would think that." A distant sadness took a hold of her still beautiful face. She gave a deep sigh. "—But you would be wrong. I am hoping not to find out. I want to imagine him ascending to wherever we go in one blaze of light, rather like a phoenix."

He thought for a long time before speaking. "In a sense, that is exactly what he did, Prime Ohnahara."

She placed one of her hands on his arm and tightened her grasp. "Thank you, Ryler. I shall never forget my wonderful, much-loved child. But he has flown up into the brightness now. Here below, life goes on. We have to move every day, however much that pains us."

He thought of Mel, who seemed to be finding that extremely difficult. "Some people can't."

"You are talking about Mel. That is something I wanted to talk to *you* about."

He looked up, surprised. "Yes?"

"Have you noticed that Mel has been much happier since she came to *Shapley*?"

Much to his chagrin, he had not. He shook his head.

The fingers on his arm tightened even more. "Stop blaming yourself, Ryler. All that happens is not your fault. You have been busy. I am not surprised that Mel's situation has rather escaped you."

"Tell me now."

"It turns out that *Shapley* is much larger than her own family shipstation. You know how badly she is claustronetic?"

"Of course. Though recently ... before Sammy's ... death ... she had improved greatly."

"Yes. However, when Sammy died she says that all the progress she had made disappeared. For whatever reason, the claustronetia came back, stronger than ever. But it was worse, because she also found herself unable to leave *Nivala*."

"So she was utterly trapped inside her own panic?"

"Exactly. Until she came onto *Shapley*. This station is so much bigger than *Nivala* that her claustronetia has receded considerably. Yet it is not so open that she is scared to be here. She has been making considerable progress. I was wondering if you would consider leaving her here with us. I would love to have her close to me, for a time. I feel she could thrive if she stayed with us."

"Have you spoken of this to her?"

Ohnah shook her head. "I wanted to run it by you first. I know she is paid by the Interstellar Enforcement Agency now. But I would be happy to match that salary, since she would be outside the usual *Shapley* personnel structure. And she could join *Nivala* if necessary for occasional missions, when you really needed her. She would not have to be tied here forever. Just until she felt confident enough to travel again, or found something else that would suit. A few years, perhaps?"

"I will talk to her. Of course it could be arranged if it is something she would like to do. In fact, it is a very good idea. She could oversee our *Bellaris* contingent for you. She is familiar with the Mallivan shipstation and would be ideally placed to help them transition to their new lives on *Shapley*."

"Good. I will leave it to you, then. And ... thank you for letting me keep my phoenix."

Her eyes weren't the only ones that were suspiciously wet. The captain swallowed. "I loved him too."

The gentle touch gave Ryler one last squeeze. "I know you did, Ryler. It is time to let the guilt go."

It was. And he did. Speaking to her, even without telling her very much, had helped enormously. He breathed in and then out and a deep feeling of peace seemed to settle over him. The sadness was still there, permeating his life. But the feeling of guilt had dissipated. He closed his eyes and took a few more deep breaths. Then he turned to thank her, but she had gone.

At last the day of the race came. The kids were so excited that their ability to concentrate was pretty much zero. Ohnah had arranged for Denaraz and Mallivan to watch it from a prime position. They were amongst those sitting in her best shuttle, along a row of comfortable seats in front of a spaceglass window larger than any he had ever seen before.

Mallivan was so used to seeing the exterior through smaller

viewports that he found it slightly disconcerting. However, the window was banked all around by screens that gave them different points of view, with close-ups and zooms of particularly difficult stretches of the race.

The small skimmers were only distinguishable by color. Giedi had a bright red one, Zenzara silver, Tally pink, Leo mustard, Alise bright blue, Orin yellow. Peetie was manhandling a copper skimmer, and Ohnah's children had gold, orange and green. Those were the ones Mallivan was trying to watch. The children from Penrose and Hawking stations were not of any great interest to him. He was rooting for his three and the others that lived on the station.

Denaraz seemed to be on the side of the Chyzar, naturally, though this was causing him a couple of problems with other parents present. They were all yelling support for their own children but looking daggers at each other when one or the other skimmer edged ahead.

Mallivan was pleased to see that Giedi and Zenzara were by far the best pilots on the course. He'd expected it of Zenzie. She had already shown him how good she was. But Giedi was a pleasant surprise. He seemed to have developed a sudden determination. His chin had been set that morning when Ryler had seen him off on the warm-ups. "I *have* to win this, Father."

"You don't. It really isn't that important."

"Yes it is. Zenzie needs to see that I am efficient. She has already done so much in her life. I can't fall behind her any more. It is time I showed what I am capable of."

Mallivan had made a moue with his mouth. "I am just not sure that winning a racer off her is going to do that."

He had hesitated for a moment. "Really? What do you think I should do, then?"

His father had shrugged. "How should I know? I was never any good with women." His children, like almost all those born to Spacelanders, had been artificially conceived in the Genetic Institute of Fertility, back on Zenubi. He had never claimed to have any understanding of relationships. "You are in uncharted territory."

Giedi had looked glum. "I know." His foot had traced a circle on the deck plating. "I thought winning would make me stand out, but if even that isn't going to work …"

"Just be yourself, Giedi. I haven't seen that crest of hers standing up when anybody else approaches."

He had reddened. "No, I guess not. I … I am just not sure if that is going to be enough."

"Something will turn up. You will have the chance to impress her one day. Probably when you least expect it."

Mallivan should have kept his mouth shut. Spacelanders have a saying. 'Never toss one neutron star at another. The gravitational waves might change your world.'

He had tossed a neutron star. He just didn't know it yet.

Peetie was out of the race before it had hardly even started. His copper skimmer shied slightly in space. He was unlucky; this close to the start line there was a concentration of ships. His skimmer just scraped that of Orin. Unfortunately that small touch was enough to propel Peetie's ship, crab-like, outside the legal course.

He was still near the starting line. From the shuttle, they could see a tiny figure thumping the console in front of him in huge frustration as all the controls went dark. The ACS was primed to kick in if any of the skimmers left the programmed course.

Ohnah gasped. "Is he all right?"

"Best thing that could have happened to him, if you want my opinion," Mallivan informed Ohnah with a wry roll of his eyes. "He has about as much idea on piloting a spaceship as Scout!"

Denaraz had not taken his eyes off the race. "Look! One of the Hawking lot is out of the race too!" He sounded almost cheery, clearly forgetting that there were delegations from both Hawking and Penrose sitting directly behind them. Ryler pressed his shoe on his brother-in-law's foot.

Denaraz's head snapped round. "What the krikk ... Oh ..." He saw Mallivan was making signs with his eyes and eyebrows. Luckily, Izan realized what he was trying to say and immediately compensated. "Bad luck!" he said fervently to those behind them. "We have lost one too!" There were murmurs of acknowledgement.

Izan turned his attention back to the window and the screens. They all did. Tally, Alisevola, Leo and Giedi were on Zenzie's heels. Zenzie was keeping her skimmer flat and fast, trimming it as hard as she could. They were in the main corridor of the race now, tearing away from the spectators towards Heisenberg's Halo, which was just visible in the northern sky. The course now demanded that they stay straight for around five thousand klicks, then loop around a small planetoid to begin the return journey.

Or rather, that was the plan.

It just never happened.

Because that is when it all went very, very sideways.

There was an urgent buzzing from Prime Ohnahara's personal communicator. She frowned, then accepted the call. Mallivan was watching her carefully as she listened, so he saw the moment when she glanced at the distant view of the skimmers through the window. He also saw the color drain away from her face. "Instigate Emergency Undocking Procedures," she snapped. "Tell all ships to clear to twenty klicks radially." She stopped for a moment to visualize what shipping she currently had docked at the shipstation. "That should be sufficient to maintain separation between each ship." She cut the connexion.

The captain leapt up and took her arm. "What is it, Prime?"

She looked in his direction, but seemed unable to see him. Her voice was dazed. "There is … we … we have to do something." She looked again towards the window.

He gave her arm a tiny shake. "Ohnah! What has happened? Please!"

A harsh and much louder alarm began to sound. It snapped her out of her brain-freeze. Her eyes focused on his face and she straightened, accepting that action was needed and preparing herself for it. "An explosive reconnection event is taking place."

Her tone told Ryler that such an event should not be possible. But the alarm still sounding made it more than clear that it was. He found himself grabbing her elbow. "What is that? What about the skimmers?" Something in his heart had leapt into his throat.

Ohnah's face was grim. "Something has caused a supershell storm. A gigantic one. There will be a tremendous build-up of magnetic energy, causing buffeting. This will then consolidate into areas of mergers, known as islands. The real danger will be the tremendous instability in the region. We could get as many as a hundred islands in a time frame of ten minutes."

"Should we give the computers control of the skimmers?"

She shook her head. "Impossible. We can't guarantee that contact can be maintained with ships in the exterior. It is extremely likely that it won't. The skimmers will have to be left on manual."

"Put me through to Giedi and Chy Zenzara!"

She held up one hand and made a signal to say that she would do that next. First she needed to speak to the station personnel in five of the skimmers. She explained quickly what was happening and instructed them to position as close as they could to the youngest participants. Their job would be to see that as little harm as possible came to the contestants.

Then she handed the hand-held comlink to Mallivan. In a few seconds he was through to his son. "Giedi?"

"Hey, Dad. What's up?"

"That whole area of space is about to get very uncomfortable. A shell storm. You are going to have to ride it out. Tell Zenzie and Alise. Tell them to take care of the rest. All the firstborns should be looking after the others. We are removing the override programs."

They could see on the screen that Giedi's skimmer had immediately slowed. "Sure, Dad. You can depend on us. We will do our best. Err ... How long will this thing last?"

Ryler raised an eyebrow at Ohnah. She shrugged. "Maybe a few hours?" She bit her lip. He could see that she was still shocked.

"Hours. Good luck."

"Thanks Dad. You too."

He was on the point of connecting with Zenzara when steel plates deployed around the visor windows, shutting out the outside. The shuttle they were on began to tremble, and the connecting link turned into useless static.

Ryler threw the comlink down onto the nearest chair and took a step towards Ohnah. "Why was this not foreseen?"

"Because there can't be collapses at this time," she snapped back. "Do you think I would be lax enough to schedule a children's race in a period of instability from the nebula?"

Shapley shipstation was located close to the planet Pyrrhus, in the area of the Landau Rift dominated by the infamous Chain Nebula. That meant that it was constantly under threat from the instabilities inherent in the region.

All Spacelanders are aware of the threat of X-point collapse and shell storm formation, but the area surrounding the Chain Nebula was a hundred times more likely to experiment such dangerous phenomena. However, it was Mallivan's understanding that such events could be predicted with extreme accuracy. It made no sense that Ohnah would have allowed a race to be held at a high-risk time.

She closed her eyes. "We are at the lowest risk we have been in for years," she said, clenching and unclenching her fists. "This is not a natural phenomenon. It cannot be."

Denaraz's hand half-pushed the captain to one side. "You mean this is sabotage?"

"I don't know. But I do know that the only way that we could see a storm as virulent as this is forecast to be is if somebody – or something – precipitated it. We are at the lowest probability of instability in the nebula at the moment. And our monitors have picked up absolutely no signs of any variations." She shook her head again. "I have no idea what can have happened, but this is not a natural event. I would stake my shipstation on it."

If this was not a natural occurrence, it must have been set off by somebody who had something to gain. Why choose this particular moment? What was special about it?

Of course! The race.

Denaraz and Mallivan stared at each other. They both came to the same conclusion at the same time.

"Chy Zenzara!"

"Zenzie!"

They swung around to the window, but of course that had disappeared behind a thick sheet of steel. They were encased inside the diminished world of the shuttle, while Zenzara was out there in grave danger in the middle of a tremendous storm, in a tiny skimmer. Somebody had deliberately caused this situation and they had no communication out or in.

Mallivan's mouth went dry as he realized that there was absolutely nothing anybody on the shuttle could do to prevent disaster.

Chapter 6

Giedi had just had time to get through to the other skimmers before the tight-beams went down.

Those nearest to his skimmer had slowed down and come to a complete halt close, but not too close to him. He knew who they were from the color of the skimmers, but they were too far away for him to be able to make out anyone inside the cabins.

Giedi wondered what he could do to help against the oncoming storm. He racked his brains to remember what he had learned about the local area they were in.

However, he wasn't needed. The gold skimmer belonging to Opaline, Prime Ohnahara's first granddaughter, skipped past him. Giedi felt relief. She had been born here, she would know much more than he did about the local conditions.

Sure enough, as she passed him, she made her skimmer tip from side to side. Then she deliberately went past Zenzie's skimmer and tipped her wings again. Zenzie positioned herself to Opaline's left. The skimmer flipped over and returned to behind Zenzie. She overtook anew, again tipping her wings. This time Zenzie dropped behind Opaline.

Opal tipped the skimmer's wings and then moved forward until she was about a hundred meters in front of Zenzie. Then she stopped, and tipped her skimmer from side to side again before putting her craft in a slow flight directly towards the Chain Nebula. It had only taken a few moments for her to get her message across. Slow, constant speed, directly facing the oncoming superstorm.

Zenzie copied Opaline. Giedi suddenly realized what the girl was trying to tell them. They should all turn to face the same direction she was in, directly towards the Chain Nebula. And they should put themselves behind one another, in a straight line, leaving the same distance between each skimmer.

He tipped his own wings and fell into line behind Zenzie, breathing a sigh of relief as he saw the rest of the competitors slowly maneuvering into a line behind him. He put his skimmer into standby and concentrated on the spacecraft in front of him.

The space around him seemed suddenly to thicken. Where before there had been nothing to block out the surrounding stars, now there was a wispy look about it. He squinted into the distance. Or was it lumpy? How could interstellar space take on a lumpy texture? He blinked, but it was still there. It wasn't his eyes.

The skimmer started to yaw from side to side, shuddering as waves of energy began to toss it about in space. Giedi clutched onto the controls, but there was nothing he could do to make the disturbances more manageable. The tiny spacecraft shied and skittered, seemingly without reason. His teeth rattled in his head and he bit his tongue twice.

And that was just the very start. It all went downhill from there. But there was still faint movement ahead of him. He could just make out Zenzie's skimmer still moving forward towards the Chain Nebula. Space was so distorted that it was hard to make out any details. It was a bit like looking at the scene through the bottom of a glass bottle. He had to squint to make out her skimmer.

Giedi managed to drag his own craft back in line with hers, matching her velocity again as best he could. Behind him, he could only hope that the next in line was following his example. He couldn't make out anything of Opaline's skimmer.

His craft was still jerking and weaving from side to side. His whole body shook as shockwave after shockwave threw the tiny vehicle into chaotic movement. His arms began to ache as he clutched desperately onto the controls.

There was a tremendous crash and he glanced upwards, horrified to see that the fuselage was bending in towards his face, dented from the outside by bursts of some sort of alarming plasma that detonated alongside the vessel. Giedi gave a gulp. It wouldn't take much more to completely obliterate the plating that kept deep space out of the tiny cabin. His heart began to obey the innate fight-or-flight response and adrenaline was making him hyper-aware. But there was nowhere to go; nothing he could do to make it go away. The only way to survive this would be to outlast it.

His white face shone back at him in the dented reflection. He looked ghostly, almost insubstantial. He certainly felt it. He wondered how Zenzie was. Her ship was still in front of his, only visible as a faint ghostly shape now. The skimmer's probes had stopped working with the first wave. He could see that her ship was still there, though he had no way of knowing whether it was intact or not.

Then there was a huge bang. His skimmer was catapulted off to the port side of the racecourse, at right angles to the previous direction of travel. He felt his head snap to one side, almost tearing the neck muscles. He hit the side of the chair and for a moment was disorientated. When he did manage to open his eyes, space was lazily cartwheeling over and over; he was spinning away from all the other ships at a ridiculous speed. He closed his eyes again, dizzy. He found himself swallowing. He tried to avoid vomiting all over the console in front of him. Although he was still strapped into his chair, he was being pulled in all directions at the same time. Had something hit his skimmer? Or had it impacted an area of such deep instability that space itself had coagulated into a physical barrier of some sort?

Giedi dragged his attention back to the visor in front of his console, struggling against his seat belt, straining desperately to see anything beyond his own skimmer. Had Zenzara been affected by the same storm front? He had to find her! She could have been hurt!

Nobody except he and Opaline would be close enough to help the Chyzar, and Opaline was too far ahead of Zenzie to have noticed anything, he thought. In any case her job was to lead the others as safely as possible through this perilous instability.

The image in front of him stuttered, turned into two then three, then finally one again. He peered out, desperately trying to locate Zenzara's skimmer. She was nowhere ahead of him.

Then he caught sight of a flash of silver to his rear. The skimmer was close enough for him to see the figure in the cockpit. He gave a sigh. Of course! She had come to rescue him, not vice versa. How could it be any other way? He gave a grim sort of laugh. And here he was, trying to be the hero of the moment. Of course it would not be him! Of course it would be Zenzara!

His skimmer was still completely out of control. It was tumbling bow over stern across the stormy sky, shuddering as smaller turbulences caught and tossed it further and further away from the track Opaline had been trying to establish. The engine had given up its struggle. His brain was beginning to tell him that it was also about to close down for the near future. So much spinning over and over was causing it to take itself off-line. A fizzy kind of lightness was threatening to overtake him.

He lifted one hand to salute Zenzie. Of all the stupid things to do, the last sparking neurons told him. Why would he do that? Waving at her like a tourist. He shook his head slowly, but that hurt.

Just as he did that, the same silver shape loomed out of nowhere, to settle directly in his path. He gave a jump. A squeak of disbelief. He clamped his hand over his eyes and twisted to one side. A crash seemed inevitable and the reptilian part of his brain told him, quite uselessly, to duck.

There was a horrid grinding of metal on metal. A shower of sparks ran across the screen. His vision was completely blocked by silver-painted fuselage.

His skimmer jarred so heavily that he was tossed into his seat belt. It cut into his IEVA suit and pushed all the remaining air out of his lungs. He struggled against it, gasping as he unsuccessfully tried to force another breath into his body.

Sweat was pouring down his face. He battled for his life, yet all he was trying to do was to take another breath. He couldn't. Everything was beginning to go black around the edges, but he thought that the wild tumbling of his shuttle was beginning to slow. It wouldn't matter. It would be too late. He still couldn't force air down into his lungs.

And then it all stopped. The rolling, the dipping, the shaking. His skimmer was finally still. He managed one breath, and then another. He prised his eyes open and blinked several times. His view out was still blocked, but he could see Zenzie in her cockpit, not three feet away from him. Her face was extremely worried.

He sighed. Being rescued by her did not make him feel great. He stared at her. She beckoned.

Trembles in the skimmer he was in made his mind snap him back into hyper-awareness. He was in a skimmer that had no engine, in the middle of a shell storm, with a dented and fragile ship that felt as though it might disintegrate any second. It was more broken than Scobis. No wonder she was signaling him to get out of it.

He grabbed the IEVA helmet from its niche in the console and rammed it down over his head. He would only be in open space for seconds; there was no need to change into full EVA. No time, either, for all he knew. His battered skimmer could disintegrate at any moment, judging by the desperate signals that were coming from the other skimmer. She was in a position to be able to see the outside of his ship. It must have been compromised more badly than he thought. Her mouth was opening and closing. He couldn't hear what she was screaming out at him, but the panic written across her face galvanized him into action. Her crest was rigidly vertical.

He ripped at his seat belt, which had locked and was hard to open. He chipped two fingernails scrabbling at it before he managed to unfasten it.

The skimmers were very small ships; far too small to boast artificial gravity. So he hung in place in front of the console. His eyes swept across it. He saw that one of the dials was showing a nasty flashing red light. He frowned, closing in slightly so as to be able to read what it said.

'Hull breach!' flashed on and off in red letters across the console.

He glanced to the right, where another red light was flashing on and off. 'Fuel containment breach!' it shouted at him.

Giedi's head was hurting, but those signs still managed to convey a sense of immediacy in his evacuation. He pushed himself away from the chair, stifling a groan of pain that came from both his right leg and his left arm. He sailed across the tiny cabin to grasp the end rung of the airlock. It was narrow, but would enable him to evacuate the ship.

He took the time to grab at the statutory roll of rope and the grappling hook. Zenzie's skimmer was only feet away, but there was no point risking any more, and the turbulence was far from over.

He activated the interior hatch and fed himself gingerly into the airlock itself. Because of the small size of the skimmer, it was only a tiny space. An adult would have had to curl themselves up into the fetal position. Giedi was able to avoid that, but he did have to pull his legs up towards his arms to fit inside the airlock.

It was such a small space that the green exterior light was soon flashing. He took a long breath, inhaling and exhaling slowly to make sure he was as calm as he possibly could be. Then he pushed the green button.

A few seconds later, he pulled himself gingerly out into open space. It was still tremendously bumpy. He was buffeted from side to side by clumps and threads of an energy burst he could not see. Space around him was opaque, yet colorless. He could feel some strange wind chivvying him as he clung desperately onto the hatch cover.

A burst of some energy hit the ruined skimmer, jarring it. Giedi's hand was ripped from the cover. He was dragged along the side of the ship's fuselage, until his suit caught on one of the many small protuberances along the hull, slowing his momentum. He scrambled for a handhold, then another, then another, until he got himself back to the open hatch again.

There was no time to waste; his IEVA suit may well have been damaged by that ill-fated slide across the outer hull plating. In feverish haste, he anchored the rope to his own skimmer and then thrust out with both feet towards the silver one. He could see that, although deep scratches were scarring the sleek sides, it had withstood the collision quite well.

The rope easily reached the second skimmer, and he was able to latch onto the fuselage with no problems. It was too early for a sigh of relief, but he breathed one anyway.

After untying the rope, it took only moments to sidle, crablike, along the small spaceship and position himself over the airlock. It opened fairly easily and Giedi slipped inside, closing his eyes momentarily in gratitude.

That was almost premature, because an anomaly hit them just as he was lowering the airlock hatch, which was torn out of his grasp. As he had hold of it, he was sucked out of the airlock like the cork from a bottle and almost lost his grip. There was a moment when his heart stopped beating. One of his hands was dislodged, leaving his whole life dependent on the tenuous link of four fingers wrapped around a handwheel.

Panic made his skin shiver, but his fingers mercifully stayed locked. Even though his legs were flung away, he managed to retain his handhold. He was able to slide back down into the airlock again.

There was no time to dither; he threw all his weight behind the hatch, slamming it shut as fast as he could.

Waiting for the green light took seconds, but it passed like hours to Giedi. His stomach was churning with adrenaline, his pulse racing. At last the lower airlock pulsed green and he was able to open the inner hatch.

He dropped down into the cockpit of the small skimmer, managing to just stay upright. He pulled off the IEVA helmet and glared at his rescuer.

"I was doing just fine!" he snapped.

Zenzie, whose crest was still vertical with fright, gaped at him. "W-What?"

Giedi felt an irrational anger sweep through him. "I said, I didn't need rescuing!"

Zenzie glared at him. "Well, excuse ME for trying to help!"

He sniffed plaintively. "I wanted to rescue YOU!"

She broke out laughing. "You are cross at me because I rescued you, when you wanted to rescue me? Is that it?"

"No. Of course not." It was, though. Giedi felt he would never live this down.

Zenzie's eyes had turned into narrow slits. "Let me get this straight. You are angry at me for saving you? You'd rather I left you to die?"

"No. I guess not." He was shifting from foot to foot now. Put like that, it did sound a little juvenile.

She shook her head to herself. He thought he heard a *sub voce* comment about men and then another about the likeness between him and his father. He bristled up again, bile forming in his throat.

"I suppose you think I should thank you!"

Her face went suddenly very still. "No, why should you? I only did what anyone would have done. What you would have done, if it had been the other way around."

Damn it! She was right. He would have done the same. But he hadn't had the chance. That was what really grated on him.

"*I wanted to save you,*" he repeated, stubbornly.

"Well, hard cheese." It was her turn to snap now. "But I will attempt to put myself in danger just to give you that satisfaction, if you insist!"

He felt terrible. He rubbed a hand over his face. "I'm sorry."

She relented, just a little. After all, he had just had quite a shock. He was as white as a sheet, his hands were trembling and he had clear injuries on one leg and an arm. She gave a long sigh. "Make yourself comfortable, Giedi. That was the easy part. We have been carried way off track. We have to wait out the storm in this tin can, and there are six too many dents in the fuselage for me to feel secure inside it."

He gulped. "Thank you for saving me."

"You're welcome. Don't make me regret it." Her eyes were brittle, challenging.

He looked down. Why was he behaving like a crass idiot? He felt totally miserable. He squeezed his long lanky frame into the miniscule space behind her pilot's chair and settled in. "What happened to the others?"

She lifted her shoulders. "No idea. We have been tossed too far off the race lane. I have no probes that are working and they are too far away to see."

There was a rattle and a thump as they were hit by another anomaly. The controls were almost torn out of Zenzie's hands. Giedi reached across the back of the seat to help her, but she batted his hands away. "I can manage."

"Of course you can."

"Well?"

"Well then."

They found themselves looking at each other. Giedi swallowed again. She was almost as battered as he was, though not bleeding quite so much. A small part of her crest had been pulled out by something and it looked rather strange. He gave a weak smile and reached over to touch it, but she ducked quickly away.

"Don't do that!"

"Does it hurt?"

She shook her head. "We don't have much sensation in our crests. How much of it is gone?"

He tilted his head. "About half an inch, I would say."

She stabbed at the console in front of her. "It doesn't matter."

"It makes you look fierce!"

She forgot her anger with him, just for the briefest of moments, looking up with a grin. "Does it?" Then she remembered and her expression clouded over. "Not that I care."

"No." He folded into the most comfortable posture he could manage in the very limited space available. It was not easy. It meant half-perching on Zenzie's seat, half-crouching behind it. She shuffled over with a huff, but even so there was not enough room for both of them.

"Why did you come for me?" He said, his voice still thick with mortification.

"I really don't know," she snapped. "Maybe I shouldn't have bothered."

He grinned at that and began to laugh.

She let his shoulders shake for a few seconds in glaring silence and then relented. He heard one giggle, then another. Then, just like that, they were both completely out of control. He laughed and laughed, until tears poured out of his eyes and he could hardly breathe. She wasn't much better. Every time one of them managed to get their convulsions under control, the other would set off again. It was so painful after five minutes that they were both clutching their abdomens.

Until another anomaly hit them. There was a huge clatter, right behind Giedi's head. The engine went silent. Then they were drifting in space. In huge, wide, open, black space. An alarm began to sound on the console. It was insistent, impossible to ignore. Zenzie looked down at it. "We have a leak," she said. "If we don't do something about it, we have about six minutes of oxygen left."

Suddenly, none of it was in the least bit funny.

Chapter 7

Denaraz was staring out through the protective steel panel as if he had X-ray eyes that could penetrate it. He didn't. They couldn't. That didn't stop him from trying.

Mallivan put a hand on one of the Tyzaran's shoulders. Izan shrugged it off. "The Chyzar is in danger, and I am not there!"

"It is not your fault."

Denaraz swiveled round and glared at the captain. "Of course it is my fault! It is my *job*, for krikk's sake!"

"Zenzie is quite capable of taking care of herself. You know that, Izan. We have to have faith in her."

Denaraz was beyond rational thought. His crest was perpendicular. He clutched at the captain suddenly. "You have to get me a ship, Mallivan! Let me get out of here. I *have* to help her."

"There is no way we are going anywhere until this supershell storm is over, and you know it. Why? Do you think that the whole thing was planned to harm the Chyzar?"

Izan's gaze was frantic. "What else? If Prime Ohnahara thinks that it is a man-made phenomenon, then who could it be targeted at? They deliberately waited until this race was being held, that much is clear, is it not?"

True. And he was right. It was hard to think of anybody else who might be a target. All the same, there was absolutely nothing any of them could do. They were incommunicado, and likely to stay that way for hours, from what Ohnah had told them.

"They could be targeting the shipstation," Ohnah's voice was soft and worried. "After all, there is a reduced crew on it now."

Ryler tried that one on for size, but it was a stretch to believe. Shipstations could not be moved easily, due to their huge inertia. Their engines could be used, at a pinch, but usually only for micro-corrections to avoid future collisions. Stuff like that. And they were hardly vaults carrying huge amounts of valuables. The Vaer factions had seen to that. Anything worth a lot of money would be deposited in one of the hyper-secure facilities on Agazed. It didn't seem to fit with an attack like this. This was something that had been highly planned, something that was timed down to the last moment. This was the work of someone who was determined to get what they wanted.

Ryler hoped that wasn't the Chyzar, but even he had to admit that it most probably was.

He drew Denaraz down to sit with him on one of the long benches. "I don't know, Izan. If Scout were here I could tell you where the threat is coming from, but I left him on *Nivala*. The only thing we can do is sit..."

"... and wait," The Tyzaran finished in a gloomy voice. "Tell me something I don't know."

Ohnah walked over and sat herself down beside them. "I am so sorry," she said brokenly. "I have put all our children in danger."

The captain shook his head. The waiting had given him time to think. "Not your fault, either. Nobody could have foreseen something like this. Who even knows how to provoke a … what did you call it, Ohnah?"

"An explosive reconnection event. They can happen naturally, when the Chain Nebula provokes X-point collapse. There are probably two or three such events each decade. But we monitor those, and of course, they can be tracked. We are far enough away for us to be able to move the shipstation out of the most destructive central path, if one should happen to track in our direction. It does happen, but only very occasionally. We would have picked up any natural phenomena, no question."

Denaraz narrowed his eyes. "It sounds as though it would need a great deal of energy," he mused. "How would somebody force such an event?" His face creased up in intense concentration. He was at heart a scientist; happiest when working with algorithms and constructs. It would, at least, keep his mind busy, thought Mallivan. Algorithms and constructs had never been his own strong point.

The turbulence was stronger now. They were perfectly safe inside such a well shielded shuttle, but the notion of all those delicate skimmers trying to maintain integrity in the surrounding chaos was disturbing. Ohnah's eyes were damp. Mallivan put an arm around her, though he didn't believe that it would help much. She leant in gratefully, to his surprise.

They sat out the storm like that.

It took hours.

They had almost given up hope of normality ever returning, so the retraction of the steel plates came as a surprise. They all jumped up, eager to see what had happened. Of course, they could see nothing. There were no skimmers within sight, and that was all they had since instrumentation was still down. Nevertheless, there was a surge towards the window, where they all squinted out into the darkness beyond.

Mallivan wasn't able to pick out anything in the gloom, so he found himself turning to Denaraz. Tyzarans have better eyesight than humans. Izan shook his head. The captain's brother-in-law was still very pale.

It wasn't until half an hour later that the comlink squawked and finally came to life. Ohnah hurried across. They couldn't hear what she was listening to, but the captain did see the slump of her shoulders.

He raced across. "What? What has happened?"

She forced her eyes up to meet his and gave a gulp. "It was *Nivala* they wanted to get to. Your ship."

He heard her words, but his brain couldn't seem to process them. "*Nivala*? What do you mean? Who would want *Nivala*?"

The corners of her mouth bent towards the floor. "The Avaraks."

"The *Avaraks*? Why the krikk would they want ...? —Oh ...!"

"They have taken Segaton and Seyal. As far as the shipstation goes, two of my crew are dead. Four more are badly injured and there are still people unaccounted for."

"The skimmers?"

She bit her lip. "We don't know — yet."

"My ship?"

"It undocked before the storm hit. That is current protocol of course. They would have known that. *Nivala* was taken to a safe distance and then the crew would have locked her down. As soon as the storm interfered with all probes and communications, the Avaraks simply pulled alongside, forced their way in through one of the hatches, and fought their way onto the bridge. I am told it was very quick."

"It must have been, if they got Seyal and Segaton. If they had given her any time she could have ducked into the crawl spaces. Male Avaraks can't follow her there."

"Mel was on board and so was your wife, Denaraz."

His crest flickered. My wife? Is she all right?"

"I don't know. They are establishing a vid-link now. It is a problem, because *Nivala* had only a skeleton crew."

She didn't have to say anymore. Mallivan knew who had been behind the whole thing. There was only one Avarak sufficiently determined and twisted to do something like this. Vebor. Doctor Vebor would have something to do with it. Provoking a supershell storm just for his own ends was exactly the sort of thing he would do. The captain should have seen it before.

Seyal had been nipping away at lordly Avarak heels for over a year now. She had been trying to get the women of the species to revolt against their unfair treatment. Their lives were dictated by the males, and the treatment they were required to endure was quite shocking.

Female Avaraks are born with slightly smaller vocal chords, which give them rather harsh voices. To correct this, young girls are often subjected to treatment with injections which block signals from the nerves to the muscles of the throat. This forces the chords to atrophy, and deliver upon puberty a small, hoarse, breathy voice that the male Avaraks find more attractive. Females who have not had the injections are normally operated on in order to correct what the males consider to be birth defects.

Females are also completely different to the males. Where the males are heavy and weighty, the females are thin and almost delicate. The males have large heads with prominent features; the females have poorly defined contours that make them appear of little importance. Their facial features blur into their skin and it is extremely hard for people from other races to tell them apart. Females are only considered of importance only for breeding.

Females aren't taught Universal. Females aren't allowed to do any job considered to require decision-making. Most are conjoined to a male by fifteen, and pregnant by sixteen. As many as sixty-five percent of females die giving birth, so it is most unusual to meet one who is older than twenty, in equivalent Sol years. By then they will have given birth three times, which means that they have only around a four percent chance of reaching twenty-one. Those that do reach this age are freed from marital obligations and become midwives and advisors to the younger generations. Even so, their lifespan is short. Few live to reach thirty-five. The males, on the other hand, can reach seventy years of age and still be productive. The most venerable male Avaraks are in their eighties and nineties and absolutely huge.

Female Avaraks have no vote on anything in their world and do not enjoy emancipation. They belong to their husbands, who are free to mistreat, sell, exchange and even kill them. Nowadays this is frowned upon, but it does still occur in distant mountainous areas of Rhyveka.

A female death is not acknowledged on Rhyveka, whereas a male death requires a long ceremony, attended by all the deceased's offspring. This goes on for three days by law, and any female wives surviving him are ceremoniously auctioned off to the highest bidders. The resultant money raised is used to erect huge mausoleums to his achievements, so most Avaraks make sure they have at least ten wives at all times. They will search far and wide for the females with the most breathy voices, to ensure, if the worst should come to pass, that their resting places should be worthy of them. This means that any noble house of Avarak will have at least three seekers. These are individuals who travel the planet to find the sweetest-voiced females for the males of their houses. Seekers are highly trusted members of any house. The most supremely important male Avaraks can have up to thirty wives at any one time. Avaraks therefore look down on any female. They particularly despise any females with sharp voices. They look down on aliens with only one wife. They don't really like any aliens at all. In fact, they don't really get on with anybody except other male Avaraks, and even that conforms to a strict class structure. They have an almost military organization, one which adapts easily to war. Their leaders are based on a pyramidal concept of power. They are, in fact, fairly war-like creatures, although they would dispute this. They are not a species you want as an enemy.

And Seyal had been putting herself in their sights for months. She very definitely *was* their enemy

It was a huge relief to hear and see Mel on the comlink. "Mel? Are you all right?"

"I am, Rye. But ... But they took Seyal and Segaton ... and ... and your sister."

Blood began to pound in the captain's chest, flooding it. He certainly didn't have any in his face.

"S-S-Sib-by?" he stuttered. "They took S-Sibby?"

There was a thump and he looked around to see a hand-sized dent on one of the benches. Denaraz looking at his fist, from which was trickling a small amount of blood. "You all right?" Ryler asked.

Izan's gaze was pure stone. It could have frozen a gargoyle. "I am." He paused for a few moments, probably to let his military training overcome his emotions. Finally he let out a deep breath and uncurled his long fingers from the fists they had automatically made. "So; we have to retrieve the Chyzar and then get after the Avaraks." He made it sound as though they were simply the next two chores of the day, but Mallivan wasn't fooled. Izan's crest was actually vibrating. The captain had never seen that before, on any Tyzaran, anywhere. You live and learn.

"Gus is missing too," said Mel. "We can't find it anywhere."

"You think they took the Enif as well?"

Mel lifted her hands and grimaced. "Maybe. Or maybe it snuck on board their ship to try to help the others. Either way, it is not currently on board *Nivala*. Scout and I are the only current inhabitants."

"What is the status of *Nivala*, Mel?"

An almost pained expression flickered over her face. "They put explosives around all the bridge consoles, Mal. We won't be going anywhere until those are removed. It is a delicate job. It will take hours, if not a full day."

He found his own hand clenching into a fist. It would be more than satisfying to put another dent in the bench, but he managed to resist temptation. His head told him it wouldn't be helpful, but the fire inside him longed to strike out.

"Fine, Mel. Get *Nivala* towed back to the shipstation, will you? We will be back on board as soon as we can."

He cut the connexion, and Ohnah shot a worried look in their direction. "I will send my two best technicians to your bridge. They can get started on removing the explosives."

"Thank you, Prime. I appreciate that. Now, we need to find all the race contestants and shepherd them back to the shipstation. How are we going to do that?"

Ohnah nodded. "I will mobilize three more shuttles. All will have the capacity to scoop up two or three skimmers. We will take the lead."

"Do you have a runabout?" Denaraz's voice was harsh.

"I believe we have two."

"Then, with your permission, I shall take one. Your priority is any and all participants. Mine is just one. I am obliged to try to find the Chyzar as quickly as possible."

"Of course. I understand."

She didn't, but the prime could see that this was something that Denaraz needed to do.

Izan gave the captain a brief nod and then ran for the shuttle bay. Shortly after, a runabout passed by the window and accelerated away from their position.

Mallivan sighed. There seemed to be too many things to do, all at once. He needed to get to his ship, especially after what had happened, but the children were the immediate priority. He quickly came to an agreement with Ohnah. He would take the second runabout and assume command of one of the other rescue shuttles, leaving Ohnah with this one. They would need to act quickly. Some of those skimmers could be in critical situations.

Or worse, but he wouldn't allow himself to think about that.

Yet.

Chapter 8

Denaraz was soon upon the slowest of the skimmers. He hesitated, but saw that three of the youngest participants were already being helped, and that one of the shuttles Ohnahara had dispatched had rear bay doors open, ready to take them into safety. Two were, amazingly, still under their own steam. One was being towed in by a runabout. Those kids were going to have quite a story to tell, seemingly.

His crest refused to lie flat. He couldn't forget that Sibby had been taken from *Nivala* by the Avarak stealth team. He was terrified that something even worse than that might have happened to her. But his training had kicked in. Despite his white and strained face, Denaraz knew better than to lose focus. His job was to find Zenzara, and find her he would.

Even so, he couldn't simply abandon the other skimmers, and when he came across a distant one that was leaking atmosphere into space, he knew that the Chyzar would have to wait. From the pink color of the skimmer, he realized that this must be Mallivan's middle child, Talitha. Tally was a lovely child, if normally a little reticent. She must be scared to death.

Izan drew his runabout in alongside her shuttle. She was certainly alive, and very glad to see him, since she was jumping up and down in her seat and flapping her arms. He shook his head. Didn't she realize that to do that was to use up even more of the little air she had left?

Of course she didn't. She was almost a baby. These humans were not like Tyzaran children, who were taught to defend themselves as soon as they could walk properly. It was difficult for a Tyzaran to assimilate just how little independence these Spacelanders were given until their late teen years. By twelve, a Tyzaran was normally totally independent of their family.

Izan flipped his runabout in order to dock with the skimmer. It was a standard maneuver and within ten minutes Tally was aboard the bigger ship. She ran over to Denaraz and wrapped her arms around his neck.

"Thank you, Uncle Izan. Thank you!"

His crest wilted and his heart quivered, just a little. He hugged the tiny figure back. "Are you all right, Tally?"

"Yes. But I was getting awfully breathless. I am just glad that you arrived in time to help me. Are we going to find Giedi now?"

He hesitated. Should he take this child back to safety first, or should they carry on together with his rescue mission?

Tally herself was the one to tip the balance. "When the tight-beams came back up nobody could reach either Zenzie or Giedi." she said solemnly as she slipped into the bench seats behind him and strapped in. "We have to hurry."

He nodded. She was right. The three big rescue shuttles would soon be on scene. They were only about fifteen minutes behind him. He reported Tally's rescue together with the position of her damaged skimmer and informed the rescuers that she was with him. Then he turned to the little girl. "Did you see what happened to them?"

She shook her head. "But Leo did. He can tell you."

She leant past him and took up the comlink. Within seconds she was through to her cousin. "Leo. Where did Giedi go again? I am with Denaraz, and we are trying to find them."

Leo's voice was immediate and very relieved, although the connexion was sketchy. "Thank goodness he found you, Tally. I was worried sick that you would run out of air before they got to you. Hi, Uncle Izan!"

"She is fine, Leo. Are you all right?"

"I am. My skimmer is not functional, but I still have air and heating."

"Then you can wait for the rescue shuttles to reach you?"

There was a burst of static before his answer came through. The boy's voice was calm. "I can. Please don't worry about me."

That was a relief. "Did you see anything that would help us?"

"Giedi was hit by something. It impacted on the starboard side of his skimmer and he was propelled off-course to the left, towards Heisenberg's Halo."

Tally reached out and squeezed Denaraz's shoulder. She wanted to give him some kind of reassurance.

Leo had not finished. "But Zenzie followed him. She managed to push that skimmer of hers up to quite a lick. I am sure that she will have found him."

"Was his skimmer losing atmosphere, Leo?"

There was a crackle, silence, then another crackle. "I couldn't see that well, but I did see what looked like a wake of gas. It is possible."

Denaraz's face turned even grimmer. "Can you give me a general area to search?"

"I was at these coordinates when he was hit." The numbers arrived on the runabout's console. "I made sure I registered them. He was about a kilometer in front of me, and his skimmer was thrown off perpendicular to the course at that point."

"Thank you, Leo. Are you sure you are in no need of assistance?"

"Not immediately. Uncle Ryler has already contacted me. He has two more urgent pick-ups to effect, and then it will be my turn."

"Fine. Thanks for your help."

"You may need to hurry. Giedi's ship was pretty beat-up."

"We will."

"Good luck!"

"You too. Out." Denaraz spent a moment to calculate the intercept course to put them on the approximate path that Giedi's ship might have taken, then leant back in his seat and gave a sigh.

"Don't worry, Uncle. They will be fine."

He tried to smile. "Of course they will be, Tally. Just in case, let's get you up to speed on piloting this runabout. If I need to effect an EVA to get to them, you will be in charge of this ship."

She looked alarmed. "Me?" she squeaked. "A runabout?"

"Never piloted one before?"

She shook her head.

"Never mind. Always a first time. Look, the main differences between this and a skimmer are ..." He began to instruct her, keeping his voice calm and even.

Nothing on the control panel had come back to life. Zenzie's crest was drooping. Her eyelids were flickering a little. Giedi moved his cramped legs so that he could reach her shoulders and give her a small tug towards him.

She pushed him away. "What?"

He sighed. "I said I was sorry. Come on, Zenz. We laughed about it."

"So?" She wasn't going to make it that easy for him. "I laugh about lots of things."

"No you don't."

She sniffed. "Maybe you wouldn't either if you were a Chyzar." Her chin went up.

She wasn't wrong, at that. He would hate it. "So. What can we do?"

She bit her lip. "Pray?"

Giedi stared her down. "You're the *Chyzar*! Can't you do better than that?"

She blew out air. "I wish I could ..."

They both fell silent.

Giedi pulled her to her feet. "At least get yourself into your IEVA suit. That will give us twenty more minutes. Or more!"

She stood, swaying slightly. She was trying to get her mind to come up with a solution, but what solution could there be? You can't simply fabricate oxygen out of thin air. Literal thin air. Her shoulders slumped.

Giedi must have come to the same conclusion. His eyes were scanning the skimmer with desperation. He wouldn't find anything. There wasn't anything to find. The skimmers weren't even equipped with full EVA suits.

He turned towards her and pulled her under his arm for a sideways hug. "Are you sure you can't talk to those Chakrans of yours? Ask them to do something?"

She shook her head. "The connection isn't a two-way thing. It isn't like a comlink. It doesn't work like that."

"Pity. That would have been helpful. They could have transported us across space, like that time they saved you all." His tone was distinctly wistful.

She gave the shadow of a smile. "I don't think they can do that anymore. But it would have been nice if they could."

"I'm sorry; this is all my fault. You should never have come to save my stupid life. I was never worth it."

She turned on him in a flash. "You think I would have been happier leaving you to die, Spacelander? Really?"

"You would have been alive. You are the Chyzar. The world needs you."

"And I need *you*." She glared at him as they finished putting on the suits.

"Do you think we would have been together one day? Married, and stuff?"

The voice that answered him was very small. "Yes."

"Can I hug you? Properly?"

She sniffed, but he was pretty sure that she nodded too. He turned her towards him and folded her into a tight embrace. They touched foreheads.

"I love you, Zenzara Zylarian."

"I love you, Giedi Mallivan."

"If we get through this, I will stay with you forever."

"If we get through this, I will let you."

Giedi checked the IEVA readings. Fifteen minutes of oxygen left on his. Fifteen minutes. She would have slightly more. His throat felt thick and painful. It didn't feel fair to find the right person and then to lose both their lives. Was this some kind of gigantic joke on the part of the universe?

They stood together for a long moment, eyes closed. Zenzie was still swaying slightly, as if she could hear some kind of heavenly music playing. He let himself follow the tiny movements. Then he realized how lucky he was. He had, at least, found somebody to love and somebody who loved him. He would die holding the love of his life. A sense of calm acceptance crept over him. Love isn't measured in years, after all.

They didn't speak any more. There wasn't anything to say.

When they had taken a few more breaths, he gestured for her to put her helmet on. He knew that the 'sweet death', as it was called, could creep up on you unannounced. It was time to switch to the remaining air in their IEVA suits.

Zenzie shook her head. She wanted them to stay as they were. She didn't think fifteen or twenty minutes would make any difference.

But it was his job to take care of her. He lifted her helmet himself and fastened it in place, releasing the oxygen flow. That done, he put his own on.

Then he slipped his arms around her again.

Probably for the last time.

On the Avarak cruiser, *Daktar*, Seyal was staring in disbelief at her son.

"You did this?"

He stiffened. "I have a *right* to be with my own race. You have been keeping me away from them. Just because you are unlanded doesn't mean that I have to be as well! When Kelkator reached out to me, I realized what you had been doing. You and your so-called friends. He told me how you have been working against our people. The Spacelanders have turned you against us."

Seyal self-effaced herself so much that Sibby had a bit of a job to even see her. It was as if the female Avarak had shrunk almost out of existence. She felt sorry for her. It seemed that Segaton had a mind of his own, and could speak it. Nobody had expected that from a three-year old. Though she knew that three for an Avarak was equivalent to teenage for a Human or a Spacelander. That was a bad time for *any* species. She shook her head. Avarak males clearly grew up very fast and very opinionated.

His mother stared at him aghast for ten long seconds before she was able to formulate words again. "You told them about the race? It was *you* who gave them all the details? How could you! People will have died! The contestants are just children, like you!"

"They are Spacelanders," he hissed. "Nothing like me!"

"Oh, Segaton." She shrank into herself just a little more.

Sibby stepped forwards. "This is not your fault, Seyal. Children can be easily swayed. They will have told him whatever they thought he wanted to hear. Don't be too hard on him."

"He has endangered my friends. They are my family, now."

Segaton's eyes narrowed. "They say you have been disgracing *our* family name. *My father's* family name. You don't have the right to do that. It is an old and honorable landed name. It is mine to take, not yours to bring down. I couldn't let you ruin my father's name. I couldn't."

Seyal shook her head, dumbly, but Sibby swung around to face the Avarak boy. "You fool, Segaton! You have let them poison your mind against your own mother! You *know* that female Avaraks are persecuted on Rhyveka! You *know* how many of them die!"

"This has nothing to do with you or your Tyzaran husband. You need to keep out of it." He stared her down, his tone arrogant.

Sibby gave a gasp, then narrowed her eyes and took a deep breath, preparatory to speaking. She had quite a bit more to say, but the door to the holding area opened and three large Avarak males came in. One was walking slightly in front of the others. She heard what sounded like a whimper from Seyal's direction, so turned immediately to comfort her. Her friend was quivering.

"Come here, Segaton," the leader instructed in a gravelly, rumbling voice.

The boy obeyed.

"You have done most well. We are pleased with your cooperation. We shall find you a house that will prepare you for your future in Rhyveka."

"You shouldn't have taken my mother. Or this woman. You said nobody would be harmed!"

Vebor spread his arms. "Alas. Sometimes things do not go according to plan." His words were smooth, but Sibby could tell he was lying to the young boy. They may have told Segaton that they were merely coming to take him 'home', but it would have been Vebor's intention all along to remove Seyal. The Avarak Grand Council had offered a reward for her capture months ago. They would do anything to stop her activism. She had been actively undermining their authority on Rhyveka. Actively attempting to improve the lot of all Avarak women. Sibby gave a small snort. She herself might only have been a target of opportunity, but Seyal's capture most definitely had been planned.

"He is lying to you, Segaton," she told him quietly. "He convinced you to betray your mother in order to capture her."

"I betrayed nobody!" shouted the young Avarak. "It is my mother who has betrayed her husband. Her people! *My* people!" He turned angrily towards his progenitor. "This is your own fault, Mother. You should never have kept me so isolated. I have a *right* to be with my own race!"

"You certainly do." Vebor inclined his head. "You will lead a great House."

"I shall be Head of my own House!" The boy lifted his chin. "See, Mother!"

"It shall all be as we agreed," said the newcomer. "However, you will need more instruction before that can happen. This female," He indicated Seyal with a derogatory sweep of his hand, "has indoctrinated you with that which is contrary to our customs. You need to be re-educated."

Segaton didn't look best pleased to hear that. "I want my rightful House *now!*" he muttered.

The leader pinned him with a stern look. "That comment shows just how far you have been corrupted," he said, shaking his enormous head sadly. "That is what happens when females are allowed license. It is why all such outbursts must be stopped." He nodded to the other two Avaraks behind him. "Take them away. You know what to do."

They both nodded and approached Sibby and Seyal. The two women huddled together. They were half the size and a quarter of the weight of their kidnappers. They were hardly in a position to get into a physical struggle.

As the two women were dragged out of the hold, Seyal's eyes met those of her son. She simply gazed at him. The disappointment and pain were clear to see. Sibby reached out to try to touch Seyal's hand, but even the Spacelander's eyes were clouded with sadness.

The Avaraks tore the two women apart and tugged them out of the bulkhead doors.

Segaton frowned. "Where are you taking them?"

"I am afraid that you won't be able to see your mother for some time, Segaton, heir to the Solutor House. It would restrict your progress. But you must not worry for her. She is being taken care of as I speak. Now, would you like a tour of this ship? Your family used to have many just like it."

All was forgotten. "Really? Will I have one too? My own personal ship?"

"Of course, Segaton." A heavy hand came down on his shoulder. "You will have many more than one. As did your father, who gave his life for Rhyveka. *Avarak Karax!*"

"*Avarak Karax!*" Little Segaton's growing chest inflated with pride, and he rapidly forgot his mother as he followed the eminent doctor out of the brig. He would follow in his father's footsteps! He would be a hero, like him! He had always known he was destined for great things.

Denaraz was frantically searching the empty space in front of him. Unfortunately, the scanners he had available to him in the utilitarian runabout were not of the finest quality. More than once he had thumped the console he was sitting at in frustration. His crest was fully vertical. He had a really bad feeling about this.

"There, Uncle. Over to the left!" Tally's sharp eyes had caught a small reflection. Izan swung the sensors around to confirm that she had detected a skimmer. She had, but what he saw made his heart plummet. There were two skimmers, compacted together by loose fuselage. Neither was showing an atmosphere. He felt his heart lose a beat.

He put the runabout beyond its normal capacity, entering the coordinates to let the other search ships know that the two missing skimmers had been located. They thundered down on the two broken spacecraft, Tally's face paler than pale as she realized the situation.

"Get up here, Tal!"

She shuffled obediently behind the console. "Don't slow down," he told her. "Bring us in hard and fast. Then slam all the brakes on and take us alongside."

She showed him a terrified face. "You want me to crash into them?"

He was putting himself into an IEVA suit. "Nope. I want you to stop this thing on a dime and come alongside as fast as you can. There is still a chance they are alive. They have IEVA suits." He grabbed two spare helmets and tied them to his belt. "As soon as you come to a halt, I will take these over to them."

Her face went even whiter, if that was possible. "You are going out of the ship before we stop?"

"I am. There may not be time to do it once we are docked."

"But ... but ... but you might be killed!"

"Yeah. I might. But that is my job, Tally. It's on me, not you. Now, can you do it?"

Her whole mouth quivered. Denaraz thought for a moment that she was going to take her hands off the controls. But he had underestimated her. She looked down at her hands and swallowed, but her words were clear. "I will do my best."

He dropped a small kiss on the top of her head. "You will do great!"

The mouth wobbled again, but she corrected it. "Of course I will. It runs in the family!"

"Show me!"

Denaraz clipped his own helmet in place and made his way over to the airlock. It was much bigger than those on a skimmer, and only took him a moment to enter. Tally gave him a woebegone look. He nodded his head to her and let the corner of his eyes crinkle. It was unfair of him to ask this of such a young girl, but he could see no other option. Seconds mattered in this situation. He was putting all of their lives in her hands. He just hoped that she would not buckle under the strain. He was depending on her having inherited Ryler's dexterity as well as just the Mallivan genes.

He gave a slight wave of his gloved hand and then reached across the airlock to activate the hatch. It clamped down quickly, shutting all sight of Tally and the cabin. Denaraz released the air he hadn't realized he had been holding in. His stint in the Tyzaran Navy had taught him to discipline his body; he needed to stay relaxed.

Within two minutes he was outside the runabout. He looked up and forwards to see the two skimmers only a hundred or so yards in front. He shuffled slightly backwards to protect himself as best he could, gripping onto the slightly protruding airlock hatch and making himself as small as possible.

Inside the runabout, Tally was gripping the controls with icy, white hands. She was muttering to herself. *Not too early. Not too late.* Her heart was pounding and she was finding it difficult to breathe.

She had no idea how to get this maneuver just right. How could she? It wasn't exactly the sort of thing that you practiced doing at her age. You had to be over eighteen to get onto the periodic courses that all space-going Spacelanders were required to undertake.

She blinked furiously. Her eyes were misting up. She couldn't think of any reason they would be doing that, but they were. Then she became aware of dampness running down her cheeks. She was sweating. That would explain the eye problem.

And then it was too late to worry about anything more, because they were *there.* As if she had nothing to do with it, her hands and fingers wrenched the small craft over, spinning it up and flipping it so as to present the underbelly to the pile of scrap metal – all that was left of the skimmers.

The runabout began to tremble and judder furiously. Pieces of metal pinged off the joint wreckage as they came in closer and closer to the skimmers. At first it was just a shower of light particles, then they began to collide with large pieces of scrap and fuselage. These hammered into the outer shell of her runabout, pitting the outer skin. They rattled down like superdense hailstones. Tally found herself ducking.

Her mind drifted out to Denaraz, crouched on the outside of the craft. She dragged her concentration back. Losing it would be no help to anybody, least of all him.

The shuttle fought the final correction that brought it to a full stop from such a high entry velocity. It seemed to be rebelling against her will, eager to escape all control and batter the two skimmers as if they were billiard balls.

Tally hung onto the controls like grim death, a ghastly smile across clenched teeth. The whole console bucked and shied, but still she clung on. Even though she had to close her eyes, she hung on. As the two skimmers came closer and closer she shut out the sight. It was only going to make things worse. She knew what was happening; she did not have to see it.

The shuttle shuddered more and more. She stopped breathing altogether. There was a harsh squeal of metal against metal and she was thrown off her chair. The shuttle gave a final screech before subsiding into silence.

Tally collapsed over the controls. Then she turned and threw up.

Chapter 9

When the supershell storm first came, Gus had just rejoined *Nivala* from the shipstation. The Enif was trying to find Sibby to share the success of their joint efforts. The micro-camera on its pet sunflyer's back was installed and working, though it had taken the Enif quite a time to catch the insect after the first trial.

The Enif realized almost immediately that something was very wrong when the starboard outer hatch activated almost directly in front of it on the middle deck.

That was not logical. Caught with no weapons and no way of defending itself, it ducked silently back into the nearest shelter – starboard storage room five. The only way it had of knowing what was going on was via Toothpick's newly installed camera, which transferred tactile images through Gus's arm translator software. Gus ushered the small insect out through a chink in the door, careful not to open the locker door more than a sliver.

The sunflyer naturally followed the organics that were boarding the ship. The prospect of grazing on such large animals was too tempting to resist, so Gus soon realized that they were Avaraks. It was able to track them along the corridor and into the lifts. Toothpick shied from entering the lifts with them, which enabled Gus to sneak out of its hiding place and recover its pet.

The Avaraks had not left a sentry behind, it seemed. Gus quietly tracked back towards the entry point. The hatch had been left open. It was easy to see the inside of a large Avarak cruiser through a short concertina walkway. Because of the storm which raged around them, the docking tube shook and jittered in space.

Gus found itself with a bit of a dilemma. What should it do? It could run quickly to the nearest tight-beam and try to warn the shipstation of this intrusion. Though, if they had coupled to *Nivala* this easily, surely all of the scanners were down? Would the crew of the shipstation be able to foil the Avarak plans? Perhaps not. *Nivala* was no longer docked at the station, after all. So who could?

The conclusion was inescapable. The only member of *Nivala's* crew that was in a position to hamper the Avaraks was one very scared Enif, Gus itself.

Enif are not generally prone to fear, but Gus was still very young and had limited experience in any sort of conflict or combat situation. It had been blessed with a brilliant mind, even by Enif standards, but it had not been allowed to participate in any space training exercises. It had, after all, been expected to commit ceremonious suicide. The authorities on Enifa had not bothered with Gus's education, leaving the young Enif very much to its own devices.

With tremendous care, Gus edged its way along the hatchway, peering out into the ship beyond. Could the concertina walkway be sabotaged, perhaps? That might serve to abort their attack. Yes, that might just be possible. It crept closer.

But then a huge disturbance behind it put all thoughts of sabotage out of mind. The Avaraks were back, and from the noise, they were not alone.

In a flash, Gus ducked through the walkway and into the Avarak vessel. There, it found two hefty members of the crew, waiting. Luckily they were talking earnestly together, studying a hand-held device of some sort. Gus checked to see what was above it and easily swarmed straight up the bulkhead wall and into the ceiling recess which housed the hydraulics of the concertina walkway. There it sat, trembling.

The walkway began to jump from side to side as the Avarak team returned. Gus was horrified to see Sibby and Seyal being dragged unceremoniously along behind two of the intruders. Sibby had her arms around Seyal and was trying to prevent them from taking her. The captain's sister was shouting at the Avaraks to leave Seyal alone, but they were ignoring her totally. They were so strong that Sibby was being towed along with the group. Her shoes were scrambling against the deck plating, but she simply was not able to get enough of a foothold to make any difference. Seyal's son, Segaton, was running on his slightly shorter legs beside the first Avarak.

The leading Avarak slowed and snapped out a question. Gus, thanks to the permanent translator device which changed audio to electric impulses, and was also graduated for the Avarak language, was able to understand.

"What do we do with the Spacelander female? Shall I shoot her?"

The largest male, who was bringing up the rear, hesitated, clearly weighing up the pros and cons. Finally, he spoke in a gravelly tone loaded with authority.

"No. Bring her too. We can decide what to do with her later. I don't recognize her, and we need to get out of here as fast as we can.

It won't take long for the shipstation to recalibrate their sensors. We need to get going."

Seyal's son, who was walking immediately in front of the second speaker, stumbled, and almost fell. The large Avarak reached out to steady him and gave him a little push.

"Do try to keep up," he said, modifying his tone to as close to genial as an Avarak could get.

Gus frowned. It didn't seem as though Segaton were being forced along the docking tube. But then, perhaps the youngling was merely following where his mother was taken.

Gus's plan to cut the docking tube was now worthless. Its best hope would be to remain on board the Avarak ship, to be of use to the captain's sister and Seyal. It peered around. This position was hardly secure; within seconds the docking tube would be retracted, and there was not going to be room in this reduced space for an Enif and the tube. It looked frantically around.

A light touch on its carapace announced the arrival of Toothpick, who had tracked his owner down easily after taking off to explore its new surroundings. The sunflyer landed lightly on Gus's shoulder and began to groom himself. Gus felt a ridiculous sense of relief at not being completely alone. Suddenly, the chance to thank the captain for his trust had presented, and this Enif was not going to let him down. It would hide until it was able to save Sibeal, Seyal and Segaton, and that was that.

Gus looked quickly around. There were now several Avaraks in the passageway, but the corridor was high and the walls were painted black, which would help disguise an Enif presence. There seemed to be a slight indentation to the right, where some sort of cabling had been threaded through the ceiling. Discreetly, it shifted until it was pretty sure that discovery was impossible. Then it waited. It was hard to see just how it could manage to rescue three prisoners from a large Avarak cruiser in flight, but Gus was just going to take it step by step. Once the passageway was empty, the rescue mission could start.

Denaraz was almost ripped away from the exterior plating of the shuttle as it hurtled to a halt alongside the two downed skimmers. He was all right until the metal underbelly of the shuttle ploughed through the fuselages of the two crumpled and weirdly conjoined ships. The force of that inertial braking was enough to dislodge the tight grip on the hatch and tumble him over and over. Luckily he had foreseen this, and had fastened himself to the hatch with two long ropes. This gave him the leeway he needed to stay attached to the shuttle sleeve and prevent him being swatted effortlessly off into outer space.

It took him ten seconds to pull himself back to the hatch. Another thirty to propel himself, hand over hand, along the exterior of all three craft to find where Giedi and Zenzara were.

They were huddled together, uncomfortably, in the most structurally sound of the two skimmers. From his position it was impossible to see if they were alive or dead.

He fought to tear open the outer hatch. For once, his military aplomb had deserted him. He was terrified for his wife, and now for the safety of the Chyzar and that of Mallivan's son. His mind was screaming at him to hurry. It was refusing to listen to his logical pleas for it to calm down. The ancestral path of fight or flight was challenging his capacity to think before acting.

The airlock was being recalcitrant, but he wrenched it open, uncaring of the damage he was doing to his own hands. The protective gloves were rent in the process, causing red warnings to go off in his helmet. The suit was open to the cosmos. He didn't care.

He jammed himself into the airlock without heed for his own safety, yanking the hatch down and jabbing three of his fingers at the buttons to equalize pressure.

The next seconds felt like minutes. His hands were beginning to hurt where they had been exposed to the vacuum, but he hardly felt them. There was a shout building up inside his chest that he simply could not contain. It wasn't one that could be heard outside his own body. It was silent, but no less frightening for that. It seemed to peal on and on around his neurons.

At last the green light flickered on. He punched the inner hatch release and fell, rather than climbed, down the ladder, landing with an ungainly stumble.

He was at the couple's side with three long strides. He tore off their IEVA helmets and slammed one of the replacement ones he had brought on each of them. Then he frowned.

All IEVA helmets had to be made to the same specifications, precisely so that emergencies such as this one could be dealt with easily. According to all of the training he had undergone, the new helmets should immediately and automatically begin to force high oxygen air into their lungs. But was that what they were doing? He could see no change in Zenzara's face. It was horribly still, lifeless. It was not grabbing greedily at the new air that should be touching her nasal passages. Denaraz thumped her on the back. It made no difference.

He twisted to look at Giedi. The boy was pallid and unresponsive, even with the new helmet. Had he done something wrong? Was there a switch somewhere that he had missed? He shook the boy's thin shoulders. Nothing.

All he could think of to do was the Tyzaran unblock. There was nothing else left. He stood behind the boy, extended his arms around Giedi and placed his left hand flat just below the boy's sternum. Then he placed his right hand in a fist over that. Then he gave a succession of short, sharp pulls.

There was a gurgle as some remnant of air was expelled from Giedi's lungs. Then there was a gasp, a groan and a heave of the chest as air was drawn in with a pained wheeze.

Denaraz dropped the boy, who collapsed to the deck, coughing, and leapt across to Zenzara. He did the same to her, using even more force than he had with Mallivan's eldest. Tyzaran bone structure was stronger and far more resilient than that of a Spacelander.

The first time nothing happened. Izan began to think that he really was too late, that the young girl had slipped away from them. His eyes filled with tears. He decided to give it one more try. He pounded his fist against his open hand, using all the force he possessed. His own hand responded with a shaft of pain: he had broken one of the smaller bones in his palm.

He also thought he may have broken one of Zenzara's ribs. The blow penetrated further into her rib cage. At least, so it seemed to him. He let his arms tighten around her, hugging her thin and slumped body against him. "Please don't die, Chy Zenzara. It is not your time. It cannot be your time."

Then, suddenly, the body his arms were encircling gave a convulsion. He was taken completely by surprise, and dropped her. She slammed into the deck plating and convulsed again.

Denaraz dropped onto one knee beside the prone and writhing body, his heart exploding with hope. He propped her up against that knee so that she would have easier access to breathing.

To his great relief, her small mouth opened. She took in a trial breath of the air in the helmet, as though it couldn't be trusted. Just the whisper of a breath. He would hardly have been able to tell, had he not been searching for any sign of it. Her eyes flickered, though her crest remained flaccid.

There was a small pause, as if she were sampling the air quality. Then, to his great delight, she dragged in three huge breaths, one after another. He hugged her tightly, before realizing that to do so might impede the passage of that very life-giving air she so desperately needed. He found himself grinning inanely to himself.

He dragged the two youngsters over to the console and propped them up, side by side. Giedi seemed to be breathing with more regularity, though Zenzara would clearly need long minutes to replenish the air she her body was gulping in.

Denaraz reached for his comlink. "We were in time."

The comlink was opened from the shuttle, but he could only hear tears. Tally was sobbing. She wasn't the only one. His own face was wet. He closed his eyes for a moment. That had been far, far closer than it should have been. He breathed out. They had brought two back from the brink, but how many were still out there?

It took Gus more than five hours to find out where Sibby and Seyal were being kept and get itself there. The two captives had been thrown roughly into a holding cell on one of the lowest decks of the Avarak cruiser.

Gus thought it likely that the two women were being monitored in some way, so made no move to contact them. Instead, it worked its way around the cell slowly, checking each electric access hatch.

After another two hours it was fairly sure it had found all of the relevant monitoring. There were three hidden cameras and four additional audio links, with five separate access points.

All the while, the sunflyer had been resting on the Enif's

shoulder, showing no desire to explore the ship. Gus was happy about that. Tsuf was not like a dog or a cat; he could not be trained easily to sit or to wait.

The Enif bent its shimmering blue-black head over its dark carapace, thinking. How could it effect an escape from the Avarak cruiser?

Things would be slightly easier if the two captives could survive in outer space for long periods, like the Enif. Unfortunately, that was not the case. Both women would need full EVA suits if they were to abandon the ship. And surely, they would be detected.

Well, the first move would be to contact them and assess the situation. That would involve setting up loops on both the video and audio. That was something Gus *could* be getting on with.

It took around fifty minutes to set up video and audio loops. They were both relatively easy, because neither of the captives was moving or talking. They were both hunched against the bulkhead, each lost in her own thoughts.

Gus was about to initiate the loops when the deck plating began to vibrate under its feet. At least one of the heavy Avaraks was approaching. It scrambled up into the ceiling recesses as fast as it could, trying to position itself so as to be able to hear the exchange with the two *Nivala* crewmembers.

The Avarak that Gus had last seen bringing up the rear in the docking tube walked into view. He must have been important, because he was flanked by two guards. These took up positions stolidly in front of the cell, facing inwards.

Seyal's voice was thin, but full of loathing. "Avexk mexkkara Helekx, Vebor?" It sounded dismissive. The Avarak woman clearly knew this male and did not find him very likeable. Gus wondered where her dislike came from. The Enif was pleased to see that the translator strapped to one forearm could cope with Avarak even at that distance. That was going to prove helpful. Though Gus had no idea why Seyal would have spat 'Where is the honor in this, Vebor?' at the large leading Avarak.

The Avarak disabled the force field in front of the cell and stepped through into the area of reclusion. "I am glad you do not dare to speak Universal in front of your betters, Female!" came back the rumbling answer. "I will have you whipped if you do. It is most regrettable to find you in this position. Your husband hailed from a noble family, one which did not deserve to be implicated in your ill-judged actions. You have shown yourself to be subversive. Submission is a requirement of the law."

"Your law," said Seyal, uncharacteristically pushing her chin out.

Vebor turned slightly pink with anger at her comment. He stepped closer to her and pushed his face almost into hers. She flinched.

"My hands are tied," he spread them apart as if to emphasize that actually this was not so. "I can do nothing for you. It is my duty to inform you formally that the Grand Council has voted to take you back to Rhyveka where you will be put to death by fire."

Seyal's eyes widened. Gus found it hard not to make any sound.

"This can hardly be a surprise to you, female! You have only yourself to blame!" Vebor continued to speak from a lofty position of certainty. His lack of tone made it sound as though he were sorry for Seyal's plight. Only his eyes betrayed him. They were enjoying every single moment of the conversation.

"I know how you treat your wives, Dr. Vebor. You are a sadist. You need not play the statesman to me."

The huge chin stiffened and the eyes sparked with dislike. "You will make such good kindling," he whispered evilly, his tone so low that Gus had to struggle to hear his words. "We'll invite all of the top venerables to warm their drinks up on your bones, shall we?

There will be many who are happy to toast the end of your agitating, female!"

He rotated his giant head so that he could examine Sibby, changing to Universal so that he would be understood. "And you, Spacelander! I did hope you might prove useful, but I have already heard back from Rhyveka. They have no use for you after all. It pains me greatly to say it, but you are to go straight out of the nearest airlock." He swept an imaginary piece of fluff off his tunic. "Such a waste."

Sibby lifted her own small chin. "You think I want stay on this ship, you great lump of lard? I'd rather die looking at the stars than spend a moment in the same space as you!"

Vebor simply spread his hands. "Well, then. It seems we are all in agreement."

Seyal's broken voice interrupted. "My s-son? What is the Council going to do with my son?"

Vebor laughed. It was a brittle but booming sound which made Gus's sensitive skin crawl. The Enif gave an automatic shiver of aversion.

"Your son," Vebor said, his tone deliberately falsely jovial, "has decided to stay with his own race. He does not wish to grow up with an unhinged female dissident. He will be adopted into a strong Avarak male family until he takes control of his father's heritage." There was a long, smug pause. "What is left of his father's heritage, that is." Vebor straightened up until he towered over Seyal. "I believe there is a ship or two left." He removed another speck of something from his attire. "There was rather a feeding frenzy over his estate once you began your agitating, female!"

"You can't do that!"

"Can't?" Vebor seemed puzzled. "Can't? Do you really believe that as a female you have rights? I thought that was what you were bleating about in the first place. You have none. You never did. You have nothing, female. Even your voice is unpleasantly scraping. It offends me. You should have been operated on years ago. I can't think what your husband was thinking. Maybe I should do that before we carry out your sentence. It seems fitting. You have been using that voice too much, after all. So strident. As your doctor, I would be willing to oblige. Would you object to the usual anesthetic, I wonder? One of those rights you claim you never had? Perhaps I could be persuaded to forgo it. Just for you, you understand." The Avarak's eyes narrowed. "Solutor allowed you to remain undoctored. That alone showed him to be weak."

Seyal had been shrinking more and more throughout this diatribe. Now, she seemed almost to disappear into herself.

Vebor grinned, showing three rows of large white teeth. "Your son doesn't want to see you again. He is an Avarak male. He will never be subservient to a mere female again. He has already taken the oath."

What little was left of Seyal seemed to evaporate, Gus thought. Her whole demeanor became that of utter defeat. She looked as if she would welcome the chance to throw herself out of an airlock. Segaton had chosen his allegiance. The Avarak woman was beaten. Gus knew about the will to live. And Seyal didn't have that, not right now.

Sibby leapt to her feet. She must have been very frightened, but she wasn't showing it. She was already in Vebor's face, shouting at the enormous Avarak. Since they had reverted to Avarak she couldn't have understood what had been said, but his face had given her the gist.

"Leave her alone!" she shrieked, making the huge figure in front of her wince with disgust at the high-pitched feminine voice. "Your stupid antiquated rules make me sick!"

"And why should I care what you … a female … thinks?" rumbled Vebor, changing to Universal.

"You are Neanderthals!" she snapped. "You have no right to run about the Major Shells as if you were civilized people!"

His arm came out and swiped her aside, catching her full face. She stumbled, fell over Seyal and went full-length onto the deck plating. Had Gus been warm-blooded, it might have been tempted to leap to her defense. But as an Enif, it wasn't. It was cold-blooded. It would wait its chance to participate in unfolding events.

Sibby pulled herself to her feet and spat at Vebor. "You are no better than the Vaer!" she yelled. "Worse!"

Vebor shook his head. "I am afraid that you are merely confirming the Grand Council's decision, you know. They thought that you would be uncooperative."

"No shit, Einstein!"

"According to their wishes, you will be forcibly disembarked. I do hope there is nobody who might miss you." His sharp eyes caught her reaction. "Ahh. There is. Such a pity. Most regrettable. However, you should have stood aside when we boarded your ship. I am really afraid that you have nobody else to blame but yourself."

Sibby's eyes flashed again, but she made no further comment. Gus thought that she too must have given up hope, for her arms dropped slightly.

Vebor let the pause elongate, then turned and walked out of the cell, making sure that it was secured behind him. "I will let you ladies pray to whatever gods you may have. Once the ship reaches the Dark Confines, the Spacelander female will be ejected from *Daktar*." He gave what passed as a smile for an Avarak male. "Time to say your goodbyes."

Sibby let his heavy footsteps recede and then bent down to Seyal. "He seemed nice," she said, heavy on the irony. "I gather you have met him before?"

Seyal allowed herself to expand out slightly, though she was clearly still very affected. "He knows your brother too," she managed to get out. "He left us to die once before, only we were found by … well, never mind. Not relevant now. He's a doctor."

"Is he? I guess he had his fingers crossed behind his back when he took the Hippocratic Oath," mused Sibby. "He seems to make a habit of wanting you to die."

"I'm sorry, Sibeal. This is my fault. Maybe I should never have tried to change things on Rhyveka. What can one female do, after all?"

Sibby grinned. "You would be surprised. The Grand Council members are obviously scared of you!"

"They are?" Seyal seemed amazed at that thought.

"If not, they have gone to an awful lot of trouble to kidnap you. Yes, I suspect your campaign has had a much greater effect than you think. And don't worry about me. I have always known the risks of coming out into space." Her forehead crumpled a little. "Though I would have liked a little more time with Izan."

"I'm afraid there is no way out this time."

Gus knew that there would never have a better cue. The Enif quickly set all the loops in motion and then approached the force field that was keeping them in the cell. "About that …"

Chapter 10

It was ten long minutes before the young couple in front of Denaraz regained consciousness. Zenzara was the first. Her eyes fluttered open and then relaxed as they fell on Izan's face, which was half hidden behind his helmet.

"Giedi...?" she managed.

"Will be fine—" Denaraz smiled down at her, "—but it was a pretty close run thing."

She frowned, detecting the lurch of worry in his voice. "Thank you, Denaraz. I am sorry." Then she clutched at his arm. "I *had* to come after Giedi. I couldn't leave him to die alone. You understand?"

Denaraz thought of his wife, possibly facing death at this very moment. Without him. His face was grim. "I do."

Zenzara picked up immediately on the pain written across his face. "What is it? What has happened?"

He shook his head. "Now is not the time, Chy Zenzara. My first priority is to make sure that both you and Master Giedi here are safe."

"I'm fine." She managed to swing herself over onto her knees and shuffled over to Giedi's side. There, she stared down into his face. Denaraz was almost shocked by the tenderness he saw in hers. She had never been in the least demonstrative until now.

"I am going to marry him," she said, in a soft voice.

Denaraz blinked. "Marry him?"

"Mmm." She stroked Giedi's helmet absent-mindedly and then seemed to bring herself into sharper focus. She sat back on her haunches. "When we are a lot older, of course. In ten years."

"In ten years you will still only be twenty."

"I know. It is very young for a Tyzaran. But I also know that this will happen."

Denaraz searched her factions. "You are sure?"

She nodded, leaning down to tuck a stray hair behind the boy's ear. "I am sure."

"Then I must offer you my congratulations."

She broke into a radiant smile. "Thank you, Izan."

"So ... you have become multi-layered?"

"I have. And it is true. There really can be a joining of the souls. Is that how it is with you and Sibeal?"

He nodded. He would have answered, but a lump as big as an asteroid seemed to have lodged in his throat.

"I knew you would come." It was a simple statement of her trust in him.

"I will always come."

"I know. I just didn't think you would be in time, this time."

His face became very, very serious. "I nearly wasn't." Then he remembered. "And we must thank Tally for a very good piece of flying."

"Is she in that shuttle then? Well done for her!"

Giedi chose that moment to give a small moan. His eyes flickered open and then closed a couple of times. "Ouch!"

"Giedi!" she cried. "You are all right!"

He winced. "I won't be if you screech like that, Zenz. Can you tone the volume down, please?" He looked around gingerly. "We are alive then?"

She gave a playful punch to his shoulder. "Of course we are, silly! Denaraz and Tally came to get us."

"They did?" He tried to sit up but struggled to keep his head upright. Denaraz slipped his elbow behind the Spacelander's neck to help the boy. "Ooof! I feel like I went through a ZEPH drive backwards!"

Zenzie stared down at him, a set expression in her eyes. "Giedi, we will be getting married. That all right with you?"

"Right now?" he asked, his tone dubious. "I'm not sure I can stand up."

"No, Silly, in ten year—" She broke off, and her whole face illuminated. She turned to Denaraz, her whole countenance alight with eagerness. "Why not? We could do it now, couldn't we? There aren't any laws to prohibit a Pact of Intention, are there?" She must have caught Izan's expression, because she put up one hand. "No, I know we are too young to be physically married, but we could be soul-bonded, couldn't we?"

"I guess, but I think the Tyzaran Council and Giedi's father might have something to say about that."

"Oh, pooh. Who cares about them? If we are soul-mixed then even the stuffy old spokesdesignates will know that we are destined for each other. So will the Supreme Council. And Mallivan loves me like a daughter already, right?"

She didn't pick up on Denaraz's expression, which was expressing some doubt at that last statement. Her face was illuminated. "Good idea, Giedi! Right now it is! We will get bonded next week and then you will be able to come with me on all our adventures."

Giedi managed a weak grin. "Oh well, in that case ..."

His soon-to-be soulmate swiped at him. "Oh, you ..."

Denaraz helped the prospective bridegroom up. "I had better get the two of you back to the shuttle. You seem to have written off both these skimmers. Good job."

"There is no need to get snarky, Denaraz. I saved his life, didn't I?"

"You certainly did."

"One-zero, Gie. Your turn next."

He licked at his dried lips to wet them and then put his right hand stiffly over his heart. "I promise."

Zenzara actually managed a skip in the reduced height of the battered skimmer. "I will hold you to that!"

Denaraz, who was suddenly feeling very old, shook his head. Then he ushered them over to the airlock, which would only take two. "If I put you two in here together, are you capable of making it over to the shuttle airlock without putting either of your lives in danger?"

The Chyzar pulled herself up to her full height, hitting her head on the ceiling and giving a slight yelp, which rather ruined the solemnity of the occasion.

"Of course we are!"

Denaraz extended one arm politely. "After you, then." He checked both of their helmets. They had over fifteen minutes of air left. His own EVA suit had less than ten. He helped them into the airlock. "No dallying. You need to get inside that shuttle as fast as you can. I didn't come all this way just to see you run out of oxygen because you were too busy sightseeing."

"Bah. We aren't children, you know!"

Izan kept his smile to himself. "I realize that."

The Chyzar allowed her feet to be unceremoniously pushed into the airlock. She looked down at the tall Tyzaran. "Will you be my bridal custodian, Denaraz?"

"If the council hasn't jailed me for dereliction of duty."

"Oh, very funny."

Denaraz flipped the hatch closed and secured it. Once the two youngsters were on their way he allowed his mind to go to his wife. He wondered if she was feeling the same empty fear in her heart that he was. The same sense of desolation, of panic. It was horribly uncomfortable. Having your soul mixed with somebody else's had its drawbacks, too.

Tally was ready with a hot sugary beverage, which she shoved into Zenzie and Giedi's hands as soon as she had helped them off with their helmets. Then she hugged them both so tightly that half of the content of the cups ended up on the floor.

Her brother seemed suddenly older than he had been at breakfast that morning. "Hear you have turned into quite the pilot," he told her.

She flushed with pleasure. "I was scared out of my mind," she confessed.

He waved a hand. "Doesn't matter, Tal. You did it. That's all that counts."

"I nearly knocked Denaraz off the hatch." Seeing that they didn't know the whole story, she filled them in. Even Zenzie's eyebrows went up when she heard that Denaraz had been EVA when the shuttle landed on the skimmers. He had said it had been a close-run thing. But that was *really* close.

Too close for comfort.

In her cell, Sibeal Mallivan looked up in shock as she heard Gus's comment.

"Thagaarus," she whispered, remembering the long form of the Enif's name, much to its gratification. "How the krikk ...?" She made to leap up and then remembered the cameras, resulting in a sort of twisted motion that pushed into Seyal, causing the Avarak woman to topple over from her hunched, back-against-the-wall position on the floor. Sibby pulled her back up with both hands and patted her down. "Sorry!"

"It's all right," Gus hastened to tell them. "I have disabled the cameras and the audio links."

Both women stood up then and hurried over to the force field.

"How the Shells did you get here?" asked Sibby, again.

Gus explained, finishing, "... so I thought I might be able to rescue you."

Sibby's smile radiated around the cell. "That would be great, Gus." Then she remembered where they were. "But how can we get away? We are in the middle of empty space in an Avarak cruiser."

"Yes. That is the problem I haven't quite managed to solve yet."

Seyal gave a heavy sigh. "I can't go without Segaton."

Gus and Sibby exchanged a look. That simply wasn't going to happen. It was now obvious to the two of them, but Sibby could understand why it might not be so obvious to Seyal herself. "Err ... we might not be able to take him with us," she said quietly. "He seems to have decided to stay with the Avaraks."

"But he doesn't know what he is doing," wailed Seyal. "He is only a child."

A child who had just caused chaos and might well have led to many people dying, thought Gus. It was hard for the intensely loyal Enif to understand what motivation Seyal's son might have had.

"He seems to want to stay with his people," Sibby said in her unassuming voice. "Do you really think he would just agree to come home with us?"

"He didn't know what he was doing."

"Really? Are you sure?"

Seyal ducked, as if Sibby had taken a swing at her. Her eyes were huge and surrounded by dark shadows. The rest of her skin looked patchy and grey. She was struggling to understand what had happened. Sibby felt sorry for her.

"It is not your fault, Seyal."

"Why, then, did he do it?"

"Perhaps they contacted him? They may have made it sound like paradise. They would have told him he would have a lot of friends, a lot of toys, a lot of everything. They must have made it sound wonderful."

"On *Nivala* he had only me." Seyal nodded sadly. "He didn't have any friends of his own age."

"Exactly. They would have found it easy to manipulate such a young boy. I expect he revered his father's memory ...?"

"Yes." It was said so quietly that Gus could hardly hear her. "Then all this is my fault. I should have been thinking more about his well-being."

"Do you still want to take him with us?"

Good luck with that, thought Gus to itself. That child was definitely going to stay exactly where it wanted.

Seyal was silent for so long that Gus thought she had forgotten the question. Then, "I suppose, if he wants to live with his people, that it would be selfish of me to take him away."

Sibby simply hugged Seyal. "He will come back, you know. You just have to give him time."

"Do you think so? Really?"

"I am sure of it. But if we are going to avoid me being thrown out of the airlock and you undergoing immolation, we need a plan."

"Actually, I think the best idea is to let them throw you out of the airlock, Sibeal," said Gus.

That certainly got their attention. Gus scintillated with amusement, a rainbow of colors passing over the pitch-black shiny carapace.

"Well," it went on, the translated voice unfortunately toneless, "If the Avaraks were to suspect you had been saved, they would immediately turn this ship around. And if we were out there floating around, we would stand no chance. It would be a great opportunity for them to do some target practice."

"Segaton would never ..." began the boy's mother.

"... even know," finished Gus, severely. "They will keep him far away from any of these things."

The hope on Seyal's face vanished again. "Yes, I suppose they will, won't they?"

"Stands to reason," chipped in Sibby. "But, Gus, how do you know which airlock they will toss me out of? There must be dozens on a ship this size, surely. And if we have no protection, we will already be in extremis by the time the outer hatch is opened."

"Yes. That is a problem. I would have very little time to get to you."

They all considered that for some time.

"And you would need somewhere to put me. Somewhere pressurized and with oxygen. Until we can come back for Seyal."

"Do the Avaraks have PSAs?" asked Seyal, referring to the escape bags that could keep people alive for a short time after a hull breach.

Both the other two shook their heads. "They are too big for them," pointed out Sibby at the same time as Gus said, "I haven't seen any."

Gus scratched thoughtfully at its mandible. "I need to look around," it said. "There might be some kind of vessel I could commandeer. But it will be tricky, because we can't take anything that would be missed."

"And you have to get yourself outside the ship without setting off any alarms. All the hatches will have an alarm connected directly to the bridge." Sibby hugged her knees. "I don't see how you can do it."

"I can't break you two out now. There are hundreds of Avaraks on this ship. They would find us."

"Yes, I see what you mean. Our only chance is if they voluntary trash me. Happy thought."

Gus found that hard to understand. "It makes you happy? Good. I am glad to cheer you up." He shone with pleasure. Sibby didn't have the heart to tell him that she had been speaking with sarcasm. Denaraz would have understood immediately. He would have laughed. She wondered where he was at that moment. Whether or not he was all right. Her heart tensed and seemed to harden. It actually hurt.

She blinked the tears away. Love was only an inconvenience at this precise point in time. She needed to bring all her intellect to bear. That is what her tall husband would do. She had to be as strong as he was.

It seemed that Seyal had also reached a conclusion, because she gave a small sigh. "You are both right," she said. "Segaton cannot be removed from the Avaraks. Not at this time."

Sibby blew out air, relieved. "No, Seyal. He can't. I'm glad you can see that. It will even be hard to get *you* out of this cell. We would never find Segaton."

The Avarak woman was still staring at the deck plating. "Cards cannot be unshuffled. He will have to make his own way without me."

"He will, but you will see him again. He will realize that he was wrong."

"Avarak men do not admit to being wrong. Ever."

"Golly, they must be hard to live with!" As soon as the words were out of her mouth, Sibeal regretted them. "Oh, I'm sorry, Seyal. I know how inappropriate that was. I didn't intend to cause you any distress. Please, forgive me."

Seyal was staring at her. "You cannot know," she said finally. "Only an Avarak woman can know."

"You rarely speak about it."

Seyal hesitated, as though she were about to elaborate. Then she must have thought better of it, because she gave a slight shake of her head. "Solutor was a good husband. He allowed me to work. He allowed me to keep my voice. I was as happy as a female Avarak in Rhyvekan society can be. But yes, Sibeal, Avarak men are extremely hard to live with!"

Sibby slipped her slim arms around her friend and hugged her. They both began to giggle.

"Never mind, Seyal. I know you have started a revolution amongst the women on Rhyveka! One day, all that will change."

"I am afraid I shall not live to see it. According to Vebor, they are already building my funeral pyre."

"Nothing will stop it now, whatever happens. Other female Avaraks will continue what you have started. One day they will erect statues to you."

"Statues!" Seyal began to giggle again. "What an imagination you have!"

Gus stiffened. "Somebody is coming." The Enif quickly raced up the wall to efface itself again against the darkened recesses in the ceiling. It became completely still.

A slim figure crept cautiously into the brig holding area. It was a young Avarak woman. She tiptoed into the hold, keeping to the shadows. After assessing the layout for a few minutes, she made her way over to the cell where the two women were being kept. Like Seyal, she was self-effacing and melded very well into the shadows. Gus could hardly follow her progress.

Finally she came to the force field. Avoiding the main camera, she stayed in the shadows. She gave a small cough, just loud enough to attract the prisoners' attention.

Seyal edged up to her side of the force field. The two women began to talk urgently in soft Avarak. Sibby could hear but wasn't able to understand and Gus was too far away for the translator to pick up the whispered words.

Gus, looking down from his eyrie above, was amazed at just how difficult it was to make out either of the Avarak women. There was actually no danger, because the cameras and audio were still on loops, but the Enif was pretty sure that neither the conversation nor the presence of the other woman would have been picked up, even if they *had* still been working.

Seyal talked to the woman for around five minutes, and then nodded. The younger woman slipped backwards and vanished from the brig, as silently as she had come. Gus waited for a couple of minutes and then shinned down the wall again.

"Well?"

Sibby had come close as well. Seyal gave a half-smile for the first time that day. "Her name is Myska. She knew about us because she and her husband are going to take care of Segaton's introduction to Avarak society. Of course, her husband has no idea that she came down here to the cells. She joined the campaign after picking up one of my leaflets some months ago. Then a friend passed her my treatise on emancipation. I think she is going to help us, if she can. She is prepared to risk her life to save ours, although I did tell her that she should not."

"You see, Seyal! Other females of your species *are* ready to fight for their rights! You just can't expect things to happen overnight. Females on Rhyveka are so much weaker than the males. Of course it is going take time to counter that."

"I have asked that she find out which airlock will be used tomorrow. That should help Gus put some sort of a plan in place, at least for you. If we know the exact point of egress, there will be a better chance of saving you."

"You are right. That will help enormously. Was there anything else she could tell you?"

A darkness passed across the Avarak woman's face. "She has spoken to my son. Vebor has given instructions that he is to be presented as the heir to Solutor's remaining assets. He will stay with her family for the time being. She says he is not unhappy. Vebor has already given him clothes, a state-of-the-art gaming center and even a runabout."

"Did he look like he wanted to leave?"

"He did not. She asked him and he snapped at her. He told her that I had deprived him of his birthright, and that ..." she swallowed, "... he never wishes to see or speak of me again."

"I see. Well, it is better to know that than to be forever wondering. At least he is being well-treated." That was for Seyal's benefit. Personally, Sibby thought that a little deprivation would do him no harm, after what he had done. She kept her thoughts to herself, however, and went on, "—And if we are able to predict which hatch will be used, then perhaps we stand a chance of getting through the ordeal alive."

Gus nodded, but it was worried. Saving Sibby's life was going to be difficult. Being able saving Seyal's was quite another thing. The Enif gave an uncomfortable thrum. There were difficult decisions coming and Enif made their decisions according to different criteria than humanoids. It gave the Enif equivalent of a sigh.

Seyal suddenly became more substantial. She caught Gus's eye and said very clearly, in Avarak, "*Lataxla ker exla. Fexxkaskla nixx emtexx. Avarakx Sekelexx fotess maxinn. Dexxkelless esex mensk Enifx, suxx causexx statekkx.*" His translator provided him with the translation. 'Get her away from here. Do not try to rescue me. Avarak ships have internal sensors of both domestic and alien DNA. They are swept frequently. Either you have been lucky or Enif DNA cannot be picked up. Hers definitely will be."

The Enif was surprised that the Avarak woman had been able to think ahead to the future when her own life was under such threat. But she had. She had clearly weighed up the possibility of Sibby being caught if Gus brought her back into the ship and found it too risky. She preferred to sacrifice herself.

Both Gus and Sibby stared at Seyal, the first with surprise, the second with suspicion.

"What did you say?" asked Sibby, frowning.

Seyal didn't look away from Thagaarus. "Good luck!" she said, mendaciously. "I was just wishing the Enif good luck."

Sibby turned her gaze on Gus, who stiffened. "Thank you," it said quickly, nodding to Seyal to tell her that it had understood. "I need to go now. I will switch the loops back to live, so don't discuss any of this. Can you get back to your original positions, please? Against that wall over there? I don't want any jumps when I switch back."

Sibby looked very much as if she wanted to say something

else, but Gus was already stepping away. It was just relieved. The decision had been taken for it. And it was the right decision. If it could extract Mallivan's sister from the Avarak ship they might both live to fight another day. And while it seemed true that Gus itself could probably remain undetected on the ship for an almost indefinite time, the same would not be true for a Spacelander or an Avarak woman. Any normal scan would be able to pick up their warm blood. It was one of the disadvantages of being a mammal, after all.

But Sibby was one of the most intelligent women in the Landau Shell. She had a very good idea of what Seyal had told the Enif, and she wasn't about to abandon her friend.

"You told him to leave you behind, didn't you? Well, I won't go if that is what you told him." Her face took on a stubborn expression.

Seyal seemed to melt a little. "You must. I cannot avoid my punishment."

"Don't you want to be saved? Holy Nucleon, Seyal!"

"Don't be angry with me. That isn't who you are. Look, think about it. What do *you* think will happen to the female revolution if I run away?

Sibby shut her eyes. She didn't much like the conclusions she was reaching, and started shifting her weight from one foot to the other.

"See?" Seyal's calm voice interrupted. "You have realized it as well. If I run away, the feminist movement will fizzle out. The males will use it as weakness, as a way to sow doubt and dissention, won't they?"

"Not necessarily." But Sibby's voice held the doubt she felt. She could even hear it herself.

"Yes they will. Of course they will. They will not miss such an opportunity. I have told you before that I was prepared to die for the cause. You know that female Avaraks do not expect to live very long. I have already lived longer than the majority of my peers. I never wanted to live forever."

"But to die like that, Seyal. On a fire. I ... I cannot bear to think of it."

"You think rupturing in childbirth because the baby is too big is fun?" For the first time, Sibby heard real anguish in her friend's voice. "I have held the hand of thirty-five of my friends as they died in absolute agony. In one way, I shall be glad to join their ranks. Perhaps it will take away the guilt I feel at being the survivor."

Sibby's hand had gone to her mouth. "I never thought about it," she whispered. "Forgive me."

"See? You feel guilt for never asking. So how much more guilt is mine for living when they all died?"

Sibby bit her lip. "If we save you, you can continue the fight."

"No. I can't. It is becoming harder and harder to change minds on Rhyveka when I am exiled with what my people see as aliens. How can I blame them, when even my own son sees you as outsiders and not friends?" Her shoulders slumped. "I have failed as a mother. I was so happy as a crewmember on *Nivala* that I was sure Segaton would be too. It was selfish of me. I do not want to hide myself away any more. It is time to step out into the light. If it burns, then that is what is meant to be."

"Is this because of Segaton? He will realize his mistake, you know. He loves you, Seyal. He really does. This is just a phase he is going through. Think of how he will feel when he hears that this led to your death. He would never be able to forgive himself."

Seyal shook her head at her friend's naivety. "They will never tell him. They will give him some story that shows me in a bad light and them in a good one. The males of my species know how to use falsehoods and misrepresentation. That is how we got to where we are. Please, I beg you. Do not interfere in what must be. I became a dissident with my eyes open. Although I would not have chosen *this* for myself, it is something I have to follow through on now that we are here. But there *is* another way you can help, if you like."

"Anything."

"Spread the word of my execution. It might gain sympathy and support for our cause. I will rest even easier if I know that my death has helped change minds and hearts."

Sibby was crying openly. "I will do whatever you ask, but the hardest thing to do is not to try to save you from that."

Seyal softened and gave her a hug that was so gentle that it was almost imperceptible. "I know. But I am so grateful that our friendship is strong enough to survive this request, Sibby. You are a good friend indeed to uphold my wishes on this matter. I thank you from depths that are beyond my own poor spirit. I thank you from the threads of all the souls who culminated in me, in this cell, in this moment."

But Sibby only sobbed.

Chapter 11

Gus felt acutely alone that night. It had been accustomed, all its life, to that feeling, but to be attempting such a dangerous rescue enhanced the Enif's usual fears and anxiety. The two captives were depending on it for their very survival. Seyal's words echoed around its carapace. Would she have to be left behind? The thought brought a small tremble to its limbs and to its mind.

But the Enif are a practical race. Gus was not about to let its brain be paralyzed into inaction. It would do its very best to save two lives, but if that were not possible then it was determined, at the very least, that Denaraz should see his wife again. Worrying about Seyal's fate was not going to be helpful. This needed to be addressed like any engineering problem. Make a list of all the things to be solved, and work methodically through that list.

First up on that list was how to stop Sibby floating off into space with no protection when she was thrown out of the airlock. Second was ensuring that she could be within a safe oxygen atmosphere, third what to do then.

From what Seyal had said, bringing Denaraz's wife back on board the Avarak ship would not be an option. Regular DNA scans of the whole vessel would highlight the Spacelander's presence, and then any rescue attempt would become impossible. Although Gus hated to leave Seyal to face her fate, it could currently see no possible way to extract her. Hiding on board was not a solution, clearly. The Avaraks would be able to track her anywhere on the ship.

The Enif put its considerable brain power on figuring out just how to save *both* of the women, but after a full hour it had made no progress. Option after option was discounted as impossible or unworkable. Gus became more and more despondent.

With great regret, it finally came to the unwelcome conclusion that the only solution was going to be exactly that of Seyal: save the Spacelander and leave the Avarak. It was not a pleasant realization. Gus had not known either of the two women for very long, but they had both welcomed it aboard *Nivala*. In a way that its own people had not, they had given it a home. Leaving either of them behind was going to be extremely difficult.

Time, however, was passing. If even one of the two women were to be saved, Gus needed to stop theorizing and start finding practical solutions. The Enif began to crawl back to the stern of the ship. What was really needed was some sort of vessel small enough not to show up on the ship's sensors. Gus was capable of surviving for long periods in outer space, like any Enif. If necessary, it could do just that. However, humans were a fragile species. Sibeal would need some sort of protection immediately. Space without some sort of metal casing would be a truly perilous place for both Sibby and, long term, for the Enif itself.

The cargo deck of the *Daktar* was bulging with auxiliary craft, but they were all far too big to be invisible to sensors. Gus felt a sense of urgent desperation flood its mind.

There were no Avaraks in the cavernous hold, so the Enif was able to crawl down from the ceiling and walk normally between the large vehicles. All, of course, were Avarak-sized. Gus realized that any ship large enough to carry a few Avaraks would be picked up on sensors. That left … what? What could there possibly be on board that would resist the pressures of outer space, but was small, at least in Avarak terms?

The answer, when it came, had been staring it in the face all along. An EVA maintenance drone!

On the Spacelander ships, EVA maintenance drones were far too small to be of the least use in a situation like this, but Avarak drones were much bigger. Of course they were – their ships were vast in comparison to a Spacelander vessel.

Gus had passed dozens of interior cleaning drones already. The first few had given the Enif cause for alarm, but it had relaxed after a while, realizing that none of the drones appeared to be fitted with any sort of feedback to their handlers. They were one-way recipients of instructions, rather than two-way spies for *Daktar's* crew. That had been a tremendous relief. Now, however, Gus began to examine the drones more actively

Each was the height of an Avarak. That made them just under over two meters tall. Their diameter was slightly less and they were ovaloid. They resembled fat eggs, slightly flattened top and bottom to accommodate the basic propulsion jets.

At last Gus came across one that was still. It had apparently broken down. It was tilting out of line and showing its jets, which seemed to be clogged. The Enif quickly began to examine the drone. The interior drones would be of little use to them, it felt, but it doubted that the basic make-up would vary. The EVA drones would likely have a similar layout.

It was hard to find the access plate. This turned out to be set between the jets, presumably so as to protect it from any sort of damage by collision. The codes used were childishly simple to Enif logic, and Gus was able to crack them within two minutes. It activated the part of the screen that read 'open framework'.

The large egg split into two hinged halves, with overlapping fuselage along the join. Gus examined this attentively. Even the interior drone appeared to have spaceworthy joins. That was encouraging. Gus approved of the solid workmanship. Avarak astronauts were considered efficient space travelers. Now it was getting a glimpse as to why that was.

This particular drone was clearly merely for cleaning. The interior was hollow and at this moment half-full of rubbish. There was a further indentation in the framework, where the rubbish could be periodically ejected, presumably into a waste tube that led through the *Daktar's* hull and out into the void.

There were, however, no controls on the inside of the drone. Naturally, the idea of any living creature needing access from within the framework had not occurred to the Avaraks. So that was going to need addressing. So was the lack of an air source.

Its mind made up, Gus abandoned the large hold. Any EVA-ready drones would probably be held much closer to the fuselage, just under the skin of this behemoth of a ship.

It was already on its way out when its complex eye was caught by a rack of Avarak EVA suits, hanging ready to be donned on one wall of the hold. They were enormous. One such suit would swamp a human. All EVA suits are provided with an oxygen source, and even though Rhyveka was nominally lower in oxygen and nominally higher in nitrogen, the mix was breathable for humans. Avaraks were more resistant; they could survive indefinitely in a human nitrogen-oxygen mix, as Seyal and her son had already proved. Humans were not recommended to remain indefinitely within the Avarak mix, although a day or two should not lead to any permanent effects for Sibby.

Gus's carapace grayed slightly. If they were alone in space inside a drone for more than two days it would no longer matter what they had been breathing. It would mean that rescue efforts had not found them. Pinpointing a tiny drone in the immensity of space was worse than finding a needle in a haystack. If *Nivala* swept past their position, they would become impossible to find. The drone would become their space coffin. Because an Avarak EVA suit *might* provide them with enough air for a couple of days. It wouldn't and couldn't be much longer than that.

Gus sized up the suits. Pressed well down, it thought that two of the suits could be folded up and stowed safely inside a drone, leaving room for both itself and Sibby. It was the best it could come up with. There was nothing else at hand.

As for being found, well, that was going to have to wait until it managed to get inside an EVA drone. Clearly an interior drone had no need to be equipped with any source of emissions. It might be different for an EVA drone. They could quite easily become detached from a ship's superstructure, and may be equipped with some sort of automated distress signal. Gus would have to hope it was so, and that the signal could be interfered with easily. The Enif made a mental note to carry a set of Avarak tools inside the chosen drone. It would not do to fail in this mission because they didn't have the right screwdriver.

As soon as the idea took shape and became feasible, the Enif felt much better. It completed its examination of the interior drone and then quickly closed it back up. There was no need to take anything from this hold. There were bound to be complete EVA kits wherever the EVA drones were stored. But time was running out. It had already used up a third of the night.

Back on the *Shapley* shipstation, the race rescue mission was drawing to a relieved close. All of the participants of the race had been found. There had been two deaths and four serious injuries amongst the ships in or overseeing the race. Of the children, only two had permanent damage. One little girl who had been visiting from the Hawking shipstation had suffered a leg amputation. She would have died, except that she had been quick enough to apply her own tourniquet, and her skimmer had luckily been one of the first to be found. The other was Orin, Sibby's middle son. His skimmer had been thrown so far off course that he was only found after fifteen hours. His oxygen supply on the skimmer had been undamaged, so he had no lung damage. Unfortunately he had broken his spine when tossed over and over in the initial storm blast. It had happened just as he had decided to get some liquid refreshment from the fridge. The poor boy had been lying immobile for all of those fifteen hours, shivering with cold and shock. By the time the rescue workers got to him, he was almost in a coma. However, both Orin and the Hawking shipstation girl were expected to make full recoveries. They had been placed quickly into the *Shapley* medical center, where they had been put straight into Zeroth triage and treatment chambers. Orin was expected to be able to walk within three weeks. It would take a little longer for the Hawking girl to adapt to her artificial foot, but medical science had advanced greatly, and she would soon be skipping along the decks just like she had before.

The two deaths and two other serious injuries had all occurred in the accompanying ships. Three of the four supervising ships had managed to weather the storm. The fourth had not been quite so lucky. The ship with the remote access controls had been caught broadside by a particularly virulent storm wave.

The entire ship had been flipped end over end for long minutes, converting anything that was torn loose into a projectile. Their engineer and one of the cleaners had both been killed outright by flying fragments of metal. Another two of the crew had sustained hemorrhaging after also being struck by loose debris.

Prime Ohnahara was in the morgue when Mallivan made his way onto *Shapley*. She was attempting to comfort the bereaved families.

The captain shook their hands and gave them his condolences. Then he raised one eyebrow in the prime's direction. They moved slightly to one side.

"How is Orin?" asked Mallivan.

"He will make a full recovery. You can safely leave him with us. He will not regain consciousness for at least two days. The Zeroth chamber has put him into a light coma while the broken vertebrae in his back are replaced."

Mallivan nodded. "That's a great relief. I came to tell you that we have managed to repair *Nivala*. We will be leaving the shipstation within the hour. They already have a long start on us. Avarak ships are still slower than we are, but it will take some time to overtake them." His face grew tight with worry. "Time we may not have."

Ohnah leant forward to give him a hug. "Good luck, then, Ryler. I wish I could come with you, but there are still people to rescue here."

"On *Shapley*? I am sorry to hear that. We had no casualties on *Nivala*, despite the damage."

"*Apart* from the race casualties, on *Shapley* and its surrounds we have six more dead and many injuries, some extremely serious. Luckily, ships are bringing in extra Zeroth chambers both from Hawking and Penrose shipstations."

"They were not affected?"

"By the time the storm surges reached them the waves had dissipated greatly. There were only superficial injuries and some breakages."

"That, at least, is good news. I am very sorry for the losses here on *Shapley*, however."

Ohnah's face was sad. "As am I. I know everybody on this shipstation. It is hard for all of us."

"I feel responsible for the fact that the Avaraks decided to attack us here. This had nothing to do with any of you."

She gave him a sympathetic look. "It is not your crew's fault. But we need to know what new technology the Avaraks have. How were they able to trigger such a storm? Could they do it again?"

He nodded. "You're right." The captain appeared to be on the brink of saying something else, but thought better of it. He gave a half salute and vanished.

Twenty minutes later *Nivala* slipped her moorings and streaked off after the long departed Avarak ship. Ohnah's lips moved silently as she followed the bright streak in the sky. None of her crew could hear what she said.

It took Thagaarus another two hours to find the rack of EVA drones and go through them quickly. Each needed to be opened up so Gus could assess the amount of free space inside. There were no simple cleaning drones, so it was going to be a case of choosing the most uncluttered of the specialized robots.

That turned out to be one of the sampling drones. They were specifically equipped to cut through stone or any heavy material, take small to medium sized samples, and store them inside their shells for analysis aboard. Gus presumed that they must mainly be used when small meteoroids impacted the hull. Whatever their use, the space inside the drone's body was generous. There was certainly room for one Enif and one Spacelander. It was lucky, in this case, that Spacelanders were so much smaller than Avaraks. Otherwise the rescue mission would have been doomed at the start. Gus was forced to acknowledge that they wouldn't have been able to take Seyal with them, at least not in one drone. The Avarak woman, although less than half the size of an Avarak male, would still not have fit inside the body of the probe at the same time as Sibby.

Gus chose the least battered of the three sampling drones it had come across, and began to drag the heavy Avarak EVA suits from a nearby rack over to it. The Enif wasn't sure how the suits worked, but was able to find out that small detail very quickly indeed. It checked how the air supply could be released, and found that the mechanism was a latch that activated as the helmet was fitted into the body of the suit. There was also an exterior access in case of emergency.

Gus practiced once or twice to make sure that it knew how to turn on the air. The process was not difficult, thankfully.

Now it was also was able to store a couple of waterpacks and one full ration pack inside the drone. The latter was so large that the Enif was pretty sure it would last both of them for a week. These Avaraks clearly needed a lot of food to keep their energy levels stoked up.

It turned its interest to the rest of the drone. There was a failsafe emergency beacon, Gus was pleased to see. By dismantling another

EVA drone, it obtained a second one. This, it managed to clone to the first beacon. Gus wanted to test them, but decided not to. It seemed more than likely that an emergency signal transmitted from inside the ship would bring unwanted attention to this part of the vessel. It was only able to test the small lights that accompanied the beacons.

This limited test was a success, so the second beacon was mounted carefully outside the drone. The challenge was to find a way to turn on the beacons from inside the drone, rather than from the inset console on the outside. Even that console was only for back up. Drones such as these would obviously normally be managed remotely. That was something else Gus needed to see to. It would be extremely unhelpful if the Avaraks could simply press a button and recall the drone. It was also possible that an emergency signal would be sent out if the drone separated too far from the mother ship. That possible danger had to be circumvented too.

Work on all that took another couple of hours. It was relatively easy to decouple the sensors that would accept external direction from the ship, but it took longer to decouple a second console from a spare drone and clone it to the first. Finally, however, Gus closed up the two sides of the shell with the new console inside and went to find exactly how the drones were deployed when they were needed.

It soon found the EVA drone egress hatches. There were four of them, all extending out beyond the rest of the fuselage of the Avarak cruiser. Unlike the airlocks, which were necessary for the crew of the ship, these egress hatches did not need to have a system of equalizing pressure and atmosphere. They were protected by a sliding hatch, a further security hinged hatch and a force field.

Gus settled on top of the console and entered instructions manually. Clearly, this was not the usual way the drones operated, but it seemed that manual instructions were programmed to override any automated commands. The drone rose on the lower jets, positioned itself beneath the nearest egress hatch and lifted easily inside the tube leading from the ceiling of the small hold out through the fuselage of the ship.

Gus had to bend over to avoid being crushed against the first hatch. The Enif glanced warily around. Where were the controls to the hatch itself? There might not even *be* manual controls. If the whole process was by automated command, then the situation had just become a little bit more complex.

There was no sign of any console set into the egress tube. Gus's brain raced a little in panic. It took the Enif some effort to control the usually logical rational thought processes. Then it peered down at the console on the top of the drone. Sure enough, there was a small spaceglass cover. Once that was raised, it exposed a series of three controls.

Gus pushed the first one. A blue flash announced the activation of a force field, just above its head. It pushed the second one. The first hatch retracted smoothly sideways into the hull.

That left only the safety hatch. It was now or never. The question as to whether the drone egress hatches sounded an alarm when opened was about to be answered. It pushed the final button, not without a few qualms.

Then Thagaarus looked down at the flashing sign on the control panel and began to laugh. It was asking the question in Avarak "Override hatch warnings?"

Ignoring the *Nikxx* option, Gus pushed lightly down on *Jakxx*

The console turned green, the final hinged hatch opened and the drone, with Gus still draped over its nose, edged through the tube and into outer space.

*

The hatch resealed itself as soon as Gus and the drone had passed through. That didn't worry the Enif at all. Its job was only to tether the drone to the ship in a way that would not draw attention to its presence. That was done in a matter of seconds.

Then Gus took some time to look around the outer hull of the large ship. There were several small hatches situated on the upper side of the fuselage, and it seemed likely that there would be more on the lower side as well. However, the main hatch was right in front of him, some fifteen meters towards the bows of the ship. It was a vast hatch, big enough for hover sledges and air bikes to be used.

Gus examined a little further since Enif physiology enabled exposure to the vacuum with no side effects for many hours. It seemed unlikely that such a large hatch would be used to forcibly debark one slim woman, so it tried to get the bearings of all the exit hatches.

A small shape on Gus's shoulder flapped his wings and seemed taken aback when his wings didn't work. Toothpick buzzed against the Enif's hard skin, causing a small vibration that was noticeable to the host. The sunflyer was clearly indignant. So far into deep space, there was no stellar light to enable him to fly and no air either. He was stuck, an unwilling stowaway on the Enif carapace. Gus gave a slight ripple of its cordotonal receptors, treating the tiny insect to the Enif equivalent of a massage. Toothpick vibrated back sharply. He was not a happy insect.

Gus found no other hatches until it walked across the top of the ship and peered over the side. There, around three meters below, was an almost normal sized hatch. It was just the size that a fully grown Avarak could squeeze through.

There was a similar configuration towards the bows of the ship. This was reflected, Gus found, on the underside of the vast ship, making four places where a human girl could be ejected. There was only a one in four chance that the drone was in the right place. They definitely needed that confirmation from the Avarak female, Myska.

However, there was nothing more that could be done now. Gus made its way back to the drone egress and opened the hinged hatch. Then the small figure, accompanied by the even smaller hitchhiker, slipped back inside the Avarak ship.

The drone, tethered between the main hatch and the egress hatch, sailed placidly alongside the enormous bulk of the bigger ship, practically invisible.

Chapter 12

Sibby and Seyal had already been visited by the guards. A piece of bread and some water had been left as some sort of breakfast.

They were picking at it when their ears picked up the rustle of someone approaching. It was not the guards, who would make no attempt to cover up their arrival. This was somebody who didn't want to be noticed.

Sure enough, some seconds later, the female Avarak stepped gingerly into the shadows near the cell force field. Aware that the video and audio was on, Seyal dissimulated her own approach to the edge of the cell.

The girl, who seemed terrified, pointed upwards. Seyal gave an infinitesimal nod. Then the girl turned to face the front of the ship, moved her hand behind her and to the left. Then, without waiting to see if her message had been understood, she slipped out of the cell hold as surreptitiously as she could.

Sibby frowned. "She was petrified of being seen."

Seyal nodded. "She would be joining me in the airlock if she were spotted. We are lucky that she even came back. I just hope that what she has given us will be enough for Gus."

They had to wait for nearly another hour until Gus appeared. The Enif stopped to engage the surveillance loops again and then walked up to the force field. It gave a nod when the girls explained what the Avarak female's gestures had been.

"Yes, that helps. It means they will use the rear port side hatch. I can have the drone waiting behind it."

Both girls looked cheered, but Gus held up one of its right arms. "Sibby, I still have no way to ensure your safety until you get inside the drone body."

Sibby wasn't put off. "Tell us about your plan," she told the Enif.

Some ten minutes later she was up to date. She turned to Seyal. "I know I said I would try to do as you ask, but I can't. How can we possibly go without you?"

Gus and Seyal exchanged a look. Gus's carapace grayed slightly. "I am unable to see a way to take Seyal with us," it admitted. "Or come back for her."

"We are not leaving her!"

Seyal took Sibby's arm. "And just how are you going to save me?" she asked. "—The minute I am missed they would stop and search the ship. If I were not on board they would search all the local space until they found us. I know Vebor, I tell you. He will never give up." She stared into Sibby's horrified and set face. "I thank you for your determination, Sibby, but my only real hope is that you two are rescued before we get to the Veka system and that

Captain Mallivan can somehow come to my aid. He might be able to stop them, might be able to reason with them. It is only a faint possibility but it is my only hope. —And in order for that to happen, you and Gus need to get safely away from this ship without me. Can't you see that?"

There was a long and pained silence. Sibby finally managed a choked nod. She bit her lip so as not to break down, but she was unable to hide the tears of sadness that ran down her cheeks.

Seyal looked at Gus again and nodded for it to continue with the escape plans.

 "So, as soon as you are inside the drone, you must activate the oxygen on one of the Avarak suits," it told Sibby. "Then you will be safe. Relatively."

Sibby managed to look up. Tears glistened on her face, but she had herself under control now. Her voice was still wobbly, but her chin was up. "Right. But I don't see how I am going to get to the drone. What is to stop me spinning off into outer space?"

"Me."

She stared. "How?"

The Enif shimmered. I will attach myself to a rope and then leap out and grab you."

Sibby's face froze. "Excuse me?"

"I shall aim myself in your direction, push off with my feet and float over to you."

Mallivan's sister had gone even paler than before. "What if you miss?"

The Enif frowned. "Miss?"

"Yes, miss. How can you be sure to catch me?"

"I'm an Enif." Gus thrummed, clearly struggling to understand her doubts. "I won't miss." Then it saw that her face was still tight. "I have studied engineering for years. I hardly think I will miscalculate a trajectory like that. You won't be moving particularly quickly. At least, not relative to the ship's hull."

Seyal was also looking worried. "Take an extra rope," she said.

"I'm sorry?"

"Make sure you have two ropes. One that attaches you to the drone, and one you can throw in Sibby's direction if you miss her."

"But I won't miss her."

"You know that, but it will make us feel better if you take the extra rope. Can you do that for us?"

Gus thrummed again, this time rather shortly. "I suppose so."

Sibby's face relaxed somewhat. "Then you will simply pull me into the drone?"

"Yes. I will have the two halves open. Once we are there, I shall cut the rope tethering the drone to the ship and we will crouch inside and get the oxygen flowing. From then on, we should be safe until … until we are found."

"—If we are found."

"Yes. If we are found."

Seyal smiled at both of them. "You will be. I am sure of it. Well done, Gus. That seems like a good plan. I think you have thought of everything."

Then the Avarak woman turned to Sibby. "As soon as the outer hatch opens you know what you have to do, right?"

"I do?"

"You have to close your eyes and exhale all the air you have in your lungs. To avoid explosive decompression. You should be good for twenty seconds."

"Twenty seconds!"

Seyal looked surprised. "You won't need that long. Everything should go quite quickly."

"Yes." The Enif seemed pleased at her. "It will be plenty of time,

I believe."

"It doesn't sound like plenty of time to me!" managed Seyal.

"If I don't get you inside the drone within twenty seconds," said Gus, with a thrum, "you will be dead."

"I don't like to pick holes in your plan," said Sibby, "but ... err ... have you been practicing this ... throwing yourself at the end of a rope?"

A stillness crossed the Enif's face. "I have not, no."

"And will you have time to hone your accuracy?"

"I will not, unfortunately. I do not want to go out of the airlock again before I have to, for fear of being detected."

Sibby blew air out slowly through pursed lips. "So. I will come rocketing out of an airlock into a vacuum that will kill me in twenty seconds, and you will shoot yourself at me and somehow hope to get the trajectory right so that you can reel me in?"

"Correct."

"And it won't matter to us if you don't manage, because I will already be dead?"

"Correct again."

Sibby put a shaky hand behind her, found the wall, and slid down it. Her legs were suddenly rubbery. Her heart had decided to climb out through her throat. "That ... that sounds ... alarming."

"The possibility of success is not high," admitted the Enif. "It would help if you could try to come out of the airlock at a backwards angle. I shall be some meters to the stern, so it would be useful if you could close that distance slightly."

"I can try."

"You are angry with me." The Enif looked down. "I am sorry I have no better ideas."

Sibby bit her lip. She rather thought that she would never see her Tyzaran husband again. The prospect of dying had never scared her before, but it did now. She had found so much recently. There was a fiercely burning desire inside her soul to cling onto it. "I guess it will have to do, Gus. If I had brought one of the personal carbon clouds we made up, then you could have been waiting right by the airlock and nobody would have seen you," she said, with an ironic grimace. "But, after … after Sammy, I thought that all the danger was over. I stored them all away. At least you *have* a plan. I have none."

The three of them stared at each other. Sibby was right. Any plan had to be better than no plan. At the very least, it was a chance of survival. A slim chance, admittedly, but better than certain death, which is what Seyal had to look forward to. Sibby dropped her chin in shame. For just a moment, she had forgotten that.

Gus nodded and its color began to return. "Then we will do that," it said. "I will be careful to pick the right trajectory. However, I shall only have one chance, and this is something I have never done before." Its carapace glistened as the enormity of that calculation suddenly hit it.

"If you miss, my death will not be your fault, Gus. It is the Avaraks who are condemning us. You are the one trying to save me."

"I wish there were a safer way."

"If you were not here, there would be no way at all." Sibby was firm. "At least, now, we might have a chance. All of us. Now, let's think about this in detail. What if they equalize the outer hatch with the vacuum before opening the outer hatch? I would slowly die inside the hatch itself. I could be already dead by the time they opened the outer hatch and I floated outside."

"True, but I do not anticipate them doing that. They will override the failsafes, so as to expulse you while you still have a small atmosphere around you. The draining of that atmosphere into space will impart a small radial velocity away from the ship.

They certainly won't want to come into orbit around Rhyveka with a spare body attached, so they won't want to risk your snagging on any rigging. They will want to save themselves the trouble of sending men in EVA suits out to get rid of your remains. Overriding the failsafes is not a difficult process."

Sibby gave a wan smile. "Let's hope you are right."

"I believe that I am. There is no logic in leaving your body in the airlock itself. It goes against the space maxim."

"Expend the least organic energy possible." Sibby said slowly, with what sounded almost like a giggle. "I never thought that principal might save my life." Then her forehead wrinkled. "What about Tsuf? Will he be all right?"

"Tsuf is on my shoulder. He will stay there, I believe. He cannot fly outside, in the vacuum. In the Dark Reaches we are too far away from any starlight."

"Good. I would hate to leave him behind. Even though the idea of him grazing on the eyelids of a few Avaraks is very tempting."

Gus was insulted. "Sunflyers never hurt anybody!"

"That didn't stop the Captain from making an outcry about it."

"He was unused to the sensation. I am told that it can be quite pleasant. Perhaps it is an acquired taste."

Now Sibby really did laugh. "You don't know my brother very well if you think he will ever voluntarily offer up the grazing rights to his own face! Not going to happen."

"That is a pity. Tsuf is most fond of humanoid grazing."

Sibby looked upwards, paused, then gave a deep sigh. "All right. Tsuf, if we get out of here, I promise I will let you graze on my eyelids."

"He will like that very much."

Sibby pulled a face. "Then I almost feel good that the odds of our dying out there are so high."

Gus couldn't understand her. It was only a simple food chain. A good example of a symbiotic relationship. It had amazed the Enif that the Captain rejected such an environmentally positive process. However, Spacelanders were generally considered ornery on Enifa, so Gus was not overly surprised.

"The greatest danger will be in establishing an atmosphere within the drone," it pointed out. "You will need to do that very quickly if you are not to suffer badly from space-swell."

"Can you not do that?"

"I shall be closing the shell with the console I linked. If all goes according to plan, I will be inside with you. If there is a problem, however, I would have to remain outside, to activate the controls from the exterior panel. In that case you would be on your own inside the drone."

"Gus!" Seyal's face crumpled. "You would die!"

"I should be able to survive for almost two days, although it would not be easy on my body. I believe that is the record for an Enif in a vacuum. Sibby will not have any longer than that inside the drone, in any case. The Avarak EVA suits will only provide from forty to fifty hours of air, depending on how many of us are inside using up the oxygen."

"Please try to remain inside with me, Gus. I should hate to feel that you were subjecting yourself to the vicissitudes of empty space while I was in relative comfort inside the drone."

"Comfort is not a word I would use. The temperature inside will be very low. I calculate that the shell is made to provide an internal temperature of around two sixty Kelvin, which are basically Arctic conditions. We can consider ourselves lucky that anything lower than that would affect the tools inside the drone, so there is substantial insulation."

"No problem. I can wrap myself inside one of the space suits.

That should be enough protection. I am more worried about carbon dioxide levels."

"Yes. I have thought of that. I think it will be necessary to open the drone to space at least every two hours. After that you may be risking hazardous levels in the air you are breathing. Of course, none of this will affect me since the Enif breathe through their carapace, which filters out toxins." Gus seemed quite proud of its physiology. "We are much more resilient."

"If you do that the oxygen supply will not last for very long," pointed out Seyal. "Each time you open and close the drone it will dissipate."

"That is true, yet I have been unable to come to a different conclusion."

"It is easy," said Sibby with a sigh. "I need to put one of the EVA suits on. If I do that, the suit will make sure that the correct balance is maintained inside."

Gus stared at her. "Why didn't I think of that?" it said. "Of course. Then I can regulate the other to only a small flow of oxygen. I can survive with very little. That should extend our autonomy."

"I hope that we don't need to. My husband will be looking for us."

None of them said what they were all thinking. Nobody on board *Nivala* would have any inkling that Sibby had been thrown out of an airlock, and even if they did, they would not know where. It was going to take a miracle for them to be saved. And if they were not saved, Seyal would have no chance at all.

It turned out to be lucky that they had fallen silent. A noticeable vibration of the decking told Gus that Avarak guards were incoming. It quickly removed the loops on the audio and video feeds after signaling Seyal to shuffle further back from the force field. It was a close call; the Enif was almost seen as it swung itself back into the shadows of the ceiling. Sibby watched unobtrusively as the Enif crawled away into the shadows of the passageway.

Their visitors turned out to include Doctor Vebor. "You are lucky," he told Seyal in her own language. "The Avarak Council is prepared to be lenient with you."

"If they are, then there will be a reason."

"No doubt. Their hearts are noble."

"Noble? *Noble?* None of the Council would know noble if it came up and hit them in the face!"

Sibby, who couldn't understand a word, watched with interest. All she saw was her friend straightening up and turning an interesting pink color. Then Seyal began to talk, counting off things on her fingers. Sibby got the distinct impression that she was going through a long list of male faults and cruelties.

Vebor never let Seyal finish. He actually kicked out at the force field to make her stop. His boot shone with sparks for a moment before the doctor remembered himself enough to withdraw it. Sibby was mesmerized by the small curl of smoke that wended its way upwards from the footwear.

Vebor then spoke eloquently for quite ten minutes on the deficiencies of females.

Seyal gave Sibby an apologetic look. "Sorry," she said. "The males do like the sound of their own voices."

Sibby nodded. "I can see that." She affected a yawn. "Do you think he will ever stop?"

Vebor's diatribe turned into Universal, perhaps to be more inclusive. He continued to state quite forcibly that a) females were made so much smaller than males because they were of little importance, b) no self-respecting male Avarak could stand to listen to a female who hadn't had her voice 'improved' and c) Seyal had had no right to object to any of the laws on Rhyveka because females didn't have the vote and therefore had no right to say anything at all.

Sibby tried to think of the worst thing she could say to the Avarak. In the end, she laughed.

That stopped him in mid tirade. "How dare you laugh at me, Spacelander!" he thundered.

"If you could hear yourself, you would probably laugh too."

He stretched out one enormous hand towards the cell, and Sibby moved automatically back, despite the force field. He was so much bigger than she was that she knew he could kill her with one blow.

However, he had not come for that. He glowered down at Seyal, his eyes twin points of resentment. "I have been instructed to tell you that if you repudiate all that you have written, your sentence – and that of the human with you – will be commuted to life imprisonment." He spoke as though the words were distasteful to him. He clearly didn't agree.

Seyal turned her gaze to Sibby, who needed only a second to dismiss the offer. Firstly, she didn't trust the man to comply with it. And secondly, she actually thought that death would be better than a life wasted in an Avarak jail cell on Rhyveka. Besides, Seyal had already told her that backing down was not an option. The Avarak woman would accept her sentence with dignity, as a necessary postscript to her activism. Her friend's integrity would never allow her to accept what was on offer. Added to which, it would make a certain Enif's position completely untenable. Sibby shook her head immediately.

Seyal turned to Vebor. "No thank you. I will never repudiate what I have said. It was true. It still is true. Rhyvekan laws need to be changed."

Sibby thought she spotted the faintest of movements behind Vebor. She couldn't be sure, but she had the impression that it was the female Avarak who had helped them before. Myska. If so, the woman was being extremely careful not to be noticed. Sibby hoped that somebody was indeed listening. She also hoped that this young Avarak woman would do something about all this injustice. It was past time that these smug, hidebound males brought their society into the current century. It was, after all, something worth fighting for. So many female Avaraks still died every day.

Vebor treated them to another ten minutes of his opinions on the uselessness of the female species, before asking Seyal again to denounce the movement she herself had started.

She looked him straight in the eye. "Never," she told him in her soft, passive voice. "I would rather die." Sibby felt proud of her. She stood a little taller, too. It seemed to be the only way that she could show support for her friend.

"You will. But in your case, it will be on Rhyveka. For the humanoid, sooner. Here. In three hours." His face disgusted, he turned and stalked away.

Chapter 13

Denaraz looked around at the three minors. "How are you all feeling?"

They checked themselves over. A chorus of 'fines' answered him.

"Good. Then I will drop you off on one of the rescue ships, if you don't mind. I need to get onto *Nivala* before she leaves the system."

Zenzie frowned. "Why?"

He told them about Seyal and Sibby. Their faces went grey.

"You mean that the Avaraks set off that entire storm just to get onto *Nivala*?"

Izan nodded. "It is looking that way, certainly."

"You have got to be joking."

"I assure you, I am not."

Giedi shook his head. "We will come with you." Both Zenzie and Tally nodded energetically.

"You most certainly will not. None of you." The Tyzaran gave the Chyzar a stern look. "You very nearly died out there. You will all need to be put into Zeroth chambers. Maybe not for long, but you do need some medical attention. As soon as I am sure you will be attended to, I will leave you three on one of the rescue ships."

It was clear from Zenzie's expression that she was finding the idea of being left in a Zeroth chamber highly unacceptable. Her crest had gone up and her face was thunderous. Her voice, when she spoke, was distinctly spiky. "What about Mallivan?"

"The captain has already left the shipstation. He is taking *Nivala* to find the Avaraks."

She put her chin up. "Where he goes, I go."

Giedi put his arm around her. "Where she goes, I go."

Tally sighed. "Don't you dare leave me out of this. I want to help too."

Denaraz's jaw tightened. This was getting him nowhere. "I need to get on board *Nivala*," he said. "It is *my* wife they have taken. I will not stop until I get her back."

Zenzara put her hands on her hips. "Where you and Mallivan go, I go. You can put us in Zeroth chambers on board *Nivala*."

Denaraz stared at her then went to the console. It took some time to get through to Mallivan, on board *Nivala*, but eventually he managed it.

Mallivan's voice was as worried as his own. "Zenzara can come," he said finally. "If I leave her behind that Savior Protocol thing will probably drive her mad. Drop my two off at the rescue ship."

Giedi leapt up, smothering a cry of pain. "I am going to marry her. Where she goes I go."

There was a long silence at the other end of the line, which still crackled and had static due to the passing storm. "Excuse me?"

"I am going to marry her."

"Giedi, you are twelve."

"Yes, we all know how old we are. In Tyzar, you can marry

somebody when you are ten. Make a bond of intention with them, anyway."

"Why would you?" The captain sounded genuinely puzzled.

"Because we are soul-mixed."

"Oh no, not that again! You'll have to wait until you are fully grown. I am sorry, but it's illegal for Spacelanders to marry under twenty." He sounded relieved to be able to put the burden of denial onto somebody else.

"They would accept this. It is called a ....." Giedi turned to Zenzara, who answered.

"... Civil Juvenile Marriage Intention Protocol. It is a binding contract, with full marriage powers, but deferring a physical relationship to a future date. Spacelanders accept the concept. You just need special approval."

Mallivan blew out air. "Another protocol. You Tyzarans seem to have a lot of those. And they are all unbreakable, right?"

"Well of course they are. What is the point of a contract that is breakable?"

There was a long pause. "Look, we can talk about this later on. I suppose you can both come on board. But, Giedi, this is a giant leap of faith for me. You have no experience of life on board *Nivala*. You will be expected to behave as the rest of the crew does."

"Of course, Father. Thank you." The boy's eyes shone. He and Zenzie hugged.

Tally's small voice interrupted. "What about me? Can I come too?"

There was more silence as her father considered. Denaraz looked down at the eager little face beside him. "She has just piloted this shuttle to within an inch of its life. She played a major part in the rescue of your son and Chy Zenzara."

There was another sigh. "If Denaraz has to stop to put you on that rescue ship it will only hold us back. If you can behave yourself properly, Tally, you may come. But I shall expect you to obey all orders, and not just from me, mind."

Tally was jumping up and down on the spot. "I will. I promise."

Mallivan simply grunted and gave Denaraz coordinates for the meet. "What size is that runabout you are on?"

Denaraz told him.

"Fine. Bring her in to the shuttle bay. There should be plenty of room in there. Then report straight to sick bay. I want you all Zeroth checked before they do anything further."

Izan smiled at the three crestfallen faces beside him. "Acknowledged," he said.

They docked some two hours later, already well out of the *Shapley* area. The sky was dark and uninviting. There were no stars close enough to warm anything up. It made Tally shiver as she stared out of the runabout's viewing screen. She wouldn't like to be out there on her own. She just hoped that nobody was. Full communication had now been restored, and they had heard from the rescue ships. There was already a death toll of ten due to the storm.

She shivered again. Now that Giedi and Zenzie were safe, her whole body seemed to have shut down. It was chilled and shaky. Her teeth were chattering.

The shuttle door opened to her father and Mel, both of whom had worried expressions on their faces. Tally ran up to her father, and for the first time in her life, threw her arms around his neck.

He picked her up and spun her around. "Well done, Tally! I am proud of you."

The chills turned into a red flush of pleasure. Now she felt cold and hot all at the same time. It was a very strange sensation.

Her father put her carefully back down and walked up to Giedi, who was hobbling along just in front of Zenzara. Neither of them was in great health, and the captain's face reflected that. He gave them both a quick hug and shook Denaraz's good hand, pumping it up and down.

Denaraz's crest came up. He didn't like the attention or the hand pumping. Mallivan noticed, laughed and then withdrew his hand. "Sorry. You did a great job, my friend."

The crest began to settle. "Naturally. That is why I was chosen by the Supreme Council."

"He went outside on the shuttle as we approached the skimmers!" bubbled Tally. "I braked so quickly, I almost killed him!"

"There is no need to sound quite so ghoulish, Tal." Giedi gave her a small shake of his head.

His sister wasn't even listening. "And I docked the shuttle against the skimmers all on my own!"

"You did a great job, too. You all did." Mallivan smiled around. "I can't tell you how glad I am to see all four of you. But we have to get you checked out. Pity we only have two Zeroths on board. Mel, will you take them along to sick bay, please? Tally should only be a moment, so pop her in one of the triage machines first, will you? You too, Denaraz. I can see you've done something to your left hand. Then leave these two ..." he waved one hand to encompass the Chyzar and Giedi, "... in after you and Tally have finished. From the look of the two of them, they will both need to stay there, at least overnight." He caught the look of frustration that passed between them. "And no, nothing will happen during that time. We are far too far behind the ship that took them. Nothing more is likely to happen until tomorrow."

Mallivan and Denaraz hung back together as the others were led away by Zenzara.

"We can't find Gus," he told the Tyzaran. "It may have been taken as well."

Izan grimaced. "That sounds most unlike the Avaraks. They have a strong trading treaty with Enifa at the moment. I can't see them risking their supply chain."

"They have one with the Spacelanders. That hasn't stopped them from taking my sister."

Denaraz shook his head. "Not the same. The Spacelander pact is simply a non-aggression pact with some minimal degree of movement. The Enifa pact is essential for the Avaraks. Enifa would take the spacejacking of one of their citizens as a declaration of war between the two races. I just don't think they would have done that."

"Then ... perhaps Gus has managed to infiltrate the Avarak ship?"

The Tyzaran nodded. "Perhaps. It might have thought it could carry out some sort of a rescue attempt."

Mallivan pursed his lips. "In that case, we should be checking for signals as we follow them. It seems very unlikely that one Enif could do anything on a huge ship full of Avaraks, but I learnt long ago not to underestimate them as a race. They are a very resourceful people."

"Yes. Despite being generally pacific, they have certainly proved to us that they are not afraid to act when necessary. I am glad that Sibby and Seyal are not alone. If I know Gus, it will be determined to minimize any harm coming to them."

"Let's hope that is true. I have no idea what can have happened, or how the Avaraks knew enough about our situation and the race to act when they did."

"Yes. I have been thinking about that. I am very much afraid that they must have had information from inside *Nivala*." Izan pulled a face.

"It cannot have been Seyal herself. She is clearly the intended victim here. They must have decided that her meddling in Avarak male dominance warranted action."

"Yes. I think they have decided to prevent any further interference with their status quo. Seyal's attempts to undermine the male dominance must have been getting some traction."

Now it was Mallivan's turn to frown. "But, then … if it was not Seyal who told the Avaraks where and when we would be vulnerable, who could it … oh!" He stopped, and a pained expression crossed his face. "Oh, Segaton. Of course. That is … unfortunate."

"I think it must have been the boy, yes." Denaraz, much more used to analyzing such occurrences, had come to the same conclusion some hours earlier. It was the only thing that made sense. "I believe that Segaton may have been seduced by the idea of his father's estate. By the idea of playing with other boys his age. He may have been feeling isolated here. After all, Seyal has been having some trouble with him recently."

"If this is true, Seyal must be devastated."

Izan nodded. "Yes. I do not, however, think that the boy knows that his own mother is in so much danger. He has always been close to her. I expect the Avaraks will have been misinforming him about her future. They wouldn't consider a lie about a female to have any consequences at all. They would probably even feel justified."

"You think they will throw her in some detention center for the rest of her life?"

"They may. —Or they may decide to get rid of the threat altogether."

"Surely not? And make a martyr of her? That could backfire on them."

"You and I know that, but will the Avaraks? They are not exactly sensitive to their female population. I think they are far more likely to discount the women's movement as a nuisance that must be eradicated."

"And they will do that by eradicating Seyal." Mallivan's face was frozen.

"And Sibby. Yes, possibly. Maybe even probably."

"Then we need to hurry."

"Yes." Denaraz closed his eyes for a brief moment. "I hope we arrive in time."

Mallivan's face was equally grim. "We *have* to arrive in time."

Chapter 14

Both women were shivering with fear and anticipation by the time the Avaraks finally came for Sibby. Vebor was not with the security detail sent to fetch them. Perhaps he thought their deaths beneath his dignity, thought Sibby. She was so cold and hungry and scared that she couldn't generate the anger he deserved. She got to her feet as the guards cancelled the force field. Both she and Seyal stood close together, shivering slightly. Sibby put her arms around the puny shoulders of the woman in front of her.

"I admire you so much, Seyal. I am glad to have counted you as a friend."

Seyal hugged her back as tightly as she could. "You are my sister, Sibby. I love you. I am sorry for all that has happened. Forgive me."

"None of this was your fault. There is nothing to forgive."

They clung to each other for as long as they could, but it was not long enough. With very little ceremony, Sibby was bundled out of the cell and escorted along various passageways. The guards gave her the choice of walking or being dragged. She elected to walk, although her gait was somewhat unsteady. Leaving Seyal to confront her fate alone had left tears streaking down her face. She tried to wipe them away.

The guard detail used lifts twice, so there were two changes in deck involved. They reached the airlock some ten minutes later. Sibby had been anxiously peering around her to check the route, but there were too many twists and turns. She could no longer tell if they were taking her to the airlock Myska had indicated. If they had decided to go for another one at the last minute, it was more than possible that Gus would not be able to catch her. Her feet slowed and she stumbled slightly as she realized just how unlikely it was that she could survive the next moments. She was trying to be brave, but the truth was that she was trembling all over. She could hardly see because her vision was clouded. She was absolutely terrified.

There was a reception committee waiting for them at the airlock. Vebor was there, after all. He was standing behind a heavy figure that must have been the captain of the Avarak ship. There were ten other officers, ranged behind this figure and alongside Vebor. All were wearing identical superior expressions.

Sibby was brought in front of the captain, and told to stand up straight. She did not need telling. There was no way that she was going to bow down before these people. She straightened her neck as best she could and thought of Seyal. She would at least *try* to die proudly, she determined.

"I do not recognize your authority over me," she said.

There was a hiss of dismay from all those present. "You have not been given authority to speak, female," snapped the captain. "You will remain silent or the guard behind you will silence you."

Sibby curbed her tongue. She wasn't sure what that might mean, but she was fond of her voice.

The captain unrolled a scroll and began reading. It was in Avarak, not in Universal, so Sibby couldn't understand it. However, the captain gave her a loose translation every couple of sentences or so. His expression informed her that this was a favor she really didn't deserve.

"You have been found guilty of sedition against the Avarak people. This is a capital offense as there can be no justification for acts of this nature. *Avarak Karax!*"

"*Avarak Karax!*" chanted all the Avarak males present. The combined force of their voices made the deck plating tremble noticeably.

The captain continued reading from the scroll. "The Avarak Grand Council has commuted the usual form of capital punishment to death by vacuum debarkation. The sentence is to be carried out immediately, on the ship *Daktar*, with ten good and true Avaraks as witnesses."

At the words 'good and true', Sibby raised her head and stared at Vebor. Vebor ground his teeth and took a small step forward, only to be waved back sharply by the captain of the *Daktar*, who had not finished.

Sibby caught the look on the Avarak captain's face and mirrored it. Vebor's expression darkened, but he made no other movement. Sibby thought she detected just a touch of triumph inside her shaking body. She reached inside herself and tried to fan the spark. Mentally she called up Denaraz, imagining the tall Tyzaran beside her. She took his hand. Izan squeezed hers back. For a second she really thought she could feel him. As she shuffled closer to the airlock, she knew that she wasn't alone. She would never be completely alone. Her husband was there with her. She forced her shoulders back.

She stood calmly in front of the sentencing squad, facing them full on. Hers might be a slim, delicate figure in comparison to theirs, but she would show them that her heart was as strong as any of the towering males in front of her.

The captain went on, now reaching the conclusion of the document. His attempt at legalese in Universal was almost impossible to understand. She tuned him out until his last words. "You will therefore be summarily ejected into space, where your life will be quickly and ethically terminated." Those were clear, sharp and all too easy to understand.

Sibby gave a small snort and rolled her eyes. She giggled. 'Ethically terminated' seemed a bit of a ... what was the name for it ... oh yes, that was it ... a bit of an oxymoron."

This caused a deep silence in the passageway. The Avaraks ranged before her began to glance uncertainly at each other. Several of them began to murmur.

Ah, they didn't know what an oxymoron was and thought she had been insulting their intelligence! "Well, that too," she muttered, *sub voce.* "If the helmet fits ..."

The captain was glowering at her, but clearly hesitant to act. After all, she thought to herself, since she was already to be 'ethically terminated' there was little point applying any other punishment.

And then it was suddenly too late. The captain produced a fat finger and, after a couple of ceremonious waves in the air, pushed the airlock hatch release. The large seal rolled to one side and Sibby was thrust inside.

Her heart began to pound. She tripped and only the far side of the airlock prevented her from falling. She straightened up again and walked to the center to look up and out.

The midnight sky on the other side of the airlock was

overwhelming in its darkness. She could see no stars, no light. She had hoped that she would see some kind of majesty within it, but she found only darkness.

The Avaraks behind her did not speak as the huge circular hatch rolled back into place, cutting her off from the rest of the ship. The sound of a hidden motor starting up made her start. Almost immediately the air in the space, which was about the size of a small shuttle, began to hiss as it was sucked out of the compartment, draining the air.

Just as Sibby was wondering how long it would take, and when she should try to inhale deeply, she found there was nothing to breathe. The outer hatch rolled aside. She was faced with inky space, and nothing else. The vastness of space overwhelmed her. Like flotsam, she floated out with the last wisps of air. She felt completely alone; an insignificant speck in a sea of suffocation that pressed down on her from all sides.

She was utterly petrified.

Chapter 15

Prime Ohnah walked around the huge sickbay on *Bellaris* shipstation and felt powerless to help. The huge Zeroth chambers were coping with those injured. The station medical staff were bustling around tending to the station personnel, many of whom had suffered cuts and broken bones. The broken bones would need the Zeroth chambers when they had finished with patients who had been severely wounded, but until then were having their limbs immobilized by old-school methods.

She looked around her domain. There was nothing she could do here. But there *was* something that needed to be done. She had to find out just how the Avaraks had been able to trigger a supershell storm of such magnitude. Even now, the storm they started was rolling through the rest of the Landau Rift, diminishing as it slowly expanded. That could not be allowed to happen again. Too many had died.

Her mind made up, she walked quickly through the shipstation towards the engineering department. Although for many years she had been prime of the whole station, her background had been in spatial mechanics. She should be able to work this out, especially with the team of experts she had gathered on the shipstation over the years. *Shapley* was not a small station. It was one of the biggest there was. Home to many significant projects. She had spent years turning it into one of the greatest research stations in the Rift. She knew that the scientists on board, like her, would be working non-stop to find out exactly what had happened, and how it could be avoided in the future.

Sure enough, Engineering was crowded with many chattering technicians. They had clearly had the same idea she had.

As she walked in there was a sudden silence. She smiled around at them, reached up to a peg to grasp a lab coat and fastened it over her normal shipsuit. "What have we got so far?"

Talk resumed as a short and stocky figure stepped up to her. "Whatever they did, it was here." Brian Lasseny, station head of spatial research and development, pointed out a small cross on the chart which was projecting on the main screen. "Just to the south of the Chain Nebula and north of Pyrrhus. If it had been any further away, we would have had more time to react. As it was, we were only able to detect the incoming disturbance a few minutes before it hit us." The man looked grim. "We will have to amplify that reaction time in the future."

"Definitely. We will. But what we really need to find out is what they did and how they were able to do it. Is this type of attack limited to the proximity of instability, such as that in the Chain Nebula, or could the Avaraks trigger something like this anywhere in the Major Shells?"

Brian nodded. "I was considering taking a large shuttle out to that location. See what we can find. I believe that anything energetic enough to have caused a full-blown supershell storm will have left traces behind."

Ohnah paused, then made a decision. "I'll go with you."

The gasps of surprise around her told her that she was doing something unexpected. And she could understand. As Prime, she was not expected to leave the shipstation. But this was too important to ignore. Not only had the safety of their shipstation been compromised, but the safety of the whole of the Landau Rift. All personnel had now been accounted for. She had good people in place; they would look after *Shapley* while she was gone.

Lasseny, to his credit, showed no surprise. "As you wish, Prime. I will organize a multi-disciplinary team. We can leave within two hours."

"Good, Brian. I will be ready."

She gave an absent smile to the rest of those present, then hurried out. If she really was going to leave *Shapley* she had to make sure her deputies knew about it. And she needed to stop by the children's area to give them some reassurance, if that were possible. Her stomach gave a discontented rumble: she hadn't eaten for many long hours. There wasn't time for that now. She could catch up on sustenance once she was on board the shuttle.

When she walked into the children's area, she was surrounded almost at once. They wanted news of those who had not come back from the race. She filled them in on the progress of the two injured contestants, and let them know that the other three missing candidates were currently on board Nivala.

It was Peetie who put into words what a lot of them were no doubt thinking. "Who gets the runabout? Who won the race?"

Ohnah blinked. Of course the children were wondering about that. She had not given it a thought. She paused, rummaging through the possibilities in her mind. Then she made a snap decision.

"I guess nobody wins the runabout directly, Peetie," she told the boy slowly. "Although it was through no fault of their own, nobody finished the race. After what has happened, I am afraid that the fate of the runabout will have to wait. But I shall think carefully about what has happened, and I hope you will too. I am sure, together, we can come up with the right solution for Sammy's little spaceship."

That caused a long silence as the children digested it. Alisevola then gave a slow nod. "People died. It isn't right to even be thinking about prizes for the race. Not now. Not after everything that has happened."

Peetie sighed. "I guess not."

Ohnah felt her heart lift as she looked around at them. This was the next generation and although she could see disappointment, she could also see generosity of spirit.

They were all thoughtful now. Opaline, one of Sammy's children, finally gave a wry nod. "My dad wouldn't have wanted us to be thinking about ourselves when people have been killed. It isn't right."

"I have to leave the station," Ohnah told them all. "Can we get together after that — once I discuss what would be best with some other people?"

Opaline frowned. As the next prime, she was well aware of the unusualness of such a move. "Why are you going off-station?"

Ohnah hesitated, then decided that they all deserved to know the truth. She let them in on the cause of the superstorm, although she said nothing about the possible implication of Segaton.

Much to her surprise, the kids came to the same conclusion

she had. "Segaton has been very moody recently," Altair told her. "Avaraks grow so quickly that it was hard to know how to treat him. I mean, he is only three, which is a baby for the rest of us."

"Yes. But it is the Avarak equivalent of a teenager," murmured Ohnah, mostly to herself. Damn! She should have seen this coming. "He must have been feeling isolated, perhaps even sidelined. That shouldn't have happened. Not on my watch."

"It isn't our fault!" Peetie's face was red and angry. "I tried to get him to play with us. Only he got really angry when I wouldn't teach him to pilot a skimmer. The boy's voice became shrill. "He couldn't even *fit* in a skimmer. It was stupid!"

Now she really did feel guilty. It had never even occurred to her that a three-year-old should be included. She should have had a longer time with the child, she now realized. Then she shook her head. If his own mother and the crew of *Nivala* hadn't picked up his discontent, then it was hardly *her* job to do so. Still, she felt slightly dissatisfied with herself as she walked away. That was something that needed to be examined. There were several races working on the station, and so far it had been on a one-rule-for-all basis. That might require some significant adaptation.

She stopped off on the bridge to update her deputies, went to her cabin to throw a few essentials into a bag before making her way to the shuttle bay. She felt better now that she had a plan. Find out how this happened — then why — then implement change. Good. Her spirits lifted. Now it was just a case of one foot in front of the other.

On *Nivala*, Mallivan was peering at the scans. The Avarak cruiser was now only about six hours ahead of them; *Nivala's* ZEPH drive gave the ship a significant advantage over the Avarak cruiser for speed.

He had just asked Mel to record all the scans and mark up any anomalies, when three figures bounded onto the bridge. All were clean and were wearing new shipsuits. He grinned. "You look better."

Zenzara put her tongue out. "Giedi was in the Zeroth chamber longest. He had severe cuts and bruises. I was just a bit the worse for wear."

"I'm glad it was nothing worse. We were lucky."

Their faces fell. "Were other people hurt?" asked Tally.

"I'm afraid so." He explained about the deaths and the injuries, finishing up, "… but the rest of the competitors only suffered slight injuries, and the latest news about those of them who were hurt is more favorable."

Giedi shook his head. "I still can't believe that the Avaraks did something like this. It seems crazy. They could have started a war!"

"They still may have. They probably didn't realize just how big the anomaly would be. They wanted a way to isolate *Nivala* with few crew members on board. Perhaps they underestimated the effect of whatever it was they did." The captain wanted to believe that, but he also felt from his previous experience with the Avaraks that they could be quite single-minded about their goals, often ignoring some of the larger consequences. He had been on both sides of this.

Denaraz waved at the three new members of the crew. "Prime Ohnahara is currently investigating the cause of the storm," he told them. "She is skilled in this area, apparently, so I think we can be confident of her findings."

Zenzara moved closer to the scanner. "What do we know about the Avarak cruiser? When will we catch up with it? What is the plan of action?"

Both Giedi and Tally had been hanging back, unused to being on the bridge of an active ship. Encouraged by Zenzie, however, they moved up too.

Mel, who was piloting, waited to see what her captain would do. She could almost see him bite back sharp words. When he did eventually speak, his voice was calm. "We are following the ship, but we are much smaller than they are. It would be suicide to fire upon them. We will just have to tail them and hope that some sort of diplomatic opportunity opens up."

All three faces showed their disgust at such a feeble plan of action. Giedi huffed. "We have to do something! We can't just follow tamely after them! What if they are hurting Sibby or Seyal? We don't know what they will do to them!"

Denaraz, who actually felt much the same way, said nothing. However, Mallivan could tell that the tall Tyzaran was chomping at the bit to get on board the Avarak ship. This was not going to be easy.

"We will do whatever we can," he said. "But I cannot allow this ship to be destroyed. You do understand that, don't you?"

Zenzara caught Giedi's eye. "We do," she said. "How can we help?"

Giedi stared at the girl who was to be his wife. "Yes," he said slowly. "What can we do?"

Tally opened her mouth to protest, but her big brother elbowed her in the ribs. She closed her lips again, but treated him to a look that would have wilted a shellflower. Then she realized that he was attempting to communicate silently with her. She glanced between him and Zenzara, finally picking up that they had some kind of plan.

Denaraz, who had the thankless job of making sure the Chyzar remained intact, brought his eyebrows together. He knew Zenzie very well. She was radiating determination. He would have to keep an eye on the shuttles. He would bet his crest that she was up to something, and he really was not of a mind to rescue them all over again.

He noticed that Mallivan didn't seem to have picked up on the non-verbal agreement between the three younglings. The captain was concentrating on the data in front of him.

Mel answered the question for him. "I could use some help over here," she told them. I need somebody to analyze this scan data."

"Of course," said Zenzie. All three of the newcomers moved over to the console. "What are we looking for?"

Mel shrugged. "Any deviation from the normal, I guess. Even the slightest change might be relevant. You never know."

"We will not miss anything, Mel. I promise."

"Fine. I might, because I am flying the ship at the same time. I am depending on you, mind!"

Zenzie, who knew the workings of the ship, smiled back at her. "We want them back as well."

Mel's expression softened. "I know you do. Thank you."

Denaraz stepped back. But he made up his mind to keep a close watch on Chy Zenzara. He was pretty sure that where she led, the others would follow.

Chapter 16

Gus was in position as the hatch rolled back; even so the action came as a surprise. The Enif wasn't ready, would never be ready for this. What if it miscalculated the trajectory? What if the thrust away from the fuselage were inaccurate? What if the Avaraks had decided to use one of the other three smaller hatches? It multifaceted eyes were trying to take in all four hatches, two of which were under the ship and therefore not currently visible. It was an impossible task.

Gus had found itself feeling progressively more and more jittery, an almost unknown feeling for an Enif. Not knowing if Sibby had already been ejected into space from a different airlock, one completely invisible from its current position, was exacting a toll.

It also felt very alone, out in a space that was almost pitch black.

What few distant stars were visible were not nearly enough to give any sort of relief to the almost solid, almost tangible absence of light.

Sibby's heart gave one enormous thud in her chest as she was ejected from the space lock. She panicked. The sight in front of her was terrifying. The vacuum pressed on her insistently, suffocatingly eager to kill.

Belatedly, she remembered Seyal's instructions. She breathed slowly out through pursed lips, expelling all the air in her lungs. At the same time she closed her eyes. Not that she didn't feel compelled to see majestic unfiltered deep space, but she knew that the moisture within her eyeballs could start to boil, leaving her blind. Indeed, the water on her tongue was already starting to fizz as it evaporated in her mouth. It was accompanied by a strong burnt metallic taste. It was the strangest feeling she had ever had.

She had expected it to feel like plunging into liquid nitrogen, but to her surprise it wasn't as immediately cold as she had imagined. The tears on her cheeks had turned to ice instantaneously, yet her face still felt warm. She tried to think about why that was, but only got as far as thinking that there would be no conduction or convection in a vacuum when she realized how futile such thoughts were. If she only had seconds left in this life, she wasn't going to spend them on the physics surrounding her own death; she was going to spend them thinking about the people who loved her. The people she loved.

She surrendered herself to the elements, holding her arms out as she floated out towards the void of empty space where she would never be found. She thought quickly of Mallivan, of her children, of

Mel and Zenzara. Then Seyal, waiting back in that terrible little cell. Finally her mind grasped onto a vision of Denaraz, crest up and eyes flashing. A sensation of love flooded through her body. More tears fizzed in the corners of her eyes and then froze. Dizziness took over her brain. She had only precious seconds before she would pass out.

Suddenly she felt a hard, heavy body crash into hers. She was thrown sideways, her arms and legs tumbling over themselves. She felt a sharp pain in her side. For what seemed to be an eternity she was spinning out of control, until a jerk pulled her sideways and the last few seconds of consciousness slowly evaporated.

Gus almost missed Sibby as she suddenly appeared in front of the Enif. One second the panorama was lifeless and static, the next there was a flash of movement and the slim shape of a woman was floating away from the ship.

Gus frantically calculated the trajectory, crouching down on the fuselage of the *Daktar* as it prepared to jump. There was a moment of flashing doubt, but it tamped that down sternly. That was not the Enif way. The Enif way was to double-check the estimate and then act. Its upper arms were already checking that the rope attaching it to the drone was secure.

It crouched even lower, compressing the elongated tarsus of its legs. There was the briefest of brief pauses then it launched itself out over the hull of the ship.

Gus was able to count to three before their bodies collided. They were the second-longest three seconds in its life. The first had been when it had received the news of the disappearance of its *faliif*, Halaashi.

The Enif impacted Sibby's body with too much force. She shot away from Gus like a billiard ball from a cue and Gus scrambled to grab a hold of her before the rope jolted its body back towards the ship. If that happened, her trajectory would sweep her away. Lucky the Enif had four arms and the top arm on its left managed to latch onto her ankle just in time.

Gus clutched desperately at that leg, knowing that it would be jerked backwards at any moment. It had only managed to close two of its arms around her foot when there was a massive jolt as the rope reached its full extent. Gus knew that the digits that served as its fingers would be digging into Sibby's flesh, but it couldn't risk losing her. The girl seemed to be unconscious already; her hair was flowing out from her scalp like an aura and her arms were stretching out towards either horizon.

Gus took a brief moment to gather the inert body into a safer position against its carapace, and then began to pull them both back along the length of the rope with one free hand. The Enif found progress slower than it would have wished – it was acutely aware of the scarce seconds left for Sibby. She needed to be placed in an oxygenated atmosphere soon or her recuperation would be compromised.

The oppressive black vacuum around them luckily offered no resistance, which helped Gus to drag the inert body quickly towards the waiting drone. Within five seconds of the time the Enif's body had impacted her, they were both hovering within the open sides of the drone. It looked like two halves of a walnut, hinged together — the only safe haven within several parsecs.

Gus allowed them to crash into the back part of the drone, grabbing at one of the stowing ropes in order to steady them and prevent any sort of rebound. Then it leant out and severed the rope that tethered the drone to the mother ship, before pulling the console out of the wall, where it had been carefully stowed, and instructing the two halves of the bivalve to close around them.

It leapt to one of the Avarak EVA suits, its digits scrambling to turn on the flow of oxygen. Once that was done, it turned to the second suit and did the same thing. Then it broke open an emergency light tube and used it to examine Sibby as best it could.

The Spacelander's face was chapped and her lips were darkened. In fact, her whole face seemed almost burnt. There were the beginnings of space swell, so she didn't even look like herself. The good thing was that she had maintained her body temperature. She had not been exposed enough for any sort of freezing to take place, except for superficial water that had somehow found the way to the surface of her skin. It was as if she had been dusted by powdered ice.

Gus brushed it away from her skin. Then it pushed her gently over to the first EVA suit and began to feed her limbs inside the thick material. The EVA suit, meant for a fully grown Avarak male, was enormous compared to the slim humanoid in front of him. Both of her legs fitted into one of the suit's extremities, and her head reached only to the waist.

Gus slammed the helmet onto the EVA suit and screwed it firmly into place. Then it breathed a sigh of relief and slumped back on the second suit, taking a moment to turn off the flow of oxygen from that one. Gus would not need much of an atmosphere, at least not for several hours. It was determined to save as much air as possible. That air was vital to the survival of Sibby, after all. And not so vital to the Enif.

Gus watched the EVA suit anxiously. Its carapace was dull with worry and concern. What would have been the point of this entire exercise if Sibeal didn't wake up? Did she need some sort of artificial respiration? Surely she should have regained consciousness by now?

Just as Gus was preparing to re-open the helmet and undertake some vague attempt at heart massage, the folds of the stiff fabric began to move. They bumped out towards the waiting Enif once or twice, then there was a tremendous jerking of the suit as Sibby thrashed her arms about, clearly frantic with panic and unaware of her current surroundings.

Gus pushed the communications device on the second suit. They were on the same channel, it knew. It had checked the previous day. It depressed the button that would allow her to hear its voice.

"Sibeal, you are inside the drone. I am here with you. There is sufficient oxygen inside the suit for you, so all you need to do is breathe slowly. The suit will keep you warm and safe. Please try to relax. I believe that you to have suffered no long term damage. However, I would be pleased if you could confirm that hypothesis, once you find that you can talk. If you wish to see me, you will need to pull yourself up inside the suit until your face is inside the helmet area."

There was a long, long pause, then the struggles inside the closed EVA suit diminished.

Gus found itself able to hear its own heartbeat in the deep silence. It was most disconcerting. The seconds ticked by far too slowly, as if some sort of time dilatation were in force.

Then the EVA suit squirmed, and finally a slightly woebegone face peered out through the oversized visor of the helmet.

Seeing that she was looking in its direction, Gus gestured towards the button on the outside of her EVA suit. "You need to open a channel."

Sibby struggled with her hands. In order to switch on her audio channel, she had to push the button on the external part of the suit. She put one arm in each sleeve, but found that her hand did not have enough strength to pull one glove over to the other. She struggled for a few moments and then shook her head at Gus. She was speaking, but the Enif could hear nothing. She shrugged her shoulders helplessly. There was no way she was going to be able to press that button.

Gus took pity on her and leant forward. It pressed firmly down on the audio button with two of its own hands, and gestured to her to say something more.

"A-Are you a-alright, G-Gus?"

Inside the suit there was a very loud crackle which made her jump, before her voice blared out through the speakers of her suit, way above her head. It was deafening to both of them, but especially to the Enif, suitless in the enclosed space of the EVA drone. Gus jerked backwards and winced. There was sharp pain in its complex eyes. It reached down to adjust the controls on the suit's glove. After a screech of feedback that nearly deafened them both, Sibby's sound levels came down to something rather more bearable than hard foghorn.

"Better?" The Enif asked.

"M-Much. Yes. These Avaraks must have e-eardrums made of steel," she answered. "S-sorry."

"How are you, Sibeal? Have you performed a self-examination? A diagnostic?"

The mouth quavered a little. "I ... I ... guess I am f-f-fine." She didn't seem sure about that statement.

Gus peered at her worriedly; she didn't look fine at all. What it could see of her face was puffy and she was trembling. Was that normal for a human exposed to imminent death, or had her brain been affected? A quick test of mental acuity seemed prudent.

"What are the seven defining constants?"

She frowned in concentration. "Err ... Boltzmann's; then ...

err … the speed of light in a vacuum; the … the Planck constant; the elementary charge … err … what am I missing? —Oh, yes, the hyperfine transition frequency of cesium-133; … the … the Avogadro constant and … what is the last one? … Ah, yes! —the luminous efficacy of monochromatic radiation of frequency," she said with a slightly triumphant air.

"Yes, but I was asking for their values."

"Their values?" She stared at the Enif from behind the visor of the spacesuit. Her shocked eyes seemed huge. "You mean the actual numbers? Like three hundred thousand kilometers per second?"

"Well, I would have expected two hundred and ninety-nine thousand seven hundred and ninety-two point four five eight kilometers per second in the case of light speed, but yes, that's exactly what I mean."

"Are you serious? I don't know the actual numbers."

"Were you in the vacuum for too long?"

"No. *No!* Nobody knows the actual numbers, Gus! We don't learn them by rote."

This astounded the Enif. "You don't?"

Sibby stared back, equally amazed. "You *do*? Then what exactly is Boltzmann's?"

"One point three eight zero six four nine times ten to the twenty three joules per kelvin," it rattled off.

"And the transition frequency?"

"Nine one nine two six three one seven seven zero hertz."

She lost her balance inside the suit and had to scramble back up to the visor again. Her battered face managed the semblance of a smile. "I think, if I am capable of remembering even what the seven defining constants *are*, then we can deduce that my mind survived the void more or less intact."

Gus wasn't convinced, but remained polite. "If you say so."

"I do. Thank you. You have saved my life."

"Yes, I know."

Sibby found herself managing another faint grin. But what had she been expecting? Some sort of modest denial? That was not the Enif way. Enif always stuck to a factual interpretation, which was quite refreshing.

They were safe, but she had no idea how long that statement would hold true. Their drone cocoon would protect them from gamma rays and random space debris, but it was a temporary refuge at best. They would need even more luck if they were ever to be found, drifting as they were in the immense confines of deep space.

She dragged her mind away from such contemplations. She was here. She was breathing. She was almost warm and momentarily safe. And she was very grateful to the Enif beside her for that.

She just couldn't help thinking of Seyal, now all alone in that horrid cell and facing imminent immolation. She closed her eyes. Though the tears that slid out of them no longer turned into ice, her heart was still heavy.

Chapter 17

On the journey out to the origin of the supershell storm, Prime Ohnahara was informed of yet another death amongst the injured crew. She felt a physical weight settle on her shoulders when she was told the news. It hurt. Her crew had trusted her to keep them safe. She knew all of them so well. She knew their families. Learning of a further death was a blow.

She was worried about the three missing crew members from *Nivala*, too. Though they were theoretically under the command of Ryler Mallivan, that didn't absolve her of all blame. She could have put *Shapley* immediately on a war footing as soon as she heard of the coming storm. If the defensive force had been scrambled, they would certainly have seen the Avarak ship. Whether they would have been able to be helpful in the middle of a storm was another matter, but she couldn't help but second guess her previous choices, especially now that the true cost in lives was known. At the time, there had been no sign this was anything other than a natural phenomenon. Still, the insidious feeling of guilt crept in.

At least none of the children had died. The two who had been badly injured were now progressing adequately, and should be able to resume normal life shortly. But the continuing existence of *Shapley* had been threatened. If the Avaraks could instigate a supershell storm whenever and wherever it suited them, it would have huge repercussions. She *had* to find out exactly what had happened. She might have failed those who had already been killed; she would *not* fail those whose lives still depended upon her.

Brian Lasseny gave a grunt, pulling her out of her introspection. "Are we there?"

They peered through the forward spaceglass porthole. The inky darkness was streaked with colorful artificial auroras, still forming kaleidoscopic arcs across the sky.

"That's not good," said Ohnah, her jaw slack, "Rainbow effects?"

He nodded. "I'm afraid so. Look at that."

She stepped quickly up to the bank of consoles that were monitoring space outside the ship. She frowned at the readouts. She paled. "Surely not!"

Brian's tone was grim. "They have found a way to create crust quakes on the surface of a neutron star. In a magnetar, like this one, that necessarily precipitates a fracture of the crust and a severe storm front."

"A crust quake would require a tremendous amount of energy. I … I find it hard to believe any aware civilization would do something like that. It … it beggars belief!"

His jaw had tightened. "That trace you see there tells us how. They detonated six of their Screwdriver astronuclear devices to provoke explosive reconnection. *Six!* Residual radiation is so strong that we can only stay here for around ten minutes. The sphere of influence is enormous. It could take centuries … CENTURIES …

for the contamination to dissipate. I can't believe *any* civilization would do that." He shook his head slowly.

Ohnah was still white. "We will have to move the shipstation."

"We will. And it should have been done yesterday."

"Can we get far enough away?"

He pressed his lips together, thinking. Then he gave a shrug. "Maybe. Nuclear radiation from astronuclear devices is fifteen times stronger in space than it would be within an atmosphere, but if we get *Shapley* moving immediately, we can avoid the worst."

"How could they justify detonating SIX astronuclear devices just to kidnap one Avarak woman? It makes no sense. They have devastated this entire region for half of eternity. Surely this will mean war?"

Brian Lasseny ran his hand through his recalcitrant hair. "We need to report this."

"We certainly do. And I need to get *Shapley* moving away from here. Thank goodness the station is well shielded." She had a sudden idea. "What if we tuck the shipstation behind the Olympus Nebula? Could we do that, do you think? Would that protect us? From this and possible future attacks?"

Lasseny started to do the calculations, using the ship's consoles to deal with the many variables. Finally he sat back on his stool. "Maybe," he admitted. "In any case, the Olympus Nebula is free of magnetars. In fact, it is free of neutron stars altogether. That would make such an attack pointless. It wouldn't create a supershell storm anywhere near as big as this one, at any rate."

"Good enough. Get me a link to *Shapley,* will you?"

She was soon talking to the *Shapley* bridge crew. Her instructions were terse and to the point. Then she tabled a conference call to the Spacelander headquarters, the Tyzaran Council and the Macers. This was far bigger than she had thought. The other members of the Interstellar Alliance needed to get involved immediately. This part of the Landau Rift was about to be put out of bounds. For much more than her own lifetime. Ohnah just hoped that she would be in time to save her beloved shipstation.

Seyal was not feeling particularly animated as she crouched against the wall in her cell. Not only was she about to die, but she would die without knowing whether her friends had escaped with their lives. It hurt. It hurt that she had had to let them go without her. It hurt that her son had betrayed her, although she still believed that he hadn't known what he was doing.

She closed her eyes and tried to reason with herself. Really, she had done quite a lot in the span of years that had been allotted to her. Most of her fellow female Avaraks didn't last as long as she had. And she didn't regret her actions. Somebody had needed to stand up for the feminine half of Rhyveka's population. If it hadn't been her, who would have done it? Not many of her peers had the chance. Most of them had died during childbirth. She had been very lucky. Solutor had been an exception to the male Avarak rule. He had allowed her to become a nurse and had even turned a blind eye to her studying Universal. If he hadn't done that, she could never have become a member of *Nivala's* crew. She could never have started this small revolution.

She was pleased that he had come to an honorable end. *"Avarak Karax,"* she murmured to herself. "Segaton, if you can only become *half* the Avarak your father was …"

Her eyes had filled up with tears, despite her fingers covering them. It hurt *so* much to know of the betrayal of a child. But he was a male Avarak. Nothing could change that. She just wished he had not allowed himself to be so easily manipulated.

She sighed. He was only an adolescent. How would he know the difference? They had hung a couple of carrots in front of his face and he had obediently trotted into their stable of temptation. It was normal. He should have been warned. She herself was more than partly to blame.

The tears filtered through her fingers and dropped down onto the decking. She felt abandoned and alone, but she had insisted on being left behind, so she had only herself to blame for that. She knew that her friends would have tried to rescue her if they could have. But she couldn't let them give up their own chance at survival for her. It was time to face the music on her own. She wanted no more innocents to die for her sins. Accountability was unavoidable and it was her time now.

She heard the heavy footsteps of Avarak males approaching her cell.

She pushed herself up the side of the wall until she was standing. She rubbed at her face with her right arm, trying to eliminate the signs that she had been crying.

Vebor came to a ceremonious halt in front of the cell. "Are you happy you caused your friend's death?" he asked.

That was easy to answer. She would be giving nothing away. "No."

"That is what happens to terrorists."

She frowned. "A terrorist is somebody who uses terror to obtain their goals," she pointed out. "I have never terrorized anybody. Not once in my entire life. I merely wished to change some of the more barbaric sides of Avarak society."

"You are a terrorist because the Avarak Grand Council has decreed it so."

Seyal gave a faint smile and an even fainter shake of her head.

"You know that is not true, Dr. Vebor. The Grand Council rejects all change. But all I asked for is that we be allowed to keep our natural voices and that we be allowed to have some say in our own future. You cannot continue to use us as chattels. It is obscene."

"You are an aberration. Females should not complain. It is not their place."

"Really? You are an educated Avarak. Surely you cannot reconcile that with a medical background?"

Vebor frowned. "Whyever not? My background helps me to help people."

"No. Your background helps you to help males. Not all people. Just males. You help to perpetuate the cruel treatment of females. You operate on our voices. You allow us to die in childbirth."

"Such things are natural results of your birth defects. I do not understand why you complain. I am not a deity. I cannot change that which is."

Seyal sighed. There was absolutely no point talking to a male. It was something she had learned many, many years ago. Even Solutor had been more stubborn than a Shaulamain mule.

"Then you must do as the Council has asked."

He glared down at her. "I would hardly allow myself to be influenced by a mere female."

"No," she said sadly. "Of course you wouldn't. That is the way of our world."

She shrank back into the wall, self-effacing into her usual inconspicuous self. The habits of a lifetime were hard to break, even when that lifetime was coming to an end. She couldn't believe she had been reduced to trying to convince Vebor of anything. That had to be the absolute definition of hopelessness.

"Here." Vebor allowed one of the accompanying guards to disable a small part of the cell force field in order to pass through some victuals. "Not that you will need that for much longer. Not where you are going."

"Will you promise me one thing, Dr. Vebor?"

He looked offended. "No!"

"Will you make sure that my son doesn't know of my death? I would not want him to think he was in any way responsible."

Vebor had already been turning to leave. He paused. "As a matter of fact," he said slowly, "it has been decided that your son will not be involved in any way with your execution. So in this matter, and quite by chance, it would seem that you will get your wish."

"That is a comfort."

"You should have thought of the wellbeing of your son before you started to criticize our society. It is all that is required of a female. You are unfit as a mother."

Seyal leant even further into the wall. Life, she felt, was far from fair. She had tried to help her fellow females, but all that she had manage to do was wreck her own, and possibly her son's life.

She watched as Vebor and his escort strode confidently away. If only a fraction of that confidence had been available for the females, they could have accomplished so much!

She sank back down to the floor, ignoring the food. Where she was going she wasn't going to need it.

She spared a thought for Gus and Sibeal. At least Vebor had not mentioned them. They had not been caught by the Avaraks. But did that mean they had escaped? Where could they be?

Sibby was crouching down inside the huge Avarak spacesuit. She was lost inside it, but she was feeling much better now. Although the skin on her face and hands still felt chapped, she was breathing satisfactorily and was completely aware of her surroundings.

Gus, she saw, had not bothered to get inside the other EVA suit. It had also turned off that suit's supply of air, probably saving it for her, in case she needed more oxygen later on.

The Enif was looking worried. "Is something the matter, Gus?" she asked it.

"I have a problem with the automatic distress beacon," admitted Gus, "It doesn't seem to want to work. I have checked it out to the best of my ability, but it is probably more in your area of expertise."

"Sure. I will open the suit. Shove it in here with me. Let me see what I can do."

"Ideally, we need a strong signal that *Nivala* could pick up on. If that is not possible, see if you can set up some sort of interference pattern that might be detected by a passing ship if they were looking for something out of the ordinary."

She nodded. "Do you think we are far enough away from the Avarak ship now?"

A white wave of doubt pulsed through Gus's carapace. "I hope so. You were out of the equation for two hours. I don't think they can possibly be close enough to pick up our signal now, and even if they did, I don't think they would come back for it. It seems to me unlikely that they would link a missing EVA drone with your execution."

"Let's hope not, Gus. Have I thanked you properly for saving my life?"

Gus almost seemed to blush. "Any member of the crew would have done the same."

"Owing a life is a very important thing, Gus. I owe you mine. I shall not forget that. Every single day I exist from now on is thanks to you."

"We Enif believe that it is our duty to help the collective. If we only lived for our own benefit, we would be nothing more than Vaers."

Sibby turned her attention to the beacon. It took her almost an hour to find out why the thing had suddenly decided not to work. "Got it!" she said finally. "Look! Right here, can you see? The EVA suits inside the drone have somehow caused reverse polarity. That is why it wasn't working. I just need to ...," she fiddled with the screwdriver, and then gave a satisfied sigh, "... there, that's got it!"

Gus stretched out one hand and she passed the small beacon back out through the front fastenings of the spacesuit. Gus grinned. "I have to go outside to set this up," it told her. "Make sure you are strapped in!"

It worked at the controls of the drone and after a few moments the two halves of the casing began to open.

Sibby stared out with wide eyes. She had been outside a spaceship many times, but there had always been stars or bright nebulae nearby. The dense blackness that currently surrounded them was off-putting and rather sinister. She shivered inside the thick suit.

Gus also seemed a little intimidated by the inky darkness outside. It took the beacon and quickly shimmied out of the drone, disappearing behind one of the open casings. "I need to fasten this as securely as possible," it told her as it worked, its voice emanating from somewhere behind her head. "If *Nivala* is to have any chance of finding us, it will need to be a strong signal."

Sibby was still stuck on the immensity of the vacuum in front of her. Her heart was scrambling to keep up an even tempo. Her pulse was racing. She could feel sweat building up on her face and when she reached up to touch it, it felt cold and clammy. She was heading into a panic attack, she realized. The primal part of her brain was screaming that they weren't going to get out of this.

She forced herself to breathe in and out more gently. Then she began to laugh. Panic attacks were treated by breathing in and out of a plastic bag, she remembered. And she was currently immured in one of the biggest plastic bags she had ever seen. If that didn't settle down the annoyingly petrified part of her mind, she didn't know what would.

"Are you laughing?" Gus sounded confused.

As her pulse rate began to conform to her mental wishes, she found she was able to force air back into her uncooperative lungs. "Just a little," she admitted.

"I can't see anything very funny in our situation."

"No. There isn't anything even remotely amusing."

"Then, why are you laughing?"

She shook her head, a broad grin spreading from ear to ear. "It's a beautiful view," she said.

There was quite a long pause. Then the Enif pulled itself back into the open side of the drone and looked into her face. "Are you still suffering a deficiency of oxygen?"

"No, thank you Gus. I am fine. Just fine. It's a humanoid thing."

The Enif didn't seem convinced, but it carefully closed the doors after checking that Tsuf had not exited the drone while it had been open to space. "Well, we appear to have given ourselves the very best chance possible. "

"So, what do we do now?"

"Now, we wait."

Chapter 18

Nivala was desperately slicing through space in an attempt to catch up with the Avarak cruiser. Mallivan was pacing from side to side on the bridge. His face was tight. Denaraz was another caged lion. His crest was up and his face was like stone.

From time to time they moved to the consoles in front of them and consulted something, only to step back and resume their pacing.

Zenzara had been eyeing them for a long time now. She was worried about both of them, but she was also convinced that their concern was actually causing them to go about this in completely the wrong way. Her hand was down by her side and she was idly stroking the neck of Mallivan's pet Geiga, Scout. She was frowning as she stared down at the animal.

Giedi had caught her hesitancy. "What is it, Zenz?"

"They are just going straight at the cruiser. What if Gus has managed to get the girls off?"

"Wouldn't we pick up any vessels in the area?"

"I don't know that we would. I guess we would be able to detect anything shuttle sized, but what if they are in something smaller? What if they are in EVA suits and nothing more?"

Giedi was silent for a few moments. Then, "What do you want me to do?"

Her face illuminated. "Thank you, Gied! You have no idea what that means to me!"

He shrugged. "Well, I guess if we are soul-bound or whatever you call it, I am going to have to start pulling in the same direction as you, right?"

"It's not me," she told him, dragging him closer by his shirt so that she could lower her voice. "It's Scout."

"Scout?" Giedi stared at the Geiga. "He isn't doing anything at all. Just standing there."

"That's just it. When Geigas stand like he is doing, pointing so very deliberately in one direction, they are usually picking up some sort of danger."

"But he isn't keening. I thought they made a terrific row when there was danger?"

"They do, but only when that danger is incoming. When they feel themselves to be in danger. But they can also detect danger to other people, only it is more diffuse, more difficult to pinpoint."

"So you think that there is something out there in the Dark Confines? To starboard?"

"I do. I think something is in danger there, but we can't know if it is Gus, or Seyal or Sibby."

"Did you tell my father? And Denaraz?"

"They think I am giving Scout's direction too much importance.

But I don't think so. Look! He is slowly turning to face behind us. As though the danger is dropping behind. I think we are already past it. I have asked them both, but they won't go back."

Something cold settled in Giedi's stomach. "You want to take a shuttle and find it?"

Zenzara gave a raggedy sigh. "I wish I could. But you know about the Savior Protocol. I can't leave Mallivan alone. Not here, not now, not again."

"OK." Giedi grinned. "I'll go. Which shuttle should I take? Do I need the Geiga?"

"I'm going too." Talitha's small head appeared between the two of them. "I overheard, and you are *not* having this adventure all on your own, Giedi!" His sister caught the dubious look that Giedi shot Zenzara and stamped one foot. "If you don't let me come with you, I shall tell somebody what you are planning!"

Giedi stared at Zenzara. His mouth curved down and then he shrugged. "I guess we will both be going."

Tally jumped up and down once or twice, before Zenzara's frown made her stop. The younger girl put up both hands. "All right! All right! I won't do that anymore!"

"Don't. They mustn't suspect anything, or they will be furious. They think the whole thing is just a waste of time. I will go down to the weapons bridge and 'arrange' for the sensors to have a five minute glitch. That should be long enough for you to get away. Once those five minutes have passed, you will have to go dark for another ten, until you are out of range of any of the sensors. I will only tell them when it is necessary. Take some food and drink and make sure that whatever shuttle you decide on has at least a week's autonomy of air for four or five people."

The three friends tiptoed off the bridge. Mallivan and Denaraz didn't seem to notice. They were still pacing up and down, up and down. Zenzara made sure that her hand was on Scout's collar. The Geiga resisted a little at first, but then gave in and came with them. Denaraz frowned a little, but seemed reassured when Zenzara told them she would be back in five minutes.

Zenzie accompanied them to the cargo hold. There were several available shuttles, but the easiest was *Nivala's* main shuttle, which was currently moored first in line for launch on the FLOW stack.

She helped them load a case of water and then a case of rations. "There!" she said, "that should keep five people for a week."

"Five people and a Geiga," corrected Tally.

"Five people, a Geiga and a sunflyer," Giedi told them. "—If we get them all back."

"Don't let Scout eat Toothpick," said Zenzie.

"I won't," he promised.

They hugged each other quickly and then Zenzie hugged Tally. "Be careful!"

"We will!"

"Give me exactly five minutes to set everything up. As soon as the cargo bay door opens, you can take her out."

They nodded.

"Then just turn to our stern and take her back. At the rate *Nivala* is travelling now you will need at least a couple of hours before you reach the point where Scout began to indicate to starboard."

"Sure. Don't worry about us. We know what we have to do." Tally gave an impish grin. "After all, I already saved you two."

Giedi paused and then burst out laughing. "I suppose you did! Well, then, if the going gets tough I will let you take the decisions."

"I shall hold you to that!"

Brother and sister boarded the shuttle and Giedi began the preflight check as Zenzara made her way to the weapon's deck. She felt a bit of a traitor as she began to prepare for the shuttle's sneaky departure. It was not a pleasant feeling, particularly because of everything that both Mallivan and Denaraz had done for her.

But they had their sights stubbornly on the Avarak cruiser, and something inside her just *knew* that she was right in this instance, and they were wrong.

She shook her head to try to clear away the negative thoughts. "Just get it done," she told herself sternly. "The most important thing is to find our missing crew."

Ten minutes later she was back on the bridge having brought all the sensors back on line. Nobody had noticed anything. Giedi and Talitha had slipped away, with Scout as their main sensor. She just hoped beyond hope that they would find whoever it was that was in danger.

The *Daktar* had reached its destination, Rhyveka. There was no porthole in the cell, but Seyal felt the change in the engine noise, recognized within her the moment when they docked with the orbital platform, synchronized somewhere above the equator.

It almost didn't affect her. She had already begun to prepare for her imminent death. She felt far away from other Avaraks. It was almost a floating sensation — an evaporation of all the experiences that at one time had made her an individual. It allowed her to review the things she had liked so much: becoming a valuable member of *Nivala's* crew, making friends, learning Universal, traveling far beyond the borders of the Veka system, spending so much time with her son, being treated as an equal by aliens she admired. She pulled up memory after memory, examining each and every one and then almost bidding it farewell as she moved to the next one. She was uncomfortable, but no longer felt it. She was cold, but it no longer mattered.

When they came for her, she had already made her peace with most of her past. She got to her feet almost willingly. At least it would soon be over. At least her passage through this land of the living was reaching its end. Soon, there would be peace. The peace that eventually came to every living thing. It surely was not something to be scared of, if it happened to every single thing? Even planets and stars died. So did galaxies. Clusters, superclusters and larger scale structures. Even the universe would eventually die.

Vebor was not with the squad that came to fetch her. It was composed of fresh-faced young male Avaraks, yet they still stared at her with dislike.

It seemed strange to her now that there could be such hostility between one insignificant female and four burly young soldiers. That they had even heard of her was surprising. That they could dislike her was amazing.

Perhaps that was her one crowning achievement. To come to the attention of the males. To dare to disturb their comfortable hegemony. To have made them uncomfortable enough to notice her.

She let them lead her to the main exit of the cruiser. It would be a long way down to the ground on Rhyveka, but there was a space elevator from the main orbital platform, which is where she supposed them to be.

Her hands were free. There was not the slightest possibility that a weak female could escape from a male detail, and without Vebor there was no need for further humiliation. She was left on her own on one side of the space elevator, while the soldiers sat in an orderly file opposite her and watched her with unblinking eyes.

"Your sentence will be carried out immediately upon arrival," said the one in charge, his voice cool. He could have been commenting on the weather.

Of course. They would want to control everything. The narrative, the witnesses, the privacy. What better place than the Elevator Spaceyard? Military territory for as far as you could see. No publicity. It was an eminently logical decision.

She turned to watch the sky as the clouds of her home planet gradually came into view beneath them. Despite everything, it was a land she had loved and seeing it again was unexpected. After several minutes in transit they began to touch the white wisps, and then they were cocooned in a world of white clouds.

Seyal turned back. She had honored her husband by remembering all of his good qualities, and now there was only one person left to say her goodbyes to. Her son.

Segaton was a part of her, and she was glad that he would never know just how his mother had died. He would grow strong and fierce, as an Avarak should. Perhaps, one day, he would remember a few of his mother's values. Perhaps he would treat his own wives just that little bit better because she had been with him for these long three years? She liked to hope so, in any case.

She remembered how much she loved her son. How much she had cared for him. And she finally made her peace with his actions. For herself, she did not mind. She would have minded, very much, for Gus and Sibby. Hopefully, though, they had escaped with their lives. Hopefully this would only be a small bump in their journey, not something that truncated it.

Her lips smiled as she finalized her dissociation from the living. Now there was only the formal transfer to death to be undertaken. She was already almost gone. Merely a mist of molecules ready to blow away with the first wind. None of it mattered any longer. Nothing could touch her now. She closed her eyes, wanting to see only the soft mist inside her own head. She had gone beyond their reach, whatever they did to her body. She had moved on from the mundane. Withdrawn, in some way.

She peered downwards as the elevator drew close to the surface of her home planet. It hadn't changed much. The same beautiful mountains off to the south. The highlands surrounding the Navy yards. Then she saw a long walkway that had been hastily constructed from the space platform to an unused portion of the yards. It terminated near a small jumble of wooden logs. She realized at once that this effort had been made for her. Specially for her.

She had no wish to see any more. Her eyes remained tightly shut once the space elevator docked. She never saw the row of stolid males that had gathered to see her demise. She never saw the few distant females who had gathered in solidarity with her. She allowed herself to be led along the pathway above the ground and towards what would be the last memory she would ever face.

The walkway must have been hundreds of meters long, for it took them quite a few minutes to navigate its length. She had to open her eyes then, because one of her escorts shook her and told her to. There was a gap and a step down onto the actual funeral pyre, and they didn't want her to stumble. Ironic, she thought.

The walkway had come to an end. In front of her now was a circular pathway around a wooden post. They waited until she took that last step down and closed a small safety gate before they withdrew. She was able to walk the whole way around the pole on this small platform, which had railings so that she could not fall. She closed her eyes again, but that quick glance had shown it to be similar to the crow's nest on an old-school sailing ship, back in ancient Avarak history. She had seen pictures of them.

The walkway the detail had used to escort her to this point was being dismantled. She could hear the scraping of wood against wood as her guards removed a few meters of bridging planks to make sure of a safe gap between the walkway and the fire. It would not be long now.

This, then, was to be the end of her journey. It had taken longer than she thought, and she was grateful for the extra years. Grateful for so many things. She had got to see so much that her peers never had. Hopefully, in the future, they would see more, would be blessed like she had been.

She walked around and around the small platform, not wanting to think of what might be happening below her. She tried to close her ears to the shuffling and murmuring which indicated some sort of action. She tried to concentrate only on evaporating.

Finally she began to smell the smoke. It was dense and choking.

She welcomed it. It joined with the clouds in her soul and her mind.

She could hear the crackling as the kindling lit. But she was not scared. She knew that she would be unconscious or dead before the flames reached her. The smoke was thick. Avarak females are thin. It was to be an uneven contest from the start.

She stopped for a moment and then opened her arms and her heart, taking in a deep, deep breath. As the fumes spread into her lungs she felt a welcome separation take place within her. Her body and her soul were beginning to disintegrate. At last.

There was nothing left to do but accept. Accept that this is where her life had brought her. She tipped her head towards the sun and took another deliberate deep breath. She was already feeling dizzy. It wouldn't be long now. Another breath. It hurt, but in a distant sort of way. And another. And another.

Until she collapsed into semi-unconsciousness, sinking down onto what was left of the circular platform. As the flames reached her flesh, she embraced the gentle fizzing of the last neurons of the only life she had ever known. Then she flew. Away from the torture. Away from the bigotry. Free.

Free.

Chapter 19

Nivala was too late, even though it was only a little behind the Avaraks by the time it reached Avarak space.

Denaraz peered at the screen, his face pinched and white, as Mallivan began to talk to the controllers to begin the long process of approval for docking on the large orbital platform. They could see the *Daktar* docked in front of them, but it might as well have been on the other side of the galaxy. They were never going to get any closer to it.

"You have infringed interstellar law," snapped Ryler, his tone glacial. They had already decided not to mention Gus by name, in case they further compromised the Enif. "As representatives of the Interstellar Enforcement Agency, we demand to see our citizens."

"Hold, please."

The wait was so frustrating that they had both worn a virtual hole in the decking. It was half an hour later that the screen buzzed again, and a familiar face appeared.

"Vebor!" hissed Denaraz, his crest high. "I might have known you would have had a hand in this!"

Mallivan held out a warning hand and the Tyzaran subsided.

"Dr. Vebor," Mallivan's voice was calm. "I assume you are able to help us with our ... quest?"

The large male Avarak on the other side of the screen puffed out his chest, looking extremely pleased with himself. "If you are referring to the female Avarak subject who has just been executed, then yes, I am able to explain what has happened."

An icy silence took hold of *Nivala's* bridge. "Ex ... Executed?" repeated Mallivan, stunned.

"Why, yes. Oh, were you thinking that we would somehow extradite one of our most wanted criminals to your custody? I'm afraid not. In any case," he spread his hands, "you are too late. What a shame! I am glad to see the Interstellar Enforcement Agency taking an interest in Avarak matters, though this was a purely ... internal ... problem. Nothing to worry you about." He showed all his teeth. He seemed very pleased with himself.

The captain's jaw twitched and then went white along the bone. "I assume you have proof?" he said in a voice that sounded detached. Inside he was rigidly shocked.

Vebor gave an amicable smile. "Why, certainly," he said. He bent forward and pressed a few controls on the panel in front of him. "There you go. I don't think there will be any doubt in your minds that justice has been duly carried out." His voice hardened. "Our justice."

"And her son?" The air seemed rarified around him. Mallivan was finding it hard to breathe. He still owed Seyal a favor, and he knew what she would want him to do. She had told him, some time ago: *'If anything happens to me, I would not want my son to be alone.'*

"Segaton? He will be acclimatized to a new life without his

mother by one of my officers and his family, before taking up duties as head of his father's house. I assure you, he will be quite happy here."

"We will need proof of that."

Vebor became expansive. "Why, certainly, Captain Mallivan. However, the Avarak Council has decided to keep her fate from him at this time. I am sure you will agree that no good could come of his being informed of her execution? And that, as an Avarak citizen, the Avarak Grand Council has jurisdiction over him?"

Denaraz was quite literally hopping from one foot to another. Mallivan tried not to do the same thing. "There is also the matter of a missing Spacelander citizen ...?"

"Really? I am afraid I have no knowledge of any Spacelander citizens. How did you come to lose her? It seems rather careless, if you don't mind me saying so?"

Denaraz gave out a grunt. Zenzie pulled at him and stopped him moving forwards by dint of clutching both hands around one leg and digging her heels into the deck plating. He finally looked down at her. She saw that he was crying.

So was she, for that matter.

"I think you know very well what happened to her," Mallivan growled. "Or are you denying that you caused a major supershell storm in the Chain Nebula?"

Dr Vebor's eyebrows nearly hit the ceiling. "A shell storm? Us? the Avaraks?"

"We know that this citizen was abducted by you, Vebor. Please tell us what happened to her."

"I have absolutely no idea." He looked upwards and tapped at his own jaw in meditative fashion. "However, on a hypothetical basis ..."

"... Yes?"

"Well, Avarak policy in the event of unwanted stowaways on board any of their ships has remained unchanged in hundreds of years."

Mallivan let out a ragged sigh. "...And can you tell me what that is?"

A rather smug smile spread across the heavy lips of the face in front of him on the screen. "I am afraid they are forcibly ... spaced, I believe you call it?"

"S-S-Spaced...?"

"Well, we call it unrequested debarkation, but you get the idea."

"You threw her out of an airlock?" Now no air at all was getting into Mallivan's lungs. His mouth was open and trying to inhale, but the muscles around his chest had all blocked and were solid. He began to feel rather dizzy.

"I remind you that this is a hypothetical question, Captain Mallivan. But yes, stowaways are generally summarily debarked from our ships. After all, we have a sovereign right to protect our military secrets. And stowaways are treated as spies by our military laws."

Mallivan still resembled a fish. His skin was as clammy as any scales could be, and his mouth was opening and closing with no purpose. He was quite incapable of doing anything.

Mel, who had been at the pilot's seat the whole time, reassigned the call to her own station. "Thank you, Dr. Vebor. We will be in touch again relevant to meeting with Segaton and his new mentors."

"Acknowledged."

Mel cut the connexion and turned to the rest of the crew. None of them was able to speak. Denaraz had collapsed to his knees and Zenzara was hugging him tightly. Mallivan was staring blankly into space. And ... Mel frowned. Where were Giedi and Talitha? Surely they would not have missed this.

She looked accusingly at Zenzara and raised her chin in the Chyzar's direction, as if to say, *what have you done?*

Zenzie lowered her own gaze and thought for a moment. Then she cleared her throat. Once, and then again. "Err ...?"

That got their attention. Both men turned to stare at her.

"I believe that Sibby might still be alive," she told them. "Scout picked up a trace some light years back. I *did* mention it to you."

"Scout was only giving the weakest of signals. It could have been nothing."

"I realize that, Captain. However, we thought that it was worth investigating."

"You thought." A huge frown descended on Ryler's face. "*Who* thought?"

"The three of us." She caught their incomprehension and tried again. "Giedi, Talitha and I."

She saw the exact moment that the captain caught on. His eyes tracked around the bridge and if anything, he got even paler. "What have you done?"

"We all agreed that it was worth the risk."

"How dare you undermine my authority? I specifically said that we could not investigate that slight signal Scout was giving. Did you deliberately disobey an order?"

Suddenly the small Tyzaran girl became a blazing virago, surprising them all. "It is not my fault if you become so blinkered you are unable to see things under your own noses," she snapped back, without missing a beat. "And I am the Chyzar. I outrank *you*, CAPTAIN!"

He stood up, incandescent with rage. "This is my ship. You cannot overrule my command, Chyzar or not."

"Well I can, and I did. So there. What are you going to do about it now, Captain?"

Denaraz struggled to his feet. He clutched at Zenzara around both bony shoulders, and his fingers dug in painfully. "Did they leave the ship?" he demanded. He gave her a little shake. "Did they find anything?"

"Ouch! You are hurting me, Spokesdesignate. Kindly stop digging those talons of yours into my collar bone!"

He loosened his grip infinitesimally. "Tell me! Did they go to find her?"

"Of course they did. Neither of you would take any notice of anything we were saying!"

"We were on a mission!"

"You were blinded by one objective! You wouldn't listen!"

"That's not true!" blazed Mallivan. Then he stopped and ran a hand through his hair. "Or maybe it was. I don't know. All I do know is that we cannot leave here until we have spoken to Segaton in person. He may be an Avarak citizen, but he has lived on this ship all his life. I will not simply abandon him on a planet he doesn't want to call home. I *must* make sure that he was not coerced in any way." He looked anguished. "But you are telling me that my son and daughter have been out there in a shuttle for the last twenty-four hours? On their own? In the Dark Confines?"

Zenzie's crest, which had come up at his tone, bristled. "I am." She put her small hands on her hips. "Are you telling me that you didn't even notice?"

Mallivan reddened. "Stop trying to make me feel bad!"

Her lip curled. "Doesn't seem to take much!"

Mel suddenly exploded. "STOP! Stop all this, all of you!"

There was an immediate silence. Such strong words from such a diffident person startled them.

"Stop it, will you? We are all in denial over Seyal's death. It is making us say and do things that we normally wouldn't." Tears were beginning to track down her face. "B-But she is d-dead. The l-last thing she would want is for us to be behaving like this."

Her listeners all hung their heads.

"It doesn't matter why Giedi and Tally left *Nivala*. What matters is that they did. What matters is finding them. What matters is trying to give Sibby and Gus their last chance."

Mallivan swallowed. He looked round the bridge. They could all see that his eyes were red. "She is right. We still have work to do. Seyal is g-gone." His eyes tracked involuntarily to the station she would normally have occupied, and then dimmed with sorrow. "And nothing we can do will bring her back."

"So how can we expedite the meeting with Segaton?" asked Denaraz, whose own eyes were damp with tears.

Mel knew the answer to that one. "We agree not to mention Seyal, of course. We bow down to all of their demands. We find Segaton and ask him if he wishes to remain on Rhyveka. Now, if all of you go away and try to calm down, I will get that put into motion. I will go down to the surface of the planet, but I believe, Captain, that your presence will be necessary?"

"Yes. I should witness what the boy has to say."

"Then the rest of you should prepare for take-off as soon as we get back. Whether the Avaraks have started another war is not up to us to say, after all. Our job is to rescue whoever we can. It is too late for Seyal. It is probably too late for Segaton. We have to believe it is not too late for Sibby and Gus."

Light years away from the Veka system, a small drone was still slowly wheeling over and over in the inky depths of space as its inertia took it further and further into uncharted territory. Inside, its two occupants were in trouble.

"Are you sure it is working?" asked Sibby. "It doesn't seem to be. This console is no longer showing any readout of energy."

Gus thrummed uneasily. "I agree. It appears to have stopped working."

"But if the beacon is silent, we will never be found."

"Yes."

Sibby withdrew slightly into the heavy EVA suit that had been made for a male Avarak. Her thin body was so much smaller than the suit that she could duck her whole body down into one leg. She didn't want the Enif to see the expression on her face.

Gus couldn't blame her. The Enif was feeling a failure. It had tried its best, and had managed to pluck Sibby away from certain death without a spacesuit, only to offer her certain death with a spacesuit.

That thought made up its mind. "I shall have to go outside," it said. "But first, we will eat something and drink something. Then we will get you into the second EVA suit I brought. That will give us nearly two more days of oxygen at the current rate. I shall take that torch with me. If we get a chance of rescue, at least I shall be able to let them know where we are."

Sibby's face popped back up behind the visor of the space helmet. "You can't survive out there, Gus! Not for two days, surely?"

The Enif contemplated lying. But the truth was, it had no idea exactly how long the Enif body could exist without oxygen.

Enif are built in a different way to the humanoids. Instead of lungs, they breathe through their skin. There are oxygen-storing specialized cells just under the hard crust of their carapace. These cells are always at capacity, which means that an Enif who is exposed to outer space is able to survive for as long as the oxygen cells don't become completely depleted. For an adult Enif, that could be around thirty hours. Gus was hoping that adolescents might be able to store oxygen for much longer than that.

"I shall be all right," it said. "Remember, I can always come back inside and pop inside the first EVA suit for a short time. That will bring my subcarapacial cells up to maximum again. I think I can last for weeks if I do that." Actually, Gus wasn't at all sure it could. Subcarapacial cells were very tricky things. They needed full capacity to work correctly. It was quite possible that forcing them to work with highly reduced oxygen levels and increased nitrogen would impede the ability to top up again. Rather like over-discharged batteries, perhaps. It hoped not. A strange shiver ran right through its black body. However, there was no need to explain that to Sibby. She had enough to worry about at the moment.

"Take this suit with you." Sibby was opening the EVA suit and attempting to extricate herself.

"I can't. I need to be able to move around. I couldn't do that in one of those suits. But don't worry; I will come back inside when I need to."

"You must shut yourself inside this suit for a little while," she said sternly, her tone almost motherly. "If you insist on going out there, then at least make sure you are all topped up to start with."

Gus felt a sudden affinity to Sibby. She was in terrible shape herself, yet was still concerned for somebody other than herself. The Enif's carapace shone. It was the nearest thing to a *faliif* that it had seen in many long years.

"That is a good idea. Thank you for thinking of it."

"Of course. While you are in the suit, I will prepare us something to eat."

"You cannot be outside the suit for very long, you know. The air toxicity in the drone will spike very rapidly because of the gases you exhale."

She nodded. "I am aware. But it will be nice to stretch my legs for a bit. I find it hard to move when I am in that thing."

"Avarak males have over four times your mass. That is to be expected."

"It weighs a ton. But we will soon be opening the drone to let you out and the vacuum will remove any toxicity. I will put the other one on before that." There was silence for a short time, and then she went on, her voice small. "Do you think somebody managed to save Seyal, Gus?"

"We must hope so." It didn't, but could see no benefit in admitting that.

Sibby subjected the Enif to a long look, saying nothing. Her shoulders drooped a little further. She compressed herself against the wall of the drone so that Gus could shuffle past her and close itself inside the EVA suit. She was right, the suit was uncomfortably rigid and smelt of Avarak mixed with humanoid. At least the flow of oxygen was refreshing. It tried to relax and let its subcarapacial cells work as they should.

Sibby spent the time performing limited stretches and body twists, trying to loosen up some of the muscles that were protesting. Then she rummaged in the pack to take out two protein bars and a water pack for each of them.

The walls of the tiny drone seemed asphyxiatingly close. Thankfully, Sibby had never suffered from claustronetia, like Mel, but this was one of the most stiflingly constrictive things that she had ever done. She was very grateful still to be alive, but she would have much preferred to be anywhere else except inside this tin can in the middle of nowhere.

Her skin was turning damp and icy at the thought and she felt as though each breath was more and more difficult, so she turned her attention to the meager feast that they were about to eat. Some things are better locked behind a firewall in your brain.

After ten minutes, Gus was ready to leave the suit. It turned off the oxygen and slipped out to munch on the protein bar. Such things were quite disgusting, made as they were for Avaraks rather than the Enif palate, but there had been nothing on the *Daktar* that would have tempted an Enif's taste buds. However repulsive its taste, it was nutritious. Even Gus's body would be glad to get some fuel inside it.

Sibby was looking paler than before. She needed to get back into one of the EVA suits, clearly. Gus finished its refueling and stood up to help her into the second suit.

"Shouldn't I go back into the first one?" she asked.

Gus was firm. "No. I may be outside for some time and I want to be sure you have an ample supply of oxygen. I shall not be here to detect any changes in your breathing."

Now Sibby went even paler. "No. I suppose not."

The Enif reached over to fix the helmet securely on and to activate the tight-beam between them. "We will be OK. Someone will be out there looking for us right now. All we have to do is signal to them where we are."

Sibby tried to look upbeat, but failed dismally. "I know, Gus. They will get to us soon."

Just before Gus fastened the last tie of the suit, it paused. "Would you mind if Toothpick came in there with you?"

Sibby stared at the Enif. "In here? With me?"

"Not if you don't want to, clearly. It's just … just that I think so long out in space might be difficult for him. Bear in mind that he flies under solar power, and there are no stars close enough to us to power him. If he stays with you, at least there will be plenty of spare skin cells for him to eat."

Sibby swallowed. "S-Skin c-cells?"

"Well, if you wouldn't mind. You have no further use for them after all, right?"

"Err … no, no I suppose not." She vaguely remembered making a promise of some sort. "Sure, put him in here with me."

"He will appreciate that. These last few days have been very difficult for him."

She rolled her eyes. "Just don't tell my brother. Mall would never let me forget it!"

"Yes. He seems to have developed some sort of dislike for the sunflyer. I can't understand it."

"No, indeed."

Gus slipped the small insect into the suit with Sibby. Sibby suppressed a keen urge to cringe away. Instead she put out a hesitant finger for the sunflyer to perch on. "Can he understand me?"

"No. Sunflyers have minute brains. They are not capable of very much. Toothpick can carry a small camera, but it is impossible to direct him in any way. My experiments have not been particularly successful. He did, however, help me during the Avarak incursion, though I believe that his behavior then was purely serendipitous."

"So, in a way, he had something to do with your being on the Avarak ship?" That changed her opinion about the little being. He had played his own part in this rescue, and she ought to be grateful to him. He certainly deserved a small snack for his troubles. She closed her eyes tight shut and placed him gingerly on one eyebrow. Seconds later, she felt the gentlest of tugs on one of the hairs there and had to suppress the urge to scratch. Then there was another small tug, and then another.

"There," said Gus, pleased. "He is enjoying that snack. Your eyelids would be better of course, but eyebrows are quite tasty too,

I believe. Pity that camera of his has run out of charge. I shall have to remove it, though I can't here, of course."

"I am glad he is enjoying his feast," she replied, rather faintly.

"Right then, I believe I should leave you now." Gus checked the ties on both of the EVA suits so that they couldn't drift out to space while the two halves of the EVA drone were open to the vacuum. It took hold of the console. Seconds later, the two halves of the drone began to open.

This time, Sibby studied the sights outside. She had inched her way up the suit so that she had a panoramic view. Even through the visor it was quite impacting.

The sky was a dark slate grey as far as she could see. There were no stars immediately visible. There had to be some dim ones somewhere, but the helmet visor was probably filtering the light just enough for them not to be visible to her. She found herself staring out at the expanse of nothingness. It was majestic, almost overpowering. It really was the Dark Confines. She hoped that Gus would not be affected by the immensities out there. She shivered, awed by the vastness. It was hard to think of oneself as important while staring out directly at eternity.

She felt very, very small.

Giedi and Talitha stopped the shuttle as they finally drew close to the coordinates Zenzie had marked out for them.

"See anything?" asked Giedi of his sister.

She shook her head. "It is the anti-light out there. I have never been in a part of space that is so ... so ..."

"... black? I know what you mean. It is really depressing."

"It's known as the Dark Confines. I had never really understood that expression until now."

Giedi brought the little ship to a stop and checked the consoles. He stooped down to give Scout a pat, avoiding the long and bristly hairs on his back. "There are no signals reaching us. It is going to be up to you, Scout!"

The pet Geiga wagged his short tail, but showed no signs of marking any one direction.

Talitha sighed. "He seems to have lost the trace. What do we do now?"

Giedi pulled a face. "I guess we go looking. When he was indicating a direction, it was out to starboard, compared to *Nivala's* flight path. That means that we should go … in *that* direction." He indicated with his arm.

His sister was not particularly impressed. "You hope." She rolled her eyes. "If truth were known, you have no idea where to go."

Giedi's expression was reproachful. "Not at all. We know that when *Nivala* was here, the Geiga was pointing over … there …" he threw his arm out again. "Our best bet is to take that direction ourselves. At least for a hundred miles or so. We can always turn around and retrace our footsteps."

It sounded as good a plan as any. Tally just wished that Scout were looking more interested in that direction. Giedi should be right, if *Nivala* had been following a completely rectilinear flight path. But they didn't know that she had. The slightest deviation could put them klicks away from their goal. She bit her lip. Still, there was no other way to do it, so she needed to agree that it was as good a place to start the search as any. Because it was. Wasn't it?

"Giedi?"

"What?"

"What does this soul-mixing thing feel like?"

Her brother gave a typical boy shrug, as if it were a silly question.

"I don't know."

"Well, something has changed," Tally pointed out with her sensible voice on. "Otherwise you wouldn't know about it, now would you?"

He stuck his tongue out at her. "It just happened. My stomach got all hot and churned up and then I realized that she was the one for me."

"You didn't have to talk to her?"

He frowned, trying to remember. "No, I don't think so."

"Then it must have been like love at first sight."

His irate gaze scorched that idea into nothing. "No it wasn't. Nothing like it. Don't be silly!"

Tally opened her eyes wide. "Then, if it wasn't love at first sight, what was it?"

Her brother was not known for his eloquence, so it didn't surprise her that he needed some time to think about his answer. In the end he gave a sort of sigh. "It was like all the questions went away."

She stared. "All the questions went away?"

"You know. Like, *what will you do? Who will you be? Where will you live?* I met Zenzie, and the questions didn't matter anymore. I knew the answer. *You will be with her.* All the doubts just vanished."

"That sounds nice," said Tally, dreamily. "I wish I could meet someone who makes me feel like that."

Her brother grinned. "You won't, Tal. There isn't anybody out there who could put up with you. Except the Vaers, of course. Ow! Stop that! You shouldn't hit older and wiser brothers. They might retaliate. Like this!"

Tally reared back and hit her head against the bulkhead. "Now see what you have done!" she said, indignantly. "You made me hit my head!"

"You started it!"

"No I didn't!"

"Sure you did. Or are you telling me I can't remember what happened two minutes ago?"

"If the helmet fits ..."

"Look!"

"Don't think you can persuade me, because ..."

"No, Look ...!" He pointed down at Scout. The Geiga had turned and was facing the starboard hatch. "He is pointing at something!"

Tally dropped to her knees to hug the Geiga. "You are right. See? He is taking no notice of me at all. That is the direction! Set us on that course!"

Giedi had already programmed in the coordinates. "But now we have to slow down. I don't want us to crash into whoever is out there. We are here to save them, hopefully. Not finish them off for good."

"Agreed. You pilot us and I will set the sensor arrays to detect anything bigger than Scout. Right?"

"Fine. But to get that resolution, we will have to be pretty close. It could take us hours, depending on what proper speed they have."

"We'll find them."

Tally's voice was full of a confidence that Giedi didn't share. Because it wasn't really a question of finding them. It was a question of finding them in time.

Alive.

Chapter 20

The space elevator droned down towards the planet. Mel found herself glancing at Mallivan every few minutes. He had said nothing for the last half an hour. Of course, he may think that the elevator pod would be bugged. Anything was possible, here on Rhyveka.

She shuffled slightly on her seat. They were made for Avarak males and therefore huge. Her small frame found them extremely uncomfortable. She looked down at the floor, ashamed of herself. Seyal must have traveled down in this same elevator, going to her death. Being uncomfortable seemed such a small, selfish thing to complain about.

Her eyes filled with tears. She had liked Seyal so much. The Avarak female had changed from extreme introversion to becoming a member of the crew who could be trusted to have your back. It was unthinkable to envisage her being put to death. How must she have felt?

Then Mel remembered somebody else who had died. Someone who was never far from her thoughts, even so many months later. She realized that Seyal might have felt like Sammy had. She might have felt that dying for a good cause was a worthwhile way to end your life. Seyal had been the first of her female Avarak peers to try to improve their lot in life.

As she stared past her feet at the slatted metal floor, a thought insinuated its way into her subconscious. She gasped. Then she took a little time to let it rattle around up there. Because there *was* one thing she could do to honor the memory of her friend. One thing that might help her to assimilate another painful loss. She could help the Avarak females attain their goal.

And she knew just how she could do that. It had come to her in a flash. Of course! The one thing that might just shake those entitled males out of their smug privilege. The one thing that might further the cause of the females!

She looked towards Rye, out of the corner of her eye. No, Mallivan would not approve. He might not be able to approve. His position in the Interstellar Enforcement Agency might not allow such leeway. But there was nothing to stop *her* from stepping in.

She felt a tremendous lifting of some sort of pressure that she hadn't even known she was carrying. It was as if all the molecules in her head were suddenly standing up and cheering. And in a strange way it seemed as though Sammy was there with them. Just for a moment, she could see him as he used to be. Alive. Vibrant. His eyes wide but full of encouragement.

This could be her way to shine. To really make a difference.

It was decided in that second. She knew what she had to do. Now all that was necessary was to find a way of implementing her idea, which meant that she would need to be open to any opportunities that might present on this trip.

Mel sat for the rest of the trip with a faint smile on her lips. Yes. If she could pull it off, it would honor Seyal in a way that would also save many female lives. It would be the *perfect* homage.

Mallivan's face darkened as the space elevator dropped silently towards the planet. He felt an unhealthy mixture of sadness and rage. That was not what he needed to show Segaton. Seyal would not want her son to be made to feel guilty, even though he most certainly was.

Mallivan could almost hear his dead friend whisper gently in his ear. *Be kind to him. He is my child.*

Yet that child had been responsible for his own mother's death. It seemed a terrible betrayal. Perhaps the worst there was. The forthcoming conversation was going to be one of the most difficult that Mallivan had ever had. He took a deep breath in and then expelled it slowly, willing his anger away. He needed to attain a state of some sort of calm, a detachment that would enable him to perform his duty.

At last the elevator reached the planet's surface. They were escorted along a walkway by soldiers who had been awaiting their arrival.

Half way along the walkway, which was some twenty metres in the air, Mel stopped dead. Her hand reached back to grasp Mallivan's forearm in a death grip.

He faltered, turning with a quizzical expression. Then he saw the direction of Mel's gaze and he froze in place too.

Slightly off to one side, and slightly below them, was a huge pile of smoldering wood. Although quite a large area had been cleared for it, it had been tucked in amongst all the paraphernalia of a busy space port, and so looked completely incongruous. Wisps of smoke still wound their way upwards into the fresh Rhyveka morning air. There was the faintest of smell of smoke within that clarity.

"It was there." Mel's heart had contracted. She felt the pain of loss like a physical blow. It was not a new feeling for her. "They killed her there."

Ryler turned to the guard. "Take us closer."

The guard shook his large head. "That is not scheduled," he said.

Ryler gave something pretty close to a growl. "Take us there," he snapped. "We wish to honor our friend's passing. It is our right."

This time the guard's eyes sparked in annoyance. "She was a traitor," he said firmly. Then he gave the Avarak equivalent of a sniff. "She deserved everything she got."

Mel slipped between the two males. "We only wish to see where she was ... where she died," she said quietly. "That we should bear witness to her funeral pyre will not be unwelcome, I imagine?"

The guard hesitated, then barked a question into his right wrist, where he presumably had a comlink to his central command. After some seconds, and an answer filled with static, he gave an involuntary nod. "*Avarak Karax,*" he intoned. Mel and Ryler were treated to brief glance from under the bushy eyebrows. "You may deviate briefly to examine the sentence site."

Mallivan immediately took the smaller walkway that led down and to the left. The railings were far higher than they needed to be for two humanoids, so that the top rail come up to his neck. That was over Mel's head. But she could still see between the railings. They were taken right up to the point where the pathway stopped. The floor here was double thickness. It must have continued right onto the funeral pyre itself and then have been withdrawn once

Seyal was in position.

Tears ran down Mel's cheeks, but she never stopped scanning the area. Her sharp eyes picked up a small area down on the ground. It contained many small splashes of color.

"I want to go there," she said, pointing below them.

"That is not convenient," snapped the guard. "Some females have been permitted inside. I cannot guarantee your safety."

"Really?" Mallivan managed something like a grin. "You can't ward off a couple of weak females?"

The guard stiffened. "I can, of course. It seems unnecessary. The females are being allowed in a few at a time. There were too many of them milling around the gates. They were causing a disturbance."

"How very dreadful," mused Mel. "But then, you clearly control this whole area very tightly. No doubt that is why the sentence was carried out in the shipyards, right?"

"Naturally. We couldn't have the place overrun with keening fem—" the guard realized that such a comment was a step too far out of his remit, "—that is, there is a security risk if you are exposed to females."

Mallivan's mouth twisted. "To them or to us?" He looked away, up towards the sky. "Perhaps you should ask your command post again?"

The guard huffed and shuffled his substantial feet before claudicating. "Very well. You may descend for a few moments only. I will allow it."

Mel immediately began to run down a sloping walkway that led below. "Thank you!" she shouted over her shoulder. "I shall use the time to offer up a fitting goodbye to my friend!"

Mallivan and the guard followed at a slightly slower pace, the rest of the detail marching along behind. Ryler had no idea what Mel was up to, but he knew she was up to something. He hadn't seen her so animated since Sammy's death. His eyes narrowed, but he wasn't about to spoil her plan. She had earned his trust. She had earned so much more.

Mel skipped down the walkway as fast as she could. She wanted the chance to talk to several of the females and the longer the time she had with them, the better. She hoped that Mallivan would realize that she had run ahead for a reason. If he did, he might try to delay the rest of the group.

As she came down to city level, she saw what the splashes of color were. As far as she could see, there was a carpet of flowers. Each Avarak female was arriving with an armful of them. As they joined the other women, they quickly threaded their own offerings into a weave that left a beautiful carpet which stretched up towards the funeral pyre.

To either side, there was a female standing, almost to attention. They looked like pillars, guardians of the entry to heaven.

Mel looked towards the still smoking pile of wood. Then she turned to the nearest female. "Did anybody witness it?"

The girl, for she was only that, looked taken aback to be addressed in Universal. The whites of her eyes flashed, but she gave the smallest of signals towards the silent sentinel on the left. Mel smiled her thanks and made her way over to that side of the area, until she was standing behind the sentinel, but quite close.

"I hear that you witnessed the execution," she said, in little more than a murmur.

"I did."

Mel looked down and away. "Did she suffer terribly?"

"She seemed almost at peace. Her eyes were closed the whole

time. She collapsed long before the flames reached her, and made no noise. I believe she was unconscious for the worst of it."

"Is there any ... the slightest ... chance that she survived?"

The sentinel appeared to sway for a moment. Then she caught herself up rigidly. "None. I was here until the end. Seyal is dead. Why do you ask? Why do you expect me to speak Universal? It is forbidden to females."

"I am ... was ... a friend? She and I were crewmembers of the same ship."

That made the female look around, her face surprised. Then she caught a hold of herself and pivoted smartly back. "Then you knew her well?"

"I did."

"Are you a friend of Sibeal's too? Did you find her? Did the Enif manage to help her escape?"

Air caught in Mel's throat. "You were on that ship? How is it possible?"

The female swayed slightly again. "My name is Myska. My husband is an official of the ship that caused the anomaly. I was required on board for this trip. I was required to take care of Segaton."

"Then you know what happened to Sibby?"

"Only that she was ejected into space. The Enif had a plan to save her, but I do not know if it succeeded."

Mel's heart began beating again, but much faster than before. "Gus was not a captive?"

The woman shook her head. "No. It was hoping to save her. They wanted to take Seyal as well, but she refused." She explained all that she had seen. "You are lucky to find me still here. I have only been granted permission to be here for four hours. My husband allowed that much, but no more. He has been very generous. Many husbands have prohibited their wives from visiting this place."

Some generosity, thought Mel, privately. She didn't say anything, however. "Before you go, Myska, there is something I might … that is … I wonder if … well, I have been thinking about something that might be useful to you."

"Tell me, friend of Seyal. I am listening."

Mel explained her plan. The stiff figure in front of her began to relax as she elaborated. Mel ended up with a question. "Do you think it could work?"

Myska bent her head, as though to the funeral pyre. "It would be a fitting memorial to somebody who gave their life for the rest of us, would it not?"

"I believe so, yes. But how could it be done logistically?"

There was a long pause. Mel began to worry that the answer wouldn't come before Mallivan and the guard arrived at her position. They were already perilously close, though Ryler had stopped several times to comment on various details of the landscape.

At last the answer came, but not before the female in front of her had knelt briefly as a sign that her time as one of the guardians was at an end. Immediately, another female with her head covered in a soft draping material took her place.

Myska turned to walk away, but her eyes caught Mel's. "I have an older sister," she said quietly. "A much older sister. She is one of the very few who has been freed of marital obligations. She managed to survive three births without dying. As such, she was granted release from marriage. She is now a popular midwife. She has been posted on Tyzar for the last couple of years, to attend to any Avarak births that may arise in the diplomatic contingent. Her name is Remyka. Remyka Karysk, Midwife to the Diplomatic Commission, on Tyzar. She is constantly getting medical supplies sent to her. I believe her packages are not examined by any males."

"And she could send the ... supplies ... on?"

The female inclined her head deeply and swept past. By the time the detail escorting Mallivan came within earshot Myska was twenty feet away and had melted into the anonymity of the forty or so other females who had been allowed in the area. Mel did not watch her go. She was studiously looking to the front again, her head bowed as though praying.

She didn't feel like praying, however. She felt like dancing across the surface of the planet. She felt as though, if she did that, her steps would scorch the very soil. She felt, for the first time in a long time, liberated.

Ryler stood some distance away, his own head inclined in deep respect for the Avarak woman he had liked so much. He was aware of Mel as she moved closer to him. He was also aware of a change in her bearing. Something, finally, had gone right. He had no idea what it might be, but it filled his heart to know that Mel had found something to motivate her. Seyal had somehow, in the most incongruous of settings, managed to rescue her. He felt deeply humbled.

Sibby had been on her own for the last nine hours. She was feeling so lonely that she had begun talking to the sunflyer.

"What do you think, Toothpick? Is Gus going to come back inside soon? I would think it would be hungry, wouldn't you? I know I am."

The sunflyer, which appeared to have gone into some sort of postprandial hibernation, refrained from making any sort of a reply.

Sibby sighed. She thought she was going a little crazy. The walls of the EVA drone were closing in on her. It was so cold that her teeth were chattering, even inside the heavy Avarak EVA suit. At least she was still alive, she thought. She wondered if Seyal was.

It was hard to be optimistic right now, but she had to believe that Gus was already signaling some rescue vessel right at this moment. Maybe they would be found soon? Izan would want her to maintain hope, even when there was very little basis for it.

She reached up and rapped on the walls of the drone with the back part of her hand. The glove had a small hard ridge to protect where Avarak knuckles would fall. It took both of her hands to lift it up and rap on the outer hull, but she managed it. There was no answer. She felt a sudden wave of fear and rapped again at the hull, sending out a staccato drumbeat of worry. There was still no answer.

Was the Enif still even out there? Space – even deep space such as this – is one of the most dangerous habitats there is. Criss-crossed with tiny particles travelling so fast that they could tunnel straight through you leaving a hole. Or larger pieces of rock that could knock you unconscious. If that had happened to Gus, its body might be wheeling away from the drone even at this moment. If so, it would never be found.

She hugged her knees and rested her chin on them. She tried closing her eyes but that didn't help. She felt an absence above her and the walls closed in on her even with her eyes tight shut.

Gus was actually still on the outside of the drone carcass, perched by the control panel. It was very far from all right, though. The Enif had made one major miscalculation. And it was a miscalculation that could cost Gus its life.

Enif are a freeze-avoidant species. If they weren't, they could never survive the rigors of outer space, even for short times. When subjected to very low temperatures, they express antifreeze proteins inside their cells, enabling them to withstand temperatures approaching absolute zero while still maintaining functionality.

However, what Gus had not taken into account was that it would be perched on a curved sheet of metal. That required such a major effort at the points of contact between the Enif and the metal that the rest of its body was left with slightly too few antifreeze proteins to protect the entire body. A similar sort of process occurs in humanoids after a heavy meal. Blood rushes into the stomach, causing the heart rate to increase and blood vessels to constrict in order to maintain blood pressure. Any slight imbalance may cause fainting.

Slowly – so slowly that Gus hadn't even noticed – its core temperature had begun to sink. Its movements had become slower and slower. This included its mental capability as well

Gus clicked to itself and tried to clear what were definitely fuzzy thoughts. But it wasn't quite able to grasp what was happening. Its carapace was becoming paler and paler as the minutes passed, but it was completely incapable of reacting to the problem. Its brain was now so confused that it wasn't able to communicate any malfunction of the body.

It began, little by little, to freeze to death.

Sibby's state of worry was not getting any better. Surely Gus must have heard her battering on the hull?

She took a deep breath, holding it in and then letting it out slowly. Then again. Then again. And, suddenly, as if her heart had suddenly unfurled, she felt able to cope with everything that was happening to her. She drew in air one last time, even smiling slightly to herself. Then she gave a small decisive nod. She came to a decision, undid a small area of the EVA suit she was inside and reached over to the console that Gus had left inside the pod. Before any doubts could reassert themselves into her mind, she pressed firmly on the console. Then she whipped her arm back inside the suit and refastened it. She had been quick enough that only part of the air inside of the suit had escaped.

She pulled herself up to the visor of the suit as the two halves of the drone slowly started to open. She felt utter relief. There was no sense to it, but she felt as though she could breathe again now that the doors were open. In fact, the opposite was true, but her brain didn't want to accept that.

The sky outside was still the same unrelenting black background with no immediately visible stars. It appeared to go on forever. It was astonishingly vast. It threatened to overwhelm her senses.

She waited, sure that at any moment she would see Gus's small black face peering around the edge of one of the doors. But that didn't happen.

The determination Sibby had been feeling wavered somewhat as she waited hopefully for some sign of the Enif, but then she blew out air. "You are making me extremely nervous, Gus," she muttered. "You had better be out there. I will never forgive you if you allowed yourself to fall off this stupid drone!"

The first thing to do was to anchor herself to some part of the drone. She managed to grab the nearest of the remaining ropes and worked at feeding it behind one of the protruding battens. The fingers of the enormous gloves were useless. She found that they became tangled up in the rope, making it impossible to tie a knot.

She was forced several times to stop, go back and begin again. Finally she succeeded in looping the rope twice around and behind the batten. She risked opening the suit again to quickly tie the rope off in a quick line hitch. When she tugged on it, it tightened and held. Satisfied that she could trust her life to the knot, she tucked her hands quickly back inside the suit and fastened it.

Each time she opened the suit, icy vacuum permeated what little air was trapped inside the thick material. Even those few seconds left her trembling with cold, her fingers white and unwilling to bend.

The next stage in her plan was to get herself out of the drone and onto the exterior surface. That meant reaching the entrance, climbing one of the doors near the hinge and pulling herself up. Briefly, she considered simply launching herself out of the pod and then drawing herself in along the rope. In the end she nixed that idea. It would not actually help her to get to the top of the drone. It would simply bring her back inside the two open doors to the rope's tether.

She checked the remaining air supply in the suit, and then set off.

It took forever to untie her unwieldy EVA suit from the fastenings that held it in place inside the open shell. Then she fed as much of her body as she could into the upper part of the suit and began to sidle her way along the pod towards one of the open doors. The bottom part of the suit flopped outwards, floating in zero gravity. The weight of the material made it very hard for her to keep her grasp on the metal framework. Luckily, the inside of the drone was lined with metal strengthening struts. She was just able to fit the huge glove underneath these, so was reasonably well able to anchor herself.

"Gus?"

Surely the Enif could hear her now, if he hadn't before. Yet only silence met her attempts at contact. Her whole body became filled with dread. Something awful had happened to her friend. If not, she was sure that the Enif would not have left her completely without contact for so long. It felt like an aeon.

Her breath was coming in jagged little breaths. It was hard, even with no gravity, to move the enormous gloves which swamped her hands. The whole of her arm up to her elbow fitted inside each gauntlet.

Hand over hand and so slowly that it was enormously frustrating, she inched her way along to the point where the starboard door joined the pod. She estimated that it must have taken her nearly an hour to get herself to the topmost part of the long hinge. Now she needed to haul herself over the top of the door.

That was actually easier than she had thought it might be. There was one vertical strut that reinforced the hinge area, and once she had the bulky glove wedged behind it, it took her only a few minutes to slide that hand upwards. With no weight to pull her in any direction at all, there was little resistance.

Then she was at last able to peek over the top of the door and see the top of the drone.

She gasped.

Gus was still there, but its body was almost completely white.

Sibby was horrified. She stared.

The Enif seemed dead. Even the shiny carapace, which was usually a rich and glossy black, had been bleached of all color. The wonderful multifaceted eyes were sightless and dull. How it was still attached to the drone was a mystery, because it was quite definitely unconscious.

She became frantic in her scrabbles to reach her friend, but the suit dragged her back, flopping out and snagging on some of the door battens. She was forced to move herself around inside the suit to try to dislodge first one and then another part of it.

Eventually she managed to release the material and pull herself up and over the top of the open door. She reached up with one glove, careful not to touch Gus. She felt as though the slightest extra pressure could send it spinning off into open space.

At last she was on the same level as the Enif. She didn't even have to think about what to do. There was only one thing that she could do.

She took in a deep breath of oxygenated air, and then unfastened the entire front of the EVA suit, from collar to hip. She grabbed out at Gus and yelped as her fingers immediately stuck to its carapace.

Ignoring the pain, she drew the inanimate carapace inside the Avarak EVA suit with her. Every time it touched her, it stuck to whatever it touched. So she found herself with clothes and skin glued to the icy carapace and to the Enif's limbs.

Tears ran down her cheeks, but she couldn't stop. Her own life was now in such danger that if she even paused to consider what she was doing, it might drain away into the darkness of the surrounding space.

She spun around with the carapace, thrusting it to the back of the suit. Then she literally tore one of her hands free from the edge and reached back towards the fastenings. Her blood soaked the material as she sobbingly worked to close the suit.

It was almost impossible to work the fastenings closed now. Between the blood and the strips of skin which had been torn off the underside of her fingers, she had hardly any traction.

She was a woebegone mess by the time she finally succeeded in closing the suit. She was shivering with cold and her hands resembled something that had gone through a ZEPH drive. She was also struggling to find any oxygen in the suit.

She felt herself begin to go woozy. That rang an alarm bell inside the depths of her soul. She battled to pry open her eyes. Something was missing. They were not safe yet! There was still something to do. She had to get them back inside the drone and close the doors! Here, out in space, they were very vulnerable.

Blearily, she tried to force back the blackness that was threatening her mind. What was it that she still had to do? Oh, yes. She had to pull them back inside the drone. She mustn't lose consciousness. They wouldn't be safe in this vast emptiness.

But it was calling to her to give up, to let herself go. As she struggled for breath, that last spark of awareness fizzled in the darkness and was extinguished. Her head lolled against the material of the EVA suit and she slipped down into one of the legs of the suit.

Gus's body lodged just above the other leg, its carapace too big for it to fall inside.

The glove that had been holding them to the top of the drone slipped. The suit that now contained the inert bodies of both Sibby and Gus floated away from the drone's surface and gradually drifted backwards until it reached the full extent of the rope that Sibby had carefully tied to the drone.

Once there, the giant suit spread out until it became a parody of a space anchor, arms and legs akimbo.

There was no movement at all inside the suit.

Chapter 21

Tally was at the helm of the shuttle when she noticed that Scout's behavior had changed. She gave a shout to wake Giedi, who had been trying to catch a few moments of sleep.

"Giedi! Come quick! I think Scout can feel something!"

A rather disheveled Giedi appeared, managing to look excited, cross and tired all at the same time. "What's he doing?"

"Look for yourself!"

They both stared at the Geiga. He was pointing along their current course, all four legs firmly planted on the deck, his snout slightly raised, just as he had been for some time. But now the spiky hairs along the top of his neck had ruffled, so that his neck appeared larger than it had before.

"That's new," admitted Giedi. "Does that mean we are close?"

"I think it must, don't you?"

Giedi pulled a face. "I hope so. Does that mean I should get into a suit? Are the outer sensors picking anything up? Should we stop, do you think?"

His sister wrinkled up her own nose as she considered all these questions. She stared down at the Geiga, just in time to see him move infinitesimally towards starboard. Immediately, she brought the small shuttle to a halt in space.

"He moved! Did you see that?"

Giedi frowned. "Are you sure? I'm afraid I wasn't looking directly at him. I can't tell you if he did or he didn't."

Tally bit her lip. But she was sure. And that had to mean that they were passing whatever it was they were looking for. It had to be quite close!

She bent her head and recalibrated the sensors, trying to make them even more sensitive. Still nothing showed up.

She and her brother looked at each other. Both of them hesitated for a few moments.

Then Giedi nodded his head. "If you say he moved, he moved. I will suit up immediately. Keep us as still as you can in space until I am out there, will you?"

Tally nodded, her chest tightening with worry. She *thought* she had detected that movement, but what would happen if she had been wrong? They could be losing valuable time searching an area that was completely empty. She almost opened her mouth to tell her brother that she wasn't really sure. That she might have been mistaken. But she didn't. She couldn't. Even though she was no longer certain what she had seen, she had been sure at the time, hadn't she? And that meant that second-guessing herself could also be the wrong thing to do.

In the end she sat back down and concentrated on the sensors and the console in front of her. She had to believe in Scout. And Scout had shifted. Only a touch, but he had definitely shifted to the right. And that meant that something nearby was in danger. They *had* to investigate.

It took Giedi a little longer than he would have liked to put on the EVA suit. Although it was the smallest available, it was still too large for him, and that made it quite hard to struggle into.

At last he was in and could fix the helmet in place. He activated the tight-beam and tested it.

"You getting this, Tal?"

"I am." Her voice was rather tremulous.

"You will have full control of the shuttle, which is probably good, since you are the only one of us who has done this before."

Talitha flushed a little. His tone was one of pride. She straightened her back. She wouldn't let him down. She wouldn't let any of them down.

Giedi stomped over to the airlock and opened the hatch. For a moment he stood there, watching her. "Denaraz said you were a great pilot. You've got this, Tally."

"I know. Good luck!"

"You too." He lifted his gloved hand in a wave and then fed himself into the slim tube that was the airlock. There was a slight hiss as the hatch closed behind him. Tally turned back to the console and laid in a new course along the coordinates that Scout had been indicating. She kept the speed down to just a few meters per second. The Geiga immediately shuffled some degrees to port until it was pointing directly ahead. She stooped to give Scout a quick pat. The Geiga stilled again, but she realized that she would need to continue to proceed excruciatingly slowly and keep an eye on the direction the animal was indicating. It could be hours before they came upon the thing he was trying to pinpoint.

She face-palmed as she realized something. How silly of them! There was a *really* easy way to see if Scout had changed direction. An old-fashioned way.

She looked around for something that wrote. There was only an old marker. Nobody used hand-held writing materials these days. They had been obsolete for centuries. She was lucky to find anything at all in a modern shuttle like this.

She grabbed the marker and drew a line on the decking with it, as parallel as possible to Scout's body. There! That would help. She didn't want to be second-guessing herself any more. There was far too much riding on this endeavor. Far too much.

Satisfied that the line was as close to the new heading as it could be, she slipped back into her seat, keeping the shuttle in the lowest gear she could manage.

They began to head even further into the Dark Confines.

Giedi was becoming concerned. He been outside the shuttle for over two hours now, and there was nothing to be seen in any direction. He was beginning to feel that they had made a mistake, that Scout's slight motion had meant nothing, that he should go back inside and tell Tally to take them to a different sector.

His vision was blurring slightly as he strained his eyes against the pitch blackness outside his helmet. It was a depressing sameness. There were so few pinpricks of light to brighten the overwhelming darkness. Now he found that the small tracks of random photons resulted in long trails on the back of his retina. He could blink as much as he wanted, but they remained burnt into the membrane at the back of his eyes, a ghostly echo that confused him. He no longer trusted his eyes. If they could cling onto remnants of photons like this, it was hard to believe what they were showing him. He gave a sigh.

"Anything new, Tally?"

The disembodied voice from the cockpit below him was tense. "Nothing so far. You?"

"'Fraid not. Do you think we should keep going?"

"I don't———wait!"

Her tight-beam fell silent for quite some time. Giedi couldn't stop himself looking down as though he could see right through the fuselage into the cabin beneath his feet.

"Giedi? You there?"

"No. I decided to swim off into the void. What have you seen?"

"Scout has moved again."

"You sure? How many degrees?"

"Yes, I'm sure. I marked his direction on the decking."

Giedi raised his eyebrows. "Simple, but effective. Well done!"

"I am going to take us around now. It is about five degrees to starboard. You might want to look in that direction?"

Giedi shifted slightly, his magnetized boots scraping on the outer hull of the shuttle. He squinted. "Nope. I can't see anything right now. What is Scout doing?"

"He is beginning to pant slightly. I think we must be really close."

"All right. I will do my best."

In fact, it was another half an hour before Giedi spotted something. Or thought he did.

"Stop, Tal!"

The shuttle immediately came to a halt in space.

"I'm seeing a sort of flicker, about two degrees to port of our current course. Can you fix the sensor array on that area?"

"Sure." She did, bending at the waist to scrutinize the results better. "There is a very slight anomaly, about five klicks ahead of us."

"I have lost it. It was only visible for a second or two. But if the sensors say there is something there, then I think we must have found whatever it is that Scout is signaling."

"Ok. Five klicks? I will edge us closer then, but I don't want to run over whatever it is. Keep your eyes peeled."

Giedi gave a grunt. "That isn't as easy as you might think. But I will do my best." He checked his tanks. "Before you do that, can you wait for a couple of minutes? I want to recharge my air supply again, just in case."

He reached over his shoulder and detached a long but light tube from the oxygen supply tank. Then he studied the hull beneath him. For several generations, emergency oxygen ports had been statutory on all spaceworthy vehicles. This shuttle should be no exception.

Sure enough, the port was safely protected by the main airlock coaming. He plugged himself in and tapped his fingers in irritation as he watched the levels of air in his breathing monitor begin to climb. Now they were so close, he didn't want to lose a moment more than absolutely necessary. On the other hand, they had no idea what they were about to find. He might well need a full tank on his back.

Finally it was done. He snapped the coupling free and retracted the feed pipe back into its housing.

"OK, Tal. Take us in there. Slow as you like."

The shuttle gradually edged towards the anomaly. Tally took her time, checking both the sensors and Scout every few seconds. At five hundred meters, she stopped the shuttle again.

"Can you see anything yet?"

"I think I can. There are some faint reflections in front of us. What are the sensors showing?"

"Still only a glitch, but it hasn't changed vector, which would fit with some sort of floating container."

"Let's approach."

They did. Tally brought the shuttle in to a hundred meters. Then she stopped the shuttle again.

Giedi's mouth was wide open. He blinked. "Your sensors showing anything?"

"Just the same blip. Why? What is it?"

"I ... I'm not sure." He shook his head in wonder. "Is ... Is that a tin can? And a space suit floating along behind? Or am I seeing things? You sure you can't see anything, Tal?"

Tally peered out of the spaceglass visor. "Nope. Still can't see anything."

"There is no movement and that tin can thingy is empty. The doors are wide open."

"Then they are dead or in the space suit. I'll take us in as close as I can."

Her heart pounding, Tally took the shuttle alongside. It wasn't long before she could make out the strange, floating spacesuit and the small walnut-like drone casing. She bit her lip as she edged closer. It was very dangerous. If there *was* a person inside that floating suit, they might very well not survive the gentlest of touches by a spaceship, even one of this size. Her forehead furrowed with concentration.

Giedi breathed a ragged sigh of relief as the shuttle came alongside the suit. It was an Avarak EVA suit, and he couldn't see if it was empty or if it contained somebody. He didn't think it was an Avarak, though. The suit billowed out in a way that made it seem empty.

"I don't think there can be anybody alive inside that," he said despondently.

"Scout is still signaling danger. Surely that indicates that they are alive?"

"I don't think they can be." He stared glumly in front of him.

However, thinking wasn't doing. He needed to be doing. He checked the length of the safety rope attaching him to the shuttle, bent his legs and pushed off.

He collided with the Avarak suit with too much momentum. He should have been more gentle. Still, he opened his arms wide and managed to catch hold of it. He had a snap hook to his suit ready, and snagged it quickly onto one of the small metal rings set into the suit for that purpose. He was now tied securely to the suit. The three ropes had tangled, but that was a problem for later.

He pulled himself hand over hand up the side of the suit, until he could peer inside through the helmet, shining a light down inside it.

To his astonishment, he saw two bodies. Sibby's shining hair was visible, down by the leg of the suit. Gus's body could be seen slightly higher up, except it had a frosting of white instead of the usual black.

Giedi's pulse gave a stutter. They looked dead. Had he and Tally arrived too late?

"No-no-no-no-no!" he muttered, pulling out a knife preparatory to cutting the tie to the tin can that they were anchored to. "Come on! Hang on a little bit longer!"

"What's happening?" His sister sounded terrified.

He told her what he could see and then left the tight-beam connexion open without speaking again. He didn't have time to give her a running commentary. There was too much to do, and not enough time to do it in. They might just still be alive now. They certainly wouldn't be for very much longer.

Once Giedi had cut the rope that tied them to the tin can, which he now saw was some sort of metal drone, it didn't take him long to pull the suit across the small distance to the shuttle.

Then he needed to figure out what to do next.

In the end, he opted for the quickest option. He would take them out of the suit and put both of them in the airlock at the same time. It would be a very tight fit, but if there was one thing he was certain of it was that waiting was not an option. They might be dead already – Gus certainly looked as though it was – but hanging around making them take turns was not the way to go.

They would both be exposed to the vacuum. However, he would settle the Enif in the airlock first, since Enif were resistant to the vacuum of space. Then he would transfer Sibby from suit to airlock as quickly as he possibly could.

"It is Gus and Aunt Sibby." He explained all he could see to Tally. "They are either unconscious or dead," he added grimly. "So they will drop out of the airlock as soon as it is opened. Put something soft underneath it, and do what you can for them."

Her voice, when it came back was horrified. "What can I do? I don't have any training with humans, let alone Enif!"

"I know, Tal. Just wrap them up and put them in the fetal position. We can try to reanimate them once I get inside. We must have an emergency hand-held Zeroth machine on board. I know handhelds are very limited, but it will at least give us an idea of what we should be doing. We will just have to try whatever it says, as best we can."

He was already pulling the outer hatch open as he spoke. He grabbed the stiff carapace of the limp Enif and stuffed it into the airlock. Then he reached inside the large EVA suit and dragged Sibby's senseless body up towards him by its hair.

"Sorry, Aunt," he murmured to himself, even though she couldn't feel it. It still felt wrong to be manhandling her in this way.

She popped out of the leg and he managed to grasp her more tightly under her arms. There was a movement by her hair and a small insect flapped his wings at him in an aggrieved manner. He gave a start and almost dropped his aunt. "Toothpick!"

"What?" screamed Tally, whose nerves were by now beginning to get the better of her.

"The sunflyer. He is here. Alive."

"Does that mean that Gus and Aunt Sibby are too?"

"Not now, Tal. Quiet please!"

She subsided, feeling guilty. She shouldn't be interrupting Giedi. Not when he was so stressed. It was just so hard not knowing.

Outside the ship, Giedi was pushing his aunt into the airlock. He was pleased to see that the small sunflyer was maintaining his precarious position on her shoulder. At least he wasn't trying to fly away. Giedi was pretty sure he wouldn't have gone after the insect if the sunflyer had.

But the insect seemed quite content to enter the airlock with Gus and Aunt Sibby. Giedi quickly pushed his aunt's arm down so that the hatch could be closed and then closed it, slamming his hand against the emergency pressurization.

"Airlock pressurizing," he called out to Tally, who would be waiting on the inside to open the hatch.

In the cabin beneath him, Tally was counting the seconds.

"Fifteen supernova sixteen supernova seventeen supernova eighteen supernova nineteen supernova … time!" She stretched out her hand and pressed the green button.

The hatch opened and a tangle of limbs fell out onto the mattress she had pulled beneath it. She gasped at the color of both of them, but bent down after slamming the hatch shut again.

"Airlock free!" she called up to Giedi through the tight-beam. Then she turned her attention to the two bodies lying on the mattress. She quickly pulled Sibby onto her side, pushed her legs up towards her arms and tucked a large emergency blanket over her. Then she stared down at the Enif. Its color was absolutely horrible. It looked deader than a doornail, though what a doornail was she had no idea.

Still, she pushed it facedown onto one side of the mattress and tucked a blanket around its carapace, gently moving its appendages about so that they were covered too. Then she stared at her patients, trying to work out if either of them were breathing.

She was kneeling beside her aunt, with one hand on Sibby's arm, when the hatch opened again and Giedi made his way down the ladder.

He pulled off the helmet and knelt beside Tally. "Is she breathing?"

Tally pulled a face. I … I … think I can detect a pulse. And maybe she is breathing, but very shallowly. I don't know about Gus, but then I don't know how an Enif breathes anyway. I don't think they have lungs."

Giedi began to strip the EVA suit off. "Good job, Tally. I'll take over here, you break out the hand-held Zeroth machine, and see if you can find a manual for it. We have to do our best for them."

"On it!" She ran up to the small alcove set in the wall and pulled down the lever that secured the traveling triage machine. She had a general idea of how it worked, but took a few seconds to check the right procedure in the manual. Luckily, this opened out to a color plate of where to place the sensors. It took only a moment to attach the cables to Sibby's inert body. The machine hummed for about thirty seconds and then gave its very distinctive *beep.*

Tally read out loud from the top display, her voice breathy with fear. "Hypoxemia! Almost certain hypoxia. Hypothermia and Decompression lesions. Prognosis reserved. Keep patient warm and quiet. Fluids intravenously if possible. Extra oxygen if possible. Evacuation to full Zeroth chamber recommended but probably not essential. Triage level 4," she read out rapidly. Then her eyes flickered around the shuttlecraft's cabin. "Do we even *have* a drip?"

Giedi shook his head. "I don't think so, and I wouldn't know how to set one up anyway. I think we just leave her as is. Keep her warm and give her plenty to drink if she wakes up. What about Gus?"

But Tally was ahead of her brother and had already attached the clips to the Enif body, hesitating somewhat as to which parts of the alien to attach them to. Luckily the manual had illustrations for all the Major Shell species.

This time the machine deliberated for longer. Then it illuminated two of the clips and told her to replace them at different locations. After that, it fell silent again. Tally was shifting from one foot to the other by the time the result appeared on the hand-held screen.

"Species Enif," it told them.

"Well, thanks a lot," sniffed Tally. "It's not like we've got eyes or anything!"

The machine ignored her. "Subject alive. Diagnosis: Chill Coma. Probable tissue hypoxia. Possible brain damage. Requires urgent treatment in full Zeroth Chamber within twelve hours to avoid permanent lesions or death. Triage level 2. Interim procedure: keep still. Do not cover. Do not attempt to raise temperature. Keep chilled if at all possible."

Giedi looked up at Tally, a horrified expression on his face. Then he snatched off the blanket. "Chilled?" he repeated. "How can we keep him chilled? And what temperature is chilled?"

"Err ..." Tally scrunched up her forehead as she tried to get more answers out of the portable Zeroth, "just a moment. I think ... yes, here it is!" She looked up again with a happier expression. "Ice-cold," it says.

Giedi mumbled to himself. "So we can't put Gus outside the shuttle; it would be much colder than that." He was looking around the cabin, trying to find something that might work. "Any ideas?"

Tally was looking very dubious. "Well, there is a fridge."

Giedi stared at her. "We can't just shove Gus into a fridge!"

"We needn't close the door," she said. "That way it would still get oxygen."

Giedi's brain froze for a few seconds, and then he blew out air. "All right. I can't think of anything better. Here, you take its legs. I'll get the arms. At least, I'll get two of them. The other two will just have to flop along on the floor."

They finally managed to get Gus half in, half out of the fridge. It was the best they could do. The Enif wouldn't completely fit, even with all the shelving taken out. Shuttles had very limited facilities.

Tally's mouth curved down. "If this were a shipstation," she said sadly, "we could have pushed it into the freezer. You could get a shuttle inside *Bellaris's* freezer."

"It is all we can do. Now, put that extra blanket on top of Sibby. We need to find the nearest Zeroth Chamber. And we only have twelve hours to find it."

Tally ran back to the console, almost colliding with Toothpick, who was hovering around eye height just behind her. "Oops, sorry, Sunflyer!"

The insect hastily glided away, hovered for a few seconds, and then alighted on the back of Sibby's head – the small part that was still peeking out from under the blankets. He folded his wings and disappeared under the top fold of the blanket.

"Ugh!" Tally's eyes were wide and disgusted. "Did you see that? I wouldn't want one of those down my neck, would you?"

Giedi managed a smile. "She won't be feeling a thing. He isn't going to cause her any harm. Leave him alone."

"Ay Ay, Captain!" snapped Tally in a snarky voice. "You know best!"

"Found anything yet?"

"Why don't you come and look, if you're in such a hurry?" Then she thought better of it. This was not exactly the time to snap at your brother. "Sorry. Didn't mean that."

"S'okay, Tal. I'm worried about them too."

"We are too far away to be able to raise *Shapley* or any other ship. There is nothing on my radar at all."

"Then take us back to the vector joining Rhyveka and *Shapley*. That will put us more or less in the spot we left *Nivala*. If they are looking for us, that is where they will start. Right?"

"I guess." Tally wasn't convinced. "But won't that take too long? We don't have a lot of time."

Giedi pulled a face. "The only other choice is to put ourselves close to the cargo lanes. They traverse the Dark Confines. Ships taking provisions from The Bifold Shell to the Landau Rift use them. We could switch on a mayday signal and hope somebody will stop. Hope there is a ship near enough to even hear us. That might give us a better chance. At least there is some trans-shell traffic in this part of the Dark Confines. We are pretty much out in the sticks here."

Tally bit her lip. "But what if the only people to hear us are the Nova Vaers? We could be shipped off to Nova Vaer. You know they are like, Gied. Pirates! Dad had to lose his ship to save his and

Zenzie's lives, remember? The Vaers would never save Aunt Sibby or Gus."

Giedi felt an uncomfortable hollow doubt overtake him. He had no idea what to do for the best.

"What do you think our chances of meeting up with *Nivala* in the next ten hours are?"

Tally shook her head. "Pretty much nil. If they went as far as Rhyveka, which is what they were planning to do, they couldn't possibly get back to this area for another couple of days."

"Then we must move to the main shipping lanes and see if we can get one of the cargo ships to help us. —If there are any." He looked sadly in Gus and Sibby's direction. "It is Gus's only hope. It managed to save Aunt Sibby from the Avaraks. We *have* to save both of them, Tal."

Tally gave a curt nod. She didn't disagree but her insides shook just a little at the thought of broadcasting an emergency signal in the middle of the Dark Confines. It left them very exposed. But she couldn't see any other way that had even the slightest chance of saving Gus. And her brother was right; Gus had to be saved.

She checked the maps and plotted a path to the principal trans-shell shipping lane. "Three hours at full speed," she sentenced.

"Then let's get going. We are cutting it awfully fine."

Tally pushed the engines up to full. The little shuttle trembled a little as her speed gathered, and then shot off towards the cargo lanes.

"How many trans-shell cargo ships cross the Dark Confines along those main shipping routes?"

"Not many. I guess there is some trade between the Bifold Shell and the Landau Rift, but it is not exactly Waypoint. And there will be regular long distance supply ships, but who knows with what frequency." He blew out worried air.

Tally's stomach sank even lower. Would they find another ship? Would it be friendly if they did?

Would they be in time?

Chapter 22

el and Ryler walked into the large house on Rhyveka with some trepidation. Vebor had joined them, and was clearly there to make sure that nothing incriminating was said. Mallivan's face was set. Mel's was white. They had just come from Seyal's funeral pyre. It wasn't going to be easy to pretend that nothing had happened.

"Please to come this way," said a burly Avarak male in stilted Universal. "Segaton is playing with two of my own sons."

They followed. The house was large, but filled with heavy, dark furniture and huge pictures of previous male Heads of the House. Mel found it very oppressive. She gazed up and around at them, squirming at the prepotent air each and every one of the Avarak pictures portrayed.

Then they were escorted past a row of subservient Avarak

females, all waiting in a line, all with their heads bent in deference. Mel stared at them and felt a shaft of glee at what she had decided to do. Things simply could not, should not go on like this. These women were doing everything in their power to disappear into the wall. They were mere belongings to their powerful husband. She put her chin up as she walked past them.

Right at the far end, she spied Myska, who must have hurried back to get here before they did. Myska was effacing herself as much as possible, too. She also had her head down. But, just as Mel passed, the Avarak female looked up from under her eyebrows, her eyes full of mischief. Mel let the corners of her own mouth twitch. Nobody should be left unable to change their circumstances. Nobody.

Then they were past the row of wives, displayed for their perusal like so many statues, and into the part of the house dedicated to the nursery.

They were led into a large room where three Avarak boys were playing. Segaton was the nearest to them.

"What are you doing here?" he said in a wary voice. He stood up, looking not at Mallivan and Mel, but at Vebor. "Why have they come?"

"They merely want to satisfy themselves that you are being well looked after, Segaton. That you wish to stay with us here on Rhyveka. Once you have reassured them of your wishes, they will be leaving. Immediately."

Segaton seemed relieved. "Well you can go already. I don't know why you came. These are my people. You never were!"

Mel wanted to reach out, to convince him of the error of his ways, but Mallivan stretched out a warning arm just as she moved. She slid her eyes to his and he shook his head slightly. She moved obediently back.

"We just want to know if you wish to stay here, Segaton. We cannot compel you to return to *Nivala* with us."

"No, but I bet my mother wants me back!" The tone was bitter.

Mallivan hesitated. "We ... we haven't spoken to your mother."

Segaton looked again at Vebor. "They can't take me away. Can they? Can they?"

"Not if you wish to stay with us, no. I shall make sure that they don't."

"And you won't let my mother take me away?"

"I will never let your mother take you away, I can promise you that." Vebor carefully avoided meeting Mallivan's gaze.

Segaton seemed reassured. "Well then." He waved a dismissive arm and turned back to his console. "Tell them to go away."

Mel felt a vicious need to grab the boy by the neck and throttle him. Didn't he realize what he had done? What damage his selfish actions had caused? She could almost feel steam coming off her head.

"We are leaving." Mallivan's voice was harsh as he took Mel's upper arm and turned her away from Segaton and the other two boys. "I am glad to see that you are not alone. Goodbye, Segaton."

There was no answering voice. The boy was already immersed in his game, having lost interest in them. Vebor led them back to the guard detail and then vanished, after treating them to a sardonic grin which showed most of his teeth.

Mel and Ryler were led back to their ship by the detail. They kept their own silence for the entire journey, even when they passed the funeral pyre with its small dots of color that indicated the flowers which had been left. This time Mel kept her gaze firmly in front of her, but she couldn't hide the tears that tracked down her face. There were simply too many of them. So many of them that they spilled over and trickled down onto the walkway.

She closed her eyes. "Oh, Seyal," she murmured. "Oh, Seyal."

There was nothing else left to say.

Nivala slipped her moorings and turned back towards the Chain Nebula. Now that they were back on board, Mallivan didn't waste a second.

"We need to get back to the area Giedi and Tally left the ship."

"You mean I was right?" said Zenzara, looking smug.

"Of course you were not right."

She stamped her foot. "You should have let me come down to the surface with you. I was entitled to, under the Savior Protocol!"

"Then you shouldn't have encouraged my son to steal a shuttle, should you, Chy Zenzara?"

She reared back as though she had been hit. "You should have listened to me!"

"No. *You* should have listened to *me*."

Denaraz stepped forwards. "You have found out something? About Sibby? And Gus?"

"Sibby was thrown out of an airlock."

Two Tyzaran crests immediately stiffened vertically. "What!!??"

"She *may* have survived. Mel found out that Gus had a plan to save her. He commandeered an EVA drone. There is a chance ... only a chance, mind you, that they are both still alive."

Zenzie swiveled around, furious with him. "I *told* you so! But nobody wanted to listen."

Mallivan had gone slightly pink. "Yes. That doesn't mean that Giedi and Tally have found them, or that any of them are still alive. But we need to get there as fast as we possibly can."

Denaraz was already at the pilot's console, tapping in commands.

Nivala turned obediently in answer to his input. "Full speed?" he asked curtly.

"Ten percent over," replied Mallivan. "We are probably already too late."

Zenzara gave a sniff. "You should trust your own children more. If anybody could find Sibby and Gus, it is them. You will see!"

Mallivan met her gaze. "I hope I do," he said slowly. "I really hope I do."

Out at the boundary of the Chain Nebula, the ship containing Prime Ohnahara was ending its vigil. They had found nothing more to explain the supershell storm that the Avaraks had instigated. Nothing more esoteric than the ripping away of space itself through six carefully placed astronuclear devices. It had been a savage, unsophisticated, unsubtle attack. One that fitted very well with the basic character of an Avarak warrior. They had never been ones to fiddle and fine-tune. They had always preferred the head-on, brutal approach.

Ohnah was still vibrating with indignation. That any species of the Major Shells should have stooped to such depths was anathema to her. That they should have done this merely to get their hands more easily on one female and one boy was incomprehensible. She simply couldn't get her head around it.

Brian Lasseny had already recalled all the probes and they had been duly decontaminated and stored in the racks that held them. The data had been refined, checked and rechecked. There could be no doubt. There had been no new science behind the attack. The Avarak race had simply detonated the bombs as a diversion. They had destroyed countless square miles of space for centuries only to satisfy their own petty revenge on Seyal.

She turned to Brian. "Well? What is the Olympus Nebula looking like?"

Ohnah couldn't afford to make a mistake about this. It was a long way to take *Shapley*. The Olympus Nebula was half way between the Chain Nebula and Heisenberg's Halo, after all. Shipstations were meant to move, as their very name indicated, but a journey from Chain to Olympus would take months. Shipstations move slowly, so as to retain all their functionality.

"Can we be sure, Brian? Sure that Olympus will protect, rather than expose *Shapley*?"

The man scratched at his receding hairline. "I'm certain, Prime. Olympus is one of the most stable Nebulae in the Landau Rift. The Avaraks could drop a hundred of their most powerful astronuclear devices anywhere in that area, and they wouldn't start a storm surge like that of the Chain Nebula. That was only possible because of the particularities of Chain." The grizzled engineer pointed to a detailed map of the Olympus section of space. "And, if we reposition somewhere in this area, we would be well-protected against radiation surges from both Chain and the center of Olympus." He gave a small shrug. "I don't think we will find a better place."

"Then we have no option." She gave a sigh. "It is not what I had been hoping to hear."

"Actually, I think it is a positive result. The Avaraks have no new technology; they were simply more prepared to ruin the ecosystem of a nebula than any other Major Shell race would have been. Those Screwdrivers of theirs have been around for the last hundred years at least. There are no new threats. Only old ones applied in new ways without thought to consequences."

"That is true. Can you parcel up all the data we have collected? It must be sent to the Nepheals, the Macers, the Humans, the

Spacelanders and the Tyzarans. They will want to examine the evidence themselves."

Lasseny inclined his head. "Very well, Prime. They will have their copies by the end of the day. We have already summarized the data for them. Do you think that this will mean war with Rhyveka?"

"I doubt it. I don't think anybody wants another war so soon after the last one. I suspect there will be accusations and rebuttals, but that little will change."

"Except for *Shapley*, the casualties, and the families of the people they killed."

"You are right. It will be an enormous change for *Shapley* and for many of us. But it will be the start of a new chapter in our history."

"A safer one."

Ohnah shrugged. "There is nowhere completely safe in outer space. We all know that."

They exchanged a look, both thinking of their respective children. It was hard to keep them from harm. Perhaps parents can never fully keep their children from harm.

Chapter 23

Two hours later Tally and Giedi reached the main shipping lane that intersected the Dark Confines. It looked to be just as deserted and abandoned as the rest of the depressing space they were flying through.

Tally put the engine into idle and checked her scanners. "Now what?"

"Let me sit there."

She moved obediently away and her brother slid into the seat she had vacated. He checked the protocols on one of the screens and then began the space emergency call. "Mayday. Mayday. Mayday." He paused and then repeated the call. Then they listened. There was no reply. "Medical emergency. Space shuttle SX290 requires immediate Zeroth chamber for critically injured crew member."

He listened, then pressed a few more buttons. "There. That is being sent out in a loop, together with our coordinates. Cargo ships that are built to go through the Dark Confines are equipped with very efficient sensors. If there is anyone within a day's travel of here, they will hear us."

Tally nodded. She was bending over Gus, trying to see if there had been any change in his condition. There hadn't. The Enif was still looking terrible.

She moved to Aunt Sibby. The Spacelander was still unconscious, but at least her color had improved a little. Tally let out a shaky breath. It wasn't much, but it was at least *something*.

"We need to eat," she said, moving to the tiny galley. "Ration pack A or ration pack B?"

Giedi gave a shrug. "Whatever. I have never been able to taste the difference. Wouldn't mind a Tessara cake, though."

Tally grinned. "Can't be any of those within twenty light years."

"I shall eat six when we get home. One after the other."

"No you won't. What would your tame Chyzar think about her future husband being a glutton? I bet you wouldn't catch Zenzie guzzling six Tessara cakes."

Her brother bristled. "She might. What's so wrong about it?"

Tally shrugged. "Go ahead. You'll see. Real men don't devour six cakes. They might have one." She thought for a moment. "Or perhaps two."

"You are the silliest sister anybody could have. I think they swopped embryos in the Genetic Institute. I don't think you can be my sister."

"No," she said in a sweet tone, "—I pilot so much better than you do!"

"Do not!"

"Do too! Denaraz said so!"

"He did not! He may have praised your pilotage, but he never said you were any better than me."

"Tha—," Tally broke off as a flutter of static flooded the small cabin. She and Giedi leaped for the console at the same time, which led to a mid-air collision. It was Giedi who made it first to the chair, leaving his sister with a rueful expression, rubbing one elbow.

"Sorry!" He bent over the console. "It is coming from a cargo vessel." Then he frowned. "But it is not on the main Bifold-Landau route. It seems to be coming from above us. That's odd."

The static continued, even though Giedi was trying to recalibrate the sensors to concentrate them in that one direction. He cursed his slowness. He should have listened better in those lessons, back on *Bellaris* shipstation. At the time he'd thought them boring and irrelevant to his life. He shook his head, angry at himself. Just showed how much he knew.

Eventually his sister gave a *tsskk*, and leant over his shoulder. She fiddled with some of the controls in front of him until the sensors converged above them instead of to either side along the shipping route.

Immediately, the static ceased and became one voice.

"—help you?" it said.

Tally pressed another button and then nodded to Giedi.

"Hello? Hello? Can you hear me? Can you help us?"

There was a pause so long that the two siblings checked the console again. Everything seemed to be working correctly. They exchanged a shrug.

"—Hello! Yes, we can hear you. We are an antimatter cargo ship, coming in from the Senithan system to the Landau Rift, with a large cargo for Enifa. What is your current situation?"

Giedi eagerly supplied the coordinates and explained about Gus, adding that they also had a severely injured Spacelander who needed help.

"We have several Zeroth Chambers. Our problem is that we cannot stop our ship. It would take us one whole day to slow down and three days to get back up to speed. Are you capable of matching our speed?" The unembodied voice gave details of that velocity.

"Probably," admitted Giedi. "But it will put us right at the top of our capabilities. There will be very little extra if anything goes wrong."

"Nothing will go wrong," the voice said comfortably. "We will open our front hold and scoop you up. We can take you all the way to Enifa, if you'd like. Your most serious casualty is an Enif, you said?"

Tally looked doubtful. They had no idea if the Enifa would welcome Gus back. Dad hadn't said how it had left its home planet.

"Err ... We would prefer to contact our home ship, if it is all the same to you, Captain."

"Not the captain, lad. I'm just the Engineer. You're lucky it was my shift. I don't think the captain would have taken much notice of a mayday call. He lives eats and breathes antimatter fees. He would never risk a late arrival fee, not even to save somebody's life. I'll start a repeating signal for ... *Nivala*, you said, right?"

"*Nivala*, yes. Your captain sounds like a nice type."

"He's from Shiller's Rock. A Casino man. They don't promote nice types. I'm just here for the experience. I don't care about the money. Not much, anyway. I'm Alasdair Restar, generally known around here as Chief Restar. Nice to meet you."

Giedi had already pushed the shuttle into a fast converging heading. He introduced himself and Tally.

The chief sounded interested. "Oh, you are Spacelanders? You sound a bit young to be wandering around the Dark Confines on your own rescuing people."

"It's a long story."

The voice laughed. "I'd like to hear it." There was a pause. "Ahh. I have you now. You should be alongside us within three hours. Will that give you enough time for your worst casualty?"

"We think so. The portable Zeroth gave us a time limit of twelve hours. We will be within that. If you come from outside the Major Shells, will your Zeroth be calibratable for Enif physiognomy?"

"Sure. Zeroths are one of the things we exchange for Antimatter. Have you never heard of us?"

The two siblings shook their heads. "We didn't know anybody lived outside the Major Shells."

There was a roar of laughter. "And just where did they tell you antimatter came from? The Great Divide?"

Tally and Giedi stared at each other. "I don't think they told us anything," admitted Giedi, "—and we never thought about it."

"What you call the Major Shells are only six small bubbles in an infinite space," the voice, sounding amused, told them. "Senitha is in another bubble some distance away. I thought everybody would have heard of us. You sure you haven't? Gehenna? Jacob's Coffin? Slipstream Alley?"

"No. Sorry."

"No matter. Although I confess to being a little disappointed. I thought we were more famous. You have cut me down to size."

The words contained amusement, so Giedi knew it was a joke. He was interested, though. "Do you know much about us?"

"Oh, we know all about you. We have to. When we deliver here, we risk being attacked by Vaers, and you have just gone through an interspecies war. We don't transport antimatter into places we know nothing about. That can turn out to be very dangerous."

"You must all be very rich," essayed Tally, her forehead crinkling.

That got a genuine belly laugh. "I wish. But life in my neck of the universe can be quite challenging. There are some rich people, true, but the Fortune Syndicate and the Euthan Church have a bit of a corner on the antimatter market. People like me find jobs mending ships, mending parts. We get by, but we don't exactly live like princes."

Giedi's interest was piqued. "I would like to visit, one day."

"Well, when you do, come to Tenacity. That's a planet near Slipstream Alley. I can put you up and wine and dine you. It would be my pleasure. Don't expect beauty, though. We live in an area of space which has been chewed up over and over again by the antimatter asteroid belt. But I call it home."

"Thank you."

Two hours later, they were almost alongside the huge cargo ship. It was quite the ugliest ship that either of them had ever seen. There was a stumpy bridge section at the front, with a small ancillary vehicle, or AV, bay immediately underneath. The superstructure of the cargo part of the vessel began where the bridge ended. It consisted of a two-kilometer-long set of parallel girders. Six antimatter canisters slotted into each station of these girders, surrounding them, bristling out so that the ship resembled an elongated hedgehog.

Tally's mouth dropped open. There were canisters for as far as her eye could see. It was like nothing she had ever seen before. And she had been brought up on a shipstation, which was quite a large ship in itself. But this ... this looked like ... like an elongated bunch of grapes that went on forever. No wonder the Engineer had said it would take too long to stop and start it again. With the amount of cargo pods the ship was carrying, it was a wonder it had ever managed to get up to this speed in the first place.

"Which of us is taking the shuttle in?" she asked, fully expecting her brother to bag that right for himself. But Giedi surprised her.

"You know," he said slowly. "I already owe my life to your piloting. You take her in."

Tally felt a warm glow spread throughout her thin body. "Thanks!"

"No. No thanks. You earned it. Don't expect me to stop teasing you, though. You're my sister. You know." He gave a shrug and an eye roll.

She did know. Ribbing each other was just something the brothers and sisters had always done. She didn't hold it against him.

The warm voice on the comlink came back on. "OK, guys. All we need you to do is slide that shuttle of yours gently in front of us, just under the bridge, and let us sweep you up. Just take it easy, though. A couple of meters too high and you might crash in through my windscreen!"

The AV bay was set slightly back under the bridge. Tally edged the shuttle under the overhang until the small vessel was centered just below that. At the same time the AV doors were opening, to show a deserted hold beyond them. There were no other vehicles to avoid. Tally felt relieved.

She felt her hands stiffen up as nerves began to creep in. That wasn't good. She forced herself to take deep breaths in and out for a few seconds and waited until her hands relaxed a little. Then she let the shuttle gradually ease back. She did slip a little off-center as the door mounts slowly crept past the cabin, but finally was able to set the shuttle down more or less exactly where she had been aiming. She switched off the engines and opened the shuttle door. Then she sat back in the chair. That is when her hands really began to shake. She stared crossly down at them.

Giedi was already out of the shuttle, shaking hands with a man who looked to be in his late twenties. He must be Chief Restar.

They spoke quickly together and then both nodded. A crewmember with a floating stretcher materialized behind them. Giedi pointed inside the shuttle.

Tally leaped up as the stretcher came in. She moved to help but Restar motioned her back. "Good piece of flying," he said. "I didn't realize just how young you both were. You are very capable. Now, let *us* take it from here."

In a second, both Gus and Sibby had been manhandled onto stretchers and the stretchers had disappeared into the lifts leading out of the AV bay.

Restar watched them over his shoulder. "The Zeroths have already been programmed," he said. "And I have some good news. We have managed to contact your ship. *Nivala* is a day and a half away. We have arranged a rendezvous just outside the Slingshot Binary. The day after tomorrow. Will that suit you both?" His eyes twinkled. "They were extremely glad to hear that you were well, and even more so that you had rescued your missing crew members. You did very well. Very well indeed."

Chapter 24

Nivala's scanners picked up the transmission when she was around thirty light years out of Rhyveka. Mel was on watch. She checked her sensors and then gave a gasp. She called for the captain to come to the bridge.

Mallivan and Denaraz had been sparring with each other in the gymnasium which was set just behind the bridge. They both strode onto the bridge only moments later, still chatting about their practice. Mallivan was untying the thick combat gloves that were usual for practice bouts.

Mel broke through their chat. "They are on a cargo ship!"

"What?" Mallivan's head whipped up so fast that he cricked his neck.

"I have an incoming transmission. An antimatter ship from

outside the Major Shells. They confirm four passengers: two healthy, one in recovery and one still critical. They are asking us to rendezvous with them. Shall I pass you the coordinates?"

"One critical?" Mallivan and Denaraz were staring at each other.

"Three safe," Mel thought it important to point out.

"Yes. Three safe." Both men nodded. "Three safe," repeated Denaraz in a choked voice. "Yes. That is indeed good news." His eyes were haunted, though. "How soon can we get to that ship?"

Mel did the necessary calculations. "Twenty-nine hours," she said flatly. "They are on a course for Enifa, which is taking them away from this sector of space. They apologize, but are unable to reduce speed. I guess it must be one of those huge space tankers with hundreds of pods. You can't stop and start those very easily."

"Send our thanks for their assistance and tell them we are on our way. We should be able to meet up with them ..." he walked over to the navigation deck and studied the course Mel had just laid in, "... somewhere near the Lycara Nebula. If all goes well."

Zenzara, who had been swimming in the central pool, rushed in. "Has something happened? You called for the captain."

When she heard, she stopped dead in the middle of the bridge. "One critical?" Her crest came up and she began to tremble. "Who? Which of them?"

"We have no idea. We will have to wait."

The Chyzar had gone white. "What does that mean? Has my idea killed Giedi? Or Tally? I should never have suggested it."

Denaraz walked quickly up to the distraught Tyzaran girl and gave her a quick hug. "They have saved at least one person. Either Gus or Sibby. They managed to find them. We don't know how, and it must be quite a story if they have ended up on a trans-shell cargo ship. But think for a moment, Chy Zenzara. It means that their mission was successful. If only one person is critical, then they have saved at least one of them." He shook her gently, trying to shake her out of the doldrums. "Nothing comes without a cost. You know that from the past war."

Her shivers settled. "Yes. I do know that. It's just that I never thought … I shouldn't have …"

Mallivan interrupted. "Let's be positive. Only one of the four is critical, and the megatankers that cross from the Ankaran Shells to the Major Shells will have the very latest in Zeroth Triage Chambers. There is a very good chance that they will be able to save the person who is critical. We *have* to stay positive. Now, go get some rest, all of you. Nothing more is going to happen for a whole day. That is long enough for us to catch up on our own rest. There is nothing else we can do for anybody. Mel and I will continue here for the next eight hours, then you two can take over from us. Then we can fit in two shorter shifts before we reach the rendezvous."

Zenzara nodded. She and Izan walked slowly out in the direction of the crew quarters.

Thirty hours later, Mallivan was at the helm of the second shuttle. He had wanted to take Denaraz with him, but Zenzie had refused to let him go without her, so in the end Mel and Izan had stayed to keep *Nivala* on a steady course alongside the enormous tanker, which was called *Ankaran Trader*.

The captain gave a whistle as he slid out of the cargo hold and first caught sight of the tanker. It was huge. It was built somewhat along the lines of the asset dump they had found in the outer parts of the Sol system, Platform Six. But this ship was so long that you could either see where it started or where it ended. Not both. It appeared to go on forever. It resembled a millipede more than a ship.

They had heard no more from the *Ankaran Trader,* so had no idea what they would find when they got there.

The tanker was still cruising at top speed, but it wouldn't be long until the captain needed to instigate the slow deceleration that would enable the tanker to glide easily into Enifa-synchronous orbit. It would take at least a couple of days to lose enough momentum for that.

They docked without incident. As they walked down the gangplank, they found three figures waiting for them: one large and sturdy, two smaller and thinner.

Zenzie gave a yelp of recognition and broke into a run. "Giedi!"

One of the smaller figures detached itself and ran towards the Tyzaran girl.

They met in the middle and threw themselves into each other's arms, both jabbering at the same time. It was impossible to hear what they were saying.

Mallivan paused, then the other small figure threw itself into his arms. "Dad!"

Ryler found himself clutching onto his little daughter as though he would never let her go. "Tally? Are you all right?"

Her arms were almost crushing his neck. "Gus is really sick, Dad. It has something called Chill Coma."

Mallivan found himself inundated with so many feelings all at once that he really didn't know quite what to do with them all. So he ignored them as best he could and strode forward, hand outstretched, still carrying the limpet-like figure of his daughter.

"Captain," he said, "Thank you so much."

The face in front of him was beginning to line, despite its relatively young age. "Think nothing of it, Captain Mallivan. But I am not the captain. He is ... indisposed at the moment. My name is

Restar. Chief Restar. I am the ship's Engineer."

Mallivan pumped the hand up and down. "My mistake. Thank you for looking after my family for me. How is Gus? Is it responding to treatment?"

Restar gave a so-so grimace. "Our Zeroth tells us that the levels are almost back to normal, but we have been unable to wake it so far. The coma appears far lighter, but is persisting. It is too early to give a prognosis, however."

"I am indebted to you for your efforts. —And my sister?"

"She was suffering relatively minor injuries. The Zeroth has kept her in a machine until now just as a precautionary measure. She is due out …" he checked his electronic tablet, "… about now. Would you like me to take you there?"

"That would be kind."

As they walked along the passageway, with Zenzie and Giedi following along behind, Restar tried to explain just what was wrong with Gus.

"… So, although the Enif as a species are able to withstand the rigors of space for quite some hours, existing on the air trapped beneath the carapace, there was another factor in play.

"From what your sister was able to tell us, once she regained consciousness, Gus had gone outside the EVA drone they had escaped in. It was attempting to signal any ship that might be close enough to pick up a visual signal. However, that meant that it needed to cling onto the outside hull of the drone. This was metallic, clearly, and that must have been what caused the Chill Coma."

From the expression on his listener's face, he must have realized that more explanation was necessary. He flushed slightly. "Sorry. I am probably not doing a very good job at this. I … medicine is not one of my strong points, I'm afraid. Anyway, the problem of course is that the feet have a strong tendency to stick to the metal, so more antifreeze protein is required by the cells in contact with the metal. Now, that wouldn't be a problem for an hour or two. I gathered from Miss Sibby that Gus was outside the pod for eight hours. Gradually, over that time, the cells in the feet drained the antifreeze protein down to them, in order to avoid becoming frozen in place. Enif production of antifreeze proteins, or AFPs, are extremely limited. As the AFPs settled in the feet, they left the upper parts of the body unprotected. Most importantly, the brain was unable to keep the cold at bay. The Enif would have felt woozy and must have found it difficult to concentrate. Then it must have slipped into unconsciousness. That is the basic explanation for Chill Coma."

"So the Enif needs to be warmed up?" hazarded Mallivan.

"Absolutely not. In fact, the Enif needs to be kept cold. That stimulates the fabrication of more AFPs, which can then travel into the brain cells themselves and allow the brain to function normally. Enif can die of Chill Coma, but they can also make a full recovery. According to the machine, there is a fifty-fifty chance either way after a Coma of twenty-four hours."

"Do we know how long Gus has been unconscious?"

Restar's face drooped slightly. "At least forty-four hours."

Mallivan blew out air. Tally at last let go of his neck and he helped her slide down his chest to the ground. She looked at the deck planks. "I am sorry."

"Sorry? For stealing a shuttle and going off to look for Gus and Sibby?"

"Yes, Dad."

"Well, you shouldn't be. You found them, and from the sound of it, they wouldn't have had even a *chance* at survival if you hadn't. I was wrong. I should have sent somebody to search for them. It is something I shall always regret. I am angry that you disobeyed my orders, but pleased that you did."

"Really? You are pleased?"

He pulled a face. "Pleased and angry at the same time. It is a bit contradictory, I know. You did well, Talitha. So did your brother. I am proud of you both. Especially since you managed to find a fully functioning Zeroth machine in record time. I guess that Gus would already be dead if you hadn't."

"Thanks, Dad. I am sorry we had to go."

"Yeah, well, don't make a habit of it."

"No. I won't."

Restar extended a hand. "Your sister is in the next section. Shall we go and see if she has been released?"

"Yes please." Mallivan frowned. "Restar. Restar. That sounds like a Major Shell name. We have a small planet over in the Polar Shell that is called Restar. A little beyond Geiga. Was your own family originally from this part of space?"

"Not that I know of. I only have facts two generations back, but those ancestors were Senithan, born and bred. Still, the Ankaran Shells have been exporting antimatter to other Shells for over six hundred years. It is possible that one of my ancestors came from around here originally."

They walked through another bulkhead and down a short corridor to a closed door that was labeled *Zeroth 5*. Restar pushed the door open and let them inside.

"Aunt Sibby!" Tally pushed past the two men and ran across the distance separating her from the Zeroth machine. Sibby was sitting up inside, frowning. The medical gel was already draining away to the bottom of the machine.

"Tal. Don't jump up; you will get gel all over you. How did I get here? How is Gus?"

Then she saw her brother. "Mall? Am I dreaming? I sort of

remember being trapped inside a huge EVA suit." Then she made an evident attempt to remember all that had happened. She stiffened. "Oh, no! Gus! I couldn't make it wake up. I think something awful happened to it." Her eyes were darting around the room, trying to find the Enif. "It saved my life!"

"So did Giedi and Tally," said Mallivan with a smile. "Scout was signaling weakly. I ignored it, but they were convinced it was important. At least, Zenzie was. When I told them I couldn't take *Nivala* off our pursuit of the Avarak cruiser, they stole a shuttle and took off by themselves."

Sibby's eyebrows had crawled further and further up during that conversation. Now she looked at her niece in amazement. "S-S-Stole a shuttle! Tally! I am *shocked*!"

"Y-Y-Yes, but we ... we ..."

"Come here and give me a hug. Thank you very much for saving us. But what about Gus? How is it?"

Restar explained. Sibby's face fell, then brightened. "At least you got it in a Zeroth machine within the time. I trust science. If the Zeroth told Giedi that Gus could recover if it were put in a Zeroth within twelve hours, then I am inclined to believe it. Gus is a fighter. It fought Enif convention to get onto *Nivala*, and it will fight this too. You'll see." She ruffled Tally's hair. "Shuttle-stealer!"

Talitha looked so relieved that Ryler wanted to hug his sister all over again. Sibby had always known just what to say. He was grateful.

The chief waited to one side until Sibby had extricated herself from the tank and hugged Giedi and Zenzara. Then everybody spoke at once as they all tried to get up to date with each other. Finally, the man from across the dust spoke again. "Shall I take you to Gus?"

He was instantly surrounded. He held up his hands, laughing.

"Careful, there is only one of me and you look like a crowd right now."

They fell back and let him lead them to another Zeroth room. Here, there was another crewmember of *Ankaran Trader.* He was sitting quietly in the corner, attending to some paperwork on his tablet. He stood up as they all trooped in and nodded. "No change so far, I am afraid."

Giedi moved right up to the Zeroth tank and peered in. "His color is better," the boy pointed out. "When we pulled him into the shuttle he was white all over. Now he looks more a dull grey, except for that white patch. And there is some black shining through!"

Zenzie privately thought the Enif looked terrible, but she said nothing. That jelly-like feeling of responsibility was back in her stomach. She felt a little sick.

Sibby walked over and gave her a hug, dropping a kiss on the very top of her crest. "You did well!"

Zenzie raised her head. "I did?" She stared again at the inert Enif body lying inside the Zeroth machine. "It doesn't feel like it."

"Both Gus and I would already be dead if it weren't for all of you, so stop feeling wobbly. You *all* did very well. I shall probably spend the rest of my life paying you back. Or do you want me to enact a Savior Protocol with you?"

"No!" Zenzara reared back and then began to laugh at her own reaction. "I guess one protocol with the Mallivan Bell family is enough, thank you."

"Then accept that it all went well and stop second-guessing yourself. Though, if I were you, I wouldn't steal too many more shuttles. I don't think your captain is very happy about it."

"All isn't well." The Tyzaran girl was staring down at Gus.

"Bah! You know these Enif. Anything for a good sleep! He'll be up and around in no time."

Sibby walked away and up to her brother, who had just finished communicating the updates to Denaraz and Mel. She put one hand on his arm. "Seyal is dead, isn't she?" she said, in a quiet voice.

Her brother stiffened and then gave a short nod.

Sibby thought back to the Avarak cruiser and a slow tear tracked down her cheek. "She stayed so that I could go free," she said. "She knew that if we broke her out of the cell, the Avaraks would hunt us down. She sacrificed herself for me."

Her brother leant closer. "You should take your own advice more often," he whispered. "The truth is that she sacrificed herself for *many* people. For the rest of the Avarak females. For Segaton. And maybe for you. But you are not the one responsible for her capture. You tried to stop it, didn't you? That's why they took you with them?"

She nodded, her heart too full to be able to speak.

"I thought so. She would have died anyway, Sib. With or without you. That she chose to do it without you shows what sort of a person she was." His eyes looked away, finding the ceiling. "Rest in peace, Seyal."

His sister smiled wetly and pressed his hand. "Yes. Rest in peace, Seyal. Thank you!" Then she began to cry in earnest.

Her elder brother held her tight as shudders overtook the slim frame.

They met up with Chief Restar some ten minutes later. It was not clear what their best plan of action would be, and Mallivan had asked Sibby to study the Zeroth chamber readouts.

Now she was sitting in front of all of them.

"I believe that Gus can be moved, as long as it is not kept off a Zeroth machine for more than an hour."

Restar frowned. "You are more than welcome to remain aboard *Ankaran Trader* until we reach Enifa. That would seem to be the most prudent course."

"I agree," Mallivan told the engineer, "but unfortunately we believe that Gus would not wish to be taken back to Enifa. Although of course the facilities for such an illness would be superior on its home planet, it might face retention by the *Aliifat*, or they might even refuse any treatment at all, given that it does not have a *faliif*."

That took quite a bit of explaining. Eventually Restar understood. "I see. Those circumstances indeed change the situation. I can understand why you want to transfer it across to your ship."

Mallivan got to his feet. "I'm afraid that I can't see any alternative. Gus was not happy with the treatment it received on Enifa, and I am almost certain that it would not wish to be taken back there, even in these circumstances. We will transfer it to *Nivala*."

Restar got up too and reached out to shake all of their hands. "Then I will supply a floating stretcher. I wish you all well in the future."

They all bowed slightly. "Thank you for saving us," said Sibby. "It was kind of you."

"Nothing of the sort. You know what the unwritten space rules are. I was merely following them."

"'*Never let a spacer in need fall behind you.*'" quoted Giedi helpfully.

Restar's lips twitched. "Exactly." His eyes narrowed as he shook Zenzie's hand. "I am honored to have met the Chyzar," he said quietly. "I hope that we meet again sometime in the future. I feel that we will, though I am unable to say why."

When he reached Sibby, he bent almost as low as an old-fashioned knight might have done. "I am glad we were on hand to help you. Please take better care of yourself in the future."

She laughed. "I will try not to get thrown out of any more Avarak cruisers," she told him in a rueful tone. "There are definitely more comfortable ways to get off a ship."

His eyes crinkled with amusement and perhaps something of sadness. "I will be on the Bridge, overseeing everything." He stepped back and then walked off.

They watched him go. Zenzara gave a mischievous smile in Sibby's direction. "He liked you, you know."

"Bah! Don't be silly. I'm married. I'm soul-mixed."

"Yes, but he can't help what he felt. Until the captain told him, he had no idea you were already taken. She stared after the disappearing figure. "Pity. He looks rather a lonely person, doesn't he? I hope he finds somebody nice to share his life with."

Mallivan huffed. "Just because you think *you* have become soul-mixed doesn't mean that everybody wants to be. Some of us are much happier on our own."

Zenzie eyed him thoughtfully. "Yes," she murmured, "I know."

Ryler was left staring at her. Why did he get the feeling that she didn't believe him? "I mean it, kid. Don't even think about trying to match me off with anyone. I am simply not interested."

She held up both hands. "All right! I won't!"

He cleared his throat. "Good."

Giedi gave him a cheeky grin. "Your loss."

He rolled his eyes. "Not interested," he repeated. "Especially not when I am followed around by a nosy Tyzaran girl who won't leave me in peace."

The Chyzar tossed her head up. She walked away.

Some moments later, two crew members arrived with the floating stretcher. They pulled it alongside the Zeroth Chamber and then stood back.

Sibby pushed some buttons. The canopy on the chamber swung open and the gel began to drain away.

As it did, Gus's body became more visible. Its carapace, normally black and shiny, was streaked with grey. Its head was flopping over to one side and its appendages dangled bonelessly over the sides of the stretcher. It did not look as though it could recover, thought Sibby privately. But she was not about to give up. She ran forward to lift the trailing limbs and tenderly place them alongside the carapace.

"You saved my life, Gus," she whispered. "Keep fighting. You are getting better. They say that you can make a full discovery. You have to keep fighting. You still haven't found your *faliif*, you know. You cannot leave Halaashi alone. It may spend the rest of its life searching for you. You have to get better so that you will be here for Halaashi the day it finds you. You know that, one day, it will."

To her enormous surprise she felt a sudden ripple in the arm she was tucking safely onto the stretcher. She almost leapt backwards, but then realized that Gus might be trying to communicate. "Yes!" she whispered. "Yes, Gus, I can feel that. Are you able to hear me?"

Another faint undulation told her that it was.

Sibby couldn't keep a smile off her lips. "Gus can hear us!" she shouted over to the others, who stared down at the still inert body and then looked back doubtfully in her direction. "The cordotonal organs in its arms are moving!" She gazed around with such happiness that they couldn't question what she was saying any longer.

She bent closer to the Enif. Hoping that its translation device was still sending impulses to its brain, she explained where they were, that they had been rescued by Giedi and Talitha and taken on board a mega tanker originating outside the Major Shells. She went on to tell Gus that it was being transported back to *Nivala*; that the prognosis was great, but that it would need to rest more in another Zeroth chamber.

When she finished, there was a weak vibration again. She gave Gus's arm a quick squeeze in return. "You are going to make a full recovery. Just lie back and let your body recuperate. We won't let anything happen to you, I promise."

This time the rippling movement was so small that she wondered if she had felt anything at all. But she was still smiling. Gus was in there somewhere, and had been able to let her know. That was certainly enough for now. It was the start they needed. Now she was certain that her friend would recover. She thought back to the time in the EVA drone, out in the Dark Confines.

She gave a gasp, and her hands covered her mouth.

"What, Sibby?" Her brother looked concerned.

She spun around to face Giedi. "What happened to Toothpick?" she demanded. "Tell me you didn't leave him out there in the Dark Confines! Please!"

Giedi frowned. "No, we didn't. He was in the shuttle with us, because he wouldn't leave you. I distinctly remember seeing him wrapped up in your hair when you were lying unconscious on the shuttle decking." His whole brow wrinkled. "Yet I don't remember seeing him since." He thought some more and then shook his head, clearly drawing a blank. "Nope. Sorry. He must still be on the shuttle, though, because he wasn't here on *Ankaran Trader*, was he?"

Sibby actually looked frustrated with her nephew. "I wouldn't know, would I? I was unconscious, remember?"

"True. Oh well, if he isn't on the shuttle, he will be on Restar's ship or here, on *Nivala*, right? Either way he is safe."

Sibby's expression would have told him that she didn't agree, but since he was busy staring at Zenzara again, he didn't notice.

Mallivan did. He shook his head and gave a shrug of his shoulders. "There isn't much we can do about it now," he pointed out. I can hardly ask Chief Restar to search the whole ship for one sunflyer. If he isn't on the shuttle you came in, we can tell Restar later. I'm sure he would look after Toothpick with the greatest of care."

"Yes," Sibby admitted, "I suppose he would. Still—," she shot an accusatory glare at Giedi, "—we should have thought to check."

Giedi was hurt. "We saved your lives, didn't we? And we saved the sunflyer. I *did* forget about him after we were on board. We had some rather more urgent things on our minds, you know?"

Sibby bent her head. "Sorry, Gied. I know you did. And I am very grateful. It is just … well, it will be hard to tell Gus that his pet is not here."

Giedi flushed. "OK, I can see that, but it isn't fair to blame Tally and me. Nobody can think of everything!"

He was right. She was being completely ridiculous. They had been saved by the sheer determination of three youngsters, and here she was, berating one of them, when she should be hugging him. She rectified this immediately.

Giedi looked surprised when his aunt put her arms around him. "What's happening?"

She realized that tears were slipping down her cheeks. She was half-smiling, half-crying. "I am sorry, Gied. I guess I am still a bit woozy after the Zeroth chamber."

Her nephew was staring at her in horror. "Are you crying?" he asked, his voice going up half an octave.

"Never!" She wiped her face on the sleeve of her tunic. "Perish the thought!"

Giedi looked most uncomfortable. "If I'd known you were going to do this I would have tied that stupid sunflyer to you!"

Sibby gave a hiccup. "I'm fine."

Then she proved that she wasn't by collapsing into a sobbing heap.

By moving as quickly as they could, they managed to keep Gus's time outside a Zeroth Chamber to a very minimum. Within forty minutes of being unplugged from the machine on the *Ankaran Trader*, the unmoving body of the Enif was already plugged into an identical machine on board *Nivala*, with the gel almost covering it.

Sibby had pulled a chair up alongside the chamber and had gratefully folded herself onto it. She was feeling more fragile than she had ever done before. This shaky feeling inside was refusing to go away, especially now that her husband was standing beside her. All she wanted to do was curl up in his strong arms and forget about absolutely everything, but it wasn't feasible. She couldn't leave Gus alone. The Enif had risked its life to safe hers and she had a debt that needed to be repaid, if such a thing was even possible.

Izan had been waiting for her as she came on board. He hadn't said anything. His eyes had said it all for him. He had simply enfolded her in an embrace that crushed her to his chest. The immense feeling of relief that she felt to be held safely to him had made the tears spill out of her eyes. Then he had held her slightly away and really looked at her. She hadn't had to explain anything. He had understood anyway.

Now he stood at the door, just a quiet and calming presence. He had asked nothing from her. One glance from him had been enough to see that she needed time. And he was giving it to her. That was why they were soul-mixed, she supposed. They didn't need to talk.

She watched the gel as it crept quickly up the carapace of the Enif in front of her. When she had been in her own Zeroth chamber, the gel had been still and calm. For the Enif, however, it was bubbling and frothy. She supposed that it had to be. Enif did not breathe through their mouths. They breathed through their body. That must be oxygen fizzing up through the moving liquid. She noticed that the whole of Gus's head was being immersed. For humans, the Zeroths attached a long breathing tube before their faces were covered by the gel.

It was just another sign of how different two species could be. Yet this Enif had been willing to throw its own life away to safe hers. There was still good in the world. It was hard to accept her own good luck, however, after what had happened to Seyal.

Tears ran down her cheeks again.

Denaraz, behind her, saw them. He wanted to scoop his wife up and hug her tightly, but something was telling him not to. He compromised by putting one hand softly onto her shoulder, hoping that she would understand how much he wanted to share her pain, diminish it for her.

She nodded slightly. His heart filled with wonder. She had understood him. It felt like a tiny miracle to the soldier. How was it possible that one soft touch could convey so much?

They settled in, like that, for a long wait.

About an hour later a jubilant Giedi bustled in, his eyes victorious.

"Here he is! I *thought* he would still be on the shuttle!"

Izan had no idea what the boy was talking about, but his wife did. She turned round immediately. "Toothpick *is* here?"

Giedi extended his hand in Sibby's direction. "There you are. I think he's a bit cross. He might not like being left on his own. He had somehow got locked inside the shuttle we took."

Just as Denaraz grasped what they were talking about, Sibby extended one finger and Izan saw a small insect accept her offer. Toothpick paced solemnly along Giedi's hand and down onto Sibby's finger. She stared down at him, delighted, then lifted her own hand to place him on her shoulder.

"He kept me sane inside that EVA drone. I never thought I would say this, but having your eyelids grazed on can be very calming."

Denaraz gave a mental groan, but was extremely careful not to let anything seep out into the audible range. He could see where this was going. He closed his eyes as tightly as his mouth. Tyzaran men could cope with anything, and he had, after all, been in the army for years. So why was there a hollow feeling in the pit of his stomach?

"Does it like any particular type of eyelid?" he asked tentatively.

His wife was letting the insect bury into her hair. As he watched, it disappeared.

He stifled a shudder.

"Relax, Denaraz. He is only on temporary loan to me, I think. Once Gus is awake he will go back to his real owner." She put her head on one side. "I think he is just putting up with me for the time being."

Such a wave of relief ran through Izan's entire body that even Sibby felt it. She passed one of her hands backwards and took his hand. "Were you going to say anything?"

He shook his head, tongue-tied like a youngling.

"You are a good husband. Thank you."

Denaraz knew he had passed a test. He was glad, but he wasn't about to let his guard down. There was too much at stake.

The Zeroth chamber chimed with a gentle tone. Sibby stood up to read the machine update. "Gus is now sleeping normally!" she said, eyes wide. She managed a small skip. "It needs three or four days more in deep sleep followed by one or two in recovery, then it can come out of the chamber!"

Izan dropped a quiet kiss on the top of her head. "That is great news, Sibby. Something to celebrate."

"It is."

Yet she kept her vigil at the Enif's side.

Gus and Seyal. One to celebrate and one to anguish over.

Onboard *Ankaran Trader*, Chief Restar had his feet up on the console in front of him. His eyes were half-closed and he was mulling over recent events. It was the night watch and although he was not sleeping, he was far more relaxed than he would have been on a day shift.

Suddenly an arm appeared in his peripheral vision and slammed his feet off the console. Restar almost fell off his chair.

The Captain's thick eyebrows were almost meeting in the middle. And they were far too close to the chief's face. "What the fitz do you mean by taking on aliens and helping them? We are not in the charity business! What were you thinking? I gave no permission to do that!"

Restar sighed. He really needed to get a new job. It was time.

"International space laws require us to act in such a case, Captain."

"International space laws!" the sneer in Slande's voice was very clear. "Our deadline is the *only* thing that matters, and you know it!"

"—Which is why I didn't slow down," Restar pointed out, feeling unfairly maligned.

"It was not your decision to take. Why was I not informed?"

"You ... errr ... were resting Captain. I did not consider it to be important enough to wake you."

"Well, you were wrong, Restar, and I do not appreciate your actions. I shall have to inform the company of your behavior!"

The Chief frowned. "Oh, I don't think you will do that, Captain." His voice was suddenly steely, in marked contrast to his usual bonhomie.

"Are you threatening me?"

Restar looked gratified. "I am, actually." He stood up and took one pace towards his superior, lifting his chin. "You are a drunkard. You should not be in charge of a ship of this size. Any ship, for that matter. I have every intention of resigning my position upon completion of this trip, and I advise you to do the same. I cannot, in all conscience, allow a person so incompetent to continue in such a senior position."

"You ... you ..." Words failed Slande.

"I should have been off-shift four hours ago. Good evening." And Restar walked out. He felt clarity for the first time in months. He had been running on automatic for far too long. It was time for his future to start. Life was too short to waste it in company of people like this.

Chapter 25

Three days later, *Nivala* finally caught up with the *Shapley* shipstation. It was still on the move, and would be for several months yet. But apart from a gentle velocity towards the Olympus Nebula, it looked almost unaffected by the supershell storm. The structural damage that had been caused was slowly being smoothed away by an intense repair schedule.

Prime Ohnahara was waiting for them at the airlock. She drew Sibby into a huge hug.

"I'm *so* glad that they got you back. I'm very sorry for the loss of your friend. How is Gus?"

"Gus seems to be close to waking. It should be out of the Zeroth tank within thirty hours."

"That is great news."

"My brother will be here in a few moments. He has gone to find Scout. What about the people here, Ohnah? How is everybody doing?"

The Prime's face fell. "I'm afraid we've lost three more," she said, "so the final count is fourteen dead. Everybody else is recovering, though the last Zeroth patients will need further time in the tanks. Some will have long-lasting effects, but all will be able to lead more or less normal lives eventually."

A thundering of feet prevented the adults from further communication. Peetie arrived, shadowed by the rest of the station's youth.

Peetie ran up to Giedi and Tally. "You're back! You're back!"

Giedi fended his brother off rather easily, then gave in and bent down slightly to hug him. "Of course we are back, tadpole! Where did you think we would go?"

"We were worried about you." Peetie shifted over to hug his sister. "All of you."

Giedi puffed out his chest a little. It was hard not to be proud of their achievements. "Tally and I rescued Aunt Sibby and Gus," he told his brother. "We are fine. I don't know what you were worrying about."

Denaraz had overheard this last comment. "And Tally rescued both Giedi and Zenzara," he added, his tone a little censorious.

Giedi reddened. "Yes," he agreed hurriedly. "Tally did the best of all of us."

Denaraz smiled at him now. "You all did very well indeed."

Peetie was bouncing up and down, up and down in excitement. "Really? Will Dad let you travel with them on *Nivala*, then?"

There was a sudden silence after this artless comment. Zenzie and Giedi looked quickly at each other in hope, and Tally's face fell a little, though she masked it almost immediately.

Then they all turned at the same time to Denaraz. "Will he, do you think?" asked Giedi. "I could be taken on as a cadet, couldn't I? Am I over the minimum age?"

Izan spread his hands. "You will have to ask your father," he said. "I have no responsibilities in that area, I'm sorry to say. If it were *my* ship — the Tyzaran one — I would take both you *and* Tally on as cadets. But Tyzar accepts cadets from seven years old. Spacelander laws are different."

Tally's little face shone with pleasure. "Really?" she squeaked, "you would take *me* on as a cadet. Really?"

"I certainly would. You *both* have a lot of potential."

Peetie was duly impressed. "Wow!"

At that moment Scout skittered down the airlock ramp and onto the shipstation. Three of the children made a dive for his collar, but the Geiga easily avoided them. He put his blunt snout into the air and sniffed around. Something must have been appetizing, because he suddenly lifted his head and his little feet scrabbled at the deck as he attempted to accelerate too fast for the metal planking. It didn't slow him down very much. He disappeared along the docking passageway, his little tail waving around in excitement.

"No!" wailed Peetie. "We were just about to sit down to lunch." He sped off in the wake of the Geiga, followed by six or seven of the others.

Mallivan now walked down the docking tube and grinned after his youngest. "They will never catch up with him in time. Scout has a long history of ruining meals."

"Dad?" Giedi sidled up. "*Will* you take me with you? On *Nivala*? As a cadet?"

Ryler raised his eyebrows. "As crew? But, Giedi, you are only twelve years old."

"Zenzie is only ten"

"I know, but that is different."

Giedi put his hands on his hips and scowled. "Why?"

His father was exchanging a glance with Denaraz. "We will discuss this at a later date, Giedi. Now, take Tally and make sure that Peetie doesn't strangle Scout. I'm sure they all want to hear about your adventures."

Giedi was not disposed to leave, but his sister grabbed his hand and tugged at him. "Come *on*, Gied!"

He finally allowed himself to be led away.

Denaraz allowed himself a smile. "That conundrum is not going to go away," he murmured.

"No, I don't suppose it will." Mallivan stared regretfully after his two older children. "They grew up in a hurry, didn't they?"

"They proved themselves. They have both crossed the barrier from child to adult, I think. Now they will ask to be treated as such."

Ryler scratched his head. "I need to think about that."

Izan nodded. He checked over his shoulder, to where his wife was standing, beside the entrance to the ship. Sibby met his gaze but stayed where she was. She was not ready to leave *Nivala*. Izan thought that she would want to stay on board the smaller ship until Gus was up and about. It was only natural. He made an up and down movement with one hand to indicate that he was leaving and smiled in her direction. She noticed and nodded back.

He fell in behind Mallivan as the captain followed Prime Ohnah along the passageway away from the airlock. They all needed to get up to date. A great deal had happened in a very short time.

It was some time later that Mel came across Sibby outside the Medical bay. Izan's wife had stepped outside for a moment to do some stretches and take welcome sips from a cup of her favorite Landau coffee.

"Hi Mel," Sibby gave a warm smile. "I haven't seen you to talk to since I got back."

"No. I thought that you might want to be on your own," she hesitated for a moment or two, before going on, "and I have been working on a … on a … project."

"Want to talk about it?" Sibby tilted her head from side to side to unkink her neck muscles, then inclined her head down, pressing her chin against her throat to loosen up a little. It felt good.

Then she realized that Mel hadn't answered her question. Sibby tilted her slim neck back again to one side and left it there. "Your project?" she nudged. Then her eyes narrowed. "Is this something you don't want anyone to know about?"

Mel looked furtively both ways down the corridor, and then grabbed Sibby and hustled her inside the mess hall, closing the door firmly behind them.

She pulled the recently recovered woman over to Eshaan's painting of the Avarak fleet immolating itself to save *Nivala* from the Terran attack, back in the Adhara Corridor. The two women stared up at it, struck as much by the ironic vagaries of fate as by the mastery of the painting.

"Every time I see this I am in awe of the talent Eshaan had," said Sibby.

Mel nodded. "It makes me remember everything about that day. The smells, the sights, the noises. It brings all the emotion I felt right back. It makes me relive it."

Sibby could see that something was bothering her friend. She let the silence prompt Mel to speak.

Mel was still staring up at the painting. "You see," she said, "*I want to make a difference too.*"

Sibby raised one eyebrow.

Mel began to laugh. "Sorry. I wasn't trying to be enigmatic. I was wondering how to tell you. But I guess I should start at the beginning. I need to tell you about Rhyveka. About what they did to Seyal. Is that all right?"

A lump started in Sibby's stomach and then lodged in her throat. She could only nod dumbly.

Mel began to explain about the journey down in the space elevator, about the overhead walkway in the Rhyveka Space Yards, about the still-smoking funeral pyre. She told Sibby how the captain had given her time to go ahead, how she had spoken to Myska. She told her about the flowers that were being left, about the female Avaraks who had risked the wrath of their husbands to pay their respects. She told her how Seyal had been overcome by the smoke before the flames reached her, how she couldn't have felt pain when the fire finally devoured her.

By the time that she finished, both women were crying freely.

Mel sniffed. "That was when I realized that even somebody like me could do something. That I could continue Seyal's work. In a way."

Sibby's eyes were round. "Tell me. I'm in!"

"Really? Do you mean that?" Then Mel's face fell a little. "I have to tell you; it might be very dangerous."

"Ahh." Now Sibby was beginning to see light. "You mean, so dangerous that it is something I might not be able to tell my husband?"

"Yes!" The relief showed as Mel dropped her shoulders. Then she looked Sibby right in the eyes. "It is something we might not be able to tell anyone. Ever. So, if you need to think about it before you decide, I am fine with that."

"I'm *in!*" repeated Sibby. "If you think we can make a real difference to the female Avaraks, in Seyal's memory, it would make me happier than you can ever know." Her eyes were red with the tears now brimming out of them. "She *died* for me."

"No. She died for a *lot* of people."

"I know." Sibby tried to brush away the tears, but more simply welled up in their place. "I just feel so ... so guilty, you know? If there is the slightest ... the tiniest thing I can do to vindicate Seyal, then I have to do it. Just the *thought* of making a difference to the female Avaraks makes me happy."

Mel smiled through her own tears. "All right. I'll count you in."

Sibby steepled her hands above her face. She seemed excited. "What is the plan?"

"We are going to supply the Avarak females with enough contraceptives to make them sterile for ten years."

The silence stretched on and on as Sibby tried to grasp the concept. It felt elusive. "C-C-Contraceptives?" she stammered.

"For ten years, unless the males claudicate before that."

"Shells!" Sibeal stretched out one hand to cover Mel's. "Mel!" she breathed. "It's brilliant! Will it work?"

"Myska thinks so. She has given me an address to send them to. She has an older sister who lives on Tyzar. Remyka is a midwife there. Apparently she will be able to arrange for their distribution to all females who wish it."

"But won't the males simply look for new wives? What happens if they decide to get rid of the ones who don't give them children?"

"Myska says not. There is an old charter that says females are allowed ten years to become pregnant. It is rarely used these days, because most females are fertile, but the males will *have to* wait ten years. After that, the females would definitely be in danger. But Myska says that, if enough females are brought into the scheme, the males will have to give in to at least some of their demands."

"Are they going to admit to taking contraceptives?"

Mel grinned. "Never! They are going to suggest that the lack of children is simply a result of their mistreatment. That the operation on the throat has disastrous side effects, that continual anxiety and fear can cause infertility. Things like that. They will try to make it easy, nudging the males towards change, rather than demanding it."

"Wow! Now I understand why we can never say anything. And you are right; I can't let even Denaraz in on the plan. He wouldn't want me getting involved with anything like that."

"Will that harm your relationship?"

Sibby shook her head. "No, because I am going to tell him that I have a secret from him that cannot be explained for the next ten years. That it will not hurt anybody he cares about, but that I am sworn to secrecy. He has secrets from me, after all. He is a spokesdesignate in the Tyzaran Supreme Council. He won't press me. He respects me."

"It's not just for Seyal and the Avarak women. I am doing it for Sammy too," Mel admitted, flushing slightly. "He gave his life up willingly for a truly important cause. I don't want to let him down. This is something I *can* do. Something that will make a real difference."

"It is brilliant, Mel. I will be honored to help." She put her arms around Mel's shoulders and squeezed. They both turned back to the painting.

Mel stared up sadly at the wall. "But they will never make a painting about *this* revolution, will they?"

"No. But *we* will know. That will be enough."

"Perhaps, one day, we will make a statue of Seyal."

"That would make it all worth it!"

They sat down in the dining chairs and began to plot in earnest.

Chapter 26

Gus came to with a sensation of unbelonging that was quite alien. It took in its surroundings and moved slightly.

Immediately, there was a shuffling sound close by it.

"Gus?"

A terrific sense of relief infused its carapace. "Sibeal?"

A face appeared over the edge of what must be a Zeroth chamber. "We made it, Gus! Well done!"

"We are not dead?"

"No."

"Or enlightened?"

She laughed. "I am not sure if I would know how that feels, but no, I don't think so. We both came back, although it has taken you some time. You have been unconscious for days."

Gus struggled and managed to prop itself up on three of its arms. "What happened? What was wrong with me?"

"Chill coma."

It rifled through its memories, which were still floating around in unconnected lumps. "I ... I don't think I have heard of that."

Sibby explained what the illness was, and how serious it had been. Then she bent over the lip of the Zeroth and reached down with the whole top part of her body to give the Enif a hug. "You saved my life. Thank you."

Gus almost shied away from her. It had never been in that close contact with a humanoid before, and found the whole process extremely uncomfortable. "You're welcome," it managed, stiffly. "This is *Nivala*, isn't it? Did we save Seyal, too?"

Through the long silence that greeted his question, it realized what the answer must be. Its cordotonal organs shivered along the entire length of its extremities. "Ahhh. I was hoping that they would be in time."

"The Avaraks killed her as soon as their ship arrived on Rhyveka. As soon as the top brass could witness it in person. *Nivala* arrived too late to save her."

"And her son? Segaton?"

"Mall spoke to him. He will stay with the Avaraks. He doesn't know that they killed his mother."

Now Gus was silent for a long time. Then it gave a thrum. "I have to think," it said, "that Segaton will be able to look at himself in a mirror when he finds out, but I do not believe that he ever will be able to."

"He may never find out. It certainly sounds as though they intend to keep it from him."

There was a rustle through the translator. It almost sounded like a sigh. "Oh, he will find out. The execution, from what you have told me, was entirely public. It was not carried out in front of the general population, but many Avaraks either witnessed it or were privy to it. The boy will find out soon enough. It will be a heavy burden to bear. His mother would not have wished that burden on him."

"We are all answerable for our actions, even when we are adolescents."

"Sadly, that is true." Then Gus decided it was time to change the subject. "Have you been sitting here all the time? The whole week?"

"Pretty much. I left you to eat or to catch a few hours sleep."

"Thank you. I do not deserve such a friend."

"Well, you have one for life. Whenever you need me, I will come."

"Just don't hug me again, please!"

"You don't like it?" Sibby was downcast.

Gus tried to explain. "Enif do not like to be touched."

Sibby sat back on her haunches, aghast. "Oh, right. Sorry, I completely forgot. I know that, of course. From Eshaan and Didjal. What can I do to show you are my friend?"

The Enif thought about that. "We ripple our cordotonal organs," it told her. "Like this ..."

Sibby watched as Gus's arms appeared to show a series of small waves. Her eyes opened wide and she giggled. "I can't do that!"

"No," said Gus, rather complacently. "Only Enif can do that."

"Can we touch elbows?"

Gus looked wary. "What is an elbow?"

Sibby pointed. "This. We would just touch momentarily." She demonstrated by knocking both her elbows together. "Like that."

The Enif considered. Then it bent one of its arms rather gingerly and stuck it out of the chamber in her direction, bent at the main joint. She lowered her own elbow and skimmed it over the joint, barely touching. "That acceptable?"

Gus thrummed, pleased. "That is acceptable. As long as it is not for longer."

"The merest touch, I promise."

"It is acceptable." Then something else occurred to the recuperating Enif. "What happened to Tsuf? To Toothpick?"

Sibby's face broke into a smile. "He is fine. Look…" She put one finger on her shoulder and brought it away with a small insect perching on it. "See … he is almost over his ordeal in space."

Gus twisted inside the Zeroth tank in a slightly uncomfortable sort of way. "Do you think I should take him back to Sagrest?"

"Is that their home planet? In the Landau Rift?" Sibby frowned. "Why are you considering that?"

The Enif thrummed slightly. "I … I have been thinking. What if sunflyers have … have an equivalent to *faliif*? Or to marriage? Or just to family? I have removed him from any chance of that."

Sibby wrinkled her brow. "I suppose that is true. You think that he may have been bonded with another of his species?"

"Either that, or I may be preventing him from bonding by keeping him here."

She made a face. "Maybe."

Gus was silent for a few seconds and then his translator buzzed into action again. "Thank you. I believe I shall take him back. Repatriate him. He deserves it after all he did during the Avarak attack."

Sibby was looking at Gus strangely. "Yes. He does."

"Did you ever think about repatriating Scout?"

She nodded. "We did, yes. But it turns out that Geigas attack any of their number who have been away for more than a few weeks. They would have turned on him."

"I see. Well, he seems happy enough."

She grinned. "He does. And, if we ever find a female Geiga he likes, we agreed that we would let him go. Or let her join him, if that were more appropriate."

"But you thought about it."

She touched the Zeroth tank. "Of course. And I am glad you did, too." She got up and gave another of her sweet smiles. "You need more rest, Gus." Her eyes were suspiciously moist. "You have no idea how happy I am that you are on the way to recovery. I am going to go and tell the others that you have woken up." She bent forward to check on the console beside the Zeroth chamber. "This says you need twenty-four more hours of non-immersive treatment. Now, go back to sleep. The levels will stabilize in a moment." She slid unobtrusively out of the sick bay.

The Enif lay back in the chamber, which had now drained partially to be more comfortable for an awake Enif patient. Although it felt good to be alive, Seyal, who had been a kind friend, was dead. They had not been able to save her, after all. Gus was going to miss the Avarak woman.

Giedi was flushed. He was hotly defending his position.

"Why can't I become a cadet *now*?"

"Because Spacelanders do not embark on starships as cadets until they are fifteen or sixteen."

"Tyzarans do. Look at Zenzie."

"Zenzie is a different race. She is held by other laws. And she's the Chyzar; she could make her own."

"But why do I have to stay here on *Shapley* while she is gallivanting off all over the universe with you? It isn't *fair!*" Giedi became aware of the childishness of these words. He flushed even more.

His father took pity on him. "I am sorry, Giedi. But it is only three years. As soon as you reach minimum age, I will allow you on *Nivala* as a cadet. That is the most I can promise."

"You could let me come on board as an observer."

"I could, but I am not going to do that. You need these three years to get as much knowledge into that thick head of yours as you can. You have a basic education, but if you are sure you want to pursue a career in the Interstellar Enforcement Agency, you will need a much more profound knowledge of Quantum mechanics, Astrometrics, Cosmology and Astrophysics. Three years is actually very little time. Not if you are to pass the entry level exams in all of those subjects."

Giedi just glared at Mallivan, who ignored this and continued speaking.

"Zenzara has qualifications in all of those things, even at her young age. That is because the Tyzarans subject their children to one of the most intense educational programs in the Major Shells. Or are you happy for her to know much more than you about everything?"

"She is the *Chyzar*. Of course she knows more than me. Shells! She talks to interstellar beings!"

"Yes, but you could easily know as much as she does about Quantum mechanics. Don't you see, Giedi? If you ever want to become a captain, you will need that background. I am even doubtful that three years will give you enough of a basis."

"You just want to separate Zenzie and me!"

His father's expression turned icy. "That is not true. I have been told that you are now soul-mixed. That means that you will eventually be together. But you need to work towards that goal."

"I already get good grades!" Both of Giedi's hands had formed themselves into fists and he felt like hitting out at somebody.

"I know you do. But your grandmother was only educating you to a basic level. She was tutoring Alisevola separately to become the next prime of the *Bellaris* shipstation, even though Alise prefers engineering. Alisevola has a much better grounding than you do in space education. And you haven't even begun defense training."

Giedi felt his shoulders drop. That was true. He had never been comfortable with his cousin being singled out like that. And his father was right: he didn't want Zenzara to consider him as just some space flotsam with no mind of his own.

"I will talk to her," he said sulkily.

"I already have. She understands. The Tyzarans put great emphasis on knowledge. I have explained that if we do not do this, you will never be able to reach your full potential."

"And she agrees?" The possibility that she could yawed in front of him like a big black chasm. "She would renounce the bonding ceremony? The Civil Juvenile Marriage Intention Protocol?"

"You will have to talk to her about that. Three years sounds like forever, now, Giedi, but it is a drop in the ocean compared to the rest of your lives. We live for well over a hundred years now. You and Zenzie can still have more than eighty years together. You need some perspective."

"Says you." Giedi gave one of the consoles a kick and trudged off the bridge. He felt as though he were walking through honey. Why did everything have to be so difficult?

He took the elevator down to the shuttle bay. He knew he would find Zenzara there, and he needed to talk to her.

He had been quite content with his life before he met her. Why had all that changed so much now?

After two days, Gus was able to resume its duties. It had been left with a long white patch that traversed almost the whole of its jet black carapace on its right side. It was the most peculiar after effect of the Chill coma. Apart from that, it had made a full recovery. There was a slight residual weakness, but exercise was slowly bringing the Enif back to full health again.

Now it was making its way into the main hall on *Shapley* shipstation. There was some sort of a meeting there; its presence had been requested.

Gus looked around at the station as it made its way to the main hall. Signs of the shell storm were still visible and the station's maintenance crews were working overtime to fix it.

Despite the Avarak intentionality, it appeared that diplomatic efforts had avoided another war. The Avaraks had claimed, quite mendaciously, Gus felt, that they had been testing a new weapon and had detonated it in a completely uninhabited area of space, as Major Shell directives dictated. They expressed their regret at any loss of life but denied any wrongdoing whatsoever.

While the other races had seen through this excuse, it seemed that none of them were ready to declare war again. The humans in the Sol system had been badly hit by the last one, as had the Spacelanders. Gus's own race, the Enif, preferred to stay well away from conflicts, although they were extremely unhappy about the Avarak storm, particularly since it had affected their own part of the Landau Rift. There had been some few hundred casualties, though most were light. The Nepheals lived in a different Shell altogether and in any case were much more worried about the Vaers. The Vaers had other fish to fry and maintained their isolationist policy.

People greeted Gus as it wandered past. There were cheery shouts of welcome back, and thumbs raised. It felt a little strange to be the object of all this interest. One crewmember even clapped as the Enif went past.

All this was slightly unwelcome, but it paled into insignificance once the Enif opened the door to the main hall.

The hall was full of people.

Gus paused in the threshold. There had been an excruciatingly loud hum of humanoid conversation, almost unbearable to an Enif. All this suddenly stopped. Sibby, who had been waiting beside the door, ushered the Enif in.

Gus stared around it, hesitating to go further.

Prime Ohnahara, who had been chatting to Denaraz nearby, swept up to it. "It is wonderful to see you fully recovered, Gus. Please come with me."

She swept Gus and Sibby ahead of her, before leaving them just short of a raised platform, which she mounted. The silence was now complete. Gus found itself surrounded by a sea of other races. It went a little paler.

Sibby gave a sympathetic grin. "Don't worry, Gus. This is nothing bad."

Then why did it feel so … overwhelmed?

"This is just a ceremony. Like … Like the one the Enif held to pay tribute to Dishaan."

"But who are we paying tribute to …?"

"Hush. She is about to start."

Gus, still very uncomfortable, said nothing more. To be in the presence of so many humanoids was a sensory overload for an Enif, even one who had lived amongst them for quite some time. Aware that it was trembling with something akin to panic, it attempted to tamp down the desire to run away.

In fact, it was so ill at ease that it missed the whole of Prime Ohnahara's introduction.

"—therefore been conceded to the Enif Thagaarus, known to us all affectionately as Gus, for outstanding bravery and courage in the rescue of Sibeal Mallivan Bell from the Avarak cruiser that had captured her."

Gus froze momentarily in place. What was this? What did it

mean? Now they were all staring directly at it and were making an awful noise with their front digits. It was appalling. It blanched.

Sibby gave the Enif a nudge. Gus glanced towards her. She was nodding her head insistently in Ohnahara's direction. Gus allowed its legs to move slightly in that direction, unsure if it was reading the situation correctly or not.

Sibby nodded in an encouraging sort of way and told the Enif to follow her. She led Gus up onto the dais to stand beside Prime Ohnahara. The applause was now quite deafening. The Enif decreased the volume on its translator, which helped, but the scent and furore were still almost enough to shut down its senses completely.

The prime turned to the Enif and held out a metallic medallion, which had been hung from a long ribbon. With great solemnity, she hung the medallion over Gus's neck and then bowed her head. After that, leaving the Enif wholly confused, she took a small step back.

Sibby smiled at Gus. "They have given you a medal," she hissed, "for saving my life."

"This is a piece of metal. What does it do?"

Sibby shook her head, as though Gus were lacking in something. "It doesn't do anything."

"Then why have they given it to me?"

"Shh! I will explain it later. It is a great honor!"

"It is?" The whole process felt more like torture to Gus, but it was quite prepared to take Sibeal's word for it. "What do I do now?"

"Smile. The prime has something else to announce."

"Smile? I have not got that capability."

Sibby's face fell. "That's right. You haven't. Oh well, never mind. Can you wave a hand or something? Like this ..." She smiled at the full hall and held up one hand, moving it slightly from side to side.

"That I *can* do." Gus held up all four of its arms and vaguely moved them from side to side. There was a roar from the audience. It was an almost physical wave of sound, and it made the Enif skitter backwards.

Sibby laughed. Then, to Gus's great relief, she stepped down off the plinth and indicated that it could too. The ordeal was over.

"Can I go now?" it whispered.

Sibby shook her head. "Prime Ohnahara has something else to announce."

The prime now began to speak about the various rescues that had been undertaken, praising all of the crew who had taken part in them. There was further applause, though rather more sporadic.

Until she reached the final part of her speech.

"Finally, I would like to speak about the rescue of Sibeal Mallivan and Thagaarus, our recently decorated Enif, from their ordeal in the Dark Confines. This was done by two of our youngest members, aided by the farsightedness of the Chyzar." Zenzara, standing at the front of the audience, actually managed a blush.

Prime Ohnahara went on, "Giedi and Talitha Mallivan took a shuttle and, with the help of Scout, the Geiga, who must also be commended, tracked down the literal pin in a haystack.

"Sibby and Gus had managed to survive inside an EVA drone. They were floating with nothing around them in a five light year radius. Nothing. They were way too small for normal sensors to pick them up at such distances. Nevertheless, the two Mallivan siblings not only found the drifting drone, but managed to bring both of its unconscious occupants on board their shuttle. When that had been done, they realized that Gus was in urgent need of help. Rather than head back to safe space, they risked their own lives to try to get the Enif the help it needed.

"For this, they are both awarded the *Shapley* Shipstation Medal of Valor. Please come forward."

Tally, who had gone scarlet long before Ohnah finished the speech, stumbled a few paces up onto the plinth, joined by a Giedi whose chest was puffed out so far that his chin was hardly visible. They smiled and waved as their medals were, this time, pinned onto their tunics.

The applause was still continuing when Ohnah lifted her hand again, asking for silence. Gradually, the room settled down. Ohnah nodded to Giedi. He stepped smartly back, but the prime put one hand on his sister's arm to stop her following.

"Stay here Tally, please," she asked. The prime smiled down at her and then looked up at the audience, raising her voice so that they could all hear.

"Not only did Talitha help her brother safe their aunt and Gus, but she also played a hugely important part in saving both the Chyzar and her brother from the twisted and lethal remains of their two skimmers. I believe that Spokesdesignate Denaraz has been heard to say that it was the single best piece of piloting that he had ever witnessed. And he should know, because his own life depended on it!"

There was more applause, particularly from Denaraz, who was standing next to Zenzara at the front of the audience. Ohnahara herself joined in.

Tally's face was so red that it almost shone.

Ohnah hadn't finished. "The original race obviously lost all relevance when it was overwhelmed by the disastrous consequences of the Avarak attack. The race has been declared, logically, null and void. However, I am sure that all of you will join with me in my conviction that ownership of my late son's runabout should be passed to Talitha Mallivan, in recognition of the skills in piloting that she displayed, despite difficult circumstances and her young age. We wish her well in the future, and hope that ownership of such a craft will facilitate what will undoubtedly be a highly successful career as a pilot."

There was a huge shout of approval from the audience.

Tally didn't know where to look. Tears were running down her face.

Giedi gave a great cry of delight and ran forward to wrap his arms around his little sister. He lifted her up into the air and twirled her around and around. When he finally did put her down, she stumbled and almost fell over.

Then Denaraz vaulted lightly up onto the dais. He pumped her hand. "Very well deserved. Well done!"

Tally was soon surrounded by well-wishers. Her heart was beating so fast it felt like it might detach itself from her body and fly off into the sky. Happiness radiated out from her.

At last, a familiar tall shape made its way over to her.

She squinted up, all of a sudden somber. "Dad?"

He bent and solemnly shook her hand. "Congratulations, Tally. You deserve it. Try not to prang it the first time you take it out, will you? I don't want to have to pay double insurance premiums."

She was opening and closing her mouth prior to an attempt to assure him that she would never ever even so much as scratch the little ship when the upwards curve at the edge of his lips made her realize that he was joking. So, instead, she gave a feeble slap at his arm.

He grinned down and then spun her around much like Giedi had done.

"I am proud of you, Tal."

She was getting dizzier by the moment, she realized. "You won't be, if you don't put me down," she whispered. "I think I am going to be sick."

He hastily settled her back on her own two feet. Even so, she would have fallen if Zenzie had not scrambled to her aid.

The Chyzar gave her a hug. "Well done, Tally! Thank you for saving my life!"

Tally realized that Zenzara had received nothing. "They should have given you ..." she began.

"... The only thing I did was interpret Scout," Zenzie told her. "And I am the Chyzar. I don't think the Tyzaran Supreme Council would appreciate any intervention in what they would call 'foreign' policy. Prime Ohnahara agreed to leave me off the honors list. In any case ...," the Tyzaran girl scanned around, clearly looking for something , "... Oh good, there he is!"

Tally followed her gaze, which had landed on Scout.

The Chyzar drew a paper bag out of one of her deep pockets. "In any case," she began again, "it was really Scout who picked up that drone. All I did was watch him. So I brought my own 'medal' for him."

There was a rustle of the bag as Zenzie drew out a phyonwe fruit. She was in the process of holding it out towards the Geiga when Scout's acute sense of smell kicked in.

The Geiga gave an urgent keening scream and launched himself through the crowd onto the platform.

Giedi was knocked clean over as he barged past, and his father had to grab at Denaraz to stay upright. Zenzie was not so lucky. The Geiga took off from at least two meters away and catapulted his body at her. He impacted her one long second later and then there was a chain reaction of small incidents.

Zenzie was knocked over backwards, arms flailing out to the

side. She hit Prime Ohnahara, who was swept off her feet as well.

The paper bag exploded with a bang and the four remaining phyonwe fruit inside it pitched out and rolled off in different directions.

Scout opened his mouth so wide that both sets of teeth showed, wrenched the first phyonwe fruit out of the Chyzar's hand and bore it off triumphantly to the corner of the dais. He gulped it down and then ran after the others.

The sunflyer, which had been hovering over Gus's head, shot upwards and took refuge in the ceiling joists, chittering angrily.

Peetie, looking on from the audience, laughed so much that he had to clutch his stomach.

He hadn't told anybody, but the youngest Mallivan had been missing *Bellaris* shipstation. It had been all he had ever known. This was the first day that he realized that he could be truly happy on *Shapley*. That the new shipstation was going to give him the warmth and friendship that he had always craved.

It was a day he was never to forget.

PART TWO

Trade Center,
Tyzar City,
TYZAR

TEN YEARS LATER

Chapter 27

Sibeal Mallivan — Sibeal Denaraz as most people knew her — bent low before the figure that was standing in front of her.

"Madam Ambassador," she intoned.

The Spacelander Ambassador to Tyzar raised her eyes, huffed, and enfolded her in a tight embrace.

"Sibby! How are you? Golly, how long has it been? You look great, as always! Typical that it takes a wedding to get us together!"

Sibby grinned at the well-known face in front of her. "Mel, you look just the same, too. How are you?"

They held the hug for long seconds. It was so good to see each other again. Life and circumstances had edged them apart in the last few years, but they had never lost the closeness that had cemented a live-long friendship.

"Here, come and sit down. I ordered coffee and Tessara cake." Mel indicated the seat next to her.

"You'll never manage to get rid of me if you feed me up with cake. I'm as bad as Scout with a phyonwe fruit when you put Tessara cake in front of me."

"Have as many as you like. I hear you have been in the Dark Confines for six months. You deserve them."

"You said there was some news? Is it what we were hoping for? After all these years, I certainly hope so."

Mel's face lit up, illuminated with something that seemed to come from inside her very soul. "The very best there could possibly be. The Avarak males have agreed to sign the new charter."

"They gave in?" For a second Sibby turned back into the eager teenager she had been all those years before when they used to play together on *Bellaris* shipstation. "Really? Everything?"

The Ambassador, also looking less than venerable at that moment, shook her head. "Not quite. But the females have got most of their demands." She counted them off with her fingers. "No voice alterations from now on except for medical conditions. Such conditions to be verified by the midwives." She touched another finger, "Females to receive schooling up to ten years old, including Universal." The next finger went down. "Females to receive a small pension upon the death of their husbands, and no obligation to serve any new male. They will be exempt from being sold on." Mel smiled up, then remembered, "Oh, and the fourth thing: they have also been granted the freedom to undertake work. No husband may impede this. The males stood firm on not allowing the females to choose how many children they will have, but since they have no idea that all the females now have access to contraception, that is a bit of a false victory for them. Theoretically a woman may not limit her family, practically she will be able to if she wants to."

Sibby clapped her hands together. "This has taken such a long time. I was sure they would give in the first or second year."

Mel shrugged. "What can I say? Male Avaraks are about as stubborn as any living thing can get. It has taken them years to come around to accepting the demands. In fact, it really has only happened now because old Kelkator died and a new Grand Leader was voted in."

"Who cares why? I am just so happy it is finally over." She lifted up her coffee in a toast. "Here's to Seyal!"

Mel's face crumpled and her eyes became damp. "After all these years!" she agreed. "There were so many times that I thought it would never happen. Never could, never would. Here's to Seyal!"

There was a long silence as each of the friends remembered Seyal in their own way.

Mel was the first one to speak. "Do you think ...? Could we ...? It's just ... I wish there was a statue to remember her by. She should have one. We talked about it, remember?"

Sibby was struck by that thought. "I do. I even joked about it to her, once. Maybe it is time," she murmured. "How can I help? Where can we put it?"

Mel was silent for a few moments, then she grinned. "There is a wonderful Tyzaran artist who does very meaningful sculptures. We could commission her."

"How much do you think it would cost?"

"I think the female Avaraks would want to use part of their fund to pay for it. Although you and I set up a way to finance all the contraception years ago, the few female Avaraks who had stipends have also been paying into it. There is now a small surplus, because nobody has taken any sort of profit. I will ask Myska. I am the designated financial officer, but of course she is the clandestine head of the fund, along with her sister Remyka."

"Oh yes, the one that lives here on Tyzar. So Myska is still alive? She has done well!"

"Yes, she is. The contraception has prolonged so many female lives on Rhyveka that nearly all of them are still alive. Of course, now that will change again. You know how dangerous it is for the females to give birth."

"Surely the males must suspect that the females are using contraception?"

Mel spread her hands. "I suppose they must, but they are even more afraid to recognize the possibility openly. They are a tiny bit hidebound, you know."

"No kidding! So, they finally gave in. I am so glad."

"I just wish we could have got more concessions. It doesn't seem enough."

"Rubbish, Mel, you have achieved a huge change. "

Mel took a small sip of her coffee. "*We* have achieved a huge change," she rebuked gently.

Sibby rolled her eyes. "So, have you been happy?"

Mel drew in air, her face tilted upwards. "I think so. I enjoyed splitting my time between *Nivala* and *Shapley* for a few years, but life here at the Trade Center on Tyzar is always interesting, and I have felt so much more alive with all the Avarak intrigue. In a way, I shall be sorry to see it end." She gave a small sigh and then turned her attention back to Sibby. "I hear you've been transforming Vaer Nova in your spare time."

"We could hardly expect them to stop being pirates without enough food on their own planet for self-sufficiency."

"One-woman job, I hear." Mel's eyes crinkled at the corners.

Sibby blushed. "We already had the carbon cloud tech. It was easy to develop that into biodomes."

"Easy for you, you mean. Proud of you, Sibs."

Now Mallivan's sister really was bright red. She shifted from one foot to the other. "Thank you."

Mel grinned. "All right. I promise not to embarrass you anymore. Here, have another Tessara cake."

Sibby obeyed this command and there was a companionable silence as both women enjoyed the treat. There was a question inside Sibby's head. She thought that she probably shouldn't ask it, but it somehow bubbled up anyway.

"Do you still think about him?"

"About Sammy? Of course. But it is less now. Time lays a shroud over things. Sometimes you pull the shroud back for a moment and there they are – feelings just as sharp as ever. But most of the time they are dormant, submerged somewhere in the back of your mind."

"He would have been so proud of you."

"Yes. I think he would. I am glad to have been able to make a real difference." Mel took a sip of her coffee. "And I feel that I have helped to pay a debt that we all owed Seyal."

"I do too. I felt so guilty that I couldn't save her. I have replayed what happened over and over again, but until today that sensation of culpability never went away."

"And now, Sibby? How do you feel now?"

Sibby considered, then her face flooded with joy. "I feel free." She burst into tears.

Mel felt her own eyes well up with tears. She swallowed. She put one hand gently onto Sibby's arm. "It is over," she said softly. "We have done what we could to change the fate of the Female Avaraks. The rest is up to them."

"You are right. And it does feel good. I shall feel even better when we finally get her that statue."

"Let's make a pact. We will see each other again at the unveiling!"

Sibby smiled through the tears. "Done!"

Ryler Mallivan managed a bow. "Supreme Oznard, may I introduce you to Obari."

The leader of Tyzar inclined her head. "Ahhh. Ty Obari. A pleasure to meet the head of the Alkelalavazalan race. The people of the three suns."

Obari seemed amused at her slow pronunciation. "Please, Supreme, you may refer to us as Bezniks."

"You are too kind. I was very happy to receive the document of adhesion your people have signed. We are very happy to welcome you into the Alliance."

"It is contingent on the non-exploitation of our alkel mines," warned the Beznik leader. "All alkel must remain on our planet."

"Yes, of course. That will not be a problem. The Alliance will always respect your wishes in that respect."

Obari, who found the huge Tyzaran dome most uncomfortable, nodded to them both and then excused himself. The Bezniks were accustomed to living below the surface of their planet. To be on a different planet for long periods of time was still uncomfortable for any of them.

Oznard nodded at Mallivan. "Good job, Captain. To have welcomed another major race into the Alliance is a huge achievement."

"Thank, you Supreme." He backed away, relieved and feeling irritated. The ceremonial jacket was stiff and heavy. It itched in many places that it shouldn't. He tugged at the collar, with little effect and fell in beside his brother-in-law who had been standing close by.

"I wish they had decided to hold this somewhere else," he grumbled. "You Tyzarans are such sticklers for formality."

Denaraz, who was busy fastening his own full dress jacket, grinned. "The Supreme Council was never going to let their Chyzar get married without a whole lot of pomp and ceremony. The Supremes never let an opportunity for good publicity go astray."

"I know," said Rye gloomily. "But ... three hours! They could have made it shorter, surely."

"There is what is euphemistically referred to as a short interlude, you know."

"Yeah. I heard. A bathroom break. Terrific."

"Are you not happy that your son is marrying the Chyzar?"

"If you want the truth, I don't really see why they have to formally marry. Why can't they just live together like everybody else?"

Izan looked amused. "Because it is Chy Zenzara. It has been decided that any children must be engendered physically rather than at the Genetic Institute of Fertility."

Mallivan's face clouded over. "I don't really see what business it is of the Supremes to decide how my son should procreate!"

"They think that it is. And your Fertility Institute has agreed with them."

"I know." Mallivan let go of the collar after one final, futile tug. "I suppose we should get going then. The ceremony is almost due to start."

Denaraz nodded. Both men got to their feet. Denaraz clapped his friend on the back. "Bear up, old friend. *You are not losing a son, you are gaining a daughter-in-law.*"

"That is just what I am afraid of," huffed Mallivan. "We were always stuck with Zenzara. Now Giedi will be stuck to us like a limpet too. All because of the Savior Protocol." Then he stepped aside and gestured to Denaraz to lead the way. "Just elbow me in the ribs if I fall asleep."

Zenzie was staring at herself in the mirror. She twirled from one side to the other.

"I look great!"

Tally and Danaa both clapped their hands. "You do!" "Beautiful!"

Zenzara smiled across at them. "Thank you both for coming all this way. I really appreciate it."

Danaa smiled down at her. The Nepheal woman towered over both of them. "I wouldn't have missed it for the world. Besides, you came to the Ayaala Retreat when I was giving birth to Agraya, and also for Elyaal."

"You are my best friend. Of course I would come. How are the children doing?"

"Agraya is excelling at school. She is going to be an Orator, I believe. Elyaal is more interested in science. She has a grant to study under Ouraali in the Retreat."

"Wow! Then they are both doing tremendously well."

"Yes. I was very lucky. Two female offspring. I feel blessed."

Tally seemed confused. "Don't you want a son, Danaa?"

The Nepheal shrugged. "Maybe. One day. But a son is never a priority for Nepheal women. We would consider ourselves lucky to have any child, but female children can carry on from us. Although times are changing. There are now many more opportunities for the males. One day it is said that they will even become our equals."

Tally nodded, keeping her thoughts to herself. They were that she was very lucky to have been born a Spacelander. Avaraks were dominated by the males. Nepheals were dominated by their females. It was much better to be like the Spacelanders: any child was welcome. Anybody could lead and anybody could follow.

And then she realized that it was not so. Only the females could become Primes. Though, in the last ten years, that too had changed. Old-school shipstations were becoming few and far between. The Interstellar Enforcement Agency had, in great part, been responsible for that.

Tally herself had just come back from the Institute of Fertility on Zenubi. Soon, she herself would become a parent. Six children, three nominally in her care and three in the other donor's care.

She was lucky that things had begun to change, because her father's mother would not be taking care of any great-grandchildren on *Bellaris* shipstation. The break between the Mallivan prime and the rest of the family had not been mended. However, now there were educative centers run by dedicated people. Centers where parents could spend as much time as they liked with their offspring, but where children would be nurtured when their progenitors left. The first of these centers had opened in orbit around Pyrrhus only three years ago. Tally, after visiting, had decided that she would send her children there. Prime Ohnahara had offered to bring them up on *Shapley* shipstation, now safely tucked behind the Olympus Nebula, but Tally wanted her kids to grow up outside the constraining protocols of shipstations and primes. Salaries were becoming more common nowadays; the next generation would have the whole of the Major Shells at their feet.

Zenzara was still talking. Tally gave herself a little shake. She should stop woolgathering. This was to be Zenzie's day. And her brother Giedi's, of course.

Still, she couldn't help checking out the Nepheal woman beside her. Danaa was a bit of a legend. She was commander of a whole fleet and said to be one of the most competent Nepheals in the Atlas Shell. She had been responsible for finally capturing Captain Frynee of the Vaers. Now nobody else would have to fall victim to his cruel privateering.

Tally, who had recently graduated from the Waypoint Academy, had been awarded a grant to further her studies on Nephealis for two years. She would probably be seeing more of this woman.

Today, however, was about others. Talitha pulled at her dress a little. She so rarely wore one that she was a little uncomfortable about it. But it was only for three hours. She could put up with anything for three hours.

"Did you come in the runabout, Tally?" asked Zenzara.

"No. I had to leave it on *Shapley*. I was thinking of passing it on to somebody else now that I have graduated. I think that is what Ohnah would want, don't you? What Sammy would have wanted?"

Zenzie frowned. "I guess. But it must be getting a bit worn around the edges by now. Maybe you should just take it out from the shipstation and set it alight with a couple of fireworks?"

Tally began to laugh. "No! I could never do that. Things don't stop having value just because they're old."

"But it won't have any of the new tech."

"Maybe. It is still great for practice. You know, you have helped me decide. I shall leave it to the new school at Pyrrhus. Then all the students can use it. They can learn how to update it, too. That way it will go on indefinitely."

Zenzie's mind was on other things. "Sounds good," she said in a distracted tone.

"It does sound good." Tally was pleased. She could have left it to her brother, Peetie, but he was about to graduate from the academy too. There was nothing really either of them could gain from it anymore, and lots that it could give to the upcoming batch of children.It felt right.

"Is Prime Ohnahara here?" she asked.

"Of course. She has been very kind to me over the years. I wouldn't have wanted to get married without her."

Danaa nodded. "And Giedi's grandmother? The Mallivan prime?"

There was an awkward silence. "No," admitted Zenzara finally. "She was sent an invitation, but declined." Her chin went up in a defiant manner. "All the important people will be there."

"Good. And then you and Giedi are off on *Nivala*, right?"

"Giedi took over Mel's place when she left to become ambassador, five years ago."

"That's great. It means you won't be separated again."

Zenzie almost growled. "Just let them try!"

Mel clutched at Sibby. "Is that..? No! It can't be!"

"What? Who? Where?" Sibby squinted through the crowd.

Both women gave tandem screeches and ran across the hall, thrusting their way through Supremes, spokesdesignates and normal guests alike. Mutters of discontent and complaint followed them.

Sibby put her arms around a tall young Vaer. "Emereen! How wonderful to see you! It must be twelve years, mustn't it? What are you doing here? How are you? How are your parents?"

Mel was wreathed in smiles as she greeted Emereen's sister in a similar sort of way. "You are looking terrific, Marivee. Those feathers! I'm so glad that they all grew back. I've met your father several times recently, since he became ambassador. He told me that you and your brother were doing well, but I didn't expect to see you today. I am so happy to see you both."

"It is good to see both of you, too. Supreme Oznard invited us to the celebration, and we had to come. We wanted to pay our regards. If it weren't for all of you, we would be dead."

"What are you doing now?"

Marivee dipped her beak to attend to a recalcitrant feather. "I ... err ... I have been accepted as a sub-delegate on Vaer Nova."

"A diplomat! Fantastic! Well done. Perhaps we will meet then. What about your brother?" Mel looked over to where Emereen and Sibby were deep in conversation.

Marivee swelled with a different kind of pride, one much stronger than she had in her own achievement. "He lives on Vaer Nova," she said. "He went back after his studies. He has formed a non-profit to develop resources on Nova and help those who were trapped there – whatever race or faction they might belong to. He is doing some great work." She gazed with admiration at her brother, who also looked now to be completely cured of the feather baldness they had both suffered from. He spotted Mel, and raised his glass to her with the Vaer equivalent of a grin. She did the same.

"Sounds to me as if you both are. I am so glad. Now, if you are to be a real diplomat, you need to meet some people. Come with me ..."

Prime Ohnahara smiled and held out her hand to the tall Enif in front of her. "Gus! How wonderful to see you again!"

Gus tried not to notice the physical contact. "It is a pleasure to see you again, Prime. How is the shipstation? I hope the new emplacement has proved to be satisfactory to all?"

"Yes, indeed. It is a much more sheltered position. We have had no further incidents, I am happy to say." She looked upwards, eyes scouring the space over the Enif's head. "What happened to that sunflyer of yours? What was he called …? Something really strange, I remember."

"Toothpick."

"Yes, Toothpick. That's right! I suppose he will not still be alive, after all this time?"

"I believe he is," Gus said. "He is on his home planet, Sagrest. The last I heard was that he had become the patriarch of a huge family."

"You took him back to his home?"

"I did. I decided to give him back the life he was always supposed to have," said Gus. "It felt right."

"Yes. I can see why it might. You gave him the choice?"

"Yes. I let him free in a meadow on Sagrest and waited to see what he would do."

"And ….?"

Gus thrummed slightly. "He seemed to understand that I was giving him a choice. He played around me for some time, and then he landed on my arm. He looked directly into my face as if to say goodbye, and then he launched himself up into the cloudless blue sky and climbed higher and higher until he disappeared. Some moments later I saw a flock of sunflyers wheeling and diving in the same place. They made shapes in the sky because there were so many of them. It was one of the most impressive sights I have ever seen."

"And then he was gone."

"—And then he was gone." Gus scintillated. "Surprisingly, I felt only happiness. The loss I had expected never materialized. I realized that I had adopted Toothpick to supplement my own internal loss. Liberating him felt like some sort of Karmic redress." Then the Enif paled slightly. "Apologies. That sounds very pretentious."

"No. It sounds right. I hope he has had a good and fruitful life."

"He is equipped with a tiny chip, so I do hear of his progress occasionally. There are Enif who live on Sagrest and tend to the sunflyers when they require help. Anyway, thank you for asking about him. Now, how is everybody on *Shapley* ...?"

Giedi and his best man, Peetie, were waiting inside the large ceremonial hall, just off the spaceport. It was not the venue either bride or groom would have chosen, but neither of them put as much importance on the event as the Tyzaran Supreme Council did. Their Chyzar was marrying. She had escaped living on Tyzar. They wanted full control at least of this ceremony. Zenzie had rolled her eyes, but accepted. The last ten years had been full of dangerous moments, and she was grateful that they had not brought her forcibly back to live here. She was aware that they could have done a lot more to enforce her submission.

Thankfully, Denaraz had moderated his reports to the Supreme Council, which had allowed her to continue aboard *Nivala*.

Giedi was also uncomfortable. They had him dressed in some sort of ceremonial tunic-like thing, and he felt completely unlike himself. Peetie, who had been supplied with something very similar, was preening in the most irritating manner.

"Look at me! I am prouder than a peacock!" He did a small dance to demonstrate.

"Shut up, will you?"

"What? You don't like wearing a dress? Whyever not?" Peetie spread what certainly were very reminiscent of skirts and curtsied to his older brother, who growled back.

He might have done more, but a gong began to sound loudly in the background and a line of spokesdesignates and supradesignates began to file in.

It was beginning.

Anzany and Neema were waiting for the bride's procession. Neema was holding a groomed Scout on a sturdy lead. Nobody was willing to risk the chaos he normally caused when loose. Just in case, Anzany was carrying a small bag of phyonwe slices that could be used to bribe him if necessary. They both leaned forward and kissed Zenzara on the cheek. "You look spectacular!"

"Thank you!" She bent down to pay Scout the attention he was demanding. "I see you got the job of Geiga-sitting!"

Neema gave a rueful nod. "Mallivan can still be very persuasive, even though we no longer work onboard *Nivala*."

"He should look after his own pet," said Zenzie, rolling her eyes.

Anzany gave a resigned sort of shrug and Zenzie vocalized her implicit words. "Mallivan Bell always sidesteps that kind of thing."

Neema's eyes telegraphed amusement, but she didn't answer the comment. Instead, she touched Zenzie's beautiful red dress with just the very tip of one finger. "You look stunning. So grown-up." She examined Zenzara's face closely. "You have fewer folds of skin now."

"Of course. Though we don't get truly smooth skin until our eighties, you know."

They both leant forwards to kiss and hug her, causing Scout to attempt to jump up.

Neema jerked the lead just in time. "Down, you ridiculous animal! You can't dirty that dress – the Supreme would order us thrown into the brig. Be happy, Chy Zenzara. We wish you all happiness with your handsome new husband!"

Zenzara grinned at them, her crest twitching. The small nick in it that she had sustained in the supershell storm was hardly visible after so many years. "Not handsome to you two, surely!"

They shuffled their feet. "Maybe not," agreed Neema, a twinkle in her eye, "but we can appreciate that you would find him so."

They kissed her again and then joined the rest of the bride's group. Both walked over towards Prime Ohnahara, who was talking with Sibeal Mallivan and the Spacelander ambassador to Tyzar, Mel Estermain.

The hall was circular, with a high roof. Right in the center of the room were the three tiers of five separate chairs. The stands or bleachers were disposed in three sides of a square with the fourth side open.

The forty-five spokesdesignates and supradesignates had all taken their places in the stands and were now waiting patiently. The leader of the Supreme Council had moved to stand in front of a plinth that had been placed in the middle of the fourth side.

The sound of the gong changed, becoming two tones. Peetie and Giedi began to walk solemnly towards the centre of the square, followed first by their father and Denaraz, and then by the rest of the male participants, including Gus.

"They haven't made Gus wear anything at all," hissed Peetie in a disgusted voice. "If I'd known having a carapace would exempt me I would have grown one!"

"Shhh! They will hear you."

The entire male procession formed up behind Giedi and Peetie, on the right hand side of the empty area facing the plinth.

The gong then became three-toned, signifying the entry of the bride's procession.

Giedi's face went suddenly grey when he saw Zenzie. He had been expecting some sort of similar garb to his own, but she was wearing the most spectacular red dress he had ever seen. He swallowed, and swayed slightly.

Peetie caught the movement out of the corner of his eye and reached out a hand to steady his brother, who was looking as though he might faint. Not that he could blame him. Zenzie, who normally slopped around dressed in ship's fatigues, looked like a proper woman. It was enough to make anybody stand up and stare.

Which made him realize that she was looking over at them both with a look like a face palm, so Peetie shook his brother's arm a little to wake him up. Then he raised his right hand with the thumb up, just in case she was worried. She shook her head again as if to ask herself who the fitz she was marrying. Her expression said it all. Peetie stepped slightly back. Personally he would never have thought of marrying somebody with as strong a character as the Chyzar, but hey, that was just him. His brother clearly didn't feel the same way. Luckily. He clutched again at Giedi's elbow, and was rewarded with a resigned nod. The groom was fit to continue. A relief. There had been a moment's doubt there. Peetie was beginning to realize that best man might be a position fraught with difficulties.

Finally, the two processions filled the space in front of the dais. They came to a halt and all stood solemnly, looking forward.

Supreme Oznard began to read from what must have been the most boring document on any planet in any star system. Most of the guests' eyes had glazed over before she got through the first five minutes. It had been penned in Tyzaran, and was being simultaneously translated through headsets which had been handed out in advance to those who did not speak the language.

After the first fifteen minutes, Peetie thought *he* might pass out. In fact, he was contemplating faking passing out. Anything to stop this torture. There was a continuous drone of words from the dais in front of him, overlaid by the continual drone of translated words from his headphones. It was driving him mad. They could bottle it and use it as a torture device, he thought savagely. Shells! Three hours of this! He was never going to survive.

In the end he went into a sort of hibernation. He allowed his mind to wander wherever it wanted in exchange for it not bothering him with the monotonous monologue that was assaulting his ears. He was moderately successful at tuning it out. He dozed, his body swaying only very slightly. He was sure that nobody would even notice.

Until a sharp voice to his right interrupted his wonderful reverie. He snapped back into the room, into the ceremony, with a faint sense of resentment. What now?

He blinked blearily and then twice more. Somebody had interrupted the ceremony. He blinked again. Then frowned. Who? And why? He slid his eyes to his brother who was looking worried.

"Please stop!" Mallivan's voice was as clear as a bell. The murmur from the seated Tyzaran dignitaries was not. They clearly had not expected to have their Supreme's long monologue interrupted.

"Repeat that!" The captain was adamant. There was now hum of interest from all who were present.

"Repeat it?" The translation came through Peetie's earphones, loud and clear and very sharp.

"If you wouldn't mind."

The head dipped to the paper. "I said: Pursuant to the Savior Protocol, the signatory hereby rejects the *locum tenens* of direct parentage."

"What does that mean?" asked Mallivan. Zenzie had narrowed her eyes. Giedi could tell that this information was new to her, too.

Oznard seemed rather ill of ease, all of a sudden. "Errr … the phrase refers to the possibility of *locum tenens*."

"Which is?"

"The Savior Protocol allows for the devolvement of the protocol to the original recipient's heirs after any binding legal change." The Supreme looked up from her papers to survey the audience in front of her. "That binding legal change is normally due to severe illness or disability of the original recipient, of course."

"I see." Mallivan shot a look sideways, at the Chyzar.

Zenzie was thinking furiously. Giedi could almost hear the cogs whirring inside. His future wife shot him a look. It appeared to ask him what he thought.

He shrugged and gave a small jerk of his head towards her, trying to say that the decision was hers. She must have understood, because her features melted into a smile.

His father was still holding up a hand, symbolically stopping the ceremony. He looked at it now, and seemed surprised to see it. "May I consult with the Chyzar?"

Oznard inclined her head.

Mallivan immediately came over to Giedi and Zenzara. "Are they saying what I think they are? That we could pass the Savior Protocol from father to son?"

Zenzara had a perplexed look on her face. As if she could not quite take it in, either. "Yes, I believe they are."

Both Peetie and Giedi noticed the immediate stillness which overtook their father. "You would no longer have to stay close to me?" His voice was one of total surprise.

"It seems not. That obligation would be transferred to Giedi."

"Great! He is marrying you, isn't he? He *has* to stay close to you, right?"

Zenzie went scarlet and her crest prickled up like a hedgehog.

Mallivan didn't even notice. "It isn't going to make any difference to *him*," he insisted. He turned urgently to his first son. "Is it?"

Giedi was struggling to grasp the significance. "Here, wait a mo—"

Then a huge smile spread across his father's whole face. "No disrespect, Chy Zenzara, but I feel you should definitely pass the Savior Protocol to your husband. I am happy to exonerate you from any further protection of my person."

Zenzara was still looking slightly upset. She had gone red. "You are?"

Even Peetie could see that his father might have phrased it better. The boy cleared his throat, bringing his father's attention to him for a moment.

"I mean," said Mallivan after glancing at Denaraz and receiving a quizzical raised eyebrow, "that, much as I have been honored by the efforts of the Chyzar to safeguard me, I feel that it is now more important that she do the same for her new family. Her own family. I think, going forward, it would be the right thing to do." He lowered his eyes and stepped backward.

Denaraz couldn't help but notice that the air of exuberance hadn't quite gone. Mallivan's step was definitely lighter.

After receiving a slightly dubious nod of acquiescence from the Chyzar, the Supreme raised her eyebrows at Giedi, who held up his hands as if to say that this had nothing to do with him.

"Wh-What she says …," he managed to get out.

"Very well. This will be corrected in the marriage certificate, which means that the previous recipient will also have to ratify the document. We will now continue with the ceremony." The Supreme fixed the captain with a stare and raised her eyebrows.

He nodded. "I will try not to interrupt again." However, Ryler's voice was not as trusting as it had been before.

Zenzara also saw the need to be careful. She had noticed a sudden, speculative glint to Supreme Oznard's eye. She raised her chin. "I should just state that, since my husband will be working and living on board *Nivala*, I shall continue to do so too. There is no possibility of my coming to live on Tyzar. Do I have your word as to the continuance of that current agreement?"

The Supreme looked as if she were sucking on a lemon, but finally nodded.

Zenzie eyed her thoughtfully. "I need that in writing. I also feel I should point out that such an important clause should have been brought to our attention earlier. If there is anything else that we were unaware of in this ceremony, as Chyzar I cannot undertake to remain silent."

Giedi reached out to take his bride's hand. He was almost bursting with pride.

Prime Ohnahara couldn't help a brief smile. In her experience, the Chyzar would interrupt whenever she felt it to be necessary. That was the way it should be. The younger generation shouldn't simply accept the status quo. Customs didn't gain added value just by being old. New grass should always be encouraged to grow.

Oznard went back to her interminable reading. Those listening dozed off again to a greater or lesser degree, even after the obligatory break. Of *Nivala's* crew, the only ones to truly listen were Zenzara herself and Gus, who found such things quite interesting from a sociological standpoint.

They all woke up at the end, however. The couple walked forward to stand directly in front of the Supreme, together. Oznard motioned Denaraz, as the bridal custodian, forward. Izan took an ancient thoria from the lectern and ceremoniously handed it to Oznard. The Supreme asked Giedi and Zenzara to face each other and grasp each other's hands. She then wound the thoria carefully over and around their crossed hands until they were bound together.

The translation into Universal was beautiful. "This thoria belonged to the first Supreme ever to hold office. It is a symbol of continuity and survival, of power and of suppleness. It is a symbol that the Tyzaran people hold very dear. May these bindings hold you together in all the days to come, dark or light."

Then she bowed very low before the newly-married couple as she took a step back and left them bonded together. "The future starts today!" she intoned.

It was a fitting end to the ceremony. Zenzie and Giedi stepped closer to each other and bent so that their foreheads were touching. They were both smiling. It was on their faces and in their voices as they dutifully repeated her words, "The future starts today."

Mallivan, Mel and Sibby looked around the huge hall. So much had happened, but there was still so much to do. The words resonated with each of them in a different way. There was a certain degree of sadness, but mostly a lot of hope in that sentence.

Nobody can stop time from moving on. It is what you do with it that is important.

The future starts today.

Books in the Major Shells World:

Interstellar Enforcement Agency:
Termination Shock (Book 1)
Interdicted Space (Book 2)
Exceptional Point (Book 3)

Stand-alone interquel:
This book: Supershell Storm

Next to come:
Slipstream Alley (Early 2023)
Spectacular Error (End 2023):

Also by Gillian Andrews:

The Ammonite Galaxy series:

Valhai
Kwaide
Xiantha
Pictoria
The Lost Animas
The Namura Stone
The Trimorphs

Kelfor (A stand-alone novel)